STERLING
BOOKS

Memories of Yesterday

A Novel

Cheryl Robinson

STERLING
BOOKS

Published by Sterling Books
P.O. Box 855
Roanoke, TX 76262

You are invited to visit the author's website at:
www.cherylrobinson.com

Editor: Chandra Sparks Taylor
www.chandrasparkstaylor.com
Cover photography: Eric Luecker
Author photo: Headshotz Photography, Dallas, Texas
Book and cover design: Stacy Luecker
www.essexgraphix.com

Library of Congress Control Number: 2002092131
ISBN: 0-9720867-0-6

Printed in the United States of America.

First printing

For information regarding special discounts for bulk purchases of this book,
please contact Sterling Books via email at:
sterlingbooks@msn.com

Books are available at quantity discounts
when used to promote products or services.
For information, write to:
Sterling Books, P.O. Box 855, Roanoke, TX 76262

This book is dedicated to my brother Benjamin Robinson, Jr.
(April 24, 1958-September 19, 2001)
I miss you, brother! Your memory lives on.

ACKNOWLEDGMENTS

To God for planting the seed and placing me right where I need to be in order for it to grow. You've always been there. And Your power is awesome!

To my family: my parents, Ben and Velma Robinson, for all of your support over the years. To my aunt Billy, thank you for your insight on life and your understanding of me. You taught me that being different was okay. I love you, and I miss your husband and my uncle Sherman. To my big sister, Janice, for encouraging me to finish this book. You know how many manuscripts I wrote, how many I made you read. Sorry I couldn't share this one with you. I had to try something different. To my nephew, Sterling, don't give up golfing, and of course, study hard. Always believe in yourself because I believe in you! To my nephew, Brandon, I know I didn't get to see you much while I was in Detroit, but I love you, always believe that, and set your sights high. To my aunt Naomi and all of my many aunts, uncles, and cousins in California and Oklahoma, most of whom I've never met—maybe we can have a reunion. To my big brother, Benjamin Robinson, Jr., who passed in 2001—I'm sorry I wasn't there. I had a plan I was working on that I thought was going to make things better for you, but I guess God had a different one.

To my editor, Chandra Sparks Taylor, for her professionalism, honesty and assistance. I'm so glad I logged on to Black Writer's Alliance and found your name.

To Stacy at Essex Graphix for dealing with me when I couldn't deal with myself, for not always doing everything that I asked, but doing what you knew was best for the project.

To my sister's friend Lawanda, I'll never forget that talk you gave me. It was just what I needed to hear and right when I needed to hear it.

I've had the opportunity to relocate three times with Daimler Chrysler Services and meet some really cool people. I'd like to acknowledge quite a few of them from Michigan, New York, Kansas, and Texas who encouraged me in one way or another, including: Janet Marzet, Bob Gay, Wade Lewis, Pia Wilson-Body, Randy Gibbon, Mary Jordan, Joseph Rechtiene, Mark Chermel, Dorianne Johnson, Christine Levos, Lucinda McNuckles, Gerald Lemmons, Maurice "Stylz" Broady, Regina Smith, Nekosher Dillard, Emma Stuckey, Laverio Richardson, Gerald Leigh, Narissa Waller, Dominique Brown, Jennifer Means, Carmen Moore, Nicholas Robinson, Wayne Carter, Lester Williams, Kenny Edwards, Jeff Brown, Keisha Borders, Shayla Shannon, Tamyra Anderson, Brian Gines, Eric Patterson, Belinda Bynum, Terri Lewis, Connie Harris,

Lena Marshall, Moses Fagbeyiro, Princess Davis, Chief Itata Itata, Linda Thompson, Erica Smith, Sauna Witherspoon, Rodney Gilyard, Jarred Howard, Victor Walker, Trina Mott, Kenyea Dudley, Arnold "Zeke" Mazyck, Kevin McKeever, Vivi Congress, Donna Pack, Billy Bolin, Carrey Massey, Dymond Williams, Margarita Quiceno, Sara Karingatti, Yvonne Moore, Joe Williams, Andrea Jones and those delicious cakes that you bake, Frank Rhodes, Andrea Gross, Mary Jo Vance, Glenda Howard, Lisa Thorn, Minyaun Green, Jim Gary, Nick Miaoulis, Robert Lyles, Rod Curtis, Sylvia Williams, and Jeffrey Sparks. The entire Loss Recovery Team of Mercedes-Benz Credit, including: Valissa Armstrong, Juan Orellana, Sandy Barclay, Dewhana Jones, Agatha Clark, Cynthia Taylor, Amy Moffett, Judy Britton, Robbie Waters and Jeanene Macias. I hope I didn't forget anyone. Let's just say, and too many more to name!

To Green Moss III and his wife, Eldora—hey, what can I say but I owe y'all the world and then some! It may have seemed like I pulled a disappearing act but I had to leave Detroit and go someplace where I could focus. Dallas is that place for now. You gave me more than enough chances to try all sorts of things when deep down I know the only thing I'm fit to do with genuine passion is write. Thank you for all of the opportunities. I miss y'all.

To my good friends Shannon Scott, Sherry Fields, Jacquelyn Theoriot-Merchant, Leah Evans, Raynette Owens, and Dwayne and Charrise Walker! You're my friends for life, even if we did a poor job of keeping in touch once I left Michigan, I can still call you today and we can start talking right where we left off, that's how true friends are. I feel blessed to know each of you.

To former Detroit Firefighter, Lenard Owens for our Saturday afternoon long-distance phone conversation. Your knowledge of the fire department assisted me greatly.

To Mr. Anonymous for supplying me with so much information on dealing drugs and prison life for my second book, *When I Get Free*. It is my sincere hope and my prayer that you free your mind and allow yourself to move on. I know those memories still haunt you. As much as I want to say I understand, I haven't been where you've been. Accept my love and the love of others. You are my friend for life. Just trust me.

To author, Mary B. Morrison for always responding promptly via email to my questions on the publishing industry.

To everyone who picks up my book and decides to purchase it, for allowing me to walk one step closer to my dream of writing full-time.

Thank you and God Bless.
— Cheryl Robinson

Memories of Yesterday

PART ONE

Porter Washington

1

"That's not your baby." Damion's words were swimming around in my head while I tried to sleep, causing me to wake up in a cold sweat. I thought I was in the middle of a nightmare until I opened my eyes and realized my nightmare was sleeping right beside me. My body was locked in a fetal position. I was using my bent arm as a pillow. My girlfriend, Reesey, had the heavy comforter wrapped around her naked body like a sleeping bag. My back was facing her. It was the barrier I put up after the sex ended because I shouldn't have done it. Shouldn't have made love to her last night. Only I convinced myself that it wasn't love I was making. I was just going through the motions, and besides, she didn't know what I had planned so for once I had some power.

The RCA digital radio displayed 5:58 A.M. I reached over and pressed the on button and was greeted by loud static from the non-broadcast station of 87.5. I moved the dial to 103.9 so I could listen to Alicia Duncan's weather and traffic report. I made sure the volume was low enough so as not to disturb Reesey, but I doubt if anything could. She had her mouth wide open and eyes shut like she could lie there forever. On most days, especially Mondays, it was impossible to wake her, and nudging never helped. Neither did the alarm clock that was set to go off in about thirty minutes.

"Good morning, Detroit. Are you ready for this?" Alicia asked with enthusiasm through the airwaves. "We're barely in May and it's going to reach ninety degrees. Time for the shorts and tank tops, but not for long because tomorrow it's back down to seventy-one. No major tie-ups to report this early morning. Join me again next hour on the hour for traffic at the rush. That's your brief look at weather and traffic. I'm Alicia

Duncan, 103.9, The Real Deal." I turned off the radio and continued to lie on my side, thinking.

The real deal is I ended up with the wrong woman. I should've stayed with Pam, my first girlfriend. We started going together our freshman year at Murray Wright High School until I let a tighter pair of Guess jeans turn my head and started seeing Reesey on the sly because I could get out of her what I couldn't from Pam. I continued seeing both of them through most of my sophomore year, before I decided that sex was more important than the friendship I had with Pam and broke up with her over the phone like a punk. Pam wasn't mad. She said that she loved me too much to be mad—until she found out it was Reesey I was messing with. I thought she was going to lose her mind.

"I hate that girl. Why that girl? That slut! She switches her big ass and flings that hair down the hall like she owns the school! Why that girl, Porter?"

I couldn't answer her. Not then and not now. Why that girl? Damn, that's a good question. The same one my mother asks. My father. Almost everyone that's ever met Reesey asks me that question. "Why that girl? What you see in her? She acts so stuck up. She doesn't seem that bright. Don't seem to be worth the fancy clothes on her back." Well, whatever I did see in her, I'm blind to the shit now that I know the truth and realize that I've wasted twelve years.

Now Pam is with my boy, Damion. They're married and have two children, Damion Jr., who's seven and Keandra, who's two. They own a successful business, The Perfect Touch, a collision shop specializing in repairing luxury automobiles. I'm not hatin' on my boy. No hard feelings, I guess. Besides, I knew he was diggin' on Pam from the first time I met her. Damion is the type of dark-skinned brother who gets all bent out of shape over light skin.

Honestly, back then I liked Pam because she liked me as did most of the girls in high school, which is why I was voted Best Looking, but I wasn't really attracted to Pam. Not then. Back then I had to push her away because she wanted to get real deep and spiritual on a brother. She was a home girl to the core, grew up near me, which was not quite the ghetto, but as my mother liked to say, right behind it, right in front of it, close enough to be it. Pam kicked her conversation with a lot more intelligence than Reesey, by asking questions that took conscious thought, questions about the origins of things. She listened before she spoke, and I couldn't deal with someone like that in my life, because sooner or later she'd ask about my brother. The whats and the whys of it all. About things I wasn't prepared to answer—not then and not now.

I thought it was strange when Pam used to talk about the future. Asking me how many kids I wanted to have, what I wanted their names to be, and what I wanted our house to look like. I didn't care about those things at fourteen. I was living like there was no tomorrow because I learned early on that nobody's guaranteed a future.

Reesey was the complete opposite; she didn't ask questions. Quite frankly, she wasn't rocking with too much upstairs, but she had enough in other places to compensate for all that, which is why I had to have her, even after a few of my boys whispered in my ear, telling me to stay the hell away from that one. Said for one thing, Reesey had a personality complex and was slightly off just like her mother. Reesey is black, but Indian is the nationality she staked half a claim to, with a mother one shade away from being able to pass for white and a father she'd never seen who had to be black as midnight in order to produce the rich-chocolate color Reesey loosely held on to. Both Reesey and her mother were psychos, I soon discovered. They were the kind who talked about their own race as if they were honorary members of some other. That's why none of what I know now surprises me. Reesey picking me was the surprise. I suppose when you know how to hit a woman's spot just right, it changes everything; even her own preferences.

Ironically, in the long run Damion got the best girl when Pam could've been mine. Hindsight is a bitch. I try to tell myself if we were meant to be, we would've been, but somehow that doesn't help. Once, a few months ago, while I was making love to Reesey, I pretended it was Pam. I enjoyed it so much, I felt like I had cheated on my girl and betrayed my boy. Since that day, I'd never been able to look Pam straight in the eye, but it still hasn't stopped my fantasies.

So where does this leave me now? With Reesey, a woman I can't stand to look at, and one I'm set to leave.

I rolled over on my back and watched the ceiling fan twirling furiously. I tugged on my small Afro, ready to pull the shit out of my head from the frustration building up inside.

Time to get up and get on with it.

My feet hit the floor, pulling up the rest of me as I stretched my arms out toward eventual freedom. I walked into the bathroom and stared at myself in the mirror, smoothing my hands over my cleanly shaven face. I flexed my biceps and did a pose like I was the Incredible Hulk so I could check out my pecs. Nobody was as solid as I was. Women loved me. Yeah, women loved me. All that pussy I turned down over the years, what a fool I was, but not anymore. I plan to make up for all that and then some. Life's too short to be miserable—at least that's what I've been told.

In the shower, I mentally rehearsed how my plan was going to go down. Occasionally I'd rewind it and then play it over again. I was trying to make sure that I caught Reesey totally off guard and in a state of shock. I wanted her to feel the same way I felt the day before when Damion told me that shit. I couldn't think about anything else. Not even my next step, the one I'd have to take after I left her. Nothing crossed my mind other than my plan, and what I had found out less than twenty-four hours earlier.

I walked out of the bathroom and stood beside the sleigh bed looking down at what I used to want so badly: Reesey's dark skin, the color of Hershey's milk chocolate, which I kissed every inch of and her long black hair, which I always tugged in the heat of our passion. It was going to be so nice to let that go once and for all and for good. The only thing that bothered me was the fact that I'd need to stay with somebody while I saved up for a place. I was a firefighter for the city of Detroit, but I didn't make that much money, only twenty-seven thousand dollars a year. It's a fact that we're underpaid and overworked. Even with my other two side hustles—playing drums and sometimes the saxophone at local jazz clubs and helping my parents out at their restaurant—I was still living paycheck to paycheck. Trying to stay level with all the bills. Saks, Neiman Marcus, Marshall Fields, Citibank Visa, American Express. Why the hell did Reesey get an American Express? The whole amount is due when the bill arrives, and with our income, we can't roll like that. Between the gazillion credit card bills, my high-ass car note, the furniture bill, there's no way I can afford to move out of here and into my own place right away. Even though I won't be paying seven hundred dollars toward our thousand-dollar rent anymore, I'm still almost two months behind on the truck note that I have to do something about real soon to avoid a repo. I'll definitely need to stay with somebody.

I started going down the list of my boys. There weren't a lot of them because I preferred my own company to others unless the other was a woman—one I could trust. I have and want only a few close friends. That's how it's always been. That's me.

Damion was out because that was too dangerous. If I was living in his house, my fantasy with Pam could turn into a reality that would end in a nightmare if Damion ever found out. My boy Hoffa was also out because he was married with kids and living with his mama while he pursued his dream of becoming a comedian. Conrad, one of the brothers from the fire department, would let me crash with him, but there's something about him. I think he's in the closet, and I'm not trying to stay at his house so he can open it. I guess it's going to have to be my mother.

I pulled out a pair of FUBU denim shorts from the dresser drawer, putting them on along with my polo shirt and Jordans then went into the kitchen to fix Reesey some blueberry pancakes and hickory-smoked bacon. As I was moving around the kitchen, preparing her favorite breakfast, I thought more about today and how I wanted it to be different. How I wanted it to stick out in her mind, so it could mess with her later.

It must have been the smell of frying bacon that finally opened her eyelids because Reesey was in the kitchen before I had a chance to flip the first pancake.

"Good morning," I said cheerfully, still playing along.

"Good morning, baby," she said, stroking her small bare breasts across the back of my shirt. "I enjoyed last night. And you cookin' breakfast? I don't believe this. Why you spoilin' me?"

As usual, I remained silent. I wasn't quiet with everyone, just her ass, because she knew how to shut a brother down. She even had me insecure for a little while. She didn't like anything about me. Didn't like my hair because it was too kinky so she wanted me to go bald. Didn't like my body because she said I was too muscular. Of course, she didn't like my job because I didn't make enough money. I asked her, "Why the hell you with me? You don't like shit about me." Her reply, "I been with you this long. I guess it's meant to be." Well, she's going to have to guess again. I used to think we were meant to be. Not any more. I've been rollin' with this relationship, knowing she wasn't my wife, but too caught up into the sex to leave. I tried to make the shit work, but now I have a good ass excuse of why I'm leaving. I don't have anything more to say. I made it all of these years without saying much, and I knew it always drove her crazy. In the past I've tried to work on it. I tried to be flexible even though she never was. I guess she thought her looks meant she didn't have to be. She needs a man to constantly reaffirm her by telling her how good she looks. How pretty her long hair is. How nice her expensive designer clothes fit. I'm not into that. I'm not the type to tell a woman she looks good even if she's the finest thing I've ever seen. I figure she should already know that and if she doesn't, oh well, I guess she needs to learn to mind read.

Out of the corner of my eye, I watched her stroll into the laundry room and snatch one of my dirty undershirts from the pile to drape over her. She sat at the kitchen table with her dark brown eyes climbing my bare legs. "Is it going to be that hot out?"

I walked over to her and placed a plate of pancakes and bacon in front of her and watched her eyes expand. "Yep," I said as I gave her a peck across her lips. It took everything I had in me not to tell her how bad her morning breath was, but I didn't say a word. I simply took in air through my nose so I wouldn't pass out.

"No, it's not. You just want to show off your muscles. I saw the way you were looking at that girl at the mall."

"What girl?" I asked as I started to become irritated, almost losing my happy-go-lucky cover.

"What girl? Yeah, right. You know which one, the one with the two basketballs for a chest. You couldn't stop staring at them either. I know you like big titties." If that were true, I wouldn't have stayed with her for twelve years, but see if I say that to her, she'd probably start crying. Believe me, I wanted her to cry, just not over that. "That's okay, I'm gettin' back in shape. Just watch. But I shouldn't be eating all this food when I still haven't taken off my weight from the baby." I sat across from her with a devilish grin occupying my face. "What's so funny?"

"Nothin'."

"What's that smirk all about? What, you laughing at my size? Because if it wasn't for this pouch right here—" she rubbed the excess fat on her stomach—"I wouldn't mind the few extra pounds I put on. Nothing's wrong with being healthy."

"You're right. Nothing's wrong with it, and you *are* healthy."

"What you mean by that?"

"By what?" I asked with laughter.

"'And you *are* healthy.' I don't like the way you said that."

"You are healthy."

"Yeah, I'm healthy. And? So what. That's what the brothers like. Big ass. Big thighs. You know I'm telling the truth."

"The brothers do. The white boys don't."

"So, what I care about what a white boy like?" She darted her eyes in my direction. I shrugged. "You not making no sense, Porter. I guess you'd rather me be skinny like *Pam*."

"Pam's not skinny."

"I'd say she is," she said, turning up her nose.

"*I'd* say she's not. *I'd* say she's a nice size."

"She's built like a white girl. She don't even have an ass. But maybe you like that. Do you?" I ignored her question. She jabbed her fork into a large chunk of pancakes and swished it around her maple syrup puddle before shoving it down her throat. "You need to work on your communication skills."

"Sorry, baby, I'm really trying hard to." And she'll see just how hard I'm trying when she comes home from work this evening.

"When you getting your hair cut?" she asked, twisting her nose as she looked at the top of my dome. Once again, I ignored her question. "Aren't you eatin'?" She stuck a slice of bacon into her mouth and gobbled it down.

"I'm not hungry," I mumbled.

I walked over to the kitchen drawer and removed the Kick-N-Brass cleaner but before I could make it over to the dining room area to clean the cymbals of my five-piece drum set, Reesey said, "I know you're not about to play those damn drums this early in the morning. We got a baby. Don't forget."

Her comment pissed me off, and she said it with that ghetto attitude that I couldn't stand either, but I didn't say anything back. *Actions speak much louder than words*, I reminded myself. I didn't move after I heard the baby crying either and neither did she. Nothing was going to stop her from stuffing her face. Instead, she looked over at me as if she expected me to see about him, but that's where I drew the line.

Before she could say another word, I walked to the door leading to our attached garage. "You gonna be late again," I said as I opened the door and took the steps down.

"Let me worry about that."

I stood in the darkness of the garage for a second before I pressed the door opener, allowing my mind to rewind and play back everything Damion told me the day before when I was at his shop. Even though The Perfect Touch was closed on Sundays, we'd go there sometimes to get away from our women, in his case the kids, and in both our cases all the bullshit.

We were in his large office that he had decked out like he was Donald Trump or somebody, because that's who he thought he was. That's how he spent his money—like he was a millionaire. Once you were inside his office, you'd never think that right outside was Seven Mile Road in the heart of Northwest Detroit. If anything, you'd think you were in New York somewhere off Fifth Avenue. He made money out of that shop. How was a question I never asked, but I knew he was getting paid to the point he could afford a big house in Bloomfield Hills, a Range Rover for himself and a Porsche for Pam. They had it all and lived like there was no tomorrow with spur-of-the-moment cruises and shopping sprees. The kind of life Reesey wanted. A life I couldn't provide nor had any aspirations of achieving.

I was sitting next to Damion on the leather sofa beating him badly on Madden NFL '99 as we debated the likelihood of Barry Sanders retiring from the league this season.

"Barry's making $3.3 million a season, and he ain't giving that up," I said.

"Barry ain't hurtin' for money."

"You right, he's not, but why walk away before even breaking Walter Payton's rushing record?"

"I don't know why. I just know he is," Damion said.

"Nah, man, you don't know what you're saying."

"Man, we can sit here all day and debate this, but my sources are very reliable. Number 20 will not be on the field this season."

"So he's just going to walk away without giving any advance notice?" I asked.

"Isn't that how you quiet people do it?"

We went on with our debate for more than a half an hour. While he continued talking, trying to prove his argument, I kept shaking my head. "It's not happening. So how much you want to put down? 'Cause I need some money right now with all these damn bills of Reesey's." Damion looked at me strange when I said that, strange enough for me to notice.

"Whatever you want to put down. Don't really matter, because my pockets are deep. How about yours?"

"You already know about mine," I said.

"Man, we go way back. Do you need me to cut you off a little somethin'? A grand or two. I will. You're like the brother I never had."

"I'm straight. I don't need your money."

I may be like the brother he never had, but he was nothing like the one I had. Damion was my boy. It had been that way ever since we were twelve and his family moved into the house across the street from ours. He was a short, chubby kid that the girls still liked because he would spend his last dime trying to impress them and he's still that way. Only he's grown a few inches—he's around 5' 10", but he's still chubby—close to 300 pounds, I guess you'd call that fat, but his expensive clothes conceal it well.

Damion and I went way back, but we were nothing alike and I realize it more and more as the years pass.

"You sure you don't need no money? I know you're struggling. You need to let that woman of yours go. All she's doing is keeping you broke and busted," he said.

"You sound like my mama now."

"If I'm saying shit like your mama, I must know what the hell I'm talking about, huh?"

"No. The problem with you is, you think you know every damn thing and don't know shit."

"I know more than you do, I bet you that," he said, laughing. "I bet you that for damn sure, and you don't even want to know what I mean by that. Trust me on this one."

"Man, see that's your problem. You've let that little money of yours go to your head. You need to be thankful for what you do have. Like your wife."

"Oh, you still want my wife. Is that what it is?"

"No, I don't want your wife, never did. It's about you and the way you dog her out. Man, you out there hoeing like you're a single man. You get more pussy than I do. What's up with that?"

"I get more pussy than you because you out there acting like you married while Reesey going around acting like she's single."

"What you mean by that?"

"Nothing. Forget it," he said. "I'm not going to let you fuck with me and have me mess around and say something I want to take back later."

"You meant something. What? Go on and say it."

"Forget it. You don't want to know," he said, rubbing his goatee and looking off into the distance.

"Say it! I do want to know."

"That's not your baby," he said as he positioned his eyes on mine. "You wanted to hear it, so now there it is."

I didn't want to hear that. Not that. I didn't want to hear that a child named after me, my first child, wasn't my child at all. I looked at Damion waiting to hear him say, "I'm just bullshittin'." But I could tell from his expression that he wasn't playing one of his twisted jokes. It was Pam who told him. My Pam—his Pam now—the same Pam who works with Reesey in the Assumed Names division at the City County building. She told him that she knew for a fact Reesey was messing around with one of the big bosses, some white man named Jack. According to Pam, Reesey confided in one of the white girls at work named Trish. Nobody at the job liked Reesey because she walked around snubbing her nose at others who were making the same if not more than her. If she were fool enough to tell somebody her business, it didn't surprise me that it spun all around the building and ended up with Pam, a person most people outside of Reesey like, and a person people love to pass along confidential information to because they know the only person she's likely to tell is her husband.

Damion was telling me the exact same thing my mother had tried to tell me. That baby wasn't mine. "Take a blood test. You never know," Mom said. "I don't trust that girl and neither should you. Especially since that baby don't look like either one of y'all."

I leaned back on the sofa listening to Damion while I tired to comprehend it all. Reesey had a baby by a white man. As much as she chopped my head off with her eyes any time she thought I was looking at a white girl. Telling me I bet' not even think about it, but that's what she did.

Now that I know what went down, when I drop Reesey's ass off at work today, it'll be just like any other day, except it will be the last one she'll see me. It'll be the last time I pull my Lexus that she loves so much into this garage. The last day I have to look into the eyes of a child who shares no other part of me besides my name.

———

I drove to Kindercare relying on the R&B music coming from the radio to drown out Reesey's ghetto voice and attitude. When I pulled in front of the day care, usually I'd help her with Porter, but this time I sat in the Lexus with the engine running. I was in a zone. Not really sure if I'm coming or going. I know my body is behind the steering wheel because I could see myself, but I didn't feel my fingers resting on the wood grain. I didn't feel the back of my head leaning against the tan leather headrest. I didn't feel my bent legs. I didn't feel anything at all—until Reesey said, "Say bye-bye to Daddy." I felt a sharp pain pierce my heart then. The baby was only six months old, and too young to talk, but he didn't need to say a word because his misty blue eyes said it all. We both looked at each other the same way, because we were both being used by the same woman.

I watched Reesey prance from the SUV down the walkway and into the one-story building with her Gucci diaper bag swung over her shoulder and the baby in her arms. If I was ruthless, I would have pulled off right then, but my plan was much better. Let her ass sit around after work waiting for me. Call around and look for me, like I had done for her so many nights from the firehouse. The nights she was probably with that white man or some other man, because I'm sure he wasn't the only one she was seeing. Let her ass call day care and find out I picked up the baby. Eventually she'd call her triflin' mama and find out the baby was there. Then she'd have to piece all the shit together and try to figure out what it all meant, which her simple mind could never do.

I listened to her bitching as I drove Jefferson all the way down until we reached the City County building. I double-parked behind the meter maid who was out issuing tickets a little after eight.

"You're late," I said to Reesey as I looked at the clock on my dash.

"It doesn't matter."

"Must have a real cool boss, huh?"

"He alright. See you at five." She pecked me on the lips and left.

"See ya..." I said to her as she closed the door. "When I see you. Not."

Reesey swayed down the sidewalk. She started walking faster to catch up with a few other women who carried themselves with her same demeanor. She yelled out to them. The women stopped and looked back at Reesey with fake smiles plastered across their jealous faces. I'm sure they didn't like her either and were just pretending the same way I was today.

I placed my hand on the gear ready to shift into drive when I heard a knock on my passenger side window. I turned and saw Pam's smiling face so I unlocked the door. Her hair was in tight Shirley Temple curls and her face was Noxema fresh.

"Good morning," she said, still smiling.

"Aren't you late?"

"I don't start until 8:30, so I'm actually early." Pam looked into my eyes as if she was waiting for me to tell her something she didn't want to ask, but still wanted to know. I didn't say anything about today or my plans. She'd find out from Damion whenever I decided to buzz him with my new number. "Are you okay?" Pam asked.

"Never better as my mother would say."

"Just leave her," she said. I looked at Pam. She was staring at me with determination. She knew me too well.

"Would you leave Damion?"

"Damion can cheat on me all day, every day, but the minute I find out about it, I'm gone."

"I'm sure you don't have to worry about that," I lied.

"Who knows? Only him and the girl he's fucking, right?"

We both laughed. I laughed because she needed to put an *s* on the end of girl. She probably laughed to mask her pain. "You know it's not like that," I lied again.

She shrugged.

Part of me felt that Pam knew just how out there Damion was but refused to admit it to herself because she felt trapped by her circumstances: the two kids, the big house, the years she'd already invested.

"I guess I'd better go. I like to be early instead of late like some folks. All of us don't have an in with the big boss, if you know what I mean."

"I do now."

"Stay strong, baby," she said as she smashed in my right cheek with her full lips. I drove away quickly, allowing my heart to calm its beat. No use in staying around to watch what could have been walk away for a second time.

I walked through the side door of the Soul Station restaurant and immediately heard loud banging coming from the second level where a few construction workers were. My mother appeared from the kitchen with a frown etched across her full face and her thick hair— mostly weave—pulled back. She wasn't used to being at the restaurant on a Monday or any day this early. The Soul Station was opened from 11:00 A.M. to 10:00 P.M. Wednesday through Saturday and on Sundays from one until eight. Those hours hadn't changed in fifteen years.

"What's wrong with you?" I asked.

"Your father's getting on my damn nerves as usual. He wants this restaurant to look exactly like a fire station. We might as well buy a station and move the restaurant into it. It's foolish. Then he can't even come in to take care of the business. He wants to manage by phone and e-mail and make me come in here and deal with all this shit. That damn pole in the middle of the restaurant is going to take up too much room and mess up the flow. He should know better than anyone that the Detroit Fire Department doesn't use poles no more. So what the fuck he put one in here for?"

"It's too late for changes now. What's done is done. Concentrate on the better days," I said, using her little saying. The one I hated to hear.

Mom looked at me like she suddenly realized it was me she was talking to and not herself. "What are you doing here?"

"I need a favor."

"Why do you always need some kind of favor? When is that going to change?" She rolled her eyes and sighed. "Well, I hope it's not money, because I don't have any, and I told you not to buy that damn truck. Trying to impress that girl." Mom never liked Reesey. So instead of calling Reesey by her given name, she called her, that girl.

"It's not about the truck. I need a place to stay."

She shook her head. "You not bringing that girl in my house."

"It's just going to be me."

She put a grin on her face like the one I wore earlier. "You finally left that girl?"

I nodded. "Hallelujah. I told you that girl wasn't nothin' but trouble. If you had listened to me way back when, you wouldn't be goin' through this now. Did you take a blood test like I told you?" I shook my head. "Don't matter. I knew that baby wasn't yours. Anybody lookin'. Anybody with eyesight, a blind person could see that baby wasn't yours."

"Forget about that. Can I stay with you for a few months?"

"Look," she said, rolling her eyes and dropping the smile from her face. "I don't have room for all your shit. And if you think you're going to be banging on those drums or blowing that flute—"

"It's a saxophone."

"I don't care what it is, I don't want to hear it in my house." Her words brought back memories of a time when I was still living at home, trying to date Reesey while I was in high school and just coming into my own sense of manhood. Mom controlled me. Screened my calls. Dictated my time. You'd a thought I was her man. To go back to living with my mother was something I swore I'd never do when I moved out at eighteen.

"I'm not going to play the drums or the sax while you're in the house." *I'll walk on eggshells instead.*

She walked behind the counter and over to the calendar that was hanging on the wall, motioning for me to follow her. "Do you see this?" she asked. I walked up to her, focusing on where her finger was pointing. "What's it say?"

"May third." I knew where she was headed with this. Deadline. Everything she ever did had a deadline attached. Dad told me Mom gave him a deadline to say I do and another one when she was ready to have it undone.

"Okay, you said you need a month or two." She started counting down the weeks, flipping over the page to June. "I'll give you six weeks, which brings us to the fourteenth of June. That's when you have to be out."

"I may need a little more time than that so I can get myself together."

"Why? You're working."

"I understand that, but you know how much I make and how many bills I have."

"You were the fool who went out and bought that Lexus just because that girl wanted it. Get rid of it. Buy you a used something. Why do you have to drive around the city in something that expensive anyway? Cops probably think you're a drug dealer."

"I know most of the Detroit cops."

She puckered her lips and rolled her eyes. "Tell me what happens when you go outside of Detroit to places like Farmington Hills or Grosse Pointe? No, better yet—Dearborn. Cops will take one look at your black ass in that jazzy car and you're through."

"The windows are tinted so they can't tell it's a black man driving."

"They know what's behind the tint. This isn't Florida. In Detroit only black drug dealers tint their windows."

"I guess you should know. Your last boyfriend was pushing that E320 with tinted windows. Whatever happened to him? How come he stopped coming around? I guess the cops pulled him over, too, huh?" I was talking about Herbert. The one she nearly lost her mind over. He wasn't a drug dealer; he was an entertainment attorney who divided his time between Detroit and Los Angeles, where most of his clients lived. Mom came in contact with all types of men at the restaurant. From the rich like Herbert to the poor ones like the last dude she was seeing named Doug. Doug didn't have money, but he had something that kept Mom up crying the blues like she was one of those naïve little twenty-year-olds who always tried to holler my way. Come to think of it, she cried over nearly every man she'd been with, including my father when they were together.

"Anyway," she said. I could tell she was trying not to think about Herbert. He was her good catch she let slip away. At least she was consistent. Good or bad they all left eventually. Mom needed to learn that none of the men she met were any good, and she met a lot of them because she could cook, and I guess she didn't look half bad. I'm not in the habit of looking at my mother like that, but Damion and a few of my friends had crushes on her back in the day. Even to this day, Damion can't be in the same room with my mother without going into a trance. I hope nothing happened between them, but knowing the two of them, I wouldn't be surprised. Some say my mom looks like Pam Grier. Others say she looks better. Don't matter how good she looks or how good she cooks, she still can't keep a man. I could name half a dozen in the past two years who had literally come and gone.

"Can I stay at your house for a little while? I don't want to put a definite time on it."

"Six weeks is all the time I can give you," she said.

"Okay, cool, whatever you can give me. Now if Reesey should call over here or over to the house, act like you have no idea where I am."

"Why should she be calling anywhere looking for you? Doesn't she know it's over?" I stood beside her in silence. "Hello," she sung after she got no response. "Well doesn't she or did you just leave with no explanation?"

"I didn't feel like hearing any more of her lies."

Mom grabbed her pack of Newports off the counter, took a cigarette out and lit up. "Still playing them little games," she said, blowing out smoke. "Still can't talk. You should have told her what you knew. Called her ass out on it. Y'all be back together in less than a week. I guarantee that. She'll come up with some lie. Just like the last time. You could have been rid of that girl five years ago, but no, you had to take her ass back.

Boy, you are surely stupid. Most black men don't let a woman dog them out. What does Reesey have that all these other women out here don't? Is her pussy made of gold, diamonds, pearls, what? What is it? Tell me, because I didn't raise no fool."

Whether or not you raised me at all could be debated, and I'm sure I'd win the argument. That's what I should have said, but I didn't. I just said, "That was then and this is now."

"Do you know how many times I've heard you say that?"

"Mom, this time is different and you know it is."

She blew her cigarette smoke into my face then looked at me skeptically; she probably thought I was blowing smoke into hers. "Well, she should know not to call my house unless she wants a real good cussin' out like last time. I will be so glad when you find yourself a decent woman who you can settle down with and not no project ho."

"Reesey's not even from the projects."

"Two blocks down. What's the damn difference?"

I turned from her and headed for the door.

"You working today?" she asked. I shook my head. "What, you on a kelly?" Just because Mom was a fireman's wife for twenty-six years she thought she could talk to me in department lingo. A kelly was three days off in a row, a super kelly was five days off. Mom tried to keep Dad's schedule down as best she could so she could track his every move, but it never helped, and eventually she gave up trying so hard and started playing Dad's game, cheating just like he did.

"I'm coming off one. I'm back on tomorrow."

"Must be nice to work nine days out of the month."

"Eight this month. I got a super kelly at the end of the month."

"So where you going now? You need a key to get in the house?" I stood leaning against the side door with my hand pressing the metal bar, ready to push it open. She walked over to me with her purse in her hand. "I'll have a key made for you, but until then." She handed me hers. "You don't have to pay me any rent before next week."

"You're going to charge me as much as I help you out at the restaurant?"

"Don't I pay you for that?"

"Sometimes you do, sometimes you don't."

"I'm only asking for two hundred dollars. Where can you go for that? So don't complain. I know you and that girl were paying more than a thousand dollars, and I'm sure you let her talk you into that too. A thousand damn dollars." She shook her head. "Boy, I hope you're not as stupid the next time around."

I wanted to snatch my wallet out of my back pocket and give her the two hundred dollars right then, but I couldn't because I was broke. My cell phone bill took the last of the little money I did have.

"I know you don't have an attitude?" she asked.

"Nah," I said as I opened the door and walked out with the attitude I claimed not to have.

I was anxiously awaiting Conrad's arrival. My garage door was open and my SUV was parked under the carport that was right beside my town house. I glanced at the clock. It read 10:23 A.M. I looked out of my bedroom window and saw Conrad pulling into the driveway across from mine. He used almost the same skill that I did to maneuver the pumper truck at work, when he backed the U-Haul as far as it could go into my open garage.

If I would have stuck with taking just a few things like I originally planned, I wouldn't have needed Conrad to help me move, but the more I thought about my plan, I decided it would be even better if when Reesey opened the front door half the shit was gone. Conrad lived right down the street from a U-Haul, which is the reason I called him.

When I walked out of my front door to greet him, he rolled his window down.

"How we gonna do this, bring everything out through the garage or what?" he asked.

He got out of the truck holding a king-size Snickers. Every time I saw Conrad, he looked like he was getting heavier and older, and I knew he wasn't that old, mid to late thirties. He was just out of shape.

He immediately started asking questions, wanting to know why Reesey and I were moving on such short notice. I didn't feel like telling my business, even if he was one of the brothers, so I just told him I was downsizing. "I know you're not downsizing after you just had the baby," he said as he jogged up the garage stairs behind me, stopping halfway to catch his breath.

"Man, you need to start working out. What if this was a fire you were responding to? You can't be stopping on the stairs, but then again, you just stand outside with the prep radio in your hand any damn way." I opened the door to enter the town house and picked up my bass drum case, which was right inside.

"I can't help if they got me as the boss." He didn't know how to be a boss, just like he didn't know how to fight a blaze, which is probably why they had him as the acting boss at the scene on a regular basis, so he could sit around and do nothing. He'd been a firefighter for about fourteen years, and in that time he had stories of rescues that no one but him could recall. "So, why didn't Reesey take today off for the move?" I just looked at him and didn't say shit, because it was none of his business. He'd catch the hint eventually and change the subject.

With the two of us working together, it took under an hour to move out what I needed. I could come back later for my clothes. As long as I was gone for good by 4:30, there was no reason to worry.

———

We drove to my mother's house and started unloading in her driveway. "At least I'm getting my exercise," Conrad said as we each grabbed an end of my solid oak desk and walked out of the truck, down the driveway, and through the side door of the house,"even though I need to do a whole lot more if I'm trying to drop fifty pounds by Christmas."

"You got seven months. That's about seven pounds a month. You can do that."

"Easy for someone like you to say. How many days a week do you work out?"

"I work out at Gold's almost every day."

"Maybe you can train me, man."

"I'm not a trainer. I just know how to train myself."

"Yeah, I see," he said, staring at the muscles in my arms. It was that kind of shit that caused me to wonder if his ass was gay. It wasn't the first time I caught him looking my way. I couldn't stand that shit. I swear to God if Conrad ever came on to me I'd fuck him up.

We set the desk down in the kitchen, took a few quick breaths, and continued moving in the rest of the things. It took us a little longer to unload everything without the luxury of an attached garage, but after two hours and several breaks, we were finally finished.

I took out two bottles of Evian water from the fridge, walked over to the den's entranceway, and threw one over to Conrad.

He was standing in the den staring at my mother's eleven-by-fourteen Glamour Shot that was hanging in a wooden frame on the wall. "Is this your mother?"

"Yeah." I looked at him with one eyebrow slung in a question mark.

He walked up to the picture to get a closer view. "Didn't you say your mom and dad were divorced?" My parents had been divorced for almost three years, but I didn't respond, because I knew where his question was headed. I'm not sure why Conrad was trying to front so hard like he was into women, but I'd let him pretend. "What's your mom's name?"

"Jolene."

"Hook a brother up with Jolene. This woman is fine."

"Hook a brother up? You must be crazy. Stop looking at my mom's picture."

"I'm for real, man. Hook us up. Your mother's fine."

"Man, she's too old for you."

"Too old? Nigga, I'm thirty-seven. I'm not your age. Besides, I love an older woman. That's all I date."

"Ain't no way you're going to meet my mom."

"Just because of my age?"

"No, just because of you." I stood drinking my bottled water, daring him with my look to press the issue.

"What's wrong with me?"

Since I couldn't say what I wanted to, I didn't answer him right away. Instead, I drank nearly half the water down before I pulled it away from my mouth and let out a refreshing sigh. "Just forget it, all right. It's not going to happen. Besides my mom doesn't like big men."

"Maybe I can convince her otherwise."

"Don't go there when you're talking about my mom."

"Alright. Look, it's forgotten. So tell me what happened between you and Reesey."

"I don't recall telling you something did happen." I sat on the love seat, flipping the empty water bottle around.

Conrad sat in the matching love seat across from me. "Something must have happened, because you didn't tell me to take any of her things."

"That's not what she's going to say. She thinks all that shit is hers. Anyway, you don't want to know, believe me. And even if you do, I don't feel like talking about it."

He was staring at the wall, focusing on our family portrait.

"Is that your brother?"

"Yeah," I said quickly. "Thanks for helping me move."

"Oh, man, forget about that. Y'all look just alike. Is he older?" I ignored the question. "Does he live in Detroit?" He asked more questions than a woman, and it was getting on my nerves.

"No. Not anymore."

"What, is he the black sheep of the family or something? You never talk about him." Conrad stood, walking closer to the picture, paying more attention to my mother. "Y'all were a nice-looking family, mom and dad with the two sons. Too bad all families can't stay together. A family is a beautiful thing. "

A family is a beautiful thing. When it's a family, I guess it is. I glanced over at the picture. It was such a lie. Whenever I looked at that portrait I thought about my mother leaving my brother and me at our grandmother's house, dropping us off when I was six and my brother Richard was nine. Mom told us that she and Dad were going through some things but as soon as they worked them out, one of them would be back to get us. Two years later she pulled up, but she didn't take us right then, and she didn't say when or if she was coming back. One week after that she showed back up, I guess to get us, but by that time the house was on fire, and it was too late to get us, at least both of us.

"Earth to Porter. You didn't hear a word I just said, did you, man?"

"What you say?"

"I asked you if you left Reesey because you found out that wasn't your baby." He watched my expression change.

"How you know that?"

"Anybody can look at that baby and see he's mixed. Didn't you think that?"

"Her mom's mixed so I didn't pay that any mind, but you're right, he's not mine."

"Damn," he said, shaking his head, "that's some shit for your ass. Ain't every day a sister leave a brother for a white man. "

"She didn't leave me. I left her."

"I can't believe Porter, the man voted Detroit's Most Handsome Firefighter for two years straight got played." He shook his head. "Porter the drummer man got played. It's got to be more to it. You had to be stepping out, weren't you? I know you were. Women be slinging their pussy at you, don't they?"

I didn't like the way he said that. I didn't like the way he was trying to pry into my sex life like he had an ulterior motive for wanting to know. It wasn't his business about what women did or what I was doing. Maybe I did step out a time or two, even three, but it was a while ago, more than five years to be exact and during one of our frequent monthlong breakups so it didn't constitute cheating in my mind. I never got a woman pregnant. Come to find out, not even my own woman.

"Porter, my man, if a woman will play you, I'm not sure I need to date."

"It's not about being played. It wasn't any love there. That's all. And when it's no love, anything's subject to happen."

———

It was a quarter to five. I was rushing to get a few things that I had forgotten from the town house. The last thing I needed was Reesey pulling up with one of her coworkers while I was pulling out, but by the time she realized that I wasn't picking her up, most, if not all of her coworkers would be long gone, including her boyfriend, who had to rush to his stay-at-home wife.

I deviated slightly from my original plan. Instead of picking up her baby from day care and taking him over to Reesey's mother, I left him there. I knew if I took him to her mother's, she would buzz Reesey at work and I wanted Reesey to be caught totally off guard, standing in front of the City County building waiting and wondering. So when I was on the expressway heading to my mom's from the town house, I called the day care from my cell phone and instructed the young girl who answered the phone to call Porter's emergency contact immediately, hanging up before she could ask my name. It felt so good to be rid of Reesey and that baby that wasn't mine.

———

It was time for the after work Matchmaker show, a condensed version of the one that aired Saturday on the urban station 103.9 and was hosted by the sexy-voiced Nikki Taylor. I listened regularly. It was set between old slow jams and current chart-topping love songs. Between Nikki's voice and the music, anyone could be put in the mood for love on any day. It was good to listen to other people who believed in that love bullshit. Personally, I would never call in and tell female listeners about myself, tell them who, if anyone famous, I resembled, trying to sell myself so women would write to a P.O. box for a chance to meet a voice. I never wrote in response to any of the women I heard either, but I listened and tripped out on what I did hear because at least I knew or kept the hope alive that black people hadn't given up and were willing to follow a voice and the words being spoken over a face or a body. Maybe it meant real love wasn't dead yet and people were still searching for it by any means necessary, even if it probably didn't exist.

My cell phone started beeping, letting me know I had a message waiting. I pulled into the Mobil gas station so I could call my voice mail without concentrating on the traffic. I had one new message that was received at 4:20 P.M. while I was still at the town house packing my clothes.

"Hey, drummer man," Jade's flamboyant voice rang out. He sounded just like a woman. "I see you're going to be performing at Baker's tonight. I never heard you play the saxophone so I'm coming down to check you out and I'm bringing one of my girlfriends. Can't wait to see you. Tell your mother I said hey." Damn fliers posted all over Detroit. Baker's Keyboard Lounge loved to promote its local performers. I hated that because it always brought out people I didn't want to see, and Jade was one of them. I didn't mind seeing him, but not at Baker's. Like the old saying goes, there's a time and a place for everything. Now was not the time and Baker's wasn't the place.

2

There wasn't a stage at Baker's Keyboard Lounge, just a platform set off to the side a few feet away from the entrance and not too far from the bar. The club held close to one hundred and fifty people, but from the looks of it, there were a lot more than that inside.

Everyone seemed to be into the music. I noticed most of them grooving while they sipped on their drinks or threw out their pick-up lines.

When my part came, I stepped to the center of the platform, lifted my saxophone and placed the mouthpiece between my lips.

I was in my zone again so I didn't hear what the audience heard. I didn't hear whatever it was that made some people rise from their seats and stand to cheer me on. I didn't hear the music. Instead, I concentrated on the thoughts running through my head as I blew my sax, trying to make it speak words that I couldn't. I had on dark shades and a big floppy patchwork hat. I was glad to be incognito, 'cause then I could really let loose. I know that I could have been as big as saxophonist James Carter if I had simply let my mind concentrate longer on music than my past. What happened between Reesey and me hurt a little, but I have too much other pain occupying my heart to take on any more.

After my set, I walked off the platform and immediately saw Jade staring in my direction, looking as feminine as he wanted to in his bright orange halter top and tan calf-length pants. He wasn't alone. He was with some dude that had on false eyelashes that were so long I saw the curve from across the room.

I stayed by the bar, trying not to look at them. Hoping they wouldn't come over to me, but my hopes went out the window after I heard Jade's whiny voice sing out my name. "Porter, aren't you going to speak to your friend? I saw you looking."

"What's up, Jade?" I asked, turning to face him.

"Nothing. You were so good on stage. You can blow that horn. I especially liked the way you licked your lips right before you put your mouth on it. Now that's a blow job."

Jade was just a queen, that's why I didn't let him bother me. He was one of those flaming types that liked to flirt with straight men hoping to turn them out one day, but not this one, no matter how hard he tried—and he'd tried several times.

He used to work for my parents at the Soul Station as the catering director, and that's the only reason we knew each other and the only reason I even tolerated his gay ass. He was a damn good catering director, but my mother had to fire him after she caught him having sex in the utility closet with one of her married male customers about five months ago. I don't know what he's been doing since but he never looks broke. I felt sorry for Jade because I figured he was mentally ill and needed help. This was a young dude, a few years younger than me. He didn't need to be gay.

"Where's your friend?" I asked. "That dude you were with."

"You mean my girl. Um. I'm sure she's lookin' for some big dick to suck." He rolled his tongue slowly over his teeth and let his eyes roam down to my crotch. "I told her I knew where she could find some, but she said you looked too straight to fuck with, which was unusual because she loves her a straight nigga. I told her you ain't that straight though."

"Shut the fuck up, alright. I am that straight."

He rolled his eyes. "Mmmhmm. Yeah right, you and me both. Any way, boo, I need a ride home."

"How many times do I have to tell you not to call me boo? I ain't your fuckin' boo, man!"

"Calm down." Jade surveyed the area. "Don't have the folks looking. It won't look right. It was just a term of endearment."

"Use it on somebody else."

He put his hand on his hip and started rocking his head back and forth. "Can I get a ride home or not?"

"How you get here?"

"My girl, but I told you what she's in here looking for. You scared or something? My little ass can't do nothing to you."

"Nah, I ain't scared of you," I said, looking at him like he was pathetic.

I knew he was going to invite me in. I'd been to his place several times but never this late and not since he was fired. Usually when I came over it was for a meeting dealing with an event the restaurant was catering and he wanted to run his ideas by me. Somehow he'd get to how much he was attracted to me, and I'd tell him to shut the fuck up then we'd go back to business. He was harmless.

"You want to come in?" he asked after I pulled into his driveway.

"No," I said quickly.

He sighed. "Porter, come on in. We haven't talked in a long time. I'm not going to bite you—unless you want me to."

"See, that's why I'm not coming in. I don't like that kind of talk."

"Porter, remember the last conversation we had when you were trying to pry into my business about why I was gay and I just didn't want to talk about it?" I nodded. "I can talk about it now."

"Yeah, right."

"What are you worried about? You think you gonna get tempted and want to try it out."

"Hell no!"

"Okay then. Come in. Shit." Jade got out of the truck looking back at me, motioning for me to come along. I turned off the engine, said what the hell and went in. His place was real nice. I hadn't been over since he got fired, and it looked like he had new furniture. Imported-looking shit. That's the one thing I noticed about gay men, they always seemed to dress nice, have nice places, and expensive cars. Nice things in general. Maybe that was a stereotype but that's how it seemed to be. I knew he wasn't going to talk about why he was gay right off the bat. Instead Jade offered me a glass of wine, which I kindly declined, but he poured himself a glass, and by the time he was on his third one he started spilling his guts.

"I'm gay. I'm homosexual. I'm a faggot. I love dick. What else do you want to know, Porter? Why I'm this way?"

"Yeah, why?" I looked at him, waiting intensely for his response. He poured his fourth glass of wine and sat on the sofa beside me. I scooted over so his leg would no longer be against mine.

He sighed. "I was abused as a child."

"I knew it," I said, pounding my fist into my open hand. "And that made you gay?"

"I don't think it made me gay, but I do think it assisted. I'm sure if I hadn't been abused I wouldn't have even thought about having sex with

a man. I would have been like you, but that's right, I don't really know
what you think about."

"I don't think about having sex with a man."

"Porter, this is Jade you're talking to. You can't lie to me. I was the
one who showed you your first homosexual porn movie. Remember
that?"

"Shut up. That shit was foul, and I had you turn it off. I'm not talking
about me. I'm talking about you. Who abused you?"

"Let's see." His eyes roamed as if searching for the answer. "First it
was my stepfather, then a choir director, and after that I was pretty much
no longer being abused and I just made a choice to fuck men. Is that what
you want to hear, Porter? Well, I'm sorry, it's a lie. Nobody abused me.
I've known I was gay since I was five years old."

I shook my head. "That's sad. You don't even have to be gay, man,"
I said.

"And you don't even have to be straight, man."

"Please." I rolled my eyes. I didn't want to think about being with a
man, someone who had the same thing I did.

"Porter, let me just suck your dick."

"What? Hell no!"

"That won't make you gay, Porter. Just let me suck your dick."

"Why should I let you suck my dick? I can have a woman do that."

He shook his head. "You ain't had your dick sucked until you let a
man do it, believe me. Besides, a lot of so-called straight men get their
dick sucked by gay men."

I started shaking my head. "I don't want that. No."

"Then what do you want, Porter? Why am I your friend? And why do
you call me from time to time and come over? I don't work for your
mama anymore."

"I just want to help you."

"No. You want to help yourself. People don't care about other people.
When the shit all boils down, it boils right back down to them. I'm fine
with who I am. You want to fuck a man, and you know you do, but you're
scared of being gay."

"I'm not gay! I fuck women. Not men," I said, defensively.

"That don't mean shit!" He wiggled in his seat while he sipped the
last of his wine. "I want to suck your dick. I'll pay you. I know you need
money. I'll pay you. I'll pay you five hundred dollars."

"I don't need money that bad."

"A thousand."

"Nope."

"How much?"

"A million dollars," I said.

"So you do have a price?"

"For a million dollars you can have it. I'll cut it off and put it on a silver platter for you."

"I thought money didn't mean anything to you."

"It doesn't. I'm just bull-shittin'."

"Porter, please let me. I need you." He looked at me like he was possessed, and then he took his hand and grabbed between my legs, cupping my dick.

I pushed his hand away and stood. "Motherfucka, I will fuck your ass up!" I said, pointing my finger down in his face. My nostrils were flaring. Jade was cowering like a scared child. "Don't ever come on me like that! You don't know me like that, motherfucka! I'm not to be fucked with. I'm a crazy motherfucka. You understand?"

He nodded. I could tell he was real scared. He hadn't seen me like this before. I had snapped, and my voice was completely different. It was loud and deep and more street. "I will fuck your skinny ass up if you ever put your motherfuckin' hands on me again! Grabbing my shit. I will kill your punk ass! Do you understand me?" He nodded, trying not to establish eye contact with me. "Look at me." I started beating my chest. "I'm six-two, 245 pounds of pure muscle. Why the fuck would you think I need to be with you or any man? My shit is for a woman. Do you understand me? It's for a woman! I was just trying to help your punk, sissified ass, but fuck it. Shit! I'm out this bitch."

3

I pulled up to the fire station on Tuesday at 7:00 A.M. and noticed two heads in the front seat of a burgundy Monte Carlo that belonged to Reesey's girlfriend, Tonya. Their doors were opened and closed before I could even think about getting out of my Lexus, and they proceeded to walk toward my truck. I'd never seen Reesey look so run-down. Her jeans were strangling her fat behind and thick thighs, and the faded Patti LaBelle T-shirt that she was wearing was stained.

"Get out the damn truck!" Reesey yelled with Tonya backing her up.

"I don't believe this shit," I mumbled to myself as a small crowd of firefighters formed out front. It's funny how anger energizes a person. On any other day, Reesey's ass would still be in the bed snoring.

"Get out!" she repeated, kicking my tire.

"What do you need, Reesey?" I asked as I let down my window.

"What do I need?" She turned and looked at Tonya. "Do you hear this motherfucka asking me what do I need? An expladamnation!" she said hysterically. "That's what the fuck I need! How could you do this to me?"

"Do what?" I asked, staring into her big mouth, counting all six of her fillings. Nice teeth were something she didn't have on Pam.

"Don't play me like this. Explain yourself. For once, explain your-damnself!"

"There's nothing to explain. I need you to step away from my truck so I can go to work."

"Fuck this damn truck! You left my—our—baby at day care yesterday."

"You said it right the first time—*your* baby."

"What are you talking about, Porter?"

"Reesey, stop acting dumb, even if you do it well. Why don't you just stop and step away from the truck, please?"

"I said fuck this truck!" She took her purse and threw it against my windshield.

"What the fuck are you doing? Dumb—"

"Dumb what? Dumb what? Say it." She started kicking the tire on the driver's side and hitting me on my shoulder and face with her balled fists.

I grabbed her wrist and pulled her partially inside the window. "Leave before I do or say something you regret," I said, loosening my grip. She snatched herself free.

"If you do or say something, you're going to be the only one regretting it. Why don't you say something for once in your life? Express yourself, if you know how."

I raised the tinted glass and let the darkness say what I couldn't. I could see her; she couldn't see me. That's how it was, how it had been, and how it was going to stay.

"Freak. I know your problem. You're probably gay," she said just as my window closed completely.

I snatched the door open and got out of the car rushing toward her with my fist balled. "What the fuck did you just say? Why did you say that, huh?" I yanked her by the shirt and drew her in closer to me.

Zeander, the rookie firefighter, rushed over to me and pulled us apart.

"Any man who's going to leave me got to be gay or crazy."

I waved my hands in her space and walked back to the truck. I felt like this could turn into a bigger scene than it already was so to prevent that, I pulled away. I was hoping the brothers back at the station would detain Reesey and Tonya so they wouldn't jump in the car and follow me.

On the way to my mother's house, I made a detour down East Outer Drive and passed the empty lot where my grandmother's house used to be. I was surprised by my lack of emotion this time. Each year made the reality of my brother's death easier to accept but impossible to deal with.

At the red light, I let down my window and slid in Boney James' *Body Language* CD, advancing to track eight, "I Get Lonely."

I heard a faint voice over the lyrics. Suddenly I noticed arms flapping from my side view. I turned my head slightly and saw a young lady in the passenger side of a convertible Vette. She was young. Had to be. Any woman who would go that far out of her way to meet somebody in traffic was young. "Can you pull over?" she asked after I turned down the music. "Pull over so my twin can meet you."

I smirked. "Why your twin? Why not you?"

"Oh, I'm married."

I leaned my head closer to the steering wheel, trying to get a better look at her twin to make sure they were identical, but she kept her head turned away from me, and her long hair was shielding her face.

"Are you sure she wants to meet me?"

"Yeah, she's shy. Pull over."

I pulled into the McDonald's lot just passed the light and parked in the first available space.

She stayed in the car talking to her twin so I turned the volume up to my music and entered into my own world, transforming my hands into drumsticks; I had left this universe for a moment.

"Hello," she sang. I opened my eyes, not realizing I had closed them until I heard her voice. "What, are you a drummer or something?"

I turned the music down. "Yeah, I'm a drummer."

She smiled. "That's sexy."

"Really, you think so? I'm a firefighter too."

"Oh, that's real sexy."

"So your shy twin wants to meet me? Well let me ask you something, if you're married and she's the one who wants to meet me, why is she the one wearing the big-ass rock? I can't see her face, but I can sure see that ring that's blinding me."

She hesitated. "Uh, we're playing a trick on my husband this week." It didn't take her long to admit that she was the one who wanted to meet me and that her twin was married to Tony Turn, the middleweight champion of the world. Her conversation was slightly juvenile. She asked me where I was from and told me that she thought I was from New York or California because she didn't know there were any fine black men living in Detroit. I was used to being complimented by women on my looks but not by someone who was as fine as this woman. Reesey never would've said anything close to that. Not when Brad Pitt, David Justice, and Harry Connick, Jr., were her pretend men.

The woman's name was Stacy Valentine. She was only nineteen. I knew baby girl was young, but nineteen in my eyes isn't even legal. Isn't even drinking age. When I told her my name, age, and that they called me the drummer man, she got excited because she had seen me perform down at Baker's the previous night.

"You probably still living at home with your mama," I said.

"No, actually, I have my own house."

"At nineteen?"

"You ask a lot of questions. Let me start asking you a few. Are you married?"

"Nope."

"I know you have a girlfriend."

"Not anymore."

"Mmm, I'm shocked. Well, since you don't have a girlfriend…"

"What about you? You got a man?"

"I'm seeing somebody. Nothing serious." I turned the music back up.

"Turn it down. For real, it's nothing serious. I'm just seeing some-body. We date. Go to movies, Baker's. Things like that. Please turn the music down," she said, reaching through my window. I grabbed her wrist, as her hand got closer to my sound system. "Mmm, I love a forceful man."

"Let me have your number," I said as I turned off the music and released her wrist. "I'll call you and maybe we can get together sometime."

"How about tonight?"

"You sure you not gonna be with your man?"

"I don't have a man, per se."

"Does Per Se know that?"

"You're silly. Call me tonight so we can get together, okay? Do you have something to write with?"

I handed her a pen and a take-out menu from the Soul Station. Asked her again if she was nineteen and not sixteen, because I could never be too sure these days, and then I told her straight up, "I may have a Lexus but I don't have money like Tony Turn."

"So. My twin can marry ugly, I can't."

"As fine as you are, what difference does it make?"

"I'm fine and I like to look at fine, too, just like men do. Some ugly, crusty negro thinks he gonna crawl up next to me is wrong, but you, drummer man, are a whole 'nother story, and I can't wait 'til tonight."

"Why is that?"

"You'll see." She handed back my pen and menu with her name and number scribbled across it. "Don't lose my number, cutie." She kissed me on the cheek, opposite side from Pam's, and skipped back to her car with her long hair galloping in the wind.

I made it to Stacy's house around eleven; late enough so she wouldn't think we were going out. I was surprised when I pulled in front and saw how run-down the house was. She lived on a street between Hamilton and Woodward, only a few blocks away from Boston and Chicago boulevards where all the mansions were. It shouldn't have surprised me though, because that's how a lot of Detroit was. Nice areas sprinkled between run-down ones. I felt like leaving because I didn't think my Lexus was safe.

I called her on my cell phone. I didn't want to tell her the truth, that her house was too jacked up for me to stay, however, I didn't have time to figure out a good enough lie.

"What's wrong?" she asked. "Aren't you getting out? Don't tell me you're afraid to park your Lexus in my driveway."

I cleared my throat. "Why would you say that?"

"Because you're the typical Detroit man with a nice ride—paranoid. My sister parks her Vette over here almost every day."

"This ain't day, it's night. Besides, she's got money."

"And you've got insurance, don't you?"

"I got insurance." I had insurance. I guess Reesey paid it. I hoped she did since I gave her the money last month, but she probably spent it on a new pair of shoes and another purse.

"Then come on in here and get this."

"Get what?"

"What you think? I'm standing behind the front door, butt naked with nipples so hard they feel like bullets. So what you want to do about that? You need to get this."

I cleared my throat again. "I guess I'm going to park." She was right. I needed to go and get that. I needed to be with another woman besides Reesey, and it had been so long since I had.

"I tell you what, I'm going to open the garage so you can pull your truck in there 'cause I don't want your mind on anything but pleasing me."

She hung up the phone and seconds later I saw her prancing out of the side door wearing a red satin robe with a pair of matching hooker shoes, the kind that had the heel out. She unlatched the fence and slid the gate back far enough for me to drive through.

I left my headlights on and watched her prance her tight ass down toward the one-car garage and stoop to raise it, exposing her bare butt cheeks.

She pulled her late-model convertible Mustang out and parked it to the side on the grass so I could pull my truck into the garage.

As I stepped out of the truck, she walked over to me and pinned her body against mine on the driver's door.

"You thought I was lying about being butt naked," she said as she stood back and loosened her satin belt to flash me, bouncing her fake breasts around. "Peekaboo."

"Damn, I see you."

"You gonna feel me in a minute."

———

The next morning I overslept because I didn't get home until a little after three in the morning. Now it was almost two in the afternoon, and I felt like I had a hangover even though I didn't drink one sip of liquor. Maybe it was all that rough sex the night before in every position imaginable and a whole bunch of unimaginable. Come to find out, Ms. Stacy Valentine was a stripper at the Black Orchid. Figures. Not that I'm worried. I definitely used protection. The sex wasn't bad, but it wasn't that good either because she was talking too damn much, telling me she liked it rough, biting my nipples so hard I thought she had ripped them off. Then she told me to take her in the ass. I wasn't going there. No way. Not after Jade and Reesey both called me gay. I wasn't going there, not even with a woman, but I did eat her pussy. I had to eat her pussy in order to get the taste of Reesey's out my mouth. Damn, I don't think you can get AIDS from eating pussy. Besides, I read somewhere that it was harder for a man to get AIDS from a woman. I know for a fact I read that somewhere. I hope it was true. I don't know about that girl. To only be nineteen I get the feeling she's been around the block more than a couple dozen times.

I rumbled around the bed, trying to avoid the springs that poked my side all night. Waking up in my old bedroom in a double-sized bed with a fifteen-year-old lumpy mattress and my junk leaning against the wall or crammed inside of the tiny closet wasn't the best experience.

"Mom, you home?" I yelled out to hollow silence. I got out of the bed and walked down the hall to her room. The door was open and her bed was made, which meant she was gone. Good. I had the whole place to myself. I didn't have to worry about hearing my mother screaming and yelling about when I was moving out.

My cell phone was ringing off the hook. I started not to answer it when I saw Stacy's name and number come across the display.

"Hello, Porter. This is Stacy."

"I know."

"Well, I thought I'd tell you so you wouldn't have to rack your brain trying to figure out which ho it was."

"It's not even like that."

"Mmmhmm. I'm sure it's not. I called to see if you're coming back over tonight."

"Stacy, you gonna get tired of a brother."

"Not you. You can move in if you want."

"Let's slow it down. A brother ain't trying to shack."

"You're living with your mama now."

I told her too much of my business. Even told her a little about Reesey, since she asked. One thing I will say about her, she asked enough questions. She wanted to know everything about me after we had sex. It seemed like she was trying to cram six months worth of dating into thirty minutes. She wanted to know about my last relationship and why it ended, and whether or not I was still in love with Reesey. I told her that I was never in love with Reesey, and I honestly believe I wasn't.

"Yeah, I'm living with my mother now, but that's only temporary. I'm having a little set back, but I'm going to get myself together real soon. And when I do, it'll be time to be by myself for a change," I said.

"Not if I can help it. Bring your ass over here right now."

"I can't see you tonight or this week, baby. I'm working."

"You not working seven days. Firefighters don't even work like that."

"How do you know? You know some? You dating some?"

"Just you."

And we're not dating, I thought, *just fucking.*

"We'll I'm on a new schedule. Seven days straight," I lied.

She sighed. "So what am I supposed to do for the next seven days?"

"I don't know. Call Per Se."

"You won't let that slide, will you? Even when I'm trying to be serious."

"I'll be talking to you," I said.

"Can't you call me from the station so we can have phone sex?"

"You think I'm going to have phone sex from my job? I could get fired for doing that."

"Y'all don't do nothin' down there anyway if you're not called out to a fire. You're either watching television, playing cards, eating, or sleeping. Must be nice, but I know you're probably more into drumming than being a firefighter, right? Since you're so good at it, huh?"

"I'm good at everything I do, baby."

"You can say that again."

"I'm good at *everything* I do. I play the saxophone too."

"I know. Remember, I heard you play at Baker's. So which one do you like better, the drums or the sax?"

"I'm known for drumming, but I love the sax."

"I love the sex too. Ooh, do I love the sex."

"I got to go," I said with a smile.

"Call me on your next off day, okay?" she asked.

"I'll try." Not. I doubt if I'd be calling her at all. She was a little too swift for me, and only nineteen. She'd be used all the way up by the time she hit thirty.

I went to work on Thursday and would be off on a kelly Friday, Saturday, and Sunday. Our schedule was on a day, off a day, on a day, off three days.

The volume on the radio was turned all the way up. A few of the other brothers and I were listening to the Matchmaker show on 103.9. Most of them weren't looking to be matched up, at least I hoped not since most had wives or longtime girlfriends they were committed to.

"As I promised our male listeners, Faithful is on the line. Hello, Faithful. How are you?" Nikki Taylor asked.

The female caller claimed to be twenty-five but had the voice of a ten-year-old.

"I couldn't listen to that voice all day," I said to a few of the brothers standing around.

"It's hard for me to listen to it right now," Conrad said as he walked over to join us. He was stuffing his face with one of the Subway sandwiches that Zeander brought back for us.

I ignored him. I felt my fist tighten and my blood rush to the vein protruding from my forehead. According to some of the brothers around the station, Conrad was telling my business. Telling them the reason Reesey had been up here a couple of days ago acting a fool. Telling them about the baby and how I moved out.

I kept listening to code name Faithful discuss her pet peeves about men. Top on her list were men who played games. Next were men who lied. After she was done with her long list, Nikki asked her to describe herself. She paused for too long to be telling the truth. Finally, she said that people referred to her as the black Jennifer Lopez. She said she wore a size twelve, whatever that was. The only thing I knew about women's sizes was that my mother wore a fourteen and complained every day and Reesey used to brag about being a size eight until she gained forty pounds after the baby, and never discussed her dress size again.

"Turn it up, I might write her," Conrad said between bites of a sandwich.

"What happened to you only date older women?" I asked.

"Oh, that's right, I do. Thanks for reminding me."

I started to ask him if he was sure it was older women and not men he dated, but I didn't want to start mess at the station. That wasn't even my style so I kept my mouth shut and continued listening to Faithful.

"How do you think a woman should treat her man?" Nikki asked in that sexy voice I loved to listen to.

"Like I treat my man—like a king," Faithful said, but she didn't sound like a ten-year- old when she answered that question. Nah, she sure didn't. She sounded like she was at least out of high school.

"Can you give us some examples?" Nikki asked.

"Bathing him. Full-body massages. Cooking a good meal. And never holding out the loving." Maybe she was nervous in the beginning, because that girl had suddenly become a woman.

"I might have to drop a line to the black Jennifer Lopez," Conrad said right after he took another large bite of his sandwich.

"She don't want you," I said with attitude, because I was tired of hearing him talk, especially while he was eating, but any time really, because he always got on my damn nerves.

"Oh, now you the expert on what women want?" he asked.

"Yeah, I sure am."

"You the expert on what women want all of a sudden?" he asked again while tiny strips of lettuce fell from his mouth.

"Didn't your mama teach you any manners? Like not talking while you're eating your damn food."

He stood in front of me. Staring me down in silence as he chewed. He had a smirk on his face right before he swallowed. "Yeah, my mama taught me manners. Now let me ask you something. If you're such an expert on what women want, how come you didn't know your woman really wanted a white man?"

My face hardened. I slammed Conrad's back against the wall, causing what was left of his sandwich to fly out of his hands, and then I jammed my arm under his throat before he could get out all of his laughter.

"Come on, man," Conrad said, choking on the words. "What you so sensitive about? It's only fair that the sisters start diversifying too."

"If you got jokes, get your fat ass on stage with Hoffa. See how many people laugh at your stale ass."

Conrad shook himself back together after Zeander pulled me away from him.

"Calm down, man. You okay?" Zeander asked in the cool voice he always maintained. He brushed me off and patted my back. "Don't let words get to you." I'm sure scripture was soon to follow. That's all Zeander did was pray and quote scriptures. Must have been a hell of a past he was trying to erase. I didn't ask Zeander too many questions. If we weren't out fighting fires, I liked to stay clear of him, because any conversation with Zeander always led straight to God.

"I'm okay, man." I rotated my shoulders. "But I don't feel like jokes, especially about my personal life."

"This is a family. We're all brothers here," Zeander said. "All one big family."

"Shit," I said. "Ross, you and me are a team, the hell with Conrad. His punk ass doesn't know how to fight a damn fire." I allowed my words to bounce off Conrad's back as he walked into the kitchen.

The bar that was rigged to the printer hit the ground around one in the morning. Even though the department rule was for someone to be near the printer twenty-four hours a day in order to hear the ticket print out from central office alerting us to a fire, we relied mostly on the echo from the metal bar dropping to the ground, and since it was after midnight a high-pitch tone came over the radio to ensure we received notification.

I was the first one up and in uniform. I ran downstairs, pulling the paper off the printer. It was a house fire a few blocks from where my grandmother used to live.

"Let's go!" I yelled up to Zeander, Ross, and Conrad, clapping my hands. "It's time to roll." They came running down the stairs seconds later. Ross was assigned the F.E.O (fire engine operator), which meant he was the one driving the engine truck, and he'd be the one to hook the hose to the hydrant. Conrad was the boss, which meant he'd stay outside with the handheld radio giving and awaiting instructions. Zeander and I would fight the blaze.

"Let's go. Let's go!" I shouted as I hopped on the engine truck.

When we reached the burning house, Zeander, Conrad, and I jumped off the truck. I sized up the house. It was a small colonial, probably two or three bedrooms upstairs with one full bath up, possible half bath down at the most. Just like my grandmother's. At this time of night, if there were anyone inside they'd most likely be on the second floor in one of the bedrooms.

I was dragging approximately one hundred and fifty feet of line in my arm, and as Ross drove to the hydrant he was supplying us with more line by flaking off about eighteen additional feet.

Conrad stood back with the prep radio in hand. I heard Ross talking to central office through Conrad's handheld radio. "Notify," Ross said. "I'm committed and hydrant isn't pulling water. I need arriving engine to hook to hydrant."

"Was it tagged?" Conrad asked Ross through the prep radio. There should never be a situation where we pull up to a hydrant and there's no water because we should know in advance through our regular checks and tag that hydrant.

"No tag," Ross said. Since it was May, that was possible because we didn't do as much checking that month. In fact, we rarely checked then, but still it was going to be our ass.

There was a large crowd of neighbors pouring into the streets.

"There are two kids inside. Those kids are in there by themselves!" one of the neighbors shouted. "They don't have no electricity and they keep candles burning all through the house. I know that's what started it." How did she know? Our training taught us not to listen to what people on the scene said. Question everything. Two kids inside without adults. Why? It really didn't matter if there were people inside. What mattered was whether we could save a life and bring ours back with it. At least that's what we were taught, but kids mattered to me.

"Why ain't none of y'all going inside?" another neighbor yelled out.

"I'm going in," I said to Conrad.

"You're staying here and waiting for the next engine."

"I'm going in," I said firmly.

"I'm the boss and I said nobody's going in. We're waiting."

"Save those kids in there," a few neighbors yelled.

I was supposed to listen to the boss, but in this case the boss was Conrad, and even if it wasn't Conrad, once I heard that there were kids inside that changed the whole scope of things. A house could burn, but there was no way in hell I was letting kids go with it. My adrenaline started pumping. I didn't care what Conrad said. I knew what I was going to do. I dropped the line and ran to the truck to get a tool. Another department rule: never enter a scene without a means of egress. I grabbed an ax and ran from the engine to the door, knocking it down with my foot.

"Wait a minute," Zeander shouted. "I'm going in with you." I wanted to go alone, even though the rule was to never freelance, but Zeander was fresh out of training, and the academy didn't prepare the rookies to battle real fires. I didn't want him risking his life. He had a wife and newborn baby to consider, which were two big reasons to live. All I had were the memories of yesterday haunting me. It would be much better for someone like me to die a hero than Zeander.

Nothing was visible through the thick smoke covering the bottom floor. The only sounds were from the loud crackling of fire and compressed glass. I stayed low in front of Zeander, crawling with my hand against the wall, following it. Zeander was keeping in contact behind me with his hand touching my foot.

We crawled upstairs and then splintered off, which was something we were never supposed to do, but time wasn't on our side. We had three bedrooms and one bathroom to check, and a fire in the back of the house growing out of control. All of the doors were closed. I continued crawling until I reached the door to the bedroom facing the front of the house. I opened the door and went inside. There was no fire in the room and very little smoke. I immediately closed the door so I wouldn't let in any of the smoke. I stayed low to the ground, still feeling around until I felt some braids, and a tiny face. I grabbed the child and made it over to the window, raising it.

"I need a ladder," I yelled through the window after taking off my mask. Ross had to climb up the ladder while Conrad just stood watching like always. When Ross took the little girl, she looked at me and said, "My brother. Don't forget to save my brother."

"Where's your brother?" I asked.

"I don't know." I saw the tears well in her eyes.

I pulled my mask down over my face, went back to the ground, and continued searching.

In the hallway as I moved along staying low, I felt something. Another person. My initial plan was to grab him and get him to the window and hand him off like I did his sister, but I could tell just from feeling his arm that he was a big kid, too large to get through one of those tiny bedroom windows.

"Listen to me, young man," I said, removing my mask. "We're going to take turns breathing through this mask, okay?"

"Okay," he said, coughing.

"Follow me. Start crawling. Stay low right alongside me, close to the wall. Stay in contact with my foot." I didn't know where Zeander was. I could only hope he had already made it out. We crawled down the stairs, still sharing air from the mask. The back section of the house was collapsing and the flames were spreading. "Run out the door," I said as we reached the last step. I let the boy go first to ensure he made it all the way out, then I went, praying Zeander was outside too.

When I first made it out, I looked around for Zeander, circling the perimeter with my eyes. Since the fire was classified as a box alarm, the street was packed with three engines, a truck, and a squad. I walked over to the squad to see if Zeander was being administered first aid inside, but there was no sign of him. I started to run back in, amid the high-powered water being sprayed over the scene. If he died, I'd be the one responsible, and I couldn't have another death hanging over my head. Before, I could catch my breath in order to go in again, Zeander came tumbling down the front steps. Three of us carried him away from the house and over to the squad.

"I'm fine," he said. "I just couldn't find anybody."

"They got out," I said. "We all got out. Thank God."

4

"We're having our first annual Meet Your Mate this Thursday at Ballers," Nikki Taylor's voice spoke through the airwaves.

It was Friday night a little past seven. I was off until Monday. I was in my bedroom in total darkness, stretched across the worn, red-carpeted floor listening to the portable boom box that was by my side. I was wondering what Reesey was doing and trying to figure out why I cared. For the first week, Reesey called my cell phone every day. When I was almost ready to change the number, she stopped calling and leaving threatening messages on my voice mail. Stopped calling my mother's house, probably because she couldn't leave any messages there because Mom didn't believe in answering machines, only Caller ID. The few days after the breakup, Reesey called my mother's house upwards of thirty times a day. Could've been more, but that's all my mother's display box could hold and Reesey wouldn't have been herself if she didn't go to the Soul Station to once again confront my mother about what a terrible job she did as a parent by not teaching her son how to respect a beautiful black woman.

"So now you want to claim black?" Mom asked her. "I taught my son how to respect women that aren't confused and claiming things they're not. What your mama teach you? How to be triflin'?"

I started dialing Stacy's number on my cell phone. Who else was there? I wish I could answer that question. I wish I had a spare to call, but I didn't. Let's see, how long have we known each other, about a week and one or two days? Not two weeks, that's for sure. I doubt we will make it to two weeks. I feel a ditch coming on, a disappearing act I'm about to pull, as my mother would say when she's talking about the actions of her men.

Stacy and I talked long enough to arrange another late-night visit to her place. This time her car was already going to be parked on the grass and the gate and garage door would be open awaiting my arrival. All she wanted in return was a corn-beef sandwich on rye with Swiss cheese and coleslaw, a slice of pound cake, and a twenty-ounce Pepsi from Mr. Foo Foos. That's all she wanted. Still, it was too much to ask.

I left at 9:00 P.M. heading to Stacy's. I even called in the order to Mr. Foo Foo's, but instead of driving to her house, I picked up the order and drove to Belle Isle, my favorite spot to chill and think. I parked by the water facing Canada's side and ate her sandwich and pound cake, and then washed it all down with the Pepsi before I burped.

After an hour had almost passed, Stacy started calling my cell phone. I didn't want to pick up, but that would be too rude and immature, and I didn't consider myself to be either. "Hello," I said, trying to sound rushed so she would think something had happened to detain me.

"You're not coming, right?" she asked.

"Nah, I'm not. I can't make it."

"I knew it. I don't want to see your black ass anymore."

"Look, I'm sorry. I really wasn't in a good mood tonight."

"Yeah, you rarely are, and there isn't a special shift at the fire department that works seven days. Who do you take me for, a fool? The more I hang around you, the more I might start thinking it's me, and it isn't me. It's you! I know I look good. I got my own house. It may be in what you call a jacked-up neighborhood, but it's mine. I'm not renting and I'm not staying with my damn mama!"

"Okay, I deserve that."

"No, I'm not downing you. I understand you're still hurt over your last relationship."

"No, I'm not," I said firmly.

"Yes, you are. But one day, Porter, you'll look back and think about me and think about how good of a woman I was, but I'm not waiting for that day, so good-bye." I heard the dial tone, and I knew she meant what she said, so I dialed her back, but she didn't answer. Instead she let it go straight to her voice mail. So what? She was young, and after listening to her every word, seeing how free she was with her body and the things she did to mine, I decided that she was another Reesey, so why bother. I had spent—I mean, wasted—twelve years with the same woman, but in my mind, I remained faithful mostly that whole time. Women always complain about how they get dogged by men, I guess they don't believe there are brothers out there who don't do any dogging, brothers like me who end up with women like Reesey and then what do we do after we get dogged? We start dogging. I didn't want that to be the case, but what goes around comes around one way or another, and since I'm not happy and I feel this big void, I need something. Might as well be sex. Time to let the ladies of Detroit experience a real man in uniform.

I called Jade on my cell phone and let it ring five times. I wanted to apologize for the way I acted. I flew off the handle like I was homophobic or something and I heard some expert on TV say that men who act like that are frightened of their own sexuality, but I knew that was bullshit because I knew where I stood with mine. Dick couldn't do shit.

"Hello," Jade's voice sang out.

"What's up, man?"

"Hey," his voice dragged.

There was silence for a moment. "What's up?" I repeated.

"Nothing," he said dryly. "What's up with you? Have you calmed down?"

"I'm cool."

"I thought you were going to kill me the other night. I really did."

"Nothing like that."

"Well what is it, Porter? It's something. I can tell you got some deep issues. If you didn't have issues you wouldn't be calling me, and you wouldn't feel so strongly about why men are gay. So what is it?"

"I have issues, but it's nothin' that words can fix. I'm just fucked up."

"So am I. So is everybody in one way or another."

"I just wanted to call you and tell you I'm sorry for trippin' like that."

"I want to apologize too. I shouldn't have touched you like that. That wasn't right so I deserved all that shit you were talking."

"So what you about to do?" I asked.

"You don't want to know."

"What? It's cool. It's your life."

"I'm going to a bathhouse on Eight Mile."

"A what?"

"It's a place where gay men go to have sex. It's almost like a big orgy."

"They got some shit like that on Eight Mile? West or East?"

"West. Why, you want to go?"

"Hell no, and you don't need to go, either. Man, gay is one thing, but why you got to be a ho?"

"I'm a single man and I like to fuck. I'm a ho because I'm fucking men but I wouldn't be one if I was fucking a bunch of women, now would I?"

"That's different."

"No lecture, okay. I'm 'bout to get paid."

"So that's how you get your money."

"You damn right. It's nothing in there but a bunch of old, rich white men. I'll come home with five thousand dollars tonight guaranteed."

"Watch yourself, okay?"

"You care about me?"

"In a way."

"Why?"

"I just do…and not the way you think. I just think you don't have to be the way you are. I don't even think you want to be. You didn't have a choice. You don't know what you like. You've never been with a woman."

"And I don't want to be with one either. I got to go. Call me tomorrow, and I'll tell you how much money I made."

5

I had forgotten Thursday night was Meet Your Mate at Ballers, and even if I had remembered I hadn't planned on going. Only reason I rolled through was because Damion called and wanted me to meet him for some drinks and to watch Hoffa perform. Maybe liquor and laughs were exactly what I needed.

I had never been to Ballers, a medium-size club owned by Rick Slade, a retired football player. Supposedly, it was a cool place to hang, drawing a mixed crowd. Athletes, wanna-bes, groupies, and perpetrators of all races frequented his establishment. It was the place to be on Thursday because it had two-for-one drinks, no cover, and the finest women in the metro area. I wasn't trying to meet a mate, but I did see some women I didn't mind mating with.

Hoffa was due on stage at ten. He was a real funny guy. He told jokes, but his specialty was impersonations, and he did everyone from Michael Jackson to President Clinton.

When I walked in, I stood near the back of the club. Hoffa was already walking off the stage engulfed in roars, handclaps, and a standing ovation. It was a good thing Hoffa had a gift to make people laugh and he could cap at the spur of the moment without talking too harshly about a brother, if he didn't, he'd have to duck for days on the insults that would be thrown his way because he wasn't much to look at. When I think bucked teeth and Coke-bottled glasses, I see Hoffa.

Damion was near the front of the club by the stage on his feet, whistling through his fingers.

"What's up, Hoffa, man?" I asked him as he staggered toward me. Hoffa had to, as he says, "light his mind" before going on stage, which meant he would put down some alcohol. He claimed to be a schizoid and gin and tonic was his medication.

"What's up, drummer man? You run that idea by Big D, yet?"

I looked into his glassy eyes. "Not yet. Soon though, real soon." Hoffa wanted me to talk Damion into investing roughly a hundred thousand dollars in a comedy tour of the black college campuses. I told Hoffa I would run it by Damion, but honestly Hoffa's alcohol addiction made him less than reliable. I did notice that Hoffa was trying to get closer to Damion. Trying to get an in. Used to be a time when Hoffa never went by Damion's crib, but now he plays cards every week with him and two of Damion's boys. Pretty soon, he'd feel comfortable enough to ask Damion himself—cut out the middleman. Doesn't matter, I wouldn't see any money from the whole deal anyway.

"Cool. I'm anxious to get things rolling. I know I'm the funniest cat around. I'm funnier than all them Chrises."

"Maybe Rock, not Tucker."

"Shit. You better open up your eyes and recognize."

Hoffa had gotten so far into the party scene and forty-five-minute stand-up routines at local clubs performing for close to nothing that the brother lost his drive and was willing to settle for seventy-five dollars to perform his best material. Meanwhile, we would turn on the television and hear some other comedian telling Hoffa's jokes. I tried to tell him good jokes can travel fast, and I also told him he could rest assured those dudes on TV weren't getting paid seventy-five dollars.

"You hear the crowd. They loved me, man. Did you hear me tonight? Wasn't I funny as hell, man?"

"I missed your show. I thought you came on at ten."

"I do. Your ass can't tell time and you're wearing a damn Rolex," he said, looking down at my wrist. "Must be fake."

"It's the real deal bought on credit."

"At least you can get credit," Hoffa said, "Only credit I get is credit for taking care of my kids. So what am I supposed to do, take one of my kids to JC Penny and let them swipe 'em instead of the Visa I don't have?"

"Man, you're crazy."

"Let your old high school buddy hook you up with a drink. Let Class Clown hook Class Best-Looking up with a drink. But you know what I don't understand? How did you beat me out of that shit? How were you Best-Looking? Who was the judge and jury over that? That's what I want to know. Shit, I know I look good. I bet it came down to a tie."

"You think so?" I asked.

"Had to. How else could you explain it? You want a drink?"

"Hell yeah. You treatin'? I want a rum and Coke."

"Wait a damn minute. Ain't you a firefighter? Drinking on the job. No wonder this city is burning, bunch of drunk asses. I'm getting your ass some lemonade."

"Nigga, I'm off until Sunday. I want a rum and Coke. Hook it up."

"Lem and ade. I'll have my girl Marla hook you up." Hoffa yelled to the waitress across the room then edged away.

I tried to make it over to Damion's table, but before I could, I noticed a young lady standing across the room dressed in a conservative outfit, a nice knee-length skirt with a short-sleeve aqua blouse. She was looking in my direction. I wanted to walk over to her, but I didn't know what to say.

Marla, the waitress, walked over with my drink, but I could tell from looking at it that it wasn't a rum and Coke. It was too light and the glass was too tall, and it sure wasn't lemonade.

I wrinkled my nose. "What's this?" I asked, after taking it off the tray.

"It's a Long Island Iced Tea. The lady in the aqua blouse sent it over. Her name is Adrienne, and she said to tell you that you're gorgeous, and she's right."

I glanced over at Adrienne, who was sipping on her drink still staring at me. "Thank you, but no thank you." I put the glass back on her tray. "I don't drink Long Island's."

"I can bring you something else." She smiled.

"What happened to the rum and Coke Hoffa said you were going to hook me up with thirty minutes ago?"

She scratched her beehive hairdo, making it move around her head. "Thirty minutes? Not hardly. Try five, if that. Anyway, Hoffa said to bring you a lemonade."

"Life is a joke to Hoffa. Rum and Coke please."

"You get two for one. What are you going to do with your other one?" she asked, batting her short lashes.

"Drink it."

She puckered her lips. "I'll be right back."

I played it cool. I didn't look back in Adrienne's direction again. Instead, I flirted a little with the white girl in front of me by telling her she had an ass like a sister. She smiled and we started making small talk until I felt a tap on my shoulder. I turned around and saw Adrienne. She wasn't as attractive close up. Her main flaw was her bad skin that she tried to conceal with heavy makeup. Her shoulder-length hair was decent, but she wore braces. It was strange to see a grown-ass woman with metal in her mouth, which is why I couldn't stop staring directly into her mouth every time she spoke.

"I'm sorry, I didn't know what you liked to drink so I took a guess," she said.

"You didn't have to send me a drink at all, but thank you. It was a nice gesture."

The white girl was still standing beside me until Adrienne tossed her one of those sista-girl glares to make her leave.

"So, you like white girls, huh?" she asked in a lifeless monotone.

"Why do you say that? Because I was having a conversation with one?"

"I'm just curious."

I shook my head. "Sistas need to calm down a little in that area. The brothers still love y'all."

"It's hard to tell," she said, eyeing me skeptically. "Maybe you need to borrow my *Rosewood* video to refresh your memory on some things because you black men act like you have amnesia."

I was silent after her last comment because I didn't come to the club for a damn history lesson, and I could tell that she was the type who would probably stay on that subject longer than necessary. She must have picked up the hint because she changed the subject. We stood for several minutes talking and ordering more drinks until a nearby table became available. She was working on her second Long Island, and judging by all that she was telling me, I'd say she was way passed being tore up and all the way over to fucked up. First she was talking real basic. She told me that she was a teacher at Hamilton Middle School, and almost off for the summer, still debating whether she should teach summer school. Somehow, the fact that she was a teacher reminded her that her boyfriend of seven months dumped her without an explanation.

"It wasn't like he knew I was pregnant. I could understand that because he always said he didn't want kids and if I got pregnant he would leave, but he didn't even know." After he left, she decided to get an abortion rather than become a single parent. All this happened way before she was saved. She started slurping down her third Long Island, motioning her hand for the waitress to bring her over another. "You don't need any more," I said. Two for one she reminded me, waste not, want not. I wasn't going to let her drink a fourth one. I got the sense that she always ran her mouth like this and she probably used the drinks as an excuse. I also got the sense that she was a nagger and a bragger because she had to let me know that she had a master's degree and earned more than fifty thousand dollars a year, which was more than Reesey and I made combined.

"What are you doing after this?" she asked.

"I don't have any plans. Probably hang out with my boy."

"Hang out with me. My apartment is right upstairs. Do you want to go up?" She giggled. "Did you hear what I said, do you want to go up?" She slapped my thigh. "I should have said do you want me to go down. Oops, I'm sorry, that was nasty. I'm trying not to backslide, Lord."

"I need to go holler at my boy for a second. I was supposed to meet him down here, and I haven't had a chance to talk to him yet."

"Men and their boys. What can your boy do for you?"

"I'll be right back." I walked over to Damion's table. He had a woman on either side of him, and neither one was Pam, and there was another fine woman standing beside him.

Damion and I slapped hands and said a few words to each other. He introduced me to the woman standing over him, who was none other than the sexy-voiced Nikki Taylor, and her voice wasn't the best part of her—everything was.

"Nikki, this is my boy, Porter Washington. You need to hook him up. Find him somebody to love. I swear he's going to be a bachelor for the rest of his life."

"Um, let me think, what could be your code name?" Nikki asked, pondering the question as she studied every inch of me.

"Available, if you are," I said as we locked eyes.

"Unfortunately," she said, waving her wedding ring in my face, "I'm not."

"Figures. You're too complete of a package not to have been snatched up by now."

"But so are you. Call the show sometime," she said, slipping a business card in my pants pocket. I watched Nikki swing into a crowd of people, and then I bent down and whispered my request for a condom into Damion's ear.

"All out. Sorry."

"You don't have one?"

"I got two and I need them both. Sorry. It's not like we the same size anyway."

"You right motherfucka 'cause I need super-extra-large," I said. The woman sitting next to Damion looked up at me and smiled.

I looked down at the woman for a brief moment. She was old enough to be my mama, hanging out at a damn club. I looked over at Adrienne. Shouldn't assume because a woman invites you up to her place at one in the morning after three Long Islands that that meant anything.

"Then go to Rite-Aid and buy you a pack of super-extra-large," Damion said.

"I'm going home."

I was hesitant about going upstairs to Adrienne's loft, but I went anyway. I convinced myself that I had enough control to sit and watch television, and that was it.

I stood at her entranceway on an elevated platform, observing the large, open space with a different color used to separate each room.

She offered me a drink, but I declined because I had my fill downstairs. She walked over to me while I was standing a foot or two from the door.

"Are you going to stand there all night?" she asked as her eyes roamed freely up and down my body.

I made myself comfortable on her upholstered sofa, watching reruns of *Martin,* while she disappeared behind a door that was most likely the bathroom. She returned wearing a baggy Nike sweat suit that looked comfortable, but I was surprised she didn't go for the sexy Victoria's Secret look like most women do when they want to entice a brother.

She came over to me and sat on my lap. I let her sit there for a few minutes, but after she started wiggling her drunk ass around and crushing my nuts, I moved her to the side while I stood from the sofa, throwing the remote on the cushion and stepping toward the door.

"Where are you going?" she asked.

"It's not that kind of party. I don't have any condoms."

"I was only getting comfortable. Besides I'm on my period. Come on and sit back down." She patted the cushion. "We can talk some more."

I walked back to the sofa, even though I really wanted to leave.

6

On Saturday afternoon around two, I was pulling out of my mother's driveway when my pager went off with Damion's home number in it. I was surprised to see his number since he normally called my cell first. I returned his call when I stopped at a red light.

"Hey, Pam. Put your boy on the phone."

"He's not here. I was the one paging you."

"Oh, what's up?"

"That's what I want to know. Can you come over here?"

"Sure, but what's up?"

"I'll tell you when you get here."

I hung up the phone knowing it was going to be some mess that I didn't want to be put in the middle of. I hadn't talked to Damion since Thursday at the club, but I knew he was letting this one honey who he met two months ago at The Kings of Comedy concert down at the Fox Theatre, open his nose. I told him he needed to be careful because she was trying to possess him. He never lied to any of the women about being married, but this was the first one I'd seen who seemed to be working on reversing that. For some reason, Damion thinks that he has everything under control.

While I was on my way to their house, I was paging Damion and calling his cell so he could fill me in on what was going on. I knew when I got there Pam was going to start questioning me about his whereabouts. Maybe that's not why she wanted me to come over. Maybe it was for sex. I should be so lucky.

Pam was waving good-bye to her sister and the kids as they pulled out of the driveway.

I blew my horn at Pam's older sister, Patricia, after she waved at me. Patricia backed her Expedition out of the driveway and pulled alongside my Lexus, letting the passenger window down.

"Your boy is trippin'," she said to me.

"Why you say that?"

"I have the kids. I can't say much more than that. Pam will tell you, but I'm sure you already know." She rolled her eyes at me then drove off.

When I pulled into the driveway, Pam was standing on the grass with her arms folded. "What's up, baby girl?" I asked after I parked.

"I want to know where Damion is. Who is he with? I know you know."

"What do you mean? Isn't he here?"

"No, he's not. I haven't seen him since Thursday evening. He called me on Friday with some bullshit about being out of town on business, and I was okay with it for a second but now it's Saturday and he hasn't called. Something ain't right."

We walked into the house and before I had a chance to say anything she pushed me off balance. "What was that for?" I asked.

"You're protecting him. Don't protect him, Porter. Tell me where the hell he is. I have two kids with his ass. Don't protect him. When did you see him last?" she asked, sharply.

I rolled my eyes because I was pissed that Damion was putting me in this trick bag. I didn't know if Pam even knew he went to Baller's on Thursday so what was I supposed to say? "I don't know."

"You don't know when you saw him last?" She gave me a you-don't-really-expect-me-to-believe-that grin.

My eyes widened. "I guess Thursday."

"You guess Thursday? You guess? Well where do you guess that was?"

"I can't really remember," I said as I scratched the back of my head.

"You can't really remember? Well try real hard."

I rolled my eyes toward the ceiling and puckered my lips. Shit. Why me? "At Baller's." No need to lie. Pam knew Damion went to clubs.

"Where? See that nigga ain't shit. I can't stand his ass. At Baller's! And who was he with?" she asked irately. *Oh well, I thought she knew.*

"I-I don't know," I stuttered. "He was with his boys."

"His boys. You're one of his boys. Was he with you?"

"Y-Yeah, he was with me."

"You know what? You never could lie to me. Every time you tried, you started stuttering just like you are now. Tell me the truth," she shouted.

"He was with his boys," I repeated only this time much louder because I was becoming impatient with the whole scene.

"What you yelling for? You don't have shit to be pissed about—I do. Give me names."

"Hoffa."

"I already called Hoffa. Hoffa doesn't know where he is. Who else?"

"Pam, I don't know. I didn't know them other dudes." I turned away from her because I felt a smile beginning to surface and I didn't want her to think I was laughing about the situation. It was just a bad habit that I had. I smiled when I was either real upset or nervous.

She turned right along with me so we were still facing each other. "Something funny?" she asked. "I know one thing. When you leave here you better hit that nigga on his cell phone and tell him he got one hour to get his ass home. I don't give a damn if he's in Japan. Do you hear me?"

"I hear you, Pam," I said, dragging out the words.

"Alright then. Thank you for coming by."

7

I slid across the hardwood floor into the kitchen in my white socks, opening the refrigerator in search of something to fill my empty stomach, but there was nothing inside but cold air and light. I looked in the cabinets and found a box of Ritz crackers that were one week past the expiration date and some Jiffy peanut butter that was practically empty except for what I could scrape off the sides to use for peanut-butter-cracker sandwiches.

Two weeks had passed. It was Saturday again and I had one day off, but after I worked the next day I'd be off again for five days. I talked to Jade the other night. I wanted to hang up in his face, but I could tell he needed someone to listen. He was telling me how much money he almost made at the bathhouse. He went to a new one near Dearborn but he wasn't going back. He met a rich man of foreign descent. He wasn't quite sure what country the man was from, just that his skin was dark. The man offered to pay Jade a thousand dollars if he could suck Jade's dick. Jade said he didn't like having his dick sucked. He wasn't used to that because Jade considered himself to be the woman, but the man insisted, telling Jade if he came inside of his mouth he would give him two thousand dollars. Jade couldn't even get hard. The man got mad and beat him up, then left without giving him a dime. I warned Jade about going to those places. "I'll be careful," he said.

"It's not about being careful. You don't need to go, period."

He brushed it off like those were the risks that every gay man took because as he put it, there's a lot of men floating around who are just experimenting and after they finish their experiment they take their frustration out on the one who helped them perform it. I didn't understand how a man could want men instead of women. I didn't understand it and I never would.

My cell phone rang, but I wasn't in a rush to answer because I figured it was Adrienne who had already called umpteen times and left pitiful messages on my voice mail. I didn't give any of these women who I met lately my phone number, but shit, they all probably have Caller ID. Nothing happened between Adrienne and me that first night because she was on her period, but after that, she called a lot. I could tell she'd probably cling to a brother like a piece of lint on a black wool sweater, still I talked to her each and every time she'd call. Even when she'd hang up and call me right back. Maybe I was lonely.

Adrienne was different from Stacy in that she didn't only want sex; she wanted to go out to the movies, to dinner, comedy clubs. On every one of my off days we were together, going somewhere after she got home from work. She even already had plans for the upcoming week because she was better then my mother with keeping track of my schedule, and she knew I was off for five days straight on a super kelly. We'd already had sex. She came off her period the day after we met and by the next day, I was already up in her stuff, getting a little something. Now, the girl won't let my phone rest. I'm not playing a game with her head. I'm just not trying to be tied down.

The phone stopped ringing but started up again seconds later. "This is Porter." I decided to deal with her now so she'd stop calling.

"What up, my nigga?" Damion asked. "Coming by the crib to play some spades or what? Hoffa's over and Kyle, another one of my boys is here too."

"Man, I'm chillin'."

My other line clicked.

"Is that yours or mine?" Damion asked.

"Mine. You know what, I think I will come over." I don't know how Damion did it. I don't know how he worked his way back into his house, because I never got in touch with him that day after I left Pam, but I know he didn't get home in an hour. He got home Monday night with some lame excuse that I didn't even want him repeating. All I know is that he greeted Pam with a diamond bracelet that looked like it cost more than a hundred thousand dollars and he said that put a smile on her face. I didn't think Pam was materialistic, but maybe she'd changed over the years.

———

My pager was blowing up. Dancing across Damion's dining room table while I collected the book of cards I'd won from that round. Tupac was blasting from Damion's speakers like he was still in the hood instead of an exclusive subdivision.

"You need to use the phone?" Damion asked.

"Nah, I got my cell."

"You better call that girl," Hoffa said. "She seems like the type that slashes tires."

"You got the worse luck with women, man, but I got somebody for you to meet," Damion said as he cut my ace of clubs with a ten of spades.

"Not interested, " I said.

Hoffa looked over at me like I was crazy. "Oh, you interested in this one because she's fine."

"She sure is. I hired her to run the front desk," Damion said. "It always looks good to have a fine lady at your front desk. She's a red bone, too, man. Lighter than Pam."

"Lighter than Pam? What the fuck is she, albino?"

"I heard that," Pam yelled from the kitchen.

"My bad," I said. "That's what you like," I said to Damion. "I like 'em dark. Always have."

"Man, you dark. You supposed to like opposite of you. Just meet her. Her name is Kyla Adams. You should be interested, if you not."

"Shit, if he not, I am," Hoffa said.

"Man, you married," Damion said.

"And, so are you? So what does that mean? Not a damn thing. Besides, me and my wife have issues," Hoffa said.

"It should mean a lot," Pam shouted from the kitchen on a late response. Y'all in here talking about women." She pranced into the dining room sporting a fresh new haircut.

"I like your hair," I said to Pam.

"You do?" She stroked her closely cropped style. "Damion hates it. He hates short hair, don't you, honey?"

"Woman, don't you know you can't enter the room when men are playing cards?" Damion said. "I don't care what you do with your head, because I know you, next week it'll be in a weave down your back."

"Please." She rolled her eyes. "I'll enter any room in my house at any time I want. All you playin' is spades. Real men play poker."

"You want a wife and two kids, man?" Damion asked.

"I'll take Pam and the kids any day." I winked at Pam.

"And we'll take you, too, cutie."

Damion looked back and forth at us, wondering if we meant what was being said.

"Alright now. Don't make me get out my gun."

I heard my cellular ring.

"Yes, " I said after snatching it off the table.

"Porter, is something wrong?" Adrienne asked.

"What?" I asked, shouting. I could barely hear her with Damion's rap blasting.

Damion used the remote on the table to lower the volume to his CD player.

"Is something wrong?" she asked.

"Why do you think something's wrong?" I asked.

"You aren't returning my calls, and I've left you several messages. I even paged you."

"My cell phone and pager haven't been working."

Damion, Hoffa, and the other guy burst out laughing while Pam simply shook her head.

"What was all that?" Adrienne asked.

"What?" I asked.

"All that laughing in the background."

"I'm over my boy's house playing cards, and we're just having a good time."

"Yeah, right. You expect me to believe that?"

"I don't have to lie to you." She kept rambling so to shut her up, I asked, "Do you want company?"

"Yes."

"Let me finish up this game and I'll be over."

"What time?" Adrienne asked.

"As soon as I finish up this game."

"You can't give me a time?"

"No, I can't."

"Don't tell me you're coming over if you're not."

"I'm coming, I promise." I hung up.

"Man, if you got to go, we can let you go, " Damion said.

"If I had to go, I wouldn't be here," I said.

"I'm so glad I'm married and don't have to put up with that mess anymore," Pam said.

I looked at Hoffa, who looked at Damion who was staring at his hand. "Whose deal?" Damion asked as he threw his cards in the middle of the table.

―――――

When I walked into Adrienne's apartment, she had soft instrumental jazz playing, rose petals leading to her bed, and a sweet fragrance filling the air. The mood was right, but she was all wrong for me. She held my hand and led me to her bedroom. She held me as if once she let go I might flee.

"This is nice. What's the occasion?" I asked.

"You." She pushed me on the bed and tore off my clothes. The buttons from my shirt flew over her room.

"This is an expensive shirt."

"I'll buy you another one." She yanked off my belt, slashing my zipper down. I took over undressing from there. "You are so damn fine! I hate it," she said.

I was getting tired of women calling me fine. That was supposed to be my line.

She slipped out of her black velvet spaghetti-strapped dress, her bra, and panties, and jumped on the bed, crawling toward me.

After I put on a rubber, I got on top of her, parting her long, slender legs like a wishbone I was trying to snap in two, thrusting my dick inside her, allowing her moans to take center stage. Soon her sounds collapsed with one long and pleasurable sigh. I felt that I had accomplished my deed for her, but I would need to force myself to shrink. The only way I could was to picture myself making love to Pam, and as wrong as it seemed, as much as I knew I shouldn't have, I did. I pictured myself making love to Pam.

"I love you," she whispered into my ear and watched my face turn to stone. "You don't believe that I love you?"

"It's too soon to claim that. Besides, why does it always have to be about love?"

"Because that's what life's all about."

"Is it really?"

"If it's not about love, what else could it be about?"

I heard my cell phone ringing. "It's about how I'm so tired of my cell phone because it never stops ringing. That's what it's about."

"Don't answer it."

"I have to answer it," I said, jumping off the bed. I knelt down to retrieve the phone from my pants pocket and Adrienne gave me a hard smack across my ass and laughed.

"Did it hurt?" she asked.

"Shh, be quiet, let me answer the phone."

"It better not be a woman."

"This Porter."

"Porter?" a woman asked.

"Yes. Who is this?"

"Reesey. You forgot my voice already."

"Reesey?" I started to hang up, but decided I'd hold on and see what she wanted.

"Are you still there?"

"Yeah, I'm here. What's up? Why did you call?" I asked.

"I was thinking about you, wondering how you're doing."

"I'm doing fine. Never better, but you caught me at a bad time because I'm over my woman's house right now." I looked over at Adrienne who was beaming brighter than the industrial light she had just turned on in her kitchen.

"Your woman? We've barely been apart for a month and you already have a woman?"

"That's right. What do you need, Reesey?" I asked coldly.

"We need to talk."

"That's what we're doing."

"In person."

"About what?"

"I don't want to talk over the phone."

"We don't have shit to talk about."

"I'm pregnant. So we do have shit to talk about."

"No, we don't. What you telling me for? Call the father."

"I am. You're the father."

"Just like I was the last time."

"This one really is yours."

"Oh, that's your way of finally admitting that the other one wasn't?"

"I didn't mean it that way. It came out wrong."

"Wrong because it was the truth? This one ain't mine either."

I handed the phone to Adrienne who was pacing restlessly in front of me. "Listen, don't call my man again, tramp. Don't call him again. Do you understand me? Hello. Hello. She hung up; I guess she understood. What was she saying?"

"Nothing."

"Was she trying to say she was pregnant?"

"I don't know what she was trying to say."

"Porter, don't mess with my head, all right?"

"What are you talking about? Nobody's messing with your head. Chill out." I started putting on my clothes, getting ready to leave.

"Where do you think you're going? You don't come over here and fuck me without spending the night. I'm turned out now because you have skills that are unimaginable. I'm not trying to say I've been with a lot of men, but I've been with enough to know they don't have shit on you."

"So you like me for sex?" I asked.

"No, but I do like the sex."

"Well then why do you like me?" I was waiting to hear her reply since she knew absolutely nothing about me, other than I was a firefighter. She didn't know where I lived or with whom. She didn't know who my friends were. She didn't know where I went to high school, if I went to college. She didn't know if I had any siblings. She didn't know my birthday. How old I was. All she knew was I had a big dick and I could fuck. "Why do you like me?"

"You're good to be with."

"Why? How? In what way?" I really wanted to hear her answers because when we were together, she was the only one who did the talking. It was all about her and her day, about the kids at school, about how she was trying to become an administrator, her sorority, her good credit, the house she was building. The only thing she wanted to know about me was when I was coming over to fuck her. "In what way am I good to be with?"

"You just make me feel like a woman, Porter."

"*I* make *you* feel like a woman? I don't need a woman to make me feel like a man, baby, and you shouldn't need a man to make you feel like a woman."

"I know."

"Are you sure you know?" I looked at her. My eyes narrowed with disgust. I continued getting dressed. I was ready to leave. Tired of both her and our conversation.

"Yes. I do. Can't you just spend the night this one time?"

I shook my head. "I can't spend the night. That's too intimate."

"Too intimate? So what did we just finish doing? Wasn't that intimate?" She didn't understand. Now was not the time to ask me questions because I was in my funky mood and I'd give her the answers, just not the ones she wanted to hear. "Wasn't it? Answer me." She pushed me, and it was on after that.

"No, that wasn't intimate, that was a release like jacking off. I had on a condom. I didn't cum inside you. Did I even kiss you? Have I ever kissed you?"

"No, but I just thought you didn't like to kiss."

"Did you ask me to find out? I'm going to tell you something that insecure women need to work on. When you need to know something about a man, why don't you ask him instead of making up an excuse for him? I love to kiss, but I don't know you, and I don't know where your mouth has been. All I know is you sucked my dick without a condom and let me cum inside of your mouth. Do you really think I think I'm the only man you let cum inside your mouth?" I laughed and shook my head. "Kissing is too intimate. I'm not kissing a woman who I don't feel is my wife. Anything else you want to know?"

"No."

"I want to know something. Why can't women just tell a man no? I want a woman to tell me no so bad, just so I know how that feels. I want a woman to tell me to wait until marriage."

"No, you don't."

"Yes, I do, or at least until we're engaged. I'm tired of banging a woman on the first night, first week, first month. I can wait. I really believe a woman thinks if she fucks you good enough, the man is going to stay. Like she's the only woman in the universe who knows how to move those hips. You feel like that, don't you?" She shrugged. "Maybe you don't feel like that, because you haven't fucked me good yet." With that I left.

"Call me when you get home or I'll call you," she said as I walked out the door.

8

I slumped in my barber's chair, undecided about the clippers that were nearing the left side of my head ready to shave clean my Afro, which I kept shaped tighter than Steve Harvey's. I was certain about one thing. This was the new me, the one willing to approach the world with a bald head and be proud that I had gotten rid of all those dead cells in my life. At least that's how I was trying to look at it.

My hair fled quickly and stacked against the shop's floor, falling in front of my disbelieving eyes. When my eyes met center with the mirror in front of me, I saw what Reesey had always wanted. Something I fought because if I went bald it had to be for me, and not for an insecure, materialistic, mixed-up black woman who'd rather be white.

No doubt these females I had in my life now would all be a thing of the past, especially Adrienne, but I still had to keep it real. In the three and a half weeks since I'd broken up with Reesey, I'd been with four women, three were one-night stands, and the other one, Adrienne, was simply hanging on, for what, I don't know. I was getting tired of it, but all it took was one pretty girl smiling in my direction and I'd get caught up all over again.

With twenty days off a month, I had nothing to do but think about what the next few years might hold, but not grasp on to my thoughts too tightly because in an instant it could all be over. I was tired of wanting. Tired of needing. Even more tired of pretending not to want or to need. I was just tired. I could save almost anybody's life but my own.

Curtis, my barber, dusted the loose hair from around my face and ears, took the cap off the High Time Bald Protective Scalp Treatment and showered my head with a light sheen.

"All set," Curtis said as he removed the black cape that was draped over my polo shirt. "It looks good."

I took a twenty from my wallet and tossed it on to his counter. He charged fifteen for the cut, and I was tipping him five.

"I'll see you in a few," I said as I walked out of his shop. I stood right outside the door looking at my reflection through the passenger window of my Lexus.

My cell phone was ringing from my belt hook. I checked the display and saw it was Stacy. I believed her when she said I'd never hear from her again. Respected her for a brief moment when the days passed and she never called. Thought maybe this nineteen-year-old had more sense than most young women her age, but now she was back ringing me up again. My finger reached for the talk button but slipped over to end.

The next call came through with a Caller ID of unknown. I started not to answer it, figured it was a bill collector, but it was Jade calling me from the hospital.

"Why are you in the hospital?" I asked.

"Just gettin' some test done." He coughed a few times.

"What kind of tests?"

"Just tests. I might be in here for a few weeks." Mmm-hmm. Just as I suspected, his little ass has AIDS. He was so little, built like a skinny woman. There wasn't one masculine thing about him. Tests? He probably had pneumonia. "Boo, I just wanted to call and let you know where I was because I know you and you'd call me before I got out of here, but when I do get out of here you'll be the first one I call, okay."

"Okay, but seriously stop with that boo shit."

"Okay, Porter. I'll talk to you soon."

PART TWO

Winona Fairchild

9

This was the day that I dreamed of ever since I was a little girl and watched *Cinderella* for the very first time. This was my wedding day and I was making Derwin my prince.

I stood at the altar in a white Alfred Angelo gown that had a long train extending halfway down the aisle. The sheer veil was concealing my thin face, and I wished I could remain hidden. I wished I had been born with a veil to hide my imperfections or given one when I was growing up to put on when the schoolkids became too cruel to bear.

My hands were trembling as they strangled the plastic bridal holder, which carried two-dozen white roses. As my grip tightened, so did I. I didn't really know what I was doing in this church, besides pretending. Pretending to be in love. Pretending to be loved. Pretending I wasn't two months pregnant. Pretending everything was going to be perfect as soon as we both said I do. Something had to be better than nothing and prior to this day, I had nothing.

There were only eleven people at the large Greater Faith Baptist Church witnessing our union. Five were members of my family. My sisters, Val and Colleen; my niece, Raven; Val's husband, Bo; and of course my mother. The other six were my best friend, Gina, and her parents, and three of Gina's girlfriends, who were all dolled up like they were hoping to snag someone but there were no available men in attendance. If Derwin had invited his friends, the inside would have been packed.

My brother, Trent, couldn't attend because he was serving in the army overseas so Bo walked me down the aisle since my father stayed at home. Probably watching television from his LaZ Boy, but I didn't care if Dad was there, because his very presence brought me down. I knew how he was when it came to money. He'd let you rot in the street before he gave up a dime, but if you somehow managed to weasel money out of him and waste it, you were dead in his eyes. I wasted far too much of my parents' money when I dropped out of Michigan State in my sophomore year so I was dead, and dead people don't get married. No, my father wouldn't be there, maybe for my funeral but not for a wedding.

My mother came, which didn't surprise me. She always tried to support her children, even when she may have disagreed with our choices. She still loved us unconditionally and provided us with an overabundance of her love. Almost smothering us with it. She considered herself the balancing act. Trying to compensate for what Dad never provided, but the scales were too lopsided. You can ruin the best of anything with too much of the same thing. I knew I had my mother's love, but I needed Dad's, and his wasn't to have. I never understood how Mom dealt with Dad's distance. I often told her that she could've done better. Of course, she'd respond by saying, "You wouldn't be here if I did." *So be it*. Besides, she knew I was telling the truth. After thirty-five years of marriage, Mom should realize that there must be more to her position as a wife than a whole lot of give and no take. That's probably why she can't understand why I wanted to be married at twenty. "Don't let a spur-of-the-moment decision ruin your entire life," she told me, and she should know because she married Dad at eighteen. I'd hardly consider this a spur-of-the-moment decision since Derwin and I had been in a relationship ever since freshman year in high school. I'll admit that it was an odd one because I wasn't his girlfriend, and only one of his friends, Mitchell Armstrong, knew anything about us. Others at Cass Tech didn't even know Derwin and I knew each other. The only reason Mitchell knew was because he was Gina's boyfriend, and she told him. Then she told me what he said: "He looked at your picture and laughed, and then he said, 'Oh, Derwin is going to hurt her feelings'."

What hurt were her comments. I knew she thought she was helping me out, and she seemed genuinely upset about Mitch's remarks, but she never took my feelings into consideration. There are some things people don't need to know and other things people don't want to know. I guess I didn't want to know that boys didn't find me attractive. I guess I've always wanted to pretend.

Derwin's real girlfriend in high school was one of the pretty people. She had long hair, light skin, and keen features. She looked better than I did. Her family had more money than mine. She had almost everything that I didn't. Still, I had one thing that she could never have, and that was Derwin's virginity. At least he claimed I was his first. I know he was mine, and with that came all sorts of sexual experimentation that I felt would ensure me a place in his heart and mind forever.

"I hate you!" Derwin said one day after we skipped school and went downtown to the Renaissance Center, snuck into one of the ladies' rest rooms in a secluded area and had sex in a stall. He couldn't stand to be with me, but he couldn't leave me either. "I don't want anybody to know we're together. Remember that. You're not my type. You're too dark. Your hair is too short. And you're skinny," he said as he wrinkled up his nose in disgust then he grabbed my face and kissed me passionately so in my mind he was confused and didn't mean any of the other things he had just said.

I ended up with Derwin because I was the only one willing to stroke his ego the way he wanted by making him believe what deep down he already thought was true: that he, not Ali, was the greatest.

We continued seeing each other through high school and then I followed him off to college. During my sophomore year, I got pregnant. If I told Derwin I was pregnant, he would have said I was trying to trap him, and that would have pushed him farther away. Nothing I could have said or done would have made him change his stubborn mind. It wasn't until Kirk, one of his teammates, fell out during basketball practice and died that Derwin started thinking seriously about life. Kirk didn't know there was anything wrong with his heart, and one day it stopped beating. After that, Derwin was lost. He walked around campus like a zombie because for one thing, he blamed himself, but it was also my fault. I was the one who sold Kirk the coke the night before their first practice. How did Derwin and I really think we could get away with selling drugs in college? It started off with just nickel-size weed bags, but then our supplier started giving us cocaine, heroine, whatever we thought we could sell.

I immediately went from selling, to selling and using. I didn't consider myself addicted. I don't think I have an addictive personality, but Gina does. She thinks I'm addicted to Derwin. "Why else would you settle for some-one that's ugly and arrogant? It's not the money because the money belongs to his parents. Has to be the sex. Has to be something I can't see."

I wasn't addicted, not to Derwin or the drugs I used. Being high wasn't all that great for me, but it was something I needed to do whenever I felt insecure about myself and my skinny little body, which was a result of genes not drug abuse; about my face, which never quite looked right when I stared into a mirror; and my crooked teeth, which prevented me from smiling or talking too much. I was ready to take anything to remove the pain. I was the child who never fit in. Not in my family or at school. I had one friend in high school and that was Gina, and I swear she was my friend only because she felt sorry for me.

I started drinking my first year in college with my roommate, Jennifer Theaters. She was a white girl from Holley, Michigan. I was the only black girl she'd been around, the only black period that she'd seen up close so I figured she was a racist, and she was living with me. How ironic. Obviously, at first, we didn't get along. Not until I told her that I knew she was racist. She ignored what I said. Ignored me. I guess the more she was around me and realized that I could read, that I was not part animal, that I laughed and cried the same way she did, and had issues with my family just like she did, the more she opened up. We started sharing our childhood memories. For her, it was lack of choice about whom she hated. Her father replaced the word *black* with *monkey* or *nigger monkey* or *beast* as far back as she could remember.

"My father wanted me to think that blacks were bad people, not people at all, just animals," she said, "but he was the one sneaking into my room at night. A black man never raped me. I didn't have a choice in the matter. I had to hate anybody who wasn't pure white. If I didn't, I'd get beat." We'd talk about our pain and drink from the same Bacardi bottle, stinging our throats with straight rum and our eyes with broken tears.

"When my father died," Jennifer said, "I put on the biggest smile at his funeral. I heard people whispering. They thought I had lost my mind from grief. Why else would I smile at my own father's funeral? If they only knew." In her junior year of high school, a couple of years after her father died, Jennifer's mother married an automotive executive. "My mother may have never had a clue but she always had a man," Jennifer said, guzzling down half the bottle.

It felt good not to worry about anything. Until the next day came and I woke up with a headache beating the inside of my head like a drum. Jennifer always woke up without a problem. She'd been drinking longer than I had—Started at ten—and I guess she built up her resistance.

Not a day went by that I wasn't getting drunk and skipping some of my classes. Then, after drinking for almost six months, I stopped cold turkey. That's because my slurred speech and giddy behavior was turning Derwin off. Wasn't too long after I got sober that Derwin filled me in on his new drug-dealing friend. I went along for the short ride. We sold drugs for almost a year, for the same amount of time I used them.

After Kirk died, Derwin panicked because he knew there'd be an autopsy. Not that they could trace the drugs back to us, God I hoped not. Still, it scared him enough to ask me to marry him, which brought us to that day.

I looked over at Derwin as he stood to my left, stiff as a corpse in his white tuxedo rental. There was no smile on his face, not a hint of one either, replaced instead by a blank expression. He was still scared, but this fear wasn't about Kirk. It was about what we were standing there doing. And as happy as this day made me, even I was nervous and wanted it to be over quickly. I wanted Reverend Sykes to hurry up and pronounce us man and wife. I wanted to say I do and throw my bouquet to Gina, who wanted marriage just as badly as I did. Then I wanted to float through the church before it emptied and disappear not to be seen again until after our Hawaiian honeymoon ended.

The palms of my hands were sweating while my moist armpits soaked into my silk and my Fashion Fair started melting off. Despite it all, I kept smiling through my veil as the reverend began reciting the vows.

I took a deep breath. Then another.

"Repeat after me," Reverend said to Derwin.

Derwin said, "I can't do this." It started as a whisper, but intensified as he turned toward my family. "I'm sorry," he said. "I'm too young and I can't do it."

"What do you mean you can't do this?" I asked. "You can and you will. Just turn around and say I do." It was so embarrassing. I was pulling on the arm of his tuxedo jacket, trying to make him turn around, but he didn't. I looked over at my mother who sat calmly in the first pew.

Finally, Derwin turned to face me. "Winona, I don't love you. I'm sorry but I don't, but you can keep the ring."

I guess I can, I bought it.

My knees began to buckle, and my stomach weakened. I felt my mind moving, traveling with all sorts of thoughts while my body remained still. This was a high like none I had ever experienced.

"How can you do this to me?" I screamed.

"Do what, Ma?"

I squinted to bring my reality into focus. Carlton, my fifteen-year-old son was standing over me. This wasn't December 10, 1982. I wasn't being stood up at the altar. My son wasn't growing inside of my belly, and I wasn't spending all of my days and nights worrying about whether the drugs I used in college were going to cause my baby to be deformed. It's the summer of 1999. June 25 to be exact. My son was only a month away from turning sixteen. I have a nine-year-old daughter named Sosha. Yet it still feels like my yesterdays. The days I regret.

I regret my life, almost all of it. I wish I could go back and start over again, now that I know what I should have done.

"Do what? I just tapped you on your shoulder like that," Carlton said, giving me another quick thump that stung to no end.

"Stop," I whined, sounding like Sosha.

"I'm trying to get you up because the movers are here."

"What movers?"

"What movers, Ma? The same movers who were here yesterday packing up most of our stuff."

"The movers are here already? What time is it?" I sat up in bed searching for the alarm clock. It was on the floor beside Samson, our black Lab, who was pawing the clock like it was one of his many stuffed toys.

"It's eleven," Carlton said.

"Eleven in the morning?" I jumped out of bed, taking part of the floral bedsheet with me. My silk gown was biting the crack of my behind so I yanked it free before Carlton noticed.

"I tried to wake you three hours ago when your alarm first went off, but you just laid there moaning and groaning. You must've been into some deep sleep or having another one of your nightmares."

"Probably so." I drug myself into my bathroom, turned on the faucet, placed my cupped hands under the warm water, and splashed it over my face. I opened the vanity. Everything inside had been packed except for the large bottle of Tylenol, which I instructed the movers not to touch. I popped two in my mouth. "It was just a dream," I said to myself as I poured a small glass of water to help down my pills.

I looked over at Carlton with my toothbrush stuck in my mouth. He was sitting on the edge of my bed with his back against the footboard. I spit out the toothpaste in the sink and rinsed my mouth with lukewarm water, a substitute for the Listerine that I was out of.

"Where are the movers now?" I asked.

"I'm not sure. They were carrying some of the boxes out to the truck."

"Where's Sosha?"

He shrugged. "I guess with her little girlfriend next door."

I opened my mouth and put my teeth together to examine them in the mirror. Three years of wearing braces finally straightened my crooked teeth, but I had to wait until I was a working adult before I could afford to correct them because during my childhood my parents always said nothing was wrong with my teeth. Just like I guess nothing is wrong with my mind now. I walked over to my garden tub and turned on the water. "What do you mean, you guess? Is she next door or isn't she?"

"I don't know. That's where she said she was going."

I walked out of the bathroom with my hand on my hip. "I want you to go next door and make sure she's there, then find out what the movers are doing," I demanded.

"I'll do that, but first we need to have a talk about something." Carlton walked over to me, draping his long arm around my shoulder as he followed me to the closet.

I pushed his arm aside when I entered my walk-in. "I know what you want to talk about and the answer is not before you get your grades up."

"I'm going to get my grades up, but in the meantime, I need a car. And since my birthday is coming up next month," he said as he rubbed his hands together in anticipation.

"Look, you're going into your junior year. How you do these next two years will determine what college you get into, that means no more D-pluses. You can't get into a university like that. You're going to end up in a community college or worse, bagging groceries at Kroger."

"I might not go to college right away. You didn't."

"Yes, I did. I just didn't finish right away. Besides, I don't want you doing what I did. You have to pull those grades up and keep them up."

I stood inside of my empty walk-in, which used to be filled with summer dresses before the movers packed them all. I kept out one pair of blue jeans and a T-shirt to wear on the road trip along with one suitcase filled with clothing. I needed to go shopping sometime before July 12 when I reported to work. I needed suits now that I was an executive. The word *executive* didn't even sound right for me.

"Nothing's wrong with my grades. I got one D-plus in geometry and that's only because my teacher didn't like me."

"How does someone get a D-plus?" I shook my head. "Every time you get a bad grade, it's because your teacher didn't like you. I'm not buying that excuse anymore so come up with a new one, like the truth. You don't study."

"It doesn't matter because I'm going to be the next Tiger Woods."

"The next Tiger Woods, huh? Well, Tiger, why haven't you started reading *The Great Gatsby*?"

"Um, probably because I'm not going back to Keller next year."

"No matter what school you go to I'm sure it's going to be required."

"No problem. I'll read it. Now, can we talk about my car? You work for Daimler Chrysler, I know you can get me into a 300 M," he pleaded. "And if you really want to be generous you can pick out something from the Mercedes lineup like that C-class. That's affordable."

"Now, you're really trippin'. Boy, go see what those movers are doing." I pointed toward the door as he stood still talking. "Get your butt out of here and do what I told you to do!" I watched him parade out of the bedroom, his short Afro nearly scraping the top of the door's moulding. He was tall and lanky like his father, but their personalities were the complete opposite. Carlton was more serious and resourceful than his father because he had to be. He didn't have rich parents like Derwin did. Carlton had me and Keith, the man he thought was his father. Only he didn't have Keith anymore because I kicked him out five years ago.

I walked over to my bedroom window and peeped through the verticals. A large Corrigan truck was parked in front of our apartment building, blocking three driveways. Two Hispanic men were carrying my leather Natuzzi sofa to the truck. They were both perspiring. The Texas heat was probably already well into the nineties.

"Offer those men something to drink," I yelled to Carlton.

"Something like what?" he yelled back.

"Carlton, don't ask me no stupid questions this morning."

I went back into the bathroom and stepped into the tub, letting the water run a few more minutes before I turned it off completely. Going back home made me feel strange. I didn't mind moving. It was heading back to Detroit that bothered me. When I left, I told myself it was for good, and that's how I wanted it, but this was an opportunity that I couldn't pass up because I would be making a lot more money, and I'd finally be able to afford to buy a home. It's not every day someone can jump from a band 90, which is one step above entry-level to a band 96 with perks like a company car, a large office, a secretary or what they refer to as an executive assistant. Since this was a new project, I guess all the rules were changed. That's what I wanted to believe, but it wasn't quite the case. The fact was I didn't have the experience, but I did have an engineering degree that it took me seven years to earn and a newly acquired master's degree in transportation design.

I had worked for Chrysler for almost ten years, spending most of that time as an executive assistant. I also had a hookup. Jennifer, my old college roommate, recommended me for the job. Jennifer and I stayed in touch over the years. Right after she graduated, she landed an engineering job with Chrysler. I'm sure it was due to her stepdad's connections. I don't see anything wrong with using your pull, because that's exactly what I did when I called Jennifer for a job. She told me she'd make a few calls for me. I told her I'd take anything, and she found me a job as a discounter at one of the Chrysler zone offices in the Dallas area, processing paperwork on new car loans. The pay was barely twenty-five thousand back then, but when Jennifer moved up the corporate ladder so did I. Within two years, I was promoted to an executive assistant. Last year, she was promoted to one of the regional vice presidents. Last month, she called me and filled me in on not her new position, but mine. The one she nominated me for. I checked Careers, our online posting system, and I didn't see a job listing for a Production Improvement Manager. Still I told her I'd take it.

It was a lot to consider, and it had all better work out. I was going to miss the security of my old job. When you were a good assistant, an executive would let you do whatever you wanted, come and go as you please, the same way he did. It wasn't a prestigious job, but it had its benefits—forty-one thousand dollars was one of them. Of course, ninety-seven thousand is a lot better. I had to remind myself once again that I was an executive so I guess that meant I could still come and go as I pleased.

In over sixteen years, I never returned to Detroit. Not for one visit. I ran away from the embarrassment and hurt of a cancelled wedding, and to avoid the wrath of my father once he discovered that I had used my parents' Visa to pay for it all. Now it hurts to think that I was so desperate to be married back then that I stole my parents' Citibank Visa and charged more than $15,000 on it for the wedding. By the time their bill arrived, I was halfway to Texas with my new man, Keith Kemp, whom I met at Sundance, a shoe store in Northland Mall on a Saturday, three weeks after Derwin dumped me. By that following Sunday I was on my way to Texas. If it weren't Keith, it would have been some other man. One thing I know for sure, almost seventeen years is a long time to most, but not to me. To me it feels like yesterday.

I stopped kicking my legs in the bathwater after I heard a familiar loud voice on the other side of my door.

It was Keith. Speak of the devil and there he was. I had asked him not to come by until the next day after six when we'd be gone. He didn't know anything about the relocation. I didn't need him flipping out, cutting up my furniture, and breaking out windows. I'd seen his temper once before—when I kicked him out five years ago from our apartment in Fort Worth and told him never to come back. He left peacefully but came back the next day drunk, kicking in the door and threatening to kill me. Even though he never laid a finger on me, one can never know for sure, which is why the kids and I had to leave town quietly.

There was a loud, steady knock at the bathroom door. "Winona, we need to talk!" Keith shouted as he turned the knob several times, but he couldn't enter because the door was locked.

"I'm taking a bath, Keith."

"Why didn't you tell me you were moving and taking my kids?"

"Keith, please wait a minute." He got on my last nerve. All he did was whine and complain from the time he opened his eyes in the morning until the first snore escaped his mouth at night. I was so glad to be rid of him. So glad that the last time we made love was so long ago that I forgot what his penis looked like and how it felt inside of me.

He started banging on the door in sections from top to bottom. When he reached the bottom the bangs turned into kicks. "What kind of shit is this?" he asked. I was dripping wet as I climbed out of the bathtub and grabbed the closest towel to wrap around my body. "So that's why you didn't want me to come over until tomorrow?"

I snatched open the door with steam coming out of my nostrils. "Get in here! You act like we're still together, but we're not."

He was looking bad and smelling worse. Wearing too much cologne as usual, and his closely shaven head was bubbling with sweat. "Nobody said nothing about us being together, but when it comes to my kids."

"Sosha is yours," I whispered firmly. I was getting tired of him claiming Carlton. Carlton had a father, the one I was now determined to find.

"They're both mine. I raised them."

"I raised them, and if you were so concerned you would have kept a job, supported your family, married me, and took care of business like a real man."

"We didn't get married because you didn't want to. Too scared that you were going to be stood up again."

I shook my head. "You know damn well why we didn't get married. Do you want me to spell it out to the world? It won't take long."

"Go ahead," he said as he used the back of his hand to remove some of the sweat from his forehead.

"I didn't want to marry you because I didn't love you. You left five years ago to pursue your music, writing, poetry, painting, and all your other dreams."

"I didn't leave. You kicked me out."

"Why did I kick you out, Keith?"

"I don't know. Why did you, Winona?"

"You left!" I finalized.

"And I came back."

"Yeah, this year looking for a place to stay when it didn't work out. Would you have come back if you had made it? Don't answer that because it's not important. The good thing is that it never hurts as bad the second time around. "

"I guess you're going back to Detroit so you can be with Derwin, huh? After all these years you probably stayed in contact with him, didn't you?

He don't want you. He didn't want you then, and he sure as hell don't want you now."

"Get out!" I shook my head so hard a few of the pins holding my hair into a ball fell out.

"Don't forget I'm the one who brought you to Texas. I saved you. Took you from Detroit and brought you here. When I met you, you were pregnant and looking like you was on the verge of a nervous breakdown. I loved you at your worse. Now you have a few things together, and it's forget-about-Keith time."

"Keith, listen to yourself. How do you sound? You have another woman and that's where you need to be right now. What do you want from me?"

"I want to see my daughter."

"She's not here, so leave!"

"I wish I would have married your ass, so I could've gotten custody of my kids, and that's the only reason, because you're too fucked up in the head to be any man's wife."

"You want custody? I'll give you custody. You want 'em? You can have them both."

He walked out of the bathroom, stumbling over the boxes right outside the door.

Now I couldn't wait to get away from him. I felt like jelly stuck between two stale pieces of bread. No matter which slice I chose, neither one was any better. If I stayed in Texas it was messy, if I went back, it was messy too. "I ain't got time to deal with your shit," he said.

"I didn't think so!" I shouted, trailing him.

"I know one thing, you better tell Carlton the truth before he meets it."

"The truth about what?" Carlton asked as Keith headed for the front door.

"Ask your mother," Keith said as he slammed the door behind him.

"What's he trippin' about?" Carlton asked.

"Who knows? I guess he's mad because he's not going."

"Going with us? Pleaaase, he left us first."

———

The movers left around seven o'clock, which is around the same time that I went to my bedroom for a quick fifteen-minute nap. Fifteen minutes turned into three and a half hours and when I woke up it was dark outside. I was curled up on a pallet, under a comforter. In the middle of one of the best fantasy dreams I'd ever had involving Denzel Washington and me, when I heard a knock on my locked bedroom door.

"Who is it?" I shouted. It had to be Sosha because Carlton went to the movies with his girlfriend for his last night in town. I made sure to tell him before he left not to do anything stupid. "You left a virgin and I want you coming back the same way."

Sosha knew when my door was locked that meant I wasn't feeling well and didn't want to be disturbed. They both knew that if they didn't know a thing. "Who is it?" I asked again.

"Daddy's at the door," Sosha said.

"Don't answer it," I instructed.

"I already did."

"Why don't you come out so we can talk?" Keith asked, slurring his words because I'm sure that he was drunk.

"Keith, why are you back? Please, go away." A thought suddenly popped into my head. He was back to kill us. Kill us all. I pictured him killing me first, and then Sosha. Then ambushing Carlton after he finally arrived home. Why else would Keith come back? I changed my tune quickly by speaking very gently. "Keith, just let me get dressed first, okay?"

"Hurry up!" he insisted.

"It'll only take a minute." I picked up the phone gently and dialed 911.

"What is the emergency?" the operator asked.

"My ex-boyfriend is inside of my apartment screaming," I whispered. "It's his second time over here today and I know he's going to do something to me and my kids."

"Has he threatened you?"

"Yes, he has."

"Does he have a weapon?"

"Yes, he does." I didn't know if he did, only suspected, but I had to say something if this was an emergency.

"I'll send an officer over. Are you at 207 Fairway Park?"

"Yes, I am. Apartment 1103."

"We have an officer in the area. He'll be there in less than five minutes."

I hung up the phone and crawled across the floor to my blinds to peep out and watch for the uniforms.

"What's taking you so long?" Keith shouted.

"I'm coming," I responded calmly. I stood, dropping the comforter to the floor. I was partially dressed. Only needed to slip into a pair of jeans, the pair I planned to wear the next day. I went into my closet and removed the jeans from the wire rack. "Here I come." I opened my bedroom door when I heard someone banging at the front door.

"Roanoke Police," a man yelled.

"Why in the hell are the police here?" Keith shouted. I grabbed Sosha and flew over to open the front door. There were two police officers standing in front of me. One had his gun drawn, and when he came through the door, he pointed it toward Keith who immediately raised both hands to surrender. "You called the police on me, Winona?"

"Keep your hands where I can see them," the unarmed officer warned as he walked over to Keith to pat search. "He's clean," he told his partner who then put away his gun.

I couldn't look at Keith; especially after I found out he wasn't armed.

"How could you call the police on me? You know what, you really are crazy."

"Do you live here, sir?" the officer asked.

"Not anymore."

"He never did," I said.

"That's my daughter," Keith said to the officer. "You gonna let my daughter see her father being treated like a criminal. Why are you doing this to me, Winona?"

"Ma'am, do you wish to press charges?"

I stood in the middle of the living room floor, blank. I felt like my thoughts were moving in slow motion. Even though I heard the officer's question, I choose to ignore it.

"Ma'am, do you want us to take him down to the station?"

"No," I said.

"Are you sure, ma'am? If we let him go, he's free to come back."

"I'm sure. Let him go," I said.

"You don't have to worry about me coming back ever again," Keith said to me. He kissed Sosha on her forehead. "Tell Carlton that I love him," he said to Sosha, "but I won't be able to see him anymore because your mother is a psychopath." Sosha started crying so hard snot was jamming the inside of her nose. Keith looked over at me. "You real crazy. I'ma have to pray for you," Keith said as he walked out of the door behind the officers.

"I don't want your prayers, Satan," I said as I slammed the door behind him. "Stop crying, Sosha. I know he's your father, but your parents can't get along, and it's nothing to cry about. Believe me."

"What's a psychopath?" Sosha asked.

"That would be me."

———

I was lying in the bed, watching the minutes on my alarm clock fly by. This time the next day, I'd be halfway to Michigan. It was too late to call

Gina, but I had to. Before she remarried, we'd call each other whenever we needed to talk. I know things were different, but I didn't understand why they had to be.

"Hello," Mark said in a whisper.

"Mark, did I wake you?" I whispered back.

"Who is this?" he asked. "What time is it?" I heard movement. Bedsheets rustling. "Do you know it's two o'clock in the morning? Who is this?"

"It's Winona."

"Winona, is something wrong? Don't you think it's too late to call someone's home?" he whispered.

"I needed to talk to Gina for a minute."

"Is everything okay?"

"Yes, everything's fine."

"Gina's asleep and I don't want to wake her. She had a hard day today. Do you want me to relay a message?"

"No. I'll surprise her. Thanks."

Gina didn't need to have hard days anymore. She didn't have to work two jobs—Detroit Edison during the day and doing hair at her home in the evenings. She could quit both if she wanted. Mark was a successful IBM sales executive. He always won free trips, drove a company car, and the month before last brought home a thirty-thousand-dollar bonus check. Gina didn't need to work, but she did, probably because the marriage was still so new. Barely two years, and just in case Mark left her like her first husband, she'd be able to adjust much better this time. I've tried to convince her that Mark is better than her first one. She no longer had to call me asking, why, like I was the psychic hot line. If she wasn't calling, I was certainly calling her with my situation with Keith and how much I hated him, or Derwin and how much I thought I still loved him. Gina and I would talk for hours on the phone. Talk so long until five cents a minute no longer seemed like a savings once I got my phone bill.

I broke down and called her even though I wanted to keep my surprise and just show up. I lied and told her I was taking the kids on a trip to Disney World and wouldn't be back for two weeks. I had to do that because as the time grew nearer for me to leave, I knew I'd get more tempted to tell her the truth, so instead I said I was leaving town, which gave me an excuse for not calling. I almost got weak. I'm glad Mark didn't put her on the phone. This way my moving back could stay a surprise. By the time Gina called me back the next day, we'd be on the road heading to Detroit.

10

W e passed the WELCOME TO MICHIGAN sign at 12:34 P.M. on Tuesday after spending the last eleven hours on the road. The first night we slept at a Comfort Inn in Missouri and argued for nearly an hour on which toppings to include on the pizza the kids ordered. By the time it arrived, I was too exhausted to eat and they fed my portion to Samson.

The only landmark that looked halfway familiar was the large Uniroyal tire off the I-94 expressway near Metro Airport. Besides that, I felt like a stranger in a new city, and my kids weren't helping matters by complaining the last three hundred miles of the trip.

"Is Detroit cold?" Sosha asked, looking over at me. "I don't want to be cold and I hate snow."

"You've really never been in snow," I said. "How can you hate something you don't know anything about?"

She shrugged.

"Detroit sucks," Carlton said. "Not only does it get cold and snow, it's ugly and so are the people."

I looked at him through my rearview mirror. "Carlton, when was the last time you've been to Detroit?"

"Never, but I know a few people who used to live here and they told me about it, and all of them are ugly."

"Find out for yourself before you take another person's word for anything. It won't be that bad, I promise." I tried not to roll my eyes for fear they'd see me. "And I'm from Detroit. Do you think I'm ugly?" Neither said a word, so I cleared my throat to signal I was waiting for their response.

"You're not ugly, Mommy," Sosha said, "but why do you always wear that ugly bun in the back of your head?"

"Ugly bun?" I placed my hand over it. "I don't know. It's convenient."

"I don't like it. It's yucky." She stuck her thumb in her mouth.

"Take your thumb out your mouth!" She snatched it out quickly. "Gina will do my hair one day this week."

"Good. Then maybe she can make you look young and pretty like Vanessa Williams," Sosha said.

My eyes widened. "Do I look old to you?"

"Yeah," she said.

"How old do you think I am, Sosha?"

She shrugged. "Is fifty old?"

Carlton fell across the backseat in laughter, disturbing Samson who had been curled up next to Carlton asleep for more than two hours. "Fifty, Sosha? No, you don't, Mama. You don't look a day over forty."

"Boy, shut up." I continued to hear his laughter, shadowing my feelings. I thought I had improved with age. In fact, I knew I had. I was thirty-seven, but I looked much better now. Like night and day, but I did need to do something with my hair. I put so much effort into getting it to grow long that now that it was, I had no idea what to do with it.

Sosha and Carlton quickly came back, throwing apologies and reassurances about my looks, but it still hurt. It hurt like it did in elementary school when I was teased about my skinny legs and nappy hair while I rode home on the yellow school bus. The taunts forced me to exit several stops before my own or walk home instead of take the bus at all if it meant I didn't have to hear those kids tease me. I looked much better today than I did even five years ago. I knew that for a fact because I put a conscience effort toward improving my looks. Changed my diet. Gave up pop and only drunk water, which smoothed my skin. The braces provided the biggest improvement, and the weight. I didn't have to try too hard to gain weight. I put that on naturally after I gave birth to Carlton. After Sosha, though, my chest blew up from barely an A cup to an overflowing C. Really more like a D, but I preferred wearing a smaller cup size because I loved the special effect it provided my chest. The only thing left to redo was my hair. I'd have Gina cut it into a style but not take too much length off. My insecurities would have to stay as-is. My kids loved me regardless, and after two huge failures with men, I didn't care what they thought anymore.

———

The step-by-step directions that I printed from the Internet were leading us to my parents' home, but I decided to take a detour and head for the Village Green of Auburn Hills to check into our corporate housing. After I connected to northbound I-75, traffic halted right before my parents' exit on Seven Mile Road.

We stood in the same spot for thirty minutes, inching along at a snail's pace.

"Why aren't we moving?" Sosha asked, wrestling in her seat. "I feel sick."

"Hold on, baby. There must have been an accident," I said.

People were getting out of their cars and looking far into the horizon.

Samson was panting and nudging the back of my head with his nose. "Take Samson alongside the embankment so he can use the bathroom, and please be careful. I don't want you bringing back a dead dog," I said to Carlton.

"I don't feel like it," Carlton said, huffing.

"I didn't ask you how you felt," I said with an attitude.

"The cops are all over. We're not supposed to let him shit on the expressway. What if they give us a ticket?"

"Just go. You're taking him off to the side and take the pooper-scooper with you. Don't mess with me today. I'm not in the mood. I don't care if they give us a ticket, because I'm not about to let Samson mess up the inside of my car." Carlton jerked the back door open and snatched Samson out by his leash. Samson moaned. "Stop doing him like that, Carlton," I said just as Carlton slammed the back door.

I picked up my cell phone and dialed 911, telling the operator that we'd been stuck on I-75 for almost a half hour because it was at a complete standstill.

The operator explained that emergency crews and police were on the scene due to a fatal accident, and that they'd shut down the northbound expressway and would reopen a lane to allow everyone to exit in forty minutes to an hour.

"That's too long," I shouted through my cell.

"Ma'am, somebody died so you need to be patient," the operator said.

———

When I ended the call, I began banging my head against the headrest. If I had taken Woodward Avenue to Squirrel Road like I started to, we'd already be checked into the corporate apartment by now, but out of fear I'd drive by my parents' once I crossed Seven Mile and Woodward, I changed my mind and took the expressway. *Always listen to your first mind,* I thought. This was an omen, and no matter how hard I tried, I wouldn't be able to avoid my parents.

This wasn't a good way to start our first day in Detroit.

I looked over at Sosha who was sitting beside me with a pool of tears filling her eyes. Reality was starting to sink in. My eyelids were heavy with doubt. I wasn't sure what I was doing here. Even though I had my children with me, and this was my hometown, I still felt totally disconnected from the environment. This was crazy.

Please don't let this be another mistake, I thought. I'd already made too many over the years. Now that I'm older, I recognize that and I want to do some good. I want to find Derwin and unite him with his son. I want to make amends with my father. I want to make a name for myself with Daimler Chrysler. If I can accomplish all of those things, a tomorrow never promised didn't feel so bad.

"Samson won't use it," Carlton said as he opened the back door and jumped inside with Samson then slammed the door.

"You didn't give him enough time, Carlton."

"I'm not going back out there. You can if you want."

"Forget it!" I said, rolling my bloodshot eyes. I was ready to get into someone's bed and sleep until the next day.

———

When the right lane finally opened up, I took the necessary precaution while changing lanes, trying to get all the way over from the far left to the right along with dozens of others.

"Carlton, do you see why it's so important to drive carefully? Especially inexperienced teenagers who get involved in more accidents," I said to him, but he ignored me.

I drove down Seven Mile, focusing on the road and the familiar side streets leading to Woodward.

"This is my old neighborhood," I said.

Carlton still didn't hear me. He was into his rap music. Master M, N, O, or P, whichever letter it was. I was sick of it. Rap was all he listened to. He played it so much that occasionally I'd catch myself nodding my head to the beat when I didn't even like that kind of music. Jazz was my thing.

"This is your old neighborhood?" Sosha asked, wrinkling her nose. "I thought you said you grew up in a nice area."

"I did. I grew up in Palmer Woods. The actual neighborhood is across Woodward, the street we're about to approach." I stopped at the red light and looked to my right at Sandpiper, the corner store. I used to go there almost every day after high school when the Woodward bus dropped me off in front of it. I'd load up on the junk food, praying that one day I'd wake up with a body just like Jill Stockton's, the girl I'd watch prance down the corridors of Cass Tech on her way to class. I'd pray to God to bless me with those curves so the boys' eyes would follow me like they did her. I honestly thought that a big bag of red-hot pork grinds, a Marathon bar, a Kit-Kat, and a large red Faygo soda pop was my magic potion.

"The lights green, Mama," Sosha said, snapping me out of my daze. "Take us to Grandma's, Mommy, please," Sosha whined as she turned her head toward Carlton.

"What?" he shouted, removing his headphones.

"Mommy's about to take us over Grandma's."

"We're going over Grandma's?" he asked.

"Not today. I'm tired. It's been a long drive," I said.

"So," he chimed in, "you can rest over there. You act like they're not even your parents. I'm sure they'll let you take a nap. Come on, might as well, we're already here."

Carlton felt extremely close to my parents, people he'd never seen outside of photographs. He'd spend hours talking to my father on the telephone about golf. My mother was always sending both the kids expensive gifts, anything she could to win their affection.

"What if they're not home?" I asked, even though I knew they'd be there on a Tuesday. Monday they golfed at Palmer Park. They took their daily walk every morning around the neighborhood between seven and eight. Friday was bridge, but nothing was scheduled for today.

"Mom, if they're not home, we'll leave. Now just take us there," Carlton said forcefully.

"No, we'll go over next week after we've settled in, and that's the end of this discussion."

Carlton shoved his headphones back on, increasing the volume so loud I thought it was coming through my speakers. "Turn down that music before you go deaf!" All Carlton wanted to do was make his way over to my parents' house so he could beg them for a car. I knew my son too well.

"I have to go to the bathroom!" Sosha shouted.

"Can't you hold it for twenty more minutes?"

"No, I can't. My doctor told me not to hold my pee. She said that was a bad thing to do. And besides," Sosha said, leaning into my ear, "my grandparents live right up the street."

"They *lived* right up the street. We're on Woodward and Nine Mile now, and I'm not turning around. I'll stop at this Pizza Hut and you can use the bathroom in there."

"Forget it," she said, throwing her back into the seat and folding her arms.

"I thought your doctor said it was bad to hold it."

"I said forget it!" Sosha shouted.

I wasn't going to forget it, because these kids were already starting to try my nerves. "You're too grown. You know that? When we get to the apartment and I put my belt to your behind you won't be too grown then, will you?" Sosha's eyes started watering. Even though I'd never spanked her, my words stung worse than a switch ever could. I knew too well about that. I learned from my father the how-to of destroying a child, but she was bad and she needed her ass beat, I just couldn't do it.

I swerved my car into Pizza Hut's parking lot and demanded that both of them exit.

Carlton wanted to stay, but I made him go anyway. I told them that they needed to use the bathroom, get something to eat or drink, do whatever they had to do inside that restaurant so that when they came back to the car they wouldn't be bugging me.

About fifteen minutes later they returned. Carlton was holding a large pizza box, and Sosha was carrying three large beverage cups.

"Don't spill anything in my car," I said as they entered. Taking two of the cups from Sosha and placing them in the holder. "And don't eat that pizza until we get to the apartment."

The rest of the drive was smooth sailing. I didn't have to listen to whiny voices or any more rap music, just the subtle sound of my V-8 engine guiding us to our destination.

11

I woke before the alarm clock buzzed at 8:00 A.M. and showered and dressed quickly. I was finding a house today if it was the only thing I did. The day before was our first full one in Michigan, and Alice, my real estate agent, took us house hunting, but it was like going on a wild-goose chase. She took us to look at all the new construction in the Rochester Hills and Auburn Hills area, trying to convince me that I needed to spend at least fifty thousand dollars more to get almost everything I wanted, which I found hard to believe because my needs were very basic: a four-bedroom house with a two-car attached garage with high ceilings and at least five thousand square feet. Supposedly the square footage was the clincher. Alice said to get a house that large I'd be paying more than three hundred thousand, which was almost double my price range. She showed me plenty of four bedrooms, but most were twenty-five hundred to three thousand square feet. I needed space. I needed that more than anything. Even if it was empty space, I still needed it.

I woke the kids so they could get ready before Alice arrived.

"Don't ooh and ah today," I said to Sosha through the closed bathroom door, "even if you think the houses are pretty. She doesn't need to think she automatically has a sale. I want her to earn her commission."

The shower water was probably drowning out my every word.

Carlton dragged himself into the dining room, sat at the table, and shoved his feet inside of his Nikes.

"Did you hear what I told Sosha?"

"Don't ooh and ah, yeah, I heard you," he said dryly.

"What's wrong with you?" I asked. "Do you have an attitude this morning?"

"Why do we always have to live so far away from black people? It was the same way in Texas. I think we were the only black folks who lived in Roanoke. Why can't we ever live in the city?"

"Public education is better in the suburbs. I'm sorry it's like that, but it's a fact."

"Then buy a cheaper house in the city and send us to private schools. You grew up in the city. You went to a public high school," he said.

"I went to Cass Tech, which is not your run-of-the mill public school. It was recognized throughout the country for academics."

"Well send me there."

"I don't want you going there."

"Why not?"

"I just don't." I didn't want my kids doing anything I did. Choose an entirely different path, maybe they'd have better results. Even though everyone in my family attended different high schools and the results seem to be close to the same—we're all fucked up, mentally. My brother, Trent, the middle child, went to Catholic Central. My older sister Colleen attended Immaculatta, and Val, the second youngest next to me, graduated from Benedictine. None of them went to college. I was the only one who even attempted to earn a college degree right after high school.

Trent decided to enlist in the army after high school, spending twenty-five years in the service. He married a woman he met overseas in Germany. Her name is Felda and she's white. I don't have a problem with that. I simply have a problem with my brother never wanting a black woman. He thinks we're too mean, and he told the family that he's never been attracted to one black woman. After being raised around a house full I took that as a slap in my face. I love my brother. I never met my sister-in-law so I can't say what I think of her, but Trent needs to realize that he's a black man who has never in his life dated a black woman and to me that means he has a problem—low self-esteem, poor self-image, something—he's fucked up.

Colleen lived with my parents until she was forty-two, even though she earned a decent income as a manager for a third-party collection agency. Everyone thought she was crazy to stay with my parents so long until she moved out with a big enough savings to purchase a three-bedroom ranch in Southfield and a Volvo 960 with cash. She's single with no kids, but she has had the same steady boyfriend for years. She's a bit eccentric and so is her boyfriend. They don't conform to society's rules. Especially when it comes to appearance. She refuses to put chemical in her hair to straighten it. She ignores fashion and any of the rules attached. She wears what she wants when she wants. Which could mean sandals in the wintertime or wool in the summertime. But she does believe in a reliable car and a nice home. Colleen's not really fucked up. She's just different.

Val, the one I love to hate got pregnant her junior year of high school but still graduated on time. She married Bo, who back then was twenty-six and seemed too old for her. Now he just seems too good for her. Last I heard, she wasn't working, and never worked. According to Gina, Val keeps a junky house and when her husband comes home from his job he starts cleaning, and most of the time he's cooking or they're going out to eat.

"I'm tired of being one of a handful of black kids," Carlton said.

"That's how it's going to be everywhere you go in this world. When you go to college, you're going to be one of a handful. When you get a corporate job, you're going to be one of a handful. That's just the way it is, so you need to get used to it now." I sounded just like my father, and it made me sick.

"It doesn't have to be that way. I'm going to a black college."

"You're going wherever you get a scholarship, Carlton. And after college you're going to go work for whoever hires you."

"If I don't make it pro, and I stress *if*, because I know I will, then I'm going to open my own business or if I have to work for somebody it's going to be a black business like *Black Enterprise*."

"Good luck getting a job at *Black Enterprise*. Besides, I thought if you didn't make it pro, you wanted to be a surgeon. Make up your mind."

"I can do anything I want to do. Anything I put my mind to." One thing my son had that I didn't was self-motivation.

"You won't be able to do anything if you don't study and apply yourself, which means a good education."

"Blah blah blah," he said, rolling his eyes.

"You know what?" I asked, raising my voice. "I've had enough with you and your sister's disrespect. You're teaching her to be that same way with me. Do you think this shit is easy?" His eyes widened. I had never cursed in front of my children before but I was at my breaking point. "I'm the breadwinner. It's me, myself, and I, and you kids. I have to support y'all. Not your father who's back in Texas still trying to find himself, holding on to old dreams that he had since childhood. You think I never had a dream? I wanted to have an adventurous life, too, but I'm back here. I chose my family over my own desires. I know what this family needs, and I also know what we can afford. Private school and city taxes aren't in the equation."

Sosha walked out of the bathroom wearing a midriff top and studded

Capri jeans. She had her long hair released from the braids and she was looking too grown. "Who you trying to be, a miniature Janet Jackson? Where do you think you're going looking like that?" I asked. "When did I say you could start wearing your hair down?"

"Seventh grade," she mumbled.

"What grade are you going in?"

"Sixth." Technically, she was in the sixth because she was double promoted twice, but my mind still considered her in the fourth. Even though, she was smart as a whip, she was still a baby and too spoiled for her own good, due mostly to her nana, Keith's mother, and also me, I must admit.

"So what does that mean?" I snapped. She shrugged. "It means I hope you know how to braid. Where did you get those clothes? I didn't buy them."

"Grandma sent them to me," she said, still mumbling.

"Who? Speak up."

"Grandma."

"Those were the clothes she sent you for Christmas? They must have been delivered when I was at work because I would have sent them right back. Get me a brush and comb and your clips so I can braid you hair back." She pouted into the bedroom. "You're taking too long."

"Dang, she just walked in there."

I threw Carlton an evil eye. "Was I talking to you?"

He shook his head. "Don't take your stress out on us."

"Oh, I guess you want to be hit, don't you?"

"Mom, you always threaten to hit us but you never do. Go on and hit me if it'll make you feel better. I just want to know what did we do to you? You made us move. We didn't have a choice in the matter. I was just trying to give my opinion on things. We spent all yesterday looking at houses, none of which you liked. You were the one who kept telling that real estate lady the houses in Detroit had more character. She even told you that you could probably find what you were looking for there. Dang, I mean, you trippin'."

Sosha ran out of the bedroom and over to hug me. "I'm sorry I made you mad, Mama."

"You got the stuff?" I asked as I unlocked the grip she had around my waist. She handed me her hair supplies. I sat on the sofa, spreading my legs. "Sit down so I can do this real quick."

"I hope you settle down, Mom, because you're driving me insane," Carlton said.

"Feed the dog!" I snapped. I hated myself when I was like this, taking my disappointments out on my children. I knew it was wrong and I wanted so bad to stop. Sometimes I could go for weeks acting completely normal, but there were the other times like these that I became a bitch.

————

After being shuffled from one new development to the next, gathering nothing more than several nicely printed brochures and a stack of floor plans with availability sheets, I decided to switch areas, and inquired about Parkside. What an interesting twist and one I hadn't considered before now.

Alice sat at her computer and pulled up one home located on Parkside Street that was having trouble selling because it needed a lot of work, but it had a good price, $150,000, which was thirty thousand dollars less than what I was willing to pay. There were two schools nearby, University of Detroit High School that Carlton could attend and Gesu Elementary for Sosha. Both were Catholic schools, so I'd be paying tuition, and living in Detroit also meant paying city taxes, two things I was dead set against, but as I studied the address that was on her monitor, unless the home turned out to be a complete dump when we drove up, I knew that was the one we were moving in. After all, that street had much significance. I left Detroit because I wanted to hide from my past, but now I was back to reclaim it, and what better way to do it than by living on that street in that neighborhood and definitely in that house.

12

The next week on Friday afternoon I pulled into the parking lot of the Century 21 real estate office in Bloomfield Hills to meet with Alice about the house. She called saying she had questions about a few things that appeared on my credit report.

When I walked into the office, Alice was finishing up with her clients and barely spoke, but when her clients walked out of the door, her attention immediately turned toward me. "Let's talk, shall we," she said, sweeping her hand in front of our path.

I didn't like her intro line. What did we need to talk about? I didn't want her starting any mess now. Not after I put a bid for $140,000 down on the house. The owners needed to get happy and accept it with all the things I found wrong with the place. If I got the house she could tell me now, and if I didn't, I wanted to know why because that would be impossible. "Did I get the house?" I asked as we walked into her small office, and she plopped down in her swivel chair.

"Your bid was accepted, but you've got credit issues, which I found quite strange because you have wonderful income and a steady job. Still our mortgage company can't get past your credit."

"I don't have any credit problems. My credit should be perfect."

Alice pulled out a manila folder that had a copy of my Equifax report.

I scooted my chair over to the side of her desk so I could look at it with her.

"You have a few things going on here. First of all, you have a lot of open credit that's sitting out there. You need to close all of it. You also have a charge-off from '93 for five thousand dollars that needs to be paid. What was that any way?"

"A business loan for my ex-boyfriend. He told me he paid it."

"This is what really surprised me." She pointed to a Chrysler Financial trade line, and to the side it read, Repossession. "You work for Daimler Chrysler and your car was repossessed in '98?"

"What is this?" I snatched the report from her and put it as close to my face as I could, hoping I would find some mistake. Then like a ton of bricks I realized it was Keith again. "I leased a Jeep for my ex-boyfriend while we were still together. When we broke up he said he was going to continue paying the note."

"You're going to have to get those things cleared up immediately and provide me with letters to that effect. You're making good income, I know I can get the deal approved, but I'm trying to get you the best possible interest rate."

"Why didn't you tell me the Jeep got repoed?" I screamed through the phone line.

"I did tell you," Keith said as he munched on what sounded like chips.

"No, you didn't. Why would you do that? That's affecting my credit. You don't have any credit so you could probably care less."

I was pacing my bedroom floor, strangling the phone cord as I dragged it around with me. Suddenly another wedding flashback entered my consciousness. This time I was pulling on Derwin's leg as he attempted to walk out of the church. What a fool I'd been.

"Remember last year, around this time, when I called you from New York and told you I was three months behind on the car note," he said, still munching.

"You did not!"

"I asked you for some money, didn't I? I asked you for eighteen hundred dollars, didn't I?"

"Yeah, you asked me for some money, but you didn't say what it was for."

His crunching continued. "You know the car note is six hundred dollars. Eighteen hundred is three car notes."

"First of all, the car note is $643 so get it right. You told me you needed eighteen hundred dollars to take care of some business. I asked you what kind of business, and you just said, 'Business. Don't worry about what kind.' Now, if you're asking me for eighteen hundred dollars and you don't tell me what it's for, do you really expect to get it? I know you did that out of spite because that lease was almost up."

"You wouldn't have given me the money no way. You told me back in '94 to get the fuck out of your face."

"I would have given it to you to save my credit."

"Well, what's done is done. And it's done now. When can I see my kids?"

"What? This really doesn't faze you, does it? You're probably happy about putting a little wrinkle in my plans. I'm sure you've got your new girlfriend getting you a car in her name now. You need to grow up! And when will you see your kids? This is when." I slammed the phone down and collapsed on the bed.

The kids were yelling they were hungry.

I yelled back, "Order pizza."

I pulled myself together and walked over to the closet to remove my scrapbook that was hidden in a Via Spaga boot box way in the back.

I took out Derwin's senior picture, which was stuck between the middle pages. It was the one thing outside of Carlton that he had given me. On the back he wrote:

WINNIE THE POOH,

YOU'LL ALWAYS HAVE A SPECIAL PLACE IN MY HEART.

K.I.T.

DERWIN, CLASS OF '80

It was Sunday, July 11. I was supposed to start work the next day, but I wasn't going in. I moved my start date back a week to get all the things situated with the house. Mainly trying to get approved. The week before I had to run around and try to take care of clearing up the items on my credit report, and I still had more to do. Alice tried to assure me that I wasn't going to have a problem, but I'm realistic if I'm nothing else. Bad credit is a problem, and a repo is bad credit. When I called Chrysler Financial to attempt to clear up the matter, I was informed that my account had been transferred to their recovery center in Jacksonville, Florida. I then called the toll-free number I was given just to find out that my information had been forwarded to the same collection agency my sister Colleen managed. All I needed was for her to find out and tell my parents. I had to make sure I cleared this up quickly.

This house had become a part of my plan. How perfect it could turn out if I lived directly across the street from Derwin's parents and let everything unfold on my own terms. Nothing was going to mess that up.

I turned on the radio, in search of some R&B or smooth jazz. That's when I heard a man describing himself. The brother was sounding good. He said he was, "Six-four, dark brown, and 220 pounds of muscle." I was getting excited as I listened to him. The announcer mentioned how women could meet this man if they were interested, but I wasn't doing that. No way.

13

It was Tuesday. We had been in Detroit for exactly two weeks and my kids had bugged me every day to take them over their grandparents. I had run out of excuses this time. It was hard to make that phone call, but somehow I got up the nerve.

Dad answered the phone initially, but as soon as he heard my voice, he quickly turned the phone over to my mother, who, as usual, had to make things all better by saying that my father was busy in the yard, which is why he didn't have enough time to even say hello.

For the first thirty minutes, I pretended as if nothing had changed. I was still living in Texas as far as they knew.

Then after Mom realized it wasn't a holiday, she yelled out, "What's wrong? Did something happen to the kids?"

"No, they're fine."

"I'm so surprised that you called."

"I wanted to find out what you and Dad were doing today."

"Nothing."

"Is it alright if we stop by?" I asked.

"We who?"

"Me and the kids."

"How are you going to do that? Are you in Detroit?"

"Yes."

"How long have you been in Detroit?"

"A couple of weeks, but I've been busy house-hunting."

"House-hunting? So that must mean you're moving here."

"Yeah, my job relocated us."

"Winona and the kids are in Detroit, Donald."

It sounded like they were in the same room, so I assumed she was outside since that's where my father was supposed to have been. Of course I knew better.

She covered the phone because I'm sure he said something rude. Then she came back on the line to ask when we were coming over. Before she had a chance to cover the phone again, I heard my father ask, "Does she have a man with her?"

"Tell him no, I don't."

"Donald, she said she doesn't. It's just her and the kids." Then my mother covered the phone again. Mom didn't understand that it was too late to protect me. I lived with Dad long enough to know that if he cared for his family, it was in his own way, and I was tired of trying to figure out which way that was.

I agreed to come over for dinner. Tried to make it for the next day but my mother and my kids insisted today.

―――――

My heart fluttered and my back tensed as I turned into Palmer Woods on Afton and drove down the long street until I came to my parents' house. More memories flooded into my consciousness. This is where my feelings of inferiority first began. It was hard growing up in a neighborhood that stood for prestige and wealth, but where I felt like less than hired help. My parents worked hard like our neighbors. Their combined income even mirrored some in the neighborhood, but their status was nonexistent. The difference was they didn't have Dr. or Judge in front of their name or Ph.D. behind it. Our family had the most modest house in the entire neighborhood. We didn't have a maid come three times a week like most did. My father mowed our lawn instead of hiring a service. I hated living in that house. Hated living somewhere I felt we didn't belong.

My mother's dream was to move up the ranks of restaurant management and one day own a McDonald's like the one she managed, but management was the furthest she ever came before retiring. I believe she'd say her biggest accomplishments were becoming a wife and mother. She was always happy around the family, even when there was no reason to be. Even when she had to hide shopping bags from the mall until Dad wasn't around so she could sneak them into the house. Where's the happiness in that? Someone works fifty hours a week to bring home a decent salary but she has to sneak in new clothes and pretend she's not spending any money. Get to the mail and the Visa bill before Dad catches onto her game. None of the clothes she bought were for her. Mom wasn't into clothes, shoes, jewelry, nothing but her family and job. Even after half of her face was burned when an angry employee flung hot grease on her, she still went back to work right after the series of skin grafts were completed. You could tell something happened to her face, but Mom was always secure within herself, and I never understood how she could be. Here I had smooth skin, but I might as well have been burned all over, the way I felt.

My father was a foreman at Detroit Edison. He's a tall, heavyset man who wears thick glasses and a bush full of black hair with a couple dozen gray strands mixed in. He has heavy marks on his face from when he was a child growing up with acne that eventually cleared but left the scars behind. There wasn't anything attractive about my dad as far as I could see. Mom said it was his reliability. He worked five, sometimes six days a week as much as twelve hours a day. Always brought home a steady paycheck. Hardly went anywhere with anyone but her, and that's what Mom needed while Dad needed a woman he could control, so they both got out of the relationship what they needed, I suppose.

The house looked unchanged. It was still the same modest brown brick colonial home with tan trim that we moved to when I was entering my freshman year at Cass Tech. Nothing to compare to the other more elaborate homes in the neighborhood.

When I pulled into the driveway, the front door opened and my mother rushed out to greet us with Dad nowhere in sight. Carlton and Sosha's eyes lit up like a star on top of a Christmas tree when they saw my mother. I sensed that Mom was at peace and still very happy. "It's so good to see everyone," she said, extending her arms. She hugged me first. Then hugged Sosha and Carlton together. I barely noticed her scar. She must be using some new makeup that blended in nicely with her cocoa-colored skin. "I called Val right after you called me and she rushed over," Mom said as she led us into the house.

"Great," I said, rolling my eyes. I was the first one through the door. Val was sitting in the den, preparing to smoke a cigarette. She must've thought she was at her house. I couldn't stand the smell of cigarette smoke and neither could Dad so after all of these years my first words spoken to her were, "Take it outside."

"I was planning on it." She stood slowly, snatched a golf ball-shaped ceramic ashtray, her lighter, and pack of cigarettes, and headed for the back door, but turned around after she heard Sosha and Carlton's voices. "Is this my niece and nephew?" she asked, opening her arms and giving them a group hug. "Both of you are so good-looking. Must take after your father," she said, turning up her nose as she looked toward me.

"Ha ha ha. I'm sure I'll be able to say the same thing to Raven and Bo Jr.," I said.

"I'm sure you will. There's no denying that my husband is fine." I couldn't help but stare Val down and wonder what possessed her to wear a pair of stretch pants and a cut-off T-shirt as big as her butt and belly were.

We all ended up outside on the back porch except for Mom who stayed inside preparing dinner. Carlton and my father were on the grass practicing their golf swings. I didn't know that much about golf, but I believed what the pros said about Carlton. His swing was flawless. Carlton knew he was good and loved the sport, but he didn't always take golf as seriously as girls. To him it was just a pastime he happened to excel in. He always talked that next Tiger Woods stuff, but he didn't really mean it. I wasn't sure what Carlton wanted to do. He mentioned becoming a neurosurgeon like the renowned Dr. Ben Carson, but he didn't have his grades up to par and science was his worst subject. I was concerned about both of my children. Sosha seemed like a little baby who would never grow up. She was nine but acted like a bad five-year-old, still trying to cling to me.

"So, you're my mother's sister?" Sosha asked, sucking on a red Popsicle with the juices dripping on to her white T-shirt as she stood in front of Val.

"Yes, I am, sweetheart," Val said.

Sosha studied every nook and cranny of my sister then said, "You don't look alike."

"Thank you," Val said.

"I thought my mother looked old, but you really look old. How old are you?"

"Go away, little girl, before I hurt you." Val shooed Sosha away.

"That wasn't a nice thing to say," I whispered to Sosha.

"But it's the truth and besides, I don't think I like her."

"I heard that," Val said. "Didn't you teach your children to respect their elders?"

"She's right, you can't speak to adults like that. Go apologize," I said to Sosha, but inside I was laughing because Val was getting back a taste of her own medicine. Val dogged me when I was a child, now my child was dogging her.

"I don't have to apologize for telling the truth." Sosha pouted, put her hand on her hip, and leaned to one side like she was daring me to make her. I was almost ready to pinch her little arm but my mother opened the screen door.

"Sosha, come help your grandmother in the kitchen."

"Okay, Granny," she said, all smiles, then jetted across the concrete and disappeared inside.

"You got your work cut out for you," Val said. "I thought Raven was bad when she was that age."

I sat down on the bench next to Val. "How is little Raven?"

"Not little anymore. She's twenty-one. And the girl did one of your numbers with college, went for a couple years then dropped out. Now, she's dating a professional football player. I don't know, supposedly she's getting married, but we both know how that can turn out."

I frowned. "Watch what you say and who you say it around." I looked at her, then over at Carlton who was still practicing his swing.

"You know what I'm saying so I don't need to say anything else," Val responded. "And Bo Jr. went out and got a girl pregnant so I'm going to be a grandmother when I turn forty. The baby's due date is October 22—my birthday."

"Val, please don't say anything around the kids because I never told my children anything."

"I said okay. You never even told Carlton?" she whispered.

"No, not even Carlton."

"So he thinks what?"

"I don't feel comfortable talking about this right now. Just make sure you never bring up Derwin's name around him. He doesn't know who that is and I don't want him asking. Tell your kids the same thing."

"I will, whenever I see them." I knew Val. If blackmail were a casino game, she'd be a millionaire by now. This would probably come up later when she needed gambling money, and it seemed she always needed that. I didn't understand why Bo was so weak to her. Too weak to say no when she put out her hand for his weekly paycheck for which he worked seven days at the Ford plant. Twenty-five hundred dollars, he'd turn it over to her just like that, every week. He'd been doing that for years, and according to Gina, he hadn't changed. No surprise to me the man's a functioning alcoholic. He needs something to drown Val's ass out.

"Why didn't Bo come over?"

"Bo's at work. At least that's where he claims to be."

"I'm sure you check the hours on his pay stub."

"You know I do."

"Are you working now?" I asked.

"You know I don't like to work."

"You know I don't either, but sometimes you got to do what you got to do."

"Well, I have a husband, so I don't have to do shit."

"Well maybe if you did, he wouldn't have to work seven days a week."

"He likes his schedule."

"I don't know anybody who likes working ten to twelve hours a day, seven days a week."

"You know, Bo, and he loves it."

"He probably likes the money he's making, but I doubt if he likes all the time he spends doing it."

Val focused her attention on her long acrylic nails as she picked under them. "You know Gina does hair out of her home. She does mine every week. That's my girl." She smoothed her hand over her French roll.

"Of course I know; she's my best friend." I looked at the top of Val's head. "But I'm not into fancy styles."

"She can do boring styles too."

"I didn't say it had to be boring."

"I remember how you are. You either liked your hair pulled back or turned under. How long is it now?" I sawed my hand across the middle of my back. "That long. Your hair has never been past your shoulders. Is it all yours?"

"All mine."

"Um. Ain't that something. How is it that your hair can grow long and mine never went anywhere? What I would give if I didn't have to buy a new bag of hair to put on top of my head every month."

"Why don't you wear your hair short?"

"I'm not a dyke."

"There's nothing wrong with short hair."

"I don't like it, and neither does my husband, and if it's nothing wrong with it, cut all yours off."

"One day I might. I'm not my hair."

"That's so easy for someone with long hair to say. I'll say one thing, you're certainly not skinny anymore, and it's a good thing because men don't like that either."

"I only wear a size ten, but you really think I don't look skinny?"

"Not at all, and a size ten is a lot better than a size zero."

"I never wore a zero."

"What did you wear a two?"

"A four."

"A four? Is that a real size? Lord knows you used to look so pitiful back in the day. You didn't even have a butt."

"Can we change the subject?"

"I'm just talking," she said, waving her hand.

"Dinner's ready," Sosha yelled through the open window. "Come on, Mama, I already fixed your plate and saved you a seat next to mine."

"She's the most precious little witch," Val said.

"Don't talk about my little girl like that."

Val grinned. "We're all family just having some fun."

I walked into the house behind Val. My daughter had set the table and even put name tags made from notebook paper beside each plate. She had my sister on the opposite side of us, down on the end next to Carlton. I guess he made her mad today.

Dad said the prayer, and we all commenced to eat mother's chicken fried steak.

We had light dinner conversation. I was mostly filling my family in on my new position. Dad seemed skeptical when I said I was an executive. He corrected me by saying, "You mean a manager, right, not executive?"

"No, I mean what I said, *executive!*"

"Mmm," he responded. "That's how it was at Edison. Had to know somebody to get them jobs. There weren't too many blacks getting hooked up with high positions. How did you say you knew that girl again?"

"We were roommates at Michigan State."

"Mmm." He held his head, probably remembering the money he wasted. "You find a place to stay yet?" Dad asked, not looking up from his greens.

"I'm thinking about putting a bid down on a house on Parkside." I never told them what I had done already. Always what I was thinking about, much safer that way and subject to less criticism.

"Parkside?" Val announced loudly. "In Sherwood Forest?"

"That's right," I said.

"What kind of money you makin' now? Shit, we didn't even buy in Sherwood and my husband makes more than a hundred thousand a year."

"I make close to that, but on a forty- not eighty-hour week."

"Um, I hope you can afford it," Val said. "You should have asked Dad before you put a bid on a home. Did she ask for your advice, Dad?"

"No, she didn't. I'm a little surprised that you would pay that much for your first house." He sounded dignified in his response for a change, but that's probably because my kids were there. If they hadn't been he would've started cursing, and say, "You're so stupid. Nothin' but a damn fool, and you still don't know what the hell you're doing. When will you learn? That's okay. You'll see when you fall on your face. Don't come back here when you do, because we're not helping you."

"You don't even know how much it is, I just said I was thinking about putting a bid down on a home."

"Well, honey, how much is it?" Mom asked, trying to keep the peace.

"A hundred and forty thousand."

"A hundred and forty thousand?" Val burst out. "What is it, a mansion?"

"You obviously don't know how much homes are going for today," I said.

"Yeah, obviously," Sosha said to Val.

"A hundred and forty thousand isn't a lot for a home in that area, that's what the homes in the University District are selling for, so what's wrong with it?" Dad asked, looking directly at me.

"It needs a little repair," I said.

"It needs a lot of repair," Carlton said.

Dad's frown settled upon his face and more of my childhood memories started coming back. "Why would you buy a house that needs a lot of repair?" Dad asked.

"Because it was a good deal and I like the neighborhood."

The kids were looking back and forth as we spoke.

"Did you say Parkside?" Val asked again.

"Yes, Parkside," I said.

"Didn't—" I threw her a quick look that zipped her mouth shut. "Nothing."

"Somebody did live on Parkside," Mom added.

"Forget about it, Mom," Val warned.

"Oh," Mom said, rolling her eyes, "that's right."

"Who?" Dad asked.

"Nobody, Donald, forget it," Mom cautioned.

"Sosha and Carlton, are you almost through with your dinner?" I asked.

"Yeah," Sosha said, "but I want dessert."

"We need to be getting back," I said.

"We can wait until I get dessert," Sosha said, rolling her big eyes.

"Sosha, I'll wrap up your dessert for you, and you can take it home. Would you like that?" Mom asked.

"I want to eat it here." She stuck out her bottom lip.

"Sosha, I wouldn't do that if I were you," I warned.

"You're not me," she snapped.

This was the time I wished I believed in beating kids. "It's time to go. Party's over!" I said, standing and heading for the door.

"She acts like that because you let her," Val said as I passed her. "If that was my child I'd beat her little ass."

I walked out of the dining room and stood in the foyer, waiting for Sosha and Carlton to get up from the table.

I heard Mom apologizing to my children, telling them that when we moved to Parkside, they could come over every day. Go ahead and make me out to be the bad guy.

Mom hurried into the kitchen, returning with two large brown paper bags stuffed with food that she handed each of them as they made their way to where I was standing.

"Maybe after you start your job you can drop the kids off and they can spend the week. It will give you a chance to adjust," Mom said.

"Okay, I'll do that," I said. She was such a good mom, a better mom than I could be. She was a good wife, too, a better one than I wanted to be. I could cook and clean if I had a husband, but I could never be a puppet to a man again. Never. Been there and done all that.

Val walked up to me. "Be sure to call Gina. Now that you're an executive you need to make sure you look the part."

14

While I still had a few days left being off work, I figured I'd go by Gina's for the first time since I'd been back to Detroit so she could work my hair into a style. Didn't think to call her because after all we'd been best friends since the fifth grade so calling before I came by wasn't a prerequisite—even on a Thursday— at 7:00 P.M. when I knew she'd be booked.

I stepped into her basement, amid the smell of no-lye relaxer, fried hair, and Dudley products. Mark had done an excellent job converting their basement into a salon. I never saw the "before," but the "after" looked like any other beauty shop I'd been in, only this one was in a house.

At first Gina didn't recognize me, and I almost didn't recognize her. She always had big hips, but these hips on her now had spread wide and were almost ready to part. Not to mention her hair. She had the kind of hair that didn't need chemicals to straighten. Most black people call it good hair so I guess that's what she had. It wasn't straight, but it wasn't nappy either. She didn't need to get a touchup every six to eight weeks like I did. Her hair had more of a wavy pattern to it and only once or twice a year did she have to slap an extra-mild Revlon relaxer in it. Today, she had it twisted around her head with a large clip attached to it. This was not the Gina I knew. It had been a long time since we'd seen each other. Close to ten years. She had come to visit me after I had Sosha. I knew she was probably looking bad today because she was busy doing folks' heads, but seeing her this way was almost impossible for my brain to comprehend because she was always the pretty one. Always!

"Your door was open," I said to Gina while she was flat ironing one of her customers with three others waiting under dryers.

"Are you Sylvia?" Gina asked.

"Sylvia? Gina, it's me. Do I look that different?" Even if I did look different, you'd think that after a twenty-six-year friendship she'd spot even the smallest feature like the flat mole on my right cheek. Something.

"I don't have my contacts on." She reached for a pair of broken glasses that were lying on the countertop beside her curling irons and put them on. "Winona? Girl, I'm going to kill you. You made it to town and didn't call me."

"Kill her, but don't burn me," her client said as she moved her head way from the flat iron in Gina's hand.

"Girl, look at you," Gina said as she put down the iron and came from around her stylist's chair with her arms extended wide.

We gave each other a long hug.

Tears filled her eyes.

"Gina, why are you crying? You are so emotional.'"

"I'm sorry. I didn't think you were ever coming back to Detroit." She took off her glasses and wiped away the tears. "I'm so happy. And you look so nice. Girl, you've picked up even more weight since the last time I saw you. You're not skinny, huh? The weight looks good on you."

"Now, I need my hair to look good on me."

"You sure do," Gina said.

"Can you do me tonight?" I asked, removing the large barrette from my hair and allowing it to fall well past my shoulder.

"Not today," she answered quickly. "How long you here for?"

"Indefinitely. I was relocated with Chrysler."

"What!" she shouted. "Oh, we're going to have too much fun."

"Gina, I need a touchup and a cut bad. I need the works."

"I'm sorry but I'm booked. I thought you were another woman named Sylvia. I wish you would have called me in advance." She went back to her client and continued to flat iron.

"I know I should have called, but I had no idea your business was booming like this. Why even work another job?"

"Because Mark and I have plenty of other things we're trying to do," she said.

"Well when can you take me?"

"In two weeks."

"Two weeks, Gina? I don't think so. After a twenty-six-year friendship, is that how you're going to do me? You're going to have to give one of your customers the boot." The woman sitting in her chair rolled her eyes my way. "Not you, honey. But one of them."

"I'll try to squeeze you in next week, but we have to get together before that."

"If you have time to get together with me, you have time to do my hair. I start work on Monday. Don't have me going in on my first day with my head looking like this."

"I only have one off day, and that's Sunday. I don't do work on Sunday, that's the Lord's day."

"Every day is supposed to be the Lord's day."

"Every day is, but Sunday is the one Lord's day that I don't work on. Why don't you come to church with me?"

"Are you still going to Butler's church?"

"If you mean Word of Faith, yes."

"That church is too big for me."

"I'm not asking you to join; I'm asking you to visit."

I went with Gina to 8:00 A.M. service. Carlton and Sosha were over at my parents' and I had no immediate plans to get them.

The church was crowded with what looked to be a few thousand people filling the seats, which shocked me. I had no idea so many people would get up this early to worship God. It was too early for me, which is why I continued yawning throughout the sermon, even when the bishop instructed us to turn to our neighbors and repeat his words. I'd turn and repeat the words— between my yawns. I was raised in a Catholic church and was used to forty-five-minute services without praise and worship and little interaction with the congregation. This was much too much. When it was over, I grabbed Gina's hand and politely pushed my way through the crowd, trying to beat everyone to the parking lot so we wouldn't get stuck in a long line of traffic. My plan came to a quick halt near the entrance when Gina ran into a pool of people she knew because they fellowshipped on a weekly basis at different people's home, what they called a touch group. Gina felt compelled to stop and talk about God and the Holy Ghost, while I stood behind her trying to soak it all in.

They mentioned going to IHOP for breakfast, and while I did want breakfast and loved IHOP, I didn't feel like the group church thing and Gina could tell because she knew how to read my eyes.

"Did you think Ernie was attractive?" she whispered as we walked out of the church and into the large parking lot.

"I wasn't really looking at any of them. Which one was Ernie?"

"The tall one in the tan suit. Most women that I know find him to be very attractive—and he's saved—and single."

"So why's he by himself?"

"I don't know. Maybe the same reason you're by yours. What is that reason, anyway?"

"Gina, how many times do I have to tell you I'm not looking for a man? Besides, I really do believe that the reason I can't find a husband is because he's already married. You know the good ones are all taken. All these other folks out here are nothing but leftovers."

"You shouldn't be looking for one, but it's not a problem if you look at one. Besides, Ernie's a real nice man. He's a cop. And you should see him in his uniform."

I rolled my eyes. "He probably beats his woman."

"Why would you say that? Ernie wouldn't beat a woman. He protects women and men."

I raised one eyebrow. "How would you know? Have you ever been his woman? I don't trust cops. Most of them have violent streaks."

She sighed. " Here we go again, Miss Know It All who doesn't know…" she paused, "a thing."

I laughed. "I bet I know what you would have said if you weren't saved."

We strolled through the massive parking lot constantly looking for my car. "Do you remember where we parked?" I asked.

"Not really, but I know it was way down. There it is," she said as she pointed to her left. "I want some breakfast."

"We can go to Bob Evans, because I don't feel like going to IHOP with all of your friends."

"Fine, be antisocial."

We sat in a family-sized booth near the back of the restaurant, debating what we should order for breakfast—waffles or pancakes. We made the waiter leave twice before finally deciding that we'd order both and share.

"Did you find a house yet?" Gina asked as she read through her notes from service.

"Yes, but don't ask me where."

"Where?" she asked, looking up from her notes to focus on me. "I hope you didn't move way out to Auburn Hills or Rochester."

"I bought a house in Sherwood Forest. We move in next week. It's been empty for a while so we got a quick closing. I was happy about that. Oh, and it's across the street from Derwin's parents."

"What? Why would you want to live there? I thought you told me just a few months ago that you were letting that part of your life rest."

"I am, right after I introduce Derwin to his son."

"You haven't told Carlton about Derwin yet?" She looked into my eyes and knew the answer. "I guess that means no. Winona, be honest with me. Do you want Derwin back after all these years?"

"Who, Derwin?" I asked, spitting out laughter. "Are you serious? I can't get back something that I never had."

"Well, you do have his son and you were crazy about the boy at one time. I remember freshman year in high school when you saw him down that hallway kissing on Rachel Turner. You didn't eat for a whole month. And you were already skin and bones. Do you remember that?"

"That was a long time ago, and I was trying not to remember, but thanks for reminding me. How are you going to do my hair when you do it?"

"Probably long and straight, possibly a wrap or maybe even all one length and some long bangs. It'll be sexy. Don't worry."

"I'm not worried about being sexy." I pulled out my Fashion Fair compact and smoothed over some Deep pressed powder with my sponge. I checked my lips and teeth before closing the compact and putting it back inside my Perlina handbag.

"I don't remember you being quite so prissy before."

"Do you remember me looking like this before?" I batted my false eyelashes that looked perfectly real.

"Okay, Miss Thang. No, I don't. The orthodontist has created a monster."

"Not just that orthodontist, honey," I discretely cupped my breasts and pushed them up a bit." I think I was rubbing things in her face because for so many years she was the pretty one. The one who all the guys wanted to meet when we went places together. Now, just today, there were two men sitting at the booth across from us and both were smiling and winking in my direction. The tables seemed to be turning a bit, and it was nice for a change. I ignored the men because neither was my type. I had concerns that they may have been bisexual. They seemed to give off that vibe, but even if they had been my type, I still wouldn't want to meet them because I was through with men. Besides, Gina was the one with a good man and all I had were bad memories and two kids who served as constant reminders.

"I've been meaning to ask you if you got implants," Gina said.

"No, I had Sosha. I guess all that milk never went down or something."

"Maybe I should have a baby."

"It doesn't work like that for all women. Some women get smaller."

"That would be my luck, but honestly I don't even know about the whole baby thing anyway. It's still hard for me to believe that I'm thirty-seven. Especially when I see people from high school with their kids and I'm reminded that it's only Mark and me."

"Gina, you just got married a couple of years ago. If I were you, I'd keep it like that for as long as you can. I love my kids, but if I could do it all over again…" I paused, searching for the best way to complete my sentence without sounding like a bad mother. "I'm not sure if I would."

"A lot of mothers say that, but I'm sure they don't mean it. You don't regret your kids, do you?"

"No, I don't regret *my kids*," I stressed. What I regretted was Derwin and Keith. "When are you having kids?"

"We don't know. When I want them, he doesn't. When he wants them, I don't. Right now, we're thinking neither one of us wants them. Wouldn't that be strange, though? Not having kids. What does a person do when they get old?"

"They get old with no kids."

"But that's a lonely life."

"Just because you have kids doesn't mean they're going to be around you when you get old," I said.

"You know your kids will be around you. Especially little mama's girl, Sosha."

"Who knows? Things change. People change. Have you seen or talked to anyone from high school?"

"Just Bridget Mason."

"How's she doing? Any better?"

"The same. Still living with her parents on Renfrew."

"Didn't she have a nervous breakdown?"

"Mmm–hmm. After she worked and helped put him through dental school, he left her for a woman that didn't look half as good as she did."

"How long have I been telling you that looks only get the man, but good sex is what keeps him?"

"Let's not forget it's Sunday."

"God knows I'm telling the truth."

"Poor Bridget. I just hate that happened to her. She was the nicest pretty girl I knew. She didn't have one arrogant bone in her body," Gina added.

"Don't worry, I believe in Karma. What goes around will come around. He'll get his."

"Does that include my ex?"

"It definitely includes Darren. When he left you, what did he tell you?"

"Have a good day, I might be a little late this evening. He was a little late all right. Good thing I didn't wait up for him."

"I mean before he actually left you. When y'all were starting to have problems and argue he said, 'you ain't never gonna find a man as good as me.' Now as I recall, brother couldn't keep a job. He was something like Keith. Mark, on the other hand, no baby's mama, owned his own home, debt-free. Oh, and he's a sales executive with IBM making six figures."

Gina started fanning herself. "Can you believe I snagged that? Go on. Keep it coming. Keep reminding me of what a good man I have."

"Did Mark not tell his woman, Gina, that he would support whatever she wanted to do? Yes, he did. So when Gina said she wanted to open up a salon in their wonderful finished basement, did he turn it into a salon for her? Yes, he did. He also told her that she doesn't have to work a second job or a first one either."

"Girl, I better go straight home and give that man some."

"Remember, it's Sunday."

"Remember, I'm married, and nothing's wrong with giving your husband some, even on Sunday."

"You got a good man. Whenever I want to just dog a brother out, I think about Mark."

"There are more Marks out there."

"I don't know about that but even if there are, I'm really not looking."

15

"Knock, knock," Beth said as she stood outside my open door. It was the first thing in the morning on my third day at work. Before I even had an opportunity to fix my imaginary cup of coffee to keep myself alert and less annoyed than usual with Beth Anne Jacobs, the assistant project coordinator, better known as secretary. From the first moment I saw her, I could tell we probably wouldn't hit it off. I wanted to take the fresh bottle of white out sitting on my desk and use it to correct her fake smile.

"Can I sit and chat?" she asked, fluttering her long eyelashes. She was a middle-aged white woman, but judging from the clothes she wore and the dye she used to cover her gray she was trying to look much younger, but the crow's feet around her eyes told the true story.

I had a lot on my mind. Today was Carlton's birthday and I had to pick up his cake and a present. I wanted to leave work early, but it probably wasn't appropriate since I had already postponed my start date. "I'm really busy trying to prepare for my first meeting tomorrow," I said.

"I understand," she said, plopping down on the leather sofa.

I took the framed pictures of my children out of my briefcase and put them next to my computer monitor.

"Pictures really should go on the credenza so everyone can enjoy them," she said, smiling quickly. "Your business cards came in." She stood the box up on her skirt so she could read the card that was stapled to it. "Production Improvement Manager. How did you luck up with such a good position?"

"I wouldn't exactly say it was luck. I met the qualifications and I was the best candidate for the job." I watched her throw another fake smile my way. I wondered what she had heard. How much she knew. The worst thing for other people who work under you to assume is that you were given a position you didn't deserve.

"I'm sure you did. Did you come from the Chrysler side, Mercedes side, or outside?"

"Chrysler side."

"What made you decide to switch to a consulting firm?"

"What do you mean?" I asked.

"What made you decide to work for Bradley Automotive Design?"

"I don't. I still work for Daimler Chrysler."

"No, you don't." She stood and walked over to me then handed me the box of business cards.

I looked at the card stapled to the front. I saw the three big fancy letters—B A D. Still, I couldn't believe it so I took a card from inside of the box. "Bradley Automotive Design, a new concept for cars," I read off the card. "This is a mistake. I still work for Daimler Chrysler. This is a big mistake." I flung the card across my desk. "Call the printer and tell him he printed up the wrong cards."

"It's not a mistake. What, did you think this was Daimler Chrysler? If that were the case we'd be working down the street at the Tech Center."

A puzzled look came across my face. "I don't understand this."

"Didn't you know what you applied for?"

"Yes, I knew," I snapped. "Can you leave my office? I need to make a call."

When she walked out of the office, my fingers couldn't dial fast enough. "Jennifer Theaters' office," the young woman said as she answered the phone.

"Yes," I cleared my throat, "I need to speak with Ms. Theaters, please."

"She's in a meeting all morning. Would you like her voice mail?"

"No, I need to talk to her right now," I insisted.

"I'm sorry, but she's in a meeting all morning with the executive board and there's no way I can reach her. Who's calling?"

"Let me have her voice mail."

"Hi, this is Jennifer. Today is Wednesday, July 21. I'll be in a meeting most of the morning but will return to my office in the afternoon. If you need immediate assistance, press zero to speak with Tonya my assistant."

I pressed zero and was redirected to the same woman I had just spoken to and she told me the same thing adding that Jennifer would be back in her office around two.

I made up some excuse to go to the Daimler Chrysler Tech Center and took Beth Anne with me to gain access since she had a temporary pass card. That way I wouldn't have to go through Jennifer and possibly have her avoid me.

I'm sure Jennifer knew what she had done. She knew she had screwed me, but the question was, why? What had I ever done to her? We were drinking buddies for goodness' sake. If that didn't count for something, what did? I hope she wasn't holding that against me. I hope she didn't think I'd tell her business. Maybe she just wanted to get rid of me now that she had risen among the ranks in the company. Maybe she was afraid I'd start telling what I knew about her past, but I wasn't like that, and she should know that.

Beth Anne had some people she wanted to visit while she was in the Tech Center, which was perfect because I was able to ditch her after we got off the escalator and continue along my journey to Jennifer.

When I reached Jennifer's floor, I had to go through a main entrance and get clearance from a receptionist because I didn't have a security badge to get through any of the other doors.

"Who are you here to see?" the woman sitting behind the large U-shaped desk asked.

"Jennifer Theaters."

"Your name?"

"Winona Fairchild."

"If you could have a seat, I'll ring her." The woman looked over at me while she held the phone to her ear. "Winona Fairchild is here to see you. Okay, I'll tell her." She hung up the phone. "Ms. Theaters said that she's coming right up."

I was too upset to respond. So upset I was shaking.

It didn't take Jennifer long to turn the corner. "Winona, how are you?" Jennifer asked as she walked over to me with a big smile covering her thin face. "Long time no see. You look great." I could have lied and said she did, too, but she didn't. She had lost all her misery weight from college, and now she looked about as thin as I used to. I stood, and before I could move another inch she hugged me. I could feel the bone in her back. "I was wondering when you were coming to see me. So have you settled in?" Jennifer asked.

"We have to talk," I said, bulging my eyes out at her to let her know it was serious.

"Okay, follow me." She immediately changed her tone to a more serious one.

I followed her down the hallway and into her corner office. As soon as she closed the door, I said, "How could you do that to me?"

"What did I do?"

"You know damn well what you did. You put my name in the hat for a job outside of the company. That's why I couldn't find it on Careers."

"Do you know who Bradley Automotive is? It brings concept cars to life. It's one of the largest minority—"

"I don't give a damn," I interrupted. "I work for Daimler Chrysler, and I did not authorize you to change the company that I work for."

"I never told you it was Daimler Chrysler."

"Of course you did. What's wrong with you, Jennifer? Are you still hitting that bottle?"

"No, I never told you it was Chrysler. And no I'm not drinking, not since sophomore year in college. What about you?"

"No, I'm not, but back to the situation at hand. Of course, I assumed it was Daimler Chrysler. Why would I think otherwise?"

"Maybe because the contract you signed didn't say Daimler Chrysler, it said Bradley Automotive. What difference does it make? You're a band 96 and you're making more than ninety-seven thousand dollars a year, not including bonuses, and you have absolutely no experience in transportation design. You couldn't have gotten that opportunity with Daimler Chrysler this soon."

"Why did you do this to me?"

"Because I've seen your portfolio. I could have pulled some strings and found you a job where you would be assisting not actually designing yet, but you're better than that. Bring one of those concept cars to life and see what happens to your career. Trust me."

I spit out laughter. "Trust you? I've already done that and look how I'm screwed."

She sighed. "You're not screwed."

"I want to come back to Daimler Chrysler."

"It's too late."

"What do you mean it's too late?"

"You signed a contract with Bradley. Remember those papers I sent you? That was a contract. You have to stay with them for two years."

"I don't have to do anything but stay black and die."

"Well, if you leave now, I guess that's what will happen. Daimler Chrysler won't take you back, and no one else is going to want you. Winona, after this contract is over, if you do what you're supposed to do, Tyler Roundship will probably double your salary."

"Tyler Roundship?" I asked with familiarity.

"Do you know him?"

"I've heard of him."

"It's half his company. You're working for a minority company. You should love that."

"Don't try to spin this."

"Here, take a look at these." She handed me a copy of the latest *Black Enterprise* and *Crain's* magazine."

"What are you doing with a *Black Enterprise*?"

"Hey, some of my best friends are black, and besides, there's an article inside on Tyler so if he happens to come in to see me, I'll have the magazine out on my desk. Be sure to bring it back."

"Is Bradley at least affiliated with Daimler Chrysler?" She looked into my eyes without answering. "Is Bradley under contract with Chrysler?"

"Not quite. At least not yet. But Tyler is working on it, and it looks good," Jennifer said.

"Well, you do have a say in who gets the contract, right?"

She gave me the same blank look. "I'm not over that division."

I stood there with my lips puckered. I left Michigan for Texas for a fool and came back to Michigan for another fool. "What happens if they don't get it?"

She sighed. "You've been in business about as long as I have. I'm sure you can imagine what would happen, but let's think optimistically," Jennifer said.

"Might as well. Don't think I'm not pissed at you, but I'm going to trust you this time, and it better work out."

"It will."

Carlton, Sosha, and I were standing at the kitchen table as I lit sixteen candles that were on top of Carlton's double-chocolate birthday cake. I went through great pains to make sure I had the perfect gift for him. It might not be a 300M or PT Cruiser like he was hoping for, but it was something that he needed—an IBM ThinkPad notebook computer.

Still, I had this feeling that he wasn't going to be happy with it. He wouldn't be happy with anything that didn't come with four wheels, a license plate, and a set of keys, but it was just too soon for him to have a car. I'd been on the road with him a few times and he wasn't the best driver. It was downright frightening watching the way he changed lanes without signaling.

I wasn't sure why I was nervous—I was the adult and he was the child. Still, I found myself with a tight chest as he blew out the candles that covered his cake and made a wish.

He kept his eyes closed for an unusually long time, which made me believe he was wishing for something that, unfortunately, I hadn't provided. I hoped I was wrong but something said that I wasn't.

Carlton interrupted Sosha and I while we sang, happy birthday. "Hand over the keys," he said, holding out his hand.

"What keys, Carlton?" I asked.

"The keys to my car. I don't care what you got me. Even the little Neon. I'll take it."

"Carlton, did I tell you I was getting you a car?"

"No, but so. You didn't say you weren't. You did, didn't you?"

"No, Carlton, I didn't." His face scrunched together so tight it was practically unrecognizable. "But look at what I did get you," I said as I walked into the den and removed the laptop box from behind a chair.

"What's that?" he asked, still scrunching his face together.

"It's an IBM ThinkPad."

"Well think about this, I don't want that shit. I want my car."

"What did you just say to me? Oh, boy, you've lost your mind. Not only are you not getting your car. I just bought myself a new laptop. Get out of my face! You kids fuck up everything."

I sat down at the kitchen table and cut the first slice of cake. I needed to feel good again, and chocolate was about the only thing that could do it for me. Soon as I put that first slice in my mouth, I didn't care anymore about what I said or what I did or didn't buy him. Not about cursing and not about eating the first piece of his birthday cake either.

I walked from the kitchen into the den and looked out of the window as I ate more cake, letting the crumbs fall into my cupped hand instead of on my hardwood. I hadn't seen anyone coming to or from Derwin's parents' house since we moved. The shades were always drawn and it seemed like the lights turned on every night at six and off at midnight like they were on a timer.

I saw Sosha's head peeking in the room I was in. "Yes, Sosha?"

"Are you mad at me?"

"Come here," I said. She walked in slowly. "Your brother is a teenager who wants to have a car to show off. It's a stage he's going through, but I don't want you to look at him and do what he does, because it's extremely disrespectful and it hurts me and I'm so tired right now, Sosha. No, I'm not mad at you, but you have to work on your attitude and so does your brother. Do you understand?" She nodded. "Okay, good."

"Can I call Daddy?"

"No."

"Why not?" she shouted.

"Didn't we just have a discussion about your attitude? You can't, because I said you can't."

"But Mommy, I want to talk to Daddy."

"Okay, fine. Go call him."

"I don't know the number."

"Get it from Carlton."

"Carlton don't want to talk to me right now. He's mad about the car."

"What do you need to talk to your dad about, Sosha?"

"He's my daddy, and I just want to talk to him."

I rubbed my hands over my eyes. "All right, I'll let you talk to him." I stormed up the stairs into my bedroom with Sosha on my heels. I took my phone book from the nightstand and opened it to find Keith's name and number. Sosha had her hand out for the phone. I wanted to give it to her because I had no interest in hearing his voice, but I knew how Keith's woman could be. I didn't want her flying off the handle on my child. As soon as I heard Keith's voice say, "Hello," I handed the phone to Sosha.

"Hi, Daddy." A large smile covered her face. "I love you, too, Daddy. I miss you too. I don't know when I can come, it's up to Mommy." *Never!* "Do you want the number here?" I shook my head. "Do you have something to write with?" I snatched the phone from her and hung it up. "Why did you do that? Why did you hang up on Daddy?"

"I don't want him to have the number here or our address. Do you understand me?"

"Why, that's Daddy?" Her face wrinkled and she looked like she was about to cry.

"I will let you call him once a week, but do not give him our number and address, and don't ask me why, just don't. And if he starts calling over here than I'll know you gave him the number and you'll be in big trouble."

"Daddy might have Caller ID."

"That's why I did a star 67 before I called. And I'm going to be the one to always call."

"You're mean. That's my daddy." The tears came quickly and ran down her cheeks. "What about Nana?"

"You've got your grandma here."

"No, I'm talking 'bout Nana." She meant Keith's mother who she'd seen regularly ever since she was born and even during Keith's five-year absence. Keith may have been a slouch but his parents weren't.

They were both retired now, but his mother had been on the Dallas city council for years and was very active in the community. His father was a pastor of Mount Savior in Irving. All of his five siblings turned out much better than Keith. For one thing they knew how to hold a job instead of filing false disability claims.

"Maybe, I'll let you go see Nana for Thanksgiving. Maybe." Sosha smiled and wiped her tears.

16

I pulled into my driveway after the end of a very long day at work. Two more days and my stressful week would be over. I stopped to focus out of the rearview mirror toward the Cloudses' home. There was a man across the street doing their lawn, so I got out of my car and walked over to get some information from him.

"I'm looking for the Cloudses. They live here in this house, right?" He turned off the lawn mover. "Do you know them? Do you know where the people are who live here?"

"They will be back in one week," the man said with a foreign accent. "The Cloudses?"

"Right, clouds," he said, looking up at the sky.

"No, not clouds from the sky, their name. Their last name is Clouds."

"That is right. Back in one week," he said, putting up a finger.

"One week," I repeated.

"One week. You come back in one week?"

"I will come back in one week."

I entered the house through the kitchen door, kicked off my heels, and flung my briefcase on the kitchen counter. Carlton was in the kitchen with a strange look on his face. "I met your boss today," he said, nodding.

"Who, Tyler?" I asked. He nodded again. "Where did you meet him?"

"At Rackham. We played eighteen holes. I beat him real bad."

"You golfed with Tyler? How did that happen?"

"I was by myself, and Tyler was with these three other dudes, and since the course was so crowded I had to finish off their foursome."

"Um, that's a coincidence. So why are you standing here looking so crazy?"

"I beat them so bad out there, Mom, it was pathetic. They were so frustrated because I was beating them so bad, especially on the back nine. I tore them up on the back nine."

"How did you know he was my boss? I never mentioned his name."

"They were asking me all kinds of questions about myself. Asking me about my family, and all kinds of stuff. I told them about you and that's when Tyler told me you worked for him. He kept asking questions. 'Where did you go to school? How did you learn to golf so well? Who's your pro? He's in Texas? Really? Give me his number I might fly him down.' Tyler wanted to know who I was. I'm so good it hurts."

"You are so cocky. And don't call him Tyler. Call him Mr. Roundship."

"Yeah, right. Anyway, I'm telling you, they wanted to know who this young man was beating them so bad. Tyler was mad because he lost so much money. He was like, I bet you can't par this hole. Then I'd par it. Sometimes I'd birdie it or get an eagle and he'd lose another fifty."

"I know you didn't take money from my boss. I know you didn't. Carlton?"

Carlton pulled out a stack of money, at least five fifty-dollar bills. "Where I come from it's put your money where your mouth is."

"Where I come from it's you sound like a fool." I snatched the money from him. "This is going back to him. That's my boss, Carlton."

"I should have never told you. He got the money. Shit, if he can fly my pro up here to teach his sorry ass how to golf, he got the money."

"What did I tell you about that cursing? Where's Sosha?"

"Probably reading *National Geographic*. She's so goofy."

"Leave her alone. She's just smart."

"And goofy. If she's so smart, when is she going to stop acting like a little baby?"

I ignored his question. "Did you feed Samson and take him for a walk?"

"That's Sosha's dog."

"He's yours, too, Carlton. I'm tired of always doing it. You kids need to learn responsibility."

Carlton whistled for Samson who came running down the stairs. Samson stood with his paws on my shoulder, licking my face. "Hi, man. How's my big man doing? They not treating you right?" I asked with baby talk as I stroked him.

"You need a man 'cause you be loving on that dog a little too much."

"Shut up and take him out."

Carlton walked to the kitchen door and opened it. "Come on, boy." He whistled. Samson flew out into the backyard. Good. I needed a break. I was headed upstairs to my bed. As tired as I was I might just sleep through dinner. The kids could order pizza as usual.

I sat behind my desk reading through my Lotus Notes email and listening to all fourteen of my work-related voice mails, including Tyler's message that he'd be working off-site today and requested a seven o'clock meeting with the group in the cigar lounge of Morton's Steakhouse in Southfield. Who did he think I was, one of the boys? I hated mingling, especially when it involved work. Being phony wasn't my best attribute, and small talk wasn't my specialty.

The Cloudses would be back the next day and that was going to be one of the first places I went after work.

I looked in my Franklin Planner. I had a doctor's appointment on Friday, but today, I had a whole lot of work to do, starting with turning my graphic design into a model.

The company was planning for a display featuring video simulation and lots of lights, something that would have the press and car industry talking. Hopefully, talking enough to capture the front page of the automotive magazine, *Show Talk*. It was mandatory that my design be selected as one of the four concept cars being introduced at the auto show that was a year and a half away. This was my only opportunity to be assured a comparable position within the Daimler Chrysler group. Otherwise, I could end up in Chicago—Bradley's headquarters so say all the rumors.

I couldn't move again. Especially not in 2001, the year of Carlton's high school graduation. While it would be a lot easier on me after Carlton graduated, I just wasn't up to another relocation. Living in Detroit had its benefits. The major one was the close proximity to my parents for my children, especially Sosha, who wanted to visit her grandparents daily. It was truly a benefit having my parents so close, even though it felt like a burden to me.

A valet ran up to my car when I pulled in front of the restaurant and politely opened my door. As soon as I got out of my car, the valet hopped inside and pulled off.

The small restaurant was smoky and crowded. I had no idea where the cigar lounge was. I looked on each side of me before realizing it was right in front of me.

I saw Tyler but I didn't go over to him. Instead, I stood near the entrance and watched him while he stood near the bar puffing on a cigar with a drink in his hand. He was talking to a few of the engineers from work, and a couple of other men whom I didn't recognize. There was something sexy about Tyler. There was so much to him that could turn a woman on. I couldn't put my finger on exactly what about him turned me on though. Whether it was the sprinkling of gray in his hair or the thousand-dollar suits he wore. Even as he puffed on his cigar and took a sip from his brandy snifter, I felt it. I especially felt it while I observed him laughing.

I thought about the meeting we had the previous afternoon. I was scared shitless to introduce myself in a room full of all white men with the exception of Tyler. I'd always hated public speaking. I remembered back to my sophomore year in high school and all the days I purposely stayed home to avoid speech class. The thought of standing up in that large class and facing one hundred students was more than I could handle back then. And the thought of introducing myself and mingling with people who were not part of my identifiable peer group was something else I couldn't stand. I had to remind myself that this wasn't for a grade. I could get a C back then and let the other classes average out my grade point, but in Corporate America every impression counts. You can't be average, especially when they're paying you the big bucks. At least someone like me can't.

I didn't feel as though I had anything to worry about. At the meeting all of us had to show our sketches to Tyler and explain in three minutes or less why our concept car design was the best logical choice. I guess I got a little beside myself after I noticed the look on Tyler's face. It wasn't like the look he had when the others showed off their designs. Tyler was sitting at the head of the conference table and when I turned over my sketchpad he leaned forward and raised one eyebrow. I was the only one Tyler questioned, "What do you call that?"

"The GXT."

"It's a good–looking car, but I'm not crazy about the name," he said. When he was wrapping up the meeting he said, "That was just a little experiment. I need each of you to check your egos at the door in the morning, because this is a team effort." Then he walked around the table and collected our sketchpads.

When a seat became available in the lounge, I took it. I sat there imagining what it would be like to have Tyler in my life, wondering how he treated the women he allowed to be a part of his world. For a quick second, I wanted to be his woman, but I changed my mind and simply wanted to leave. I attempted to do so but stumbled against the mirrored wall in the process.

Tyler glanced over at me and began gesturing for me to join the group. I didn't want to. They were probably over there talking about the baseball game or golf between breaks from discussing the project at work. I pretended not to see him as I slowly turned and walked out of the restaurant.

I handed the valet my car key along with a five-dollar tip. "Can you bring my car around quickly?"

"Sure thing," he said, as he ran across the pavement.

I felt the door open behind me, but I didn't turn around to see whom it was. I hoped it wasn't Tyler.

"Didn't you see me in there?" Tyler asked, walking into my view.

"Were you inside? I was looking all around for you, but I didn't see you anywhere."

"But you looked straight at me," he said.

"If I did, I swear to you, I didn't see you."

The valet pulled around in my car.

"Well now that you do, come on back inside."

"It's smoky and loud in there, and now I have the worst headache," I said, pressing my fingers against my temples.

"The team's inside. We're talking about the project. It's a project meeting."

"I'm sorry. I don't feel well."

"Are you sure you can't stay?" He gave me a puzzled look. I hope he wasn't trying to figure me out. When, and if, he ever did would be the day I'd get fired.

"I'm really sorry but I don't feel well at all."

"Okay, well, I'll stop by your office tomorrow and go over what we covered. This is some real important stuff, and if it's any way you can stay—"

"There's no way I can."

17

Iknew before the alarm clock sounded that I wasn't going in to work. Just didn't feel up to it. My head was pounding. I was sweating because I was nervous about the night before and today—the night before because I shouldn't have left the restaurant so abruptly, and today, because the Cloudses were supposed to be back home.

There was no need for me to call in. Bradley executives were allowed five unexplained absences. One of the many perks Bradley offered. It really wasn't a bad company to work for, but it didn't feel as secure as Daimler Chrysler.

I cleared my throat, picked up the phone, and called my mother.

It was a quarter to seven. I knew she'd be up and almost out the door with my father for their one-mile walk.

"Hello," Dad said.

"Hi, Dad."

"Hello," my mother said quickly, a few seconds later, "is everything okay?"

"Didn't Dad answer the phone?"

"Yes, but he gave it to me. You know how he is. Are you okay?"

"Can you come pick up the kids and take them back to your house? I'm not going into work today. I'm not feeling well."

"Why? What's wrong?"

"I have a bad headache. A migraine."

"Of course I can. I'm on my way. Maybe I should come over there to stay for a couple of days until you feel better."

"No, Mom, I don't need that."

"Maybe I should. You don't know what you need."

"I know what I need, and it's not that. I just need to rest."

———

When Mom came over to pick up the kids, she barged into the house and up the stairs to my bedroom, despite the fact that I told Sosha and Carlton to tell her I was in the bed resting. Her first words were, "You look like death."

"Thanks, Mom. Where are the kids?" I was sitting in the bed with my back against my headboard. My hair, which Gina had just done so nicely the week before was now tossed over my head, tangled in a silk scarf that had loosened while I slept.

"They're in the car." She walked over to me and felt my head. "You're burning up. Maybe you should go to the emergency room."

"I'm fine."

Mom was always exaggerating.

"Well, I'm coming back later to check on you," she said.

"No," I snapped. "I just want to rest."

"Are you sure?"

"I'm positive."

"I'll keep them for the rest of the week. Don't go in to work tomorrow if you still look and feel this bad. Okay, sweetie."

"Okay, Mom."

When I heard the door slam and the car pull out of the driveway, it was as if my headache pulled off with the car. I felt fine. I could watch *Oprah* later. Do some sketching. Bum around. Anything I pleased.

———

I was on the front porch, trying to get a whiff of fresh air when a car pulled into the Cloudses' driveway. Middle of the afternoon, and there it was. The first sign of life I'd seen from over there since we moved in.

A young woman got out of the car and walked around to open the back door. She leaned inside and when she straightened up she was holding a little boy around two or three.

Derwin was an only child, so she wasn't his sister.

It had to be his wife, and that little boy she was carrying had to be his child.

Nonetheless, I did something I hadn't expected. I walked off my porch and crossed the street.

By this time, she was standing on the front porch fumbling inside of her purse.

"Excuse me, miss," I said, walking quickly toward her.

She looked startled at first, but then smiled at me as if she knew who I was. Perhaps she had seen my photo. Maybe Derwin had shared our high school prom pictures, but that would be impossible, since he didn't take me to the prom.

"Hello," she said.

"I'm sorry to bother you like this," I said.

"That's okay. Are you lost?" she asked with a smile.

"No, I live across the street, and this is the first time I've seen anyone come to this home."

"I'm a flight attendant so I'm rarely here. And my husband's a pilot so he's never here either."

Derwin's a pilot? He hates to fly. "That must be hard on your child. What's his name?"

"No children yet. This is my nephew." She put the little boy down, and he held on to her legs. "So you were just coming by to introduce yourself?"

"Yes and no. I used to know a family who lived here by the last name of Clouds. Are you related to them in any way?"

"No. That's who we bought the house from."

"They don't live here anymore?" I asked.

"No, they haven't lived here in two years."

"Oh, I really wanted to see them again."

"Were you a good friend?"

"Yes, really good friends of their son."

"Oh yes. Sorry, I don't have a number or anything for them. All I know is that they moved to Houston to be closer to their son and his family."

I stood in shock, feeling like an elephant was standing on my chest. I had a million questions I wanted to ask, but my mind focused on the fact that Derwin had a family. Over the years, I convinced myself that he wasn't the marrying type and that he would never settle down. Not only was he married, he was in Houston only four hours away from where I had just come.

The baby started crying. "He's hungry. I'm sorry, I better go."

"Thank you for the information."

After she walked into the house, I stood on her porch feeling lost. She came back outside to check on me. "Are you sure you're okay?"

"I'm sorry. I'm standing on your porch like I live here. I'll go now."

"Okay," she said, pushing me away with her nods.

I walked back across the street, trekking up my driveway. Once inside, I called Gina at work, something I never do, because I know her supervisor monitors calls.

"Girl, I'm pissed," I said as soon as she answered the phone.

"What happened?"

"Derwin has a family. He's married and has children."

"Didn't you assume he would be?"

"No," I snapped. "I assumed he was afraid of marriage. I assumed that's why he didn't marry me, but now all I can assume is that it wasn't marriage he didn't want, it was me."

"Winona, he didn't want marriage at that time. He was only twenty; so were you. Besides, after all the drama he took you through in college, I never knew why you wanted him anyway. And the way he treated you in high school, girl, I wouldn't give that man the time of day."

"I never believed I could have somebody like that. The fact that he was my boyfriend made me feel special."

"Winona, let it go. He was never your boyfriend. I know you have the man's son, and maybe for that reason, I guess you should try to find him, but the best thing for you to do is start seeing somebody else so you can stop these flashbacks to Derwin."

"I'm not ready to date. I feel like I should sacrifice until both my kids are out of the house, but that's nine years away. I'm assuming Sosha will go to college."

"Girl, that's way too long."

"So what am I supposed to do?"

"Start dating and call me at home. I don't have an executive job like you. My supervisor is walking around my cubicle like she's a guard and I'm in state prison."

I heard a dial tone.

Gina was right. I should start dating. I needed to feel a man's touch. I needed to smell his scent. I needed to hear a man say that he missed me and couldn't wait to see me again. I needed all of that, but now wasn't the time and never would be.

18

It was 3:15 P.M. on Friday, the day of my doctor's appointment. I didn't go in to work and I didn't call. I figured if anyone from the job needed to reach me they had my home number, cell, and my pager. Otherwise, they'd see me first thing Monday morning.

I was sitting in the doctor's waiting area, people watching, wondering what was wrong with that one, the man whose face was sunken in. I could tell he used to be attractive, but not anymore. The woman sitting next to him was in a fog. It was hard to say whether they were together. I wondered if she was sick, too, or here for a regular checkup.

"Winona Fairchild," the nurse said as she stood in the open doorway. I took a deep breath before I stood, tossing the *People* magazine on the table. The nurse smiled and held the door open for me while I passed through. She was holding a patient's chart, most likely mine, so I studied her large eyes to see if they held any answers.

"You can go in the first room on your right."

The nurse followed me as I walked into the room, flipping pages upon pages of the chart she carried, while she raised one eyebrow. "The doctor will be in here in a minute. No need for you to get undressed." She placed the chart in a slot that was hanging on the door and left the room, closing the door behind her.

I stood near the door with my arms folded and my fingers crossed. *Please let the test results come back favorably.* My heart was beating so fast I could feel it bouncing up against my skin.

I heard a faint knock. "Come in," I said.

"Hello, Winona. How are you today?" Dr. Gant asked as he entered. He was a tall black man, probably six-four if he were able to walk straight instead of slumped over due to the curvature in his spine. He was the first black specialist I'd seen, and initially I was skeptical of how much he knew.

"Fine, doctor, and you?"

"Oh, I'm doing fine. Would you like to sit?"

I sat down in a chair next to the examining table, while he stood looking through my chart. It may have only been seconds before he spoke, but it felt like hours. As usual everything inside of the room, including Dr. Gant, seemed a blur. I didn't want to focus on things, especially not him, and not what he was saying.

"I received your chart from the other specialists, along with your most recent test results that you took before you relocated. Your CD 4 count is 340, but I'm still waiting on your viral-load results, I should have those in a few days. I'm going to go ahead and get you started on a combination of AZT, Ziagen, and Viracept." I shook my head. "Winona, we've had this conversation once before."

"I've never had to take medication before, and it's been five years."

"You're in my care now, and I'm recommending you go on medication."

"I want to wait to see the results of my viral load."

He removed his tiny square glasses. "I can't force the medication on you. I can only tell you what I feel is best. It will still be up to you to take it as prescribed. What can I do to convince you this is not the end of the world?"

"Nothing. I'm HIV-positive so for me that is the end of the world. My world."

Why was this happening to me? I was so angry with myself for trusting a man like Keith, a man who I didn't know, but whom I let convince me to leave Michigan and move with him to Texas. If I would have been thinking clearly that day, I would have said no, but instead I left. "You don't have to go back home. I'll buy you whatever clothes you need. You'll see. You'll love Texas. Things are better down south," he had said. I loved Texas; I just didn't love him.

I remember when I got sick about four or five years after Sosha was born. I realized there was something wrong. I thought I had the flu. I had a high fever and chills that I couldn't shake. At night, I'd sweat so badly I had to sleep in the nude, otherwise when I woke up my gown and sheets would be drenched. I didn't think much when Keith didn't seem concerned and didn't think I needed to go to the doctor. He said to take one of his antibiotics, which like a fool I did and before long, a matter of hours, I was bleeding down there and my period wasn't due. "Take me to emergency!" I screamed to Keith as I shook from fear. I can remember how quiet he was as we sat waiting for my name to be called. I'll never forget the look of fright that came over his face when I was finally summoned after nearly two hours.

When we arrived home, he seemed to be purposely avoiding me, staying clear of any room I entered. Finally, I caught him off guard in the bathroom as he sat on the stool with the front section of the newspaper shielding his face. He asked me what the doctor said was wrong.

"He didn't say."

"He had to say something," he said, folding the paper and dropping it to the floor. "Did they say you had the flu or what?"

"He said I had flulike symptoms, but he took my blood and said he was sending it out for testing to have it checked for other things."

"What other things?"

"Well, he did ask me when was the last time I had unprotected sex. I guess they're going to check me for AIDS." That's when I looked over at him, not expecting to see glassy eyes and a stone face. In a matter of seconds, the tears escaped his eyes and ran a marathon down both sides of his face. It's a frightening thing to see a grown man really break down. Keith was crying worse than a child. He continued for five minutes before he said a word. "What's wrong, Keith? What's wrong?" I shouted over and over. I knew whatever it was probably involved more than just himself. I could feel it.

He stood, pulling up his underwear and jeans.

He started by saying, "I'm sorry, Winona, but I'm—" and I stopped him.

"Don't say it. Please don't say what I think you're going to say. Don't say you have AIDS. Do you?" He looked down, zipping his pants and buckling his belt, purposely trying to avoid my question. "Are you, damnit?"

He nodded. "I'm HIV-positive." His voice quivered.

"For how long?" How long?" I shouted. "That means Sosha is too. I am and Sosha is."

"No, I just got it this year."

"How do you know?"

" 'Cause I know who I got it from."

"Who did you get it from, Keith?" He shook his head. Oh, he could tell me most of the truth but not all of it. I don't think so. "Who? What woman?" I read through his eyes, that he didn't get it from a woman. "You slept with a man? You're gay?"

"I'm not gay."

"You're not gay, but you slept with a man? You slept with a man!" I said, pummeling his chest.

"I just tried it one time. Okay, twice."

"How could you do this? How, Keith? Damn you! Why would you do that? You're nothing but a liar. You're just a liar. I hate you! Get out and don't you ever come back!"

"I'm sorry."

"You are sorry. You're telling the truth about that."

"I'm sorry," he said, dragging himself toward the door.

"Listen," I said, stopping him in his tracks. "You gave me something I didn't ask for so I'm giving it back. You better not tell one soul what you've got. Not one person needs to know because if you've got it they'll know I've got it, and I ain't got shit," I screamed.

He turned toward me. "We can get through this together."

I shot him a look with intentions to kill. "Together? Were we together when you got it? No. If you want to get through this with someone, I suggest you call up the man that gave it to you. I wish I would have known you were a fag before I fucked you! Just leave!"

He moved to New York to pursue his life dreams, but I suppose as the years passed and neither his dream nor the disease progressed, he decided to return home and I decided then was as good a time as any to leave Texas and go back to my home.

Keeping a disease hidden from nearly everyone was stressful in itself, but it was the only way. I couldn't worry my children with this, and I couldn't face my family and tell them. The only person I wanted to tell was Gina because I had told her everything, but I didn't want her scared of me. I didn't think she'd be like that, but I didn't want to test our friendship now, not when I needed it more than ever.

PART THREE

Porter Washington

19

It was Monday, August 2, and I was still living with my mama even though it was seven weeks past her deadline. I didn't know what time it was. All I knew was it had to either be real early in the morning or late at night because I was in the bed sleep and when I opened my eyes after my cell phone started ringing, it was dark outside.

I rustled through the sheets trying to locate the phone. When I reached over to the nightstand, I knocked the small lamp to the floor before I finally placed my hand on the cellular.

"Hello," I whispered.

"Hey, sorry for calling you so early but I wanted to let you know I was released last week."

"Who is this?"

"Jade. I tried calling you a few times last week but your cell was out of service." *Try disconnected.* "But I see it's working now."

I cleared my throat. "Jade, oh, what's up, man? So you out now, huh? That was a pretty long time. Almost two months. They find a cure for what you got?"

"Mmm-hmm. I was out and had to go back a couple weeks later, but I'm fine now." That statement was a dead giveaway. You get released from the hospital then you have to go back in, so whatever you went in for had to be serious. I knew he had AIDS.

"Why you calling so early?"

"I want to see if you can give me a ride to the bus station."

"Bus station? Where you going?"

"Chicago, to see my mama."

"Why don't you fly or drive to Chicago? It's only a few hours away."

"I don't fly and I don't want to drive by myself, unless you're going to drive me."

"I'll drive you to the bus station, that's about it."

"Well I have to be there in two hours."

"Shit." I looked at the clock. It was only five o'clock. "Thanks for the advance notice."

"My girlfriend was supposed to take me but she never called back last night, and I can't always rely on her. Do you mind?"

I sighed. "I'll be there in an hour."

I got to Jade's house a little past six. There was a Jag parked in the driveway with a personalized plate that read, Vanity. I guess his girl-friend didn't back out after all, but before I went back home I decided I better go in and make sure.

I rung the doorbell about five times, but there was no response so I turned to walk away. That's when I heard the door creak open. I turned around and this fine sista was standing in a short, tight dress. I cleared my throat. "I'm here for Jade."

"Come in," she said softly. "I'm Vanity." Just like it said on the license plate.

I walked into the house and looked around for Jade, but didn't see him anywhere. "Nice Jag."

"You like? I just got it. It was sort of a birthday present for myself."

"Oh, you just had a birthday."

"Kinda sorta."

"So are you Jade's sister?"

"Why do you ask that?"

"Because I know he has a sister and y'all kinda favor."

"Kinda favor? Well, do you think I look good?"

I smiled. "Yeah, but I'm sure you already know that."

"Good enough to date?"

My smile got wider. "I don't know. I'd have to get to know you a little better."

"Boo, you already do."

"No I don't."

"Look at me, boo."

I looked deep into the woman's eyes. "Oh, hell no. Jade? What the hell you dressed like that for?"

"Dressed like what?"

"Like you dressed…like a woman. Take that shit off. You not going on no bus looking like that. So now you're a transvestite? Isn't that what they call men that dress like women?"

"Yes, it is, but actually I'm a transsexual."

"What?" I dropped the expression I had off my face and looked him up and down. "Why were you in the hospital so long?"

"I just told you. You don't listen very well. I'm a transsexual."

"Jade, you had a sex-change operation?"

"That's what a transsexual does."

"Please tell me you're lying. Why the fuck would you do that? Please tell me you are lying."

"I'm not lying, boo." For some strange reason I didn't mind this Jade calling me boo, because it was hard for me to identify the woman standing in front of me as a man or used to be. This woman had boobs and shoulder-length hair. She even had little hips and nice legs. I didn't see an Adam's apple. She had on sandals and her toes were cute. I was totally confused. "Now, I can be your woman since you don't like men." She/he walked up to me and held on to both of my arms and tried to kiss me on the mouth.

"Jade, please." I brushed his hands off me. "I don't believe you did that. I can't believe you butchered yourself like that. Why?"

"I didn't like being a man. I didn't want one of them things between my legs." He was scrunching his face together. "It's much better this way."

"Man, please."

"Don't say man!"

"Jade, please, tell me you didn't go to that extreme." He remained quiet. "Okay, show me then. Prove it. Take off your clothes."

"Huh?" He held his hand against his chest. "Boo, we gonna make love?"

"Hell no! I just want you to prove that you got your dick cut off. Take off your clothes."

"And if I prove it, then will we?" he asked with a cheerful expression covering his face.

"Maybe," I lied, just so he would do it.

"Really?"

"Maybe. Now do it."

"Okay, boo." He started unbuttoning the sexy little dress. I had to shake my head because it was hard to believe this was Jade. I watched as he reached for the last button of the dress and shrugged it off, allowing it to drop to the floor. He was standing in front of me in a black bra and matching thong, and high-heeled sandals.

"Take off your panties."

"Boo, you say that so sexy. Are we gonna make love, for real?"

"Maybe. I need to see first." My eyes were fixed on his hand as it touched the thin elastic waistband of the panties. If he had a dick, I couldn't tell where he was hiding it because nothing was protruding.

"I got one."

"You got one of what?"

"I got a pussy."

When he said that, I felt my dick get hard. "You got a pussy? Okay, let me see it."

He nibbled on the corner of his bottom lip and then put his hands on the waistband and wiggled out of his thong panties. "See." He stood and revealed his man-made vagina.

"What the fuck is that?" My erection immediately went limp.

"What, boo? It's a vagina."

"Where's your dick? Stuffed up in there, right?"

"Why do you have to talk like that, boo?"

"Isn't that where it is? Man, I don't believe you did that crazy shit."

"Don't call me man. Do you know how long I've been saving for this operation? Do you know how long I've been taking estrogen? You don't know what I went through for three years to become the woman that I am today."

"Nigga, you ain't no woman. Do you bleed once a month? Can you give birth to a child? Does it say male or female on your birth certificate? Nigga, please."

"There are some women who don't bleed once a month."

"Yeah, old women who are going through menopause, and don't say there are some women who can't give birth, because you know what I mean."

"Boo, I'm a woman now." He took off his bra and once again I had to shake my head. "And my new name is Vanity."

"Damn. They did a good job, but you're not a woman. I know you as Jade. That's not to say you're not going to be able to find you a straight man, because you are. Looking like that, you will for sure."

"I don't want just any man. I want you, boo."

"You can't have me. I'm sorry."

"But I'm a woman now…"

I threw up my hand with a smirk covering my face. "Don't go there. Don't make me laugh in your face. Man, this is crazy. You ready to go to the bus station?"

"Yes," he whispered. He had a wounded look in his eyes.

"Put your clothes on and let's go, I'll be in the car. Good thing you're not too far away from Greyhound because it's almost six-thirty." I looked back at Jade and saw him wipe the tears from his eyes. "What's wrong with you?" He shook his head. "You better toughen up, nigga. Life is cruel. Remember that."

"Just go on to the car." he said, shooing me off.

20

It was around 1:00 P.M. on Saturday. I was at the gym bench-pressing 315 pounds. Damion was standing behind me, spotting. I was on my fifth lift when I let out a loud grunt. Damion took the bar out of my grip and placed it back on the stand between the two grooves, which was the most exercise he ever got. He came to the gym with his wandering eyes to scope out the ladies.

"Man, what if you were dating a woman and you found out she used to be a man?" I asked.

He stood back from the weights with a frown on his face. "I'd shoot that bitch. That shit ain't cool."

That's what I was afraid of. Jade's going to mess around and meet a man like Damion, then what? "But what if she was fine."

"But I found out, right?"

"Yeah."

"That's one dead bitch, why? That shit happened to you?"

"Hell no. One of my boys."

"One of your boys. Who? I know all your boys."

"You don't know this one."

"So what did he do when he found out?"

"I think he just told her to get on."

"Oh, he must've liked her."

"I said she was fine."

Damion stood looking toward the ceiling. "Damn, if she was like real super fine, I wonder what I would do. I mean technically she wasn't a man no more. I wonder how your boy found out."

"I think she told him. She broke down and told him because she didn't want to keep the secret from him."

"So damn, he couldn't even tell the difference. I don't know. I wonder what I would do. I know I'd be mad that the bitch told me, but knowing my freak ass if the bitch was fine and could turn a nigga out, I might have to say fuck it, fuck what society think."

"But she can't give you no damn babies, though."

"So, I already got two."

"And technically she's still a man. Wouldn't that fuck with you?"

"Not if the bitch was fine."

"So it's all about being fine to you?"

"Yeah, it is. I admit it. I need me a fine-lookin' bitch. I'm not exactly Denzel up in this motherfucka. It'd be different if I looked like you, Porter. Maybe I could be a little more secure with my shit and just get me a woman who loved me for me, but my shit ain't all put together right. That's why I need money and fine bitches, okay?"

"Man, damn, what the fuck is Pam doing with your sorry ass?"

"I bet she wakes up asking that question every morning," he said, laughing.

I was sitting on the bench watching a tight body walk by and wink at me. She had an Amazonian body. Her arms were almost as developed as mine. Her chest formed a V, tapering down to her flat abs. She was wearing a cropped Nike T-shirt that exposed her flat stomach. I can't say she was turning me on. Not as much as the woman who was being shown around the gym by Mike, one of the trainers.

I decided that I'm more of a potentials man. I was with every man's fantasy for twelve years and watched that beauty fade. Only someone who has gone through that can relate to what I'm trying to say. I looked at the woman being toured and I made a few subtle alterations to her appearance. I changed her hairstyle by cutting off a few inches. I was tired of women with long hair. Hard to tell if it was real or a weave and after living with my mother and sweeping up that horse hair or whatever it was from the bathroom floor, I just wanted a woman with her own hair. It didn't have to be long, but I didn't want to see her scalp. I continued looking over at the woman. She could stand to lose about ten pounds, mainly in her midsection. I could help her with that. She just needed to do anywhere from fifty to one hundred sit-ups a day and lay off the sweets. There wasn't anything wrong with her face; nothing I'd change. She barely had on makeup, just a little lipstick, and she still looked good. I watched her smile at Mike as he sat down at the pec flye machine and pulled the two pads together with his arms until they both touched in the center. He changed places with her and had her do the same.

"Mike, aren't you going to raise the seat for the young lady?" I asked as I walked over to them. Mike stood back several feet as I approached. I intimidated him because several of his clients had asked me if I'd train them. "Mike, you know the lady can't properly do this exercise if the seat is too low for her. You're about 6'1" Mike, and she's all of 5'5", 5'6". Come on now, Mike. You know better. Excuse me, miss," I said to her as I reached below her seat. She stood while I adjusted it to the proper height. "Now try that," I said with a smile.

"That feels so much better," she said to me with an inviting smile.

I put the pin in the hole of the thirty-pound weight. "Now bring them both together," I said to her, which she did easily. "Maybe you could stand ten more pounds." I put the pin in the hole for the forty-pound weight.

She squeezed the pads together with ease. It was difficult for me not to focus on her chest expanding before my eyes. Still, I tried not to look so obvious.

"Am I doing this right?" she asked.

I looked down at her and watched her press the pads together. "It depends. Where do you feel it?"

"In my chest and a little in my arms."

"As long as you feel it more in your chest than your arms, you're doing it right. What's your name?"

"Winona." She looked to her right when a young woman entered the gym.

"I'm Porter."

"Nice to meet you." She stopped exercising and waved to get the woman's attention. "Thanks for helping me with this machine," she said as she stood.

"Are you going to join or are you already a member?"

"No, I'm not a member. I think I need to start at Bally's because this place looks like it's for serious bodybuilders, but thanks again."

"What's wrong with joining a gym with serious body builders?" I asked her, but I doubt if she heard me because she had darted off so quickly. I watched Winona go over to the woman who had just walked in.

Damion came over to me. "You like that, man?"

"Yeah, but I'm sure she's probably married."

"I hope she's not a man." We both laughed.

"Wouldn't that be some shit?"

"Seriously though, man, do you want me to have Pam hook you up with one of her friends?"

"I've seen Pam's friends. No, thank you."

"I thought looks didn't really matter to you."

"Not as long as she looks decent and doesn't have two or three kids hanging off her legs." I said, still focusing on Winona.

"Snap out of it," Damion said. "She's gone."

"Yeah, I know."

———

After I left the gym, I drove around for almost an hour, trying to figure out what I was going to do about the car note I was behind on. My June payment was almost forty days past due. Even though I worked a full-time job and had my side gigs, I was still behind on those bills Reesey created. I was paying all of my creditors the minimum so I could maintain my good credit rating, but somehow I let my car note slip again. I was counting on getting a one- or two-month extension, but I already had two, which was the limit in one year.

The finance company said I could have a little extra time on my July note and August wasn't due until the twenty-ninth, which was three weeks away. I needed to get June's payment in today. Damion would give it to me without question, but I never borrowed money from him. He was my boy, but I just couldn't take from him. He had already taken from me, something way more important than money. I knew Jade would give it to me, even though he was in Chicago for another two weeks. His ass would run to Western Union and wire it to me, but I didn't want to make no deals with the devil.

I pulled into my mother's driveway and sat in the car preparing myself for the inevitable—a lecture mixed with profanity. I dragged my body out of the SUV. I was starting to feel like a little boy again instead of the man I knew I was, the man little boys looked up to and citizens respected because of my occupation.

Mom was moving from the living room to the dining room, making sure everything was in place. My eyes could barely keep up with her fast pace. "You better make it quick because when that doorbell rings I want you walking out the back door before he comes in the front. Speaking of walking, Porter, it's way past June 14."

"I'm moving real soon."

"I hope so because I've been more than generous to let you stay here as long as I have. Shit," she said, waving her fingers in the air. "I smudged my nails. Why are you just standing there? Can't you be useful and set the table so I won't have to worry about messing up my nails?"

"Do you have a date or something?"

"Yes, I do. Is that okay with you?" she asked sarcastically.

"You're acting like it's your first one, but I hope not. I hope you're not cooking for this man on the first date. Let him take you out."

"That's a young girl's game, sweetie. I've had plenty of first dates. It doesn't take much for someone to spend twenty dollars on you. Any bum can come up with that. But for your information, it's not the first date. Now, what did you need with me?"

"Debis Financial is calling me every damn day about my past due June note, which I don't have, but Damion has a CLK he can let me have for $10,000."

"First of all if you can't even pay your June car note, then how are you gonna get $10,000 for a Mercedes?"

"I'm going to sell the Lexus."

"He's going to let you have a Mercedes for $10,000? That boy is doing something illegal in that shop, I just know it. You better watch yourself."

"It's not illegal. He got it off a mechanics lien." Damion had a system. He didn't talk too much about it with me, but I knew he was scamming auto finance companies by claiming repair and storage costs that were never incurred. His boys purchased the cars fraudulently and two to three months later would drop them off at his shop for supposed repairs. He'd wait sometimes up to a year before he informed the lienholder that he had the vehicles but at the same time he would already have a mechanics lien. It sounded pretty illegal to me, but that was his business, not mine. "All I need is enough money to pay one car note so they won't repo the truck."

"How much is your note?"

"Eight hundred and seventy."

She ripped out a hardy laugh. "Dollars? It's cute, but not that cute. I just don't have that kind of money. Sorry." The doorbell cut our conversation short. She took off her apron, checked her face and hair in the hallway mirror, and proceeded to the front door to answer it.

I headed for the back door, but something stopped me. My inner voice said to go back and introduce myself to her date so that's what I did.

My mother had already wrapped her arm around his and was strolling into the living room.

I didn't get a good look at him, at least I wanted to believe it wasn't him just someone who resembled Conrad. He was grinning from ear to ear because Mom was leading him toward the sofa, making it too obvious that he could be a kid and her house was the candy store.

"Conrad?" I asked.

"What's up?" he asked, nodding.

"You dating this fool?" I asked Mom. They both sat on the sofa. Mom sat sideways, pushing her chest in Conrad's face. "How could you date this fool, Mom? Didn't he tell you he worked with me on my same shift?"

"Yes. He sure did."

"And you still decided to date him?"

"That's right. Makes no difference to me that he works with you."

"How long have the two of you been seeing each other?" I asked Conrad.

He turned and looked at my mother for the answer.

"A couple of months," she said.

"Couple of months? Well, you can leave now." I pulled Conrad's fat Humpty Dumpty ass up by his arm.

"Wait a minute. He's not going anywhere," my mother chimed in loudly. "This is my date. You can't tell him to leave." My mother snatched Conrad back down by the opposite arm.

I looked over at her. "Oh, Mama." I shook my head.

"Why are you staring me down?" she asked.

"Because you've already given this nigga some."

"It's not your business. I'm your mama. Don't talk to me like that. Have some fuckin' respect, shit."

"I already know you have." My lips were curled with disgust. "Do you know how this fool played me down at the fire station telling all my business?"

"Man, I didn't tell none of your business."

"Yeah, right," I said, giving him a sidelong glance.

"What business, Porter? I already told you anybody who saw that baby knew. You were the only blind fool. Good-bye, Porter."

I left her house, knowing she'd be sorry she didn't listen to me. If she got dogged out by that fat fool, it was nobody's fault but her own.

———

I can't remember the last time I went to see my dad, maybe a year or almost two ago, when he lived in a bungalow in Detroit off Six Mile on Ohio Street. Before all of his hair magazines took off. Before he decided to buy a two-hundred-thousand-dollar condo off Twelve Mile in Southfield, a Detroit suburb.

He didn't come by the restaurant much. He had most of his dealings with Mom through the phone, fax, or email. He concentrated more on his other ventures. I didn't care much for my father. If not for the fact that we looked almost identical, I'd deny being a part of him. He dogged my mother out when they were together so I don't have too many kind words to say about him, but I will say this—he is a good photographer.

When he worked at the fire department, he always volunteered to do the photo work for the monthly newsletter. After he retired, one of his girlfriends wanted him to take a picture of her with her fresh hairdo. A flash went off in Dad's head and that's when he started going around to beauty shops in his spare time with his first small venture, Slick Shots. He'd photograph customers and publish the photos along with shop information on the Web. That small venture turned into a national Web site. He had more than one hundred independent contractors working for him in different states. He also started a few magazines: *Motor City Hair, Hair Wars,* and the soon-to-be-released *Millennium Hair.* That's where he met all of his skeezer girlfriends. Most of them were wanna-be models looking for a sugar daddy. Dad wasn't supplying much sugar but he was spreading a whole lot of cream, and you couldn't tell him nothin', because he thought he was the big papa for real.

It had been so long since I'd seen him that I forgot the judge awarded Mom's 1996 white BMW 323 convertible to him during the divorce proceedings, but as soon as I pulled into his driveway I saw it parked beside his Seville inside the open garage. Only reason it was given to him was because Mom didn't want to take over the note.

When I walked inside, I soon discovered we weren't alone. There was a young woman parading around in a bright multicolored bikini with matching sarong, sipping on champagne and nibbling cheese like she was in the Playboy mansion while Dad was in the kitchen seasoning steaks.

"When I called you, you said you were alone," I said.

"You asked if I had company. I don't consider my wife company."

"Your wife? When did you get married?"

"A few days ago."

"A few days ago?"

"That's right. We flew to Vegas and tied the knot."

"I know you're not serious."

"I'm very serious. I'm waiting for your congratulations."

"Well, you're not gonna get it. How old is she, twelve?"

"He's so cute, Chucky. He takes after you." She stood in the hallway, posing in the large mirror. "Chucky, aren't you going to introduce us?"

"Chucky?" I looked at her like she was stone stupid. How the hell did she get Chucky from Richard? He didn't need to introduce us, because she wouldn't be around that long.

"Chucky, I'm going to let you and your son spend some time together." She grabbed the set of keys lying on the kitchen counter.

"You're walking outside like that?" I asked like she was my woman.

"You sound just like your father. I'm going to a pool party. This is what people wear to pool parties."

"How come you're not going to the pool party with her, Chucky?"

"He was invited to go, but he doesn't want to," she said.

"Like I said, *Chucky,* how come you're not going with her?"

"Because my son came over." She barely let him finish the sentence before she smoothed her red lips across his and skittered out the doorway.

"How old is she for real?"

"What difference does it make? Age ain't nothin' but a number," he said. "I may be fifty-one, but I can compete with the best of y'all."

"Okay, then how old is she?"

"Twenty-three."

"Twenty-three? She's younger than me. You know what? You and Mom are going through some kind of midlife crisis because y'all both doing the same thing."

"So she has a younger man?" He seemed concerned if not plain jealous.

"She's seeing Conrad. You know he works on my same shift, and you need to talk to her about that and tell her that shit ain't cool."

"I guess she needs somebody too. We all need somebody. When you going to settle down? You do have a baby now."

"Oh, you haven't heard? I thought Mom would have told you by now."

"What was she supposed to tell me?"

"I'm not with her anymore."

I followed him as he carried the steaks out on to the patio and threw them on the grill. We sat at the patio table.

"I don't understand. You were so excited over your son."

My eyes roamed quickly across his path. "It's her son, not mine. And you better watch out because I can take one look at what just left and tell you she definitely got a young stud on the side."

He shrugged. "I'm not worried about it. She did the begging for me. So what you come over here for anyway?"

"Two things. The first we already talked about."

"Trust me. Your mama won't listen to me. We're divorced but we just happen to run a business together, that's the extent of our relationship."

"The other thing I need is some money."

"Money? What kind of money? Gas money? Show fare? Concert ticket? What kind of money you talking about?"

"I'm not a kid. I need real money. I'm behind on my car note, and I was really hoping that you'd take it over. Really, I need you to buy it."

Dad started moving his left shoulder.

"Your back hurts? See, that's all those young girls can do for you old men, get your back hurtin'."

"My back's fine. I worked out today and it's a little stiff. Look, son, I don't need a truck."

"Well, do you know anybody who does or can you loan me money to pay the note? You know it has to be serious if I came to you."

"I know it must be because you sure don't believe in keeping in touch with your father. Why is that?"

I shrugged. I'm sure he knew how I felt about him deep down. I'm sure he knew I blamed him as much if not more than my mother for my brother's death.

"Trina Dash might. She asked if I was still selling your mama's old car." I remembered the honorable Judge Dash who presided over civil court cases in Thirty-sixth District court. She was the former wife of retired Captain Nick Dash, who's now deceased, and she had a fine daughter named Ronnie who went to Our Lady of Mercy High School. I tried to talk to Ronnie my junior year after Reesey started boring me for a second, but Ronnie never gave me the time of day.

Judge Dash could afford the Lexus, but it might be a little too jazzy for her with the tinted windows and the fancy rims. I'd really have to reach back and use the sales skills I acquired while I was at Mel Farr Ford selling used cars before the fire department called.

I pulled up to Judge Dash's home. She lived in the Ravines, a subdivision that my dad said used to be the talk of the town before all those new ones started sprouting up over everywhere.

I sat in the car, contemplating whether I should walk to her door. My mother couldn't stand Judge Dash. Swore that she and Dad did the nasty. If that were true, Mom would kill me for selling my Lexus to her, but she'd have to kill me because if anyone could afford it, Judge Dash could.

Her front door flung open before I had a chance to ring the bell. She was backing her body out as she pulled a wrought-iron cart filled with potted flowers. I braced her waist to prevent a near collision.

"Oh, my God! Jesus Christ," she said, dropping the handle and grabbing her heart.

I caught the handle to the cart before the pots tumbled out. "I'm sorry, I didn't mean to scare you. I'm Richard Washington's son."

"Little Porter?" she asked, focusing while she looked me up and down. "You not little anymore, are you?"

"No, ma'am."

"Please, you don't have to refer to me as ma'am. That makes me feel so old." She adjusted her sweatshirt by sucking in her stomach and sticking out her large chest. "And I'm really not that old, am I?" She flung her short bob around to allow more of her hair to frame her face. For a second, I almost forgot who she was. Forgot that she was a judge, my mother's worst nightmare, and my father's female friend. At that moment, I thought she was sexy and I was getting excited.

"Nah, you're not old. Besides, I only date older women," I said, stealing Conrad's line.

"Tell me anything. So, you came over to see Ronnie? Didn't your father tell you she got married?"

"Ronnie got married? Tell her I said congratulations, but I wouldn't have been coming over here to see her anyway. I never was her type."

"Well, my daughter and I always did have different taste." We exchanged scorching looks.

"Is that right?" I asked with a grin.

"So why did you come over?"

"My father said you might be interested in a car and I'm selling mine for a real good price. It's practically new with low mileage, fully loaded interior, and drives real smooth. "

"A car, not a sports utility vehicle. They're gas guzzlers," she said, dismissing my sales pitch.

"Not this one, judge."

"Honey, don't call me judge," she said as she stroked my cheek. "We're not in the courtroom. "Call me Trina."

"Trina, let me take you on a test drive."

"Let me slip out of these clothes then we can go for a spin."

I took her on a test drive, and we ended up getting a bite to eat at Nikola's, a rib and chicken joint on Telegraph close to her house. After we left the restaurant, I let her drive back so she could get a feel for the truck and how it handled on the road. I wanted her to fall in love with it, but she was too busy rubbing my thigh and moving her hand over closer to what she really wanted.

"I'm not being too forward with you, am I, baby?" she asked. I shook my head. "Good. Why don't we discuss this transaction more at my home over a glass of wine?"

When we got back to her house, she put on a George Duke CD and poured two glasses of wine. I let her drink both of them because I felt like I needed a clear head.

She slipped out of her clothes right in front of me, revealing her tight body. Not bad for someone forty-seven. She made sure she told me that she was forty-seven, one year younger than my mother. I know the defendants and the attorneys and all the people who came into her court-room daily had no idea what was under that robe. I can testify to that, because by the looks of things, there was no question that she really did work out four days a week like she claimed. Her body looked so much better than some of these young girls I'd been with, much better than Reesey's, and much better than Adrienne's, even better than Stacy's, and Stacy had a pretty tight body. "Come here," she said with a devilish grin, "and take off your clothes, or does the baby need help getting undressed?" I was young enough to be her baby, her child, but I didn't care. Not with the package she was offering.

After she lifted my shirt over my head, she took her soft hands and began rubbing my bare chest. I wanted her, but I didn't want to give in to the temptation. I had been doing so well. Almost three months without sex. I could have slept with Stacy, who kept calling, and of course Adrienne, who would probably never stop calling, but I wanted to do right. Even though, I hadn't attended church, I watched Bishop T.D. Jakes on TV, and I even ordered his *Manpower* tape series.

I knew that Judge Dash standing butt naked before my eyes was a test. In my heart and my mind, I knew that, but three months was a long time for me, someone who'd played house with a woman. I looked into Judge Dash's hazel eyes and reminded myself that I'd cheated on tests before in school and never got caught.

"You got a man, judge—I mean, Trina?" I asked as she unbuckled my belt and unzipped my jeans.

"No, but I got a *wo*man."

"Oh, you roll like that?"

"Sure do...one day I might invite you over to meet her. She'd really love you, but I'm not sure I want to share either one of you."

21

The transaction was complete. I sold the truck to Judge Dash two days after my initial visit. When I handed over my Lexus to her, she handed me a check for forty-one thousand dollars along with the key to her house and the remote control to her three-car attached garage. I took the check to Comerica Bank and converted it into a cashier's check made out to Debis Financial to pay off my loan. Damion hooked me up with the Mercedes, but he said he was holding on to the title for a year just in case the finance company tried to investigate. I took the three thousand in excess I had from the sale of my SUV, and took out a seven-thousand-dollar personal loan from my credit union to give to Damion.

Judge Dash told me before I left her house that evening that she liked to have her fire put out on Wednesdays and Thursdays, but I wasn't planning on seeing her anymore. I'd wait until I received the title to the Lexus and send that along with her remote and key with a note saying I was moving out of state.

It was Tuesday around 1:00 P.M. I had one wet foot halfway out of the shower when Mom came barging into the bathroom with the cordless in her hand. I nearly slipped on the bathtub tile and knocked myself out trying to hide.

"Damn, Mom, I'm in the shower. You heard of knocking?" I was peeking from behind the curtain.

"Boy, I didn't hear water running. Besides, you came out of me, so don't trip. Nothing you have means anything to me."

"Still, out of mutual respect."

"If you want to talk about mutual respect, why was fifty-year-old Trina Dash calling my twenty-seven-year-old son trying to sound eighteen?"

"Is she on the phone now?"

"Not anymore. What does she want with you, anyway?"

"It's probably about the Lexus."

"Is that what they call a dick now, a Lexus? Boy, you better watch yourself. Don't think a fifty-year-old can't drop a baby."

"Please," I said, scrunching my face. "Besides she's forty-seven."

"Oh, that's nasty to think about, but you can still stick it in her, huh? And if she's forty-seven, I guess I'm thirty-seven. Try fifty-one. She's older than me. She graduated high school with your daddy."

"Okay, Mom, whatever. Don't matter no more."

"Don't matter no more? Oh, you done got it and gone, huh?" She shook her head and looked at me with disgust. "I'm just telling you. Watch yourself. Too many women call this house for you. I can't even keep up with all these hoes' names. I would tell you to get your own phone, but what you really need to get is your own damn place!" She slammed the door behind her, but returned a couple of minutes later. This time she knocked before she entered. I was out of the shower and had a towel wrapped around my waist.

"Another one of your hoes is on the phone," she said as she opened the door with the receiver in her hand. My eyes expanded in disbelief. "Don't worry, it's on mute."

"You better hope so," I said.

"No, *you* better hope so. Those hoes don't do nothin' for me. And this one has a serious attitude. You better check her. Tell Sybil don't call my house with no damn attitude." She handed me the phone.

"Hello," I said to silence.

"Take it off mute!" Mom shouted.

"Hello," I said again after I pressed the mute button.

"Hey, what are you doing?"

"Nothing."

"Do you know who you're talking to?"

"Adrienne."

"Very good. I want you to go somewhere with me."

"Somewhere like where? Why aren't you at work?"

"You know school is still out for the summer. Are you going to go with me?"

"Somewhere like where?"

"It's a surprise. A very enlightening one. Trust me."

It was hard to trust someone who could be mentally ill. The other night while we were talking on the phone, Adrienne started crying out of the blue. When I asked her what was wrong, she said, "I want to be happy."

"Then be happy," I said impatiently because I didn't give a damn about how she was feeling. I had my own problems.

"I can't. Well, I can, but the only way I can is if I get married and have four boys."

"What if you get married and have two boys and two girls?"

"No, I won't be happy then. No girls. Just boys. Four of them, each two years apart."

"What happens if your first child's a girl?"

"I wouldn't be happy. I don't want any girls. It's too hard being a girl who ends up a woman who in my daughter's case ends up a black woman. It's too hard for black women." Then she started crying again. I couldn't trust a psycho like that. That shit was so crazy. I had to tell my mother about the conversation, and Mom told me to run the hell away from her psycho ass as soon as I could.

I don't know why I let Adrienne convince me to take a ride with her. I sat in the passenger's seat of her Jetta thinking that I really didn't know this girl. We met at a club a few months ago. We'd slept together half a dozen or so times the first few weeks we met, each time more uneventful than the last. When I stopped sexing her, she got more into me. We'd been out to different places, but besides knowing that she was crazy, I really didn't know much about her at all.

She pulled in front of an old high-rise off Woodward Avenue in Palmer Park. The area was filled with old apartment buildings, one after another. Street after street. The one she pulled in front of was raggedy. It had a sign out front that read, RENT MONTH TO MONTH, $0 SECURITY DEPOSIT.

I looked over at her. "Who lives here?"

"My psychic."

"Your who?"

"You heard me." She pulled the key out of the ignition, grabbed her purse, and got out of the car. "Come on." I sat in the car with my arms folded. She walked over to my side and opened the door.

"Come on," she said, tugging at my arm.

"No," I said firmly. "I don't believe in that shit."

"You don't believe that there are people in this world who were given a gift to see into the future?"

"No, I don't."

"Well there are, so come on." She yanked my arm so hard I fell out of the car slightly. To be so slim, she sure was strong.

"I think it's bad luck to read horoscopes and go to psychic readings," I said as I stood outside of the car.

"It's not bad luck, and besides if you're a Christian you shouldn't even speak of luck," she said as she walked toward the front door to the building, switching in her short-shorts.

"If you're a Christian you shouldn't go to a damn psychic," I said, trailing her.

"Just come on and go with me."

"I don't want to know about my future. What will happen will happen."

"Then just wait inside with me," she said.

We took the small elevator up to the ninth floor and walked down a long hallway that smelled like my grandmother's cedar closet used to. At the end of the hallway was a white door. Everyone else's door was brown. A young man who looked to be in his mid-twenties answered the door dressed in all white. A beautiful woman with long braids who was also wearing white stood beside him. They didn't seem like freaks so I felt comfortable enough to sit in the living room on the leather sofa and wait for Adrienne after she disappeared behind the crystal beads.

The young man sat in a leather chair across from me. I could feel him staring at my fingers as I flipped the pages of one of their psychic magazines.

"How long have you been a firefighter?"

"I'm sure Adrienne told you I was a firefighter," I responded without looking up.

"I've never talked to Adrienne. This is her first appointment."

"Yeah, right, good one." I continued reading the magazine.

"I smell smoke and fire coming from you. That's how I knew."

"You smell smoke and fire," I said, laughing. He may have looked normal, but he wasn't. "If you're a psycho—I mean psychic—then you should know how long I've been one."

"It depends. If you count how long your heart's been in it, I could say almost twenty years, ever since you lost your big brother in a house fire. If I count how long you've actually been doing it, I could say three years."

I threw the magazine aside and stared at him. "How in the hell did you know that? How did you know about my brother?"

"Now, do you believe?"

"I don't believe shit." I stood, ready to leave.

"Believe this," he said, still sitting, "you're in a very dark place right now and it's going to get darker, but eventually there's going to be a woman who needs you. She will come to you to help save her child and you will, only it's not her child you should save, it's her. You must save both her child and her in order to save yourself, and the ending you expect won't be the one you'll receive, but there will be better days."

"What did you just say?"

"Like your mother's been telling you for years, she's right, there will be better days ahead for you."

"Yeah, right," I said, walking to the door.

"Oh, and the woman with the baby. It is your baby. She will come to you, too, and you—"

"Cut it!" I snapped. "Adrienne," I yelled, "I'm out!"

I walked outside and waited at Adrienne's car with my arms folded. She was taking too long so I purposely bumped her car to make the alarm sound. That's when she stuck her head through the curtains and turned it off with her remote, but I bumped it again. We went back and forth with this about four times before she finally came running out of the old high-rise.

"I was in the middle of something good," Adrienne said to me.

"It was all bullshit. You told him about me, didn't you?"

"Told who?" she snapped back.

"That psychic."

"I didn't tell him anything."

"How did he know about my brother?"

"What about your brother? I didn't even know you had a brother."

"How did he know about him?"

"I don't know. He's a psychic. He sure didn't get any information from me. Besides, I don't know anything about your family. You still haven't introduced me to them. Why is that? When am I going to meet your mother?"

"I don't know."

"Do you know what the psychic told me?" she asked.

"No, and I don't care."

"You'll care about this because it involves us. She said I'd be married in less than a year."

"That doesn't involve me."

"It does involve you. Who else am I seeing? So it has to involve you.

I know we've had our ups and downs, even fell out, but we got back together. That's a sign of true love."

Since I left Reesey it seemed like I had gone from crazy to crazier to craziest. It couldn't get much worse. Everything happens for a reason and what happened today happened to teach my dumb ass a lesson. Stop! You can't keep meeting the same kind of women expecting different results because it's not going to happen. If I want great things for Porter Washington I need to make some sacrifices. Which one of these women makes me feel better than my saxophone or my drums? None of them, and that's pretty sad because lately my sax and my drums don't make me feel all that good either.

———

I was quietly sitting at the kitchen table at the fire station watching Zeander read the Bible. I was wondering how I was going to approach him with this. After dealing with that psychic and hearing the things he seemed to know about me, I felt that I needed to cleanse myself of that psychic nonsense. I needed to get right with God.

"I'd like to know Him," I said to Zeander.

He looked up from the Bible. "Know who?"

"You know who."

"I want you to say it."

"God. I'd like to know God."

"Praise God," he said as he closed the Book and focused on me. "He wants you to get to know Him."

"I've never read the Bible. I wouldn't even know where to begin."

"Start at the beginning, Genesis, chapter 1. In the beginning God created the heavens and the earth and the earth was without form and void; and darkness was upon the face of the deep," Zeander said from memory. "And the spirit of God moved up on the face of the waters and God said, let there be light; and there was light. And God saw the light; that it was good; and God divided the light from the darkness." He stopped and looked into my eyes. "You're moving into the light from the darkness, Porter."

22

It was almost a new year. November was here already and in a few short months Reesey was due to give birth. This was the second child she was trying to pin on me, but I was trying not to think about that. Once again I found myself at Belle Isle sitting in my car at the edge of the park. I increased the volume on the radio after I heard Luther's voice shimmer. I began singing along to "A House Is Not a Home." Before I realized it, I felt a stinging in the middle of my throat and a mist fill my eyes. Even though the song was ending, my emotions were beginning to kick in. I found myself with my head collapsed into my hand. I wondered why, if my brother was my angel in heaven, I still couldn't get my life together. Why wasn't he guiding me?

I went over Jade's when he got back in town. I almost got tempted. I swear the devil lives inside me. I looked at Jade and all I saw was a woman, and all I heard was how much she loved me and I wanted to believe her. I came so close to kissing her, but something held me back. I rushed out of the house and I haven't returned any of her/his/its calls.

I started my engine after I saw a few teenagers swaggering on foot toward me. That was my cue to pull off and ride the bridge across to Jefferson and take it home or wherever.

———

I ended up at Damion's house because I hadn't heard from him in a few days. He wasn't at the shop, he wasn't returning my pages, and no one was answering his home phone so I was a little worried. There were one of only a few blacks in his Bloomfield Hills subdivision, and Damion always complained about the cops pulling him over in his own neighborhood.

"Hey, Pam, is Damion here?" I had my hands buried inside of my leather jacket. She was gripping on to the front door too hard, like it was holding her up. Then I saw the tears.

"No, he isn't," she quivered.

"Are you okay? I mean, obviously you're not. Is Damion okay? The kids?"

"I'm not. It's me. I'm the one who's not okay. Did you know Damion had another baby across town?" she asked after she walked away from the door.

I followed her. "Another baby, by who? Hell no, I didn't know that."

"It's a little baby, an infant a few months old named Damion. Can you believe that motherfucka? Now he has two sons with the same first name. I have a gun, and I started to use it on his ass. Just like that." She snapped her fingers. "That's how quick a person can snap."

"Wait a minute. Slow down, Pam. What are you saying?" I closed her front door and stood lingering in the hallway.

She fell into my arms. "He's a fuck-up, and I wish you never would have left me because look how we both ended up. Both of us have been stabbed in the back by two evil people."

"Where are the kids?"

She blew her nose. "With Damion at his mother's. I'm giving him something to think about. I told him I need time to think all this through and if he comes within a foot of my house, I'll have him arrested."

"What are you going to do, leave him?"

"No." She unzipped my leather jacket. "I'm going to make love to you." She stood on her tiptoes and kissed me. It was soft and genuine, something I hadn't had since freshman year when the two of us were together.

"Pam, you know this isn't right."

"Please," she begged, "give me something to keep me sane."

"Not in his house, baby."

"It's not his damn house! It's our house."

"Still."

"Okay. We can go to a hotel."

I looked at her. Even with a red nose and streaks of grief painted down her cheeks, I still wanted her. I never had sex with her in high school, only listened to Damion brag after he did. She belonged to me then and now. I was just taking back what was mine to begin with. "Then let's go," I said as I watched her attempt to smile.

"You want to make love to me, Porter? Do you want me as bad as I want you?"

"Woman, you don't even know how many times I have already made love to you in my mind. Let's go."

————

Pam had me on the eleventh floor of the Westin Hotel crying like a baby. Her naked body was straddled over mine. She was swerving her hips from side to side, around, and up and down, while her breasts flapped in the air. I had never felt so loved and so wrong at the same time. My mind was playing tricks on me. I saw and heard Bishop Jakes preach as if I was in his Dallas church onstage in this bed with Pam on display for the entire congregation to judge. My mind kept repeating, *Wilt thou be made whole?* I couldn't be a Christian because I couldn't do right by God, and I couldn't do right by God because God hadn't done right by me. I shouted out like I was in church, "Hallelujah, thank You, Jesus!" I said and had Pam laughing so hard she fell off me.

I flipped her on her stomach, and had her on her knees so we could do it doggy style.

Her hands were gripping the side of the king-size mattress. Her back dipped down at just the right angle to give her ass the right height.

"Ask me whose pussy this is," she demanded.

"Whose pussy is it, baby?"

"It's yours. It's always been yours." Her words caused me to scream out louder than Michael Jackson in the "Thriller" video. I fell on to my back. Pam lay next to me, rubbing my chest with her feathery hands. "Do you ever think like, if you could do it all over—your life, I mean—how it would be?" she asked.

"Hell yeah, I think like that every day. "

23

"Two-dozen long-stem white roses, right?" Ben Sr. asked, pushing his horn-rimmed glasses farther up his nose.

"That's right."

I was at Ben's Florist, the only place I went to buy flowers for my brother's grave. I started going there once a week after Damion opened his shop across the street because it was so convenient to stop by Damion's then go to the florist, then go to the gravesite to lay the roses out. Only this week I wasn't stopping by Damion's. Hopefully Damion wasn't in his office, because if he were he'd see my car and wonder why I didn't come by.

Ben walked around the counter with the box of flowers ready for me. "This woman must be special. Every week she gets roses. What you get in return?"

"Hopefully forgiveness."

"Man, you mess up every week?"

"Just something that happened a long time ago that I'm still trying to make up for."

"Women will hold shit over your head for a lifetime, won't they?"

"I guess."

———

The old man pushed one of what seemed like a hundred keys from his large circular ring into the apartment door and opened it gently. He stood back and allowed me to enter the apartment first while he stayed in the hallway observing. I got the sense that he was afraid of me. I didn't know why. I didn't look like a thug.

It didn't take me long to look at the small studio. I walked in and around from the kitchenette to the small bathroom and the rest of the boxed area.

"How much do you want for this?" I asked. It didn't matter what he said, though. I was taking it. Mom had unofficially kicked me out. She was telling people who called for me on her phone that I no longer lived there. It was time for me to go. I had been there too long—almost seven months.

"You've got to have good credit. Do you have good credit?"

"I have excellent credit," I responded. "How much do you want for it?"

"You have to have been on the same job for at least six months."

"I've been on the same job for almost four years. How much is the rent?"

"It's $450 a month and that includes all of your utilities."

"Four-fifty and all utilities, I'll take it."

"I'll give you an application to fill out, and if it checks out you can move in on Monday."

I followed him back to the office and filled out the application in front of him. I felt him watching my every move. Here was a black man, same as me, and he seemed more suspicious of me than the whites would have been.

"You ever go to the Soul Station?" I asked.

"My wife and I went a few times before she passed. She sure did love the peach cobbler."

"My parents own the place. I'm going to give you one of our VIP cards," I said, taking a card from my wallet. "It's valid for this month for a dinner for two, any day Wednesday through Sunday."

"Your parents own this place?" he asked, taking the card from me.

"Owned and operated family business for fifteen years."

"So, son, what do you do?"

"I'm a Detroit firefighter," I said. When I handed him the completed application, he handed me a set of keys. "Don't you want to check it out first?" I asked.

"Automatic approval for firefighters. We don't pull credit anyway, only verify employment. I'm sure you work where you say; if you don't, I'll just evict you."

"You own this place, old man?"

"Names Arnold Fortier, and I sure do. Used to be me and my wife, rest her soul, but she passed away last year from cancer. Did I mention rent is due on the first and late on the third?"

"Several times."

"I have to train my new tenants. The better you're trained, the less work I have to do. When you plan on moving in?"

"Let's see. Today's Thursday, and I'm off until Tuesday. I guess on Monday."

"Well, before you move in, I'll need fifteen hundred dollars, which will cover your first and last month's rent, security deposit, and cleaning fee."

"I'll drop it off tomorrow." Fifteen hundred was more than I wanted to put down on an apartment and the other problem was I didn't have it.

———

"Boo, what's wrong?" Jade asked through the phone line.

"Nothing. I just need to move." I was lying in bed, staring at the ceiling. I called Jade, I mean, Vanity and was talking to him, I mean her, for almost an hour. My eyelids were ready to close because I was simply stressed out over the move and the money I needed.

"I'll give you the fifteen hundred dollars."

"I don't need you to give it to me, just loan it to me."

"No, I'll give it to you, but you know what I'm going to want. Two things. One I want to do to you and the other I want you to do to me."

"Forget it. It's not happening."

"Boo, who's going to know?"

"I will, God will, and my brother will."

"How your brother gonna know?"

"Because he's in heaven looking down at me."

"Boo, you never said anything about your brother before. I'm sorry. Do you want to talk about it?"

"No."

"I'll give you the fifteen hundred anyway, boo."

"That's alright. I got to go."

———

On Saturday, I arranged to meet Adrienne at 6:00 P.M. at Captain El's, an elegant new restaurant off East Jefferson on the river's edge. Even though I hadn't talked to her in almost three months, ever since she took me to see that psychic, she was excited when I called. She said the psychic told her I would call this week.

I stood to pull out her chair and remove her three-quarter-length wool coat like a gentleman should. She loved that kind of stuff. Made her feel appreciated. I knew how to handle Adrienne. Tell her whatever she wanted to hear and she'd do anything I asked.

"You finally got a little time for me," were the first words spewing from her mouth.

"I could have more."

"Is that right?"

The waitress came over to the table to take our order.

Adrienne sat across from me staring. I knew she was waiting for me to order for her, but I hated that shit. She wanted to be totally submissive to me, and I wasn't her husband so I didn't deserve it, nor did I want it.

"He's going to order for both of us," she told the waitress.

"Order whatever you want," I said as I held up the menu to shield my view of her.

"I'll just have whatever he has."

I put the menu down. "Give me the Porterhouse medium rare with blue cheese dressing on my salad, and garlic mashed potatoes."

"So, what's this all about, Porter?" Adrienne asked as soon as the waitress walked away. "Over the phone you mentioned something about needing my help. I'm very interested to find out how I can help. Does it have anything to do with Reesey?"

"No. I'm trying to put myself in a position where economically I have something. Once I'm together I can take on other responsibilities."

"Like marriage?"

"Maybe."

"Okay, how can I help?" she asked, leaning into the table.

I took a deep breath. "I need fifteen hundred dollars."

"Why are you looking over at me?" she asked as she leaned back from the table.

"If you loan it to me—" I stopped as the waitress came back to the table with our salads.

"Is there anything else I can get you?" the waitress asked.

"How about the check?" Adrienne asked. "I won't be staying for dinner."

The waitress looked over at me. "I'll handle the check. We don't need anything else. Thank you." I looked over at Adrienne. "What's wrong with you?"

"You had me drive to this restaurant so you could pimp me for some money? My psychic told me you were going to disappoint me. I was hoping she was wrong, but how could a psychic be wrong? You must think I'm really desperate. I will not loan that kind of money to any man, not even you, Porter, no one."

"How much will you loan me?"

"Nothing!" She jerked her napkin away from her lap, threw it on the table, and then stood.

"Please sit back down," I said.

She stormed through the restaurant, heading for the door.

I took out a fifty and threw it on the table then trailed out of the restaurant after her.

She was marching to her car like a soldier. Her handbag was swinging back and forth by her side as she held on to it and kept on stepping.

I ran to catch up with her and lightly jerked her arm, but the look on her face caused me to let go.

She stood in front of me, still for a moment, and then let out a big sigh. "I'm disappointed. Some of my girlfriends were shocked that I was dating a man who was as fine as you. They just knew you were using me, but no, I could proudly confess that you never asked me for one dime. Maybe they were right, a man who looks as good as you can't be up to anything good."

"Those aren't your friends if that's what they said to you."

"I'm not Janet Jackson or even close. I'm just an average-looking woman, and judging by the picture I saw of your last girlfriend—"

"How did you see a picture of my last girlfriend?" I asked, cutting her off.

"It doesn't matter. The picture proved to me that I'm probably the most average woman you've ever been with. Why else would you want me other than money? My psychic said money was going to play a major part in my decisionmaking this month."

"Stop talking about that damn psychic. I thought you were nice. It never had anything to do with money."

"I'm sorry. I want to give you the money because I really do love you, but if you can't stand here and tell me that you love me, too, I can't do it."

"You mean if I stand here and tell you I love you, you will give me the money?"

"That's right." She folded her arms and stared me down, waiting for my response.

"That's all you want to hear?" She nodded. I looked into her sincere eyes and said, "I can't lie to you like that. I don't love you, but I like you, except when you act desperate and talk about that psychic."

"Well I'm not going to act desperate today." She turned and walked away. I heard the roar of her engine and the skid of her tires as she flew out of the parking lot.

———

"Pam, baby," I said in a whisper through my cell line to hers.

"Hi," she whispered back.

"Are you alone?"

"You know I am."

"I need a favor and I hate to ask you but I swear I'll pay you back."

"Whatever you need. You know money doesn't mean a thing to me. Whatever you need."

"I need fifteen hundred dollars to move into my own place."

"Is that all? That's a good little investment. Think of all the money we'll save on hotel rooms. It's yours. Meet me at the Clarion."

24

I met Pam at the Clarion hotel in Toledo, Ohio, about an hour from Detroit. In the few weeks that we'd been seeing each other, we choose a different location each time we met. All of them were far enough from Detroit and usually in an area populated with few blacks so we wouldn't have to worry about seeing anyone we knew.

She was strip dancing for me, only instead of me putting money into her thong, she was placing hundred-dollar bills in the elephant trunk G-string that she bought for me, fifteen hundred-dollar bills to be exact.

"I feel cheap," I said, mocking a woman.

"Fifteen hundred for a piece of ass. You shouldn't feel cheap, baby doll. Now come over here and shake that trunk for me."

"Why? You want to feel me?" I asked as I danced over toward her.

"Hell yeah, I want to feel you." She reached for my trunk.

"You feel me?" I asked. That was our little saying. That, and you know what I'm saying. You're saying what you know.

"I feel you," she said.

"You know what I'm saying?"

"You saying what you know."

Pam and I started embracing. Then kissing. Foreplay had quickly become nonexistent after our first time together. Instead, we rushed in for the big sensation.

For the first time, I started feeling guilty about everything. It was a different story when Damion was out of the house, but as usual he made his way back in. She said it was for the kids, but at the same time claimed she was getting a divorce. I knew better, and even if she did divorce

Damion, I couldn't marry his ex-wife. The reality of the situation was starting to set in. I was starting to snap out of my fantasy.

I knew Pam took the money out of their bank account. I started thinking how I would feel. Even though Damion is a fuck-up, still, what if one of my boys was taking my money and fucking my wife? I'd be ready to kill somebody.

Things had been so steamy between Pam and me that I started hallucinating. That's the only word I can think to describe my feelings. I stopped using condoms. Convinced myself that Pam was my woman. Had her convinced, too, because when she told me Damion wasn't feeling on anything in their bedroom but cold sheets, I believed her. We talked about how things would change when I moved into my new place. We made plans to see each other on every one of my off days, if only for an hour or two since I only lived minutes from her job, making it convenient for her to stop by after work.

I turned on the television after we finished making love, hoping to find a good movie to watch on Pay-Per-View while Pam slept. As I flipped through the channels keeping the volume low, I saw a porno flick being advertised. A strong urge came over me. I didn't even care that Pam was lying right beside me. I picked up the phone gently and ordered it. As I was watching it, I started stroking myself. Before long I was masturbating.

"What's wrong?" Pam asked as she woke up.

My eyes expanded. "Nothing." I scrambled for the remote to turn off the television and tried to conceal the wet spot I was sitting in.

She pulled the cover back. "Were you masturbating?"

"Kinda sorta."

"Is it still hard?"

"No, but I can get it to come back up."

"I can too," she said, and disappeared under the sheets.

———

Damion insisted on helping me move, since he didn't the last time. I tried to think up an excuse. Nothing sounded right, plus, I was getting paranoid, thinking the more I avoided him, the more he might put two and two together, but I don't think he could ever put Pam and me together.

One of Damion's boys owned a moving company, Self Move, and Damion was able to get the truck for free.

"Besides, I want to see your fine mama," he said. Anybody else or any other time, I'd be mad, but what could I say under the circumstances?

When Damion walked through my mother's door, she greeted him with a warm embrace. There was no doubt in my mind after watching the way they hugged, and the way my mother leaned back from him holding on to his arms, while he kept his hands fastened around her waist, no doubt that something had happened between them. All I could do was shake my head, because I wasn't starting trouble. Not with Damion. At least none that he'd know about.

"I'm so glad you're helping Porter get all his shit out of here. It's about time. I love him." She turned toward me. "I love you, but you know it was time."

"I know. That's why I'm moving."

"I still don't know how you could go from a town house to a little studio. Seems like you could have gotten a nice one- or two-bedroom, especially since you have the baby coming," Mom said. I didn't even bother to comment. The last thing I wanted to think about with all the other shit on my mind was a baby I didn't want coming. I needed to get this move over as quick as possible so Damion could leave and I could stop feeling so bad.

My cell phone rung and it was Pam. Even though the cell phone was in my hand I felt like Damion could see the caller display from across the room.

"Hello," Pam's voice sounded through the speakerphone. I had forgotten that I had my cellular programmed to automatically answer.

"Is that Pam hunting me down?" Damion asked.

I nodded. "You know it is," I said to him. I took Pam off speaker. "Hey, Pam, Damion's here with me. Hold on."

I handed Damion the phone and started lugging my things out to the truck. I was putting an end to Pam real soon.

25

H ow you doing, Mr. Fortier?" I asked as I watched him come from his old pickup carrying a few bags of groceries. I'd been living in the apartment for almost three weeks and Pam had visited me a few times already.

"I'm fine, son. Trying to get ready for this winter is all. It's getting kind of nippy out."

"Sure is. We don't have too much longer and this year will be over. We're almost to Christmas—one more week."

"That's right, son."

"Do you need some help with the bags?" I asked.

"This is all I have but thanks for asking." He stopped in front of me with two plastic Farmer Jack bags, one in each hand. "How are you doing, son?"

"I'm fine, Mr. Fortier."

"You sure about that?"

"Yeah, I'm sure. Why?"

"I don't know. Sometimes I see you and you look like you have a lot on your mind, but if you're sure, you're sure." He started walking to the apartment building.

"I'm sure, Mr. Fortier," I said to his back. I stood outside with my bare hands balled inside my leather jacket. The chill in the air was sweeping over my cheeks. When I left from inside my apartment, it was a quarter after five. I didn't want to take my hands out of the jacket to check the time, I'd rather estimate that no more than ten minutes had passed.

I was waiting for Pam. She said she was coming over after work.

The city bus came roaring down Jefferson, stopping a few feet from the parking lot of my building. The door opened and two ladies came out, but neither one was Pam.

This was stupid and it was over. I really didn't know what I was trying to do with Pam, and the night before I finally realized that and told her over the phone that we shouldn't see each other. She started crying, telling me she'd rather be dead than be without me again. I hated to hear that. I hated to listen to her reduce herself as low as all those other knuckleheads I'd messed around with. I was having an internal conflict because in some ways I wanted to see her again, but in others I didn't, and I shouldn't, so that's what I told her. This morning when I woke up aroused from the thought of her, I was willing to postpone my decision indefinitely, just until I could get her completely out of my system. I called her at work and made her promise me that she'd come over afterward, but I knew she wouldn't. I knew it. First little disagreement and she didn't come over. I went inside.

I'd been sitting on my bed thinking about starting all over from scratch. Maybe it was all for the best, Pam not showing. I got myself all geeked up about it being over and then I heard a knock on the door.

"One minute," I said. In my mind I was thinking it was Mr. Fortier coming down to tell me I parked underneath a carport that I wasn't paying for. I looked through the peephole and saw Pam on the other side of my door. I shook my head. If I wouldn't have yelled out I could have pretended not to be home.

She knocked again.

I flung the door open and looked at her like we were both in the wrong.

"I don't care," she said to me as if she was reading my mind.

"Pam, what are you doing here?"

"Weren't you expecting me?" She walked inside.

I stood at the door with the knob still in my hand, rehearsing how I could tell her to leave. Before I could get one word out, I closed the door and walked over to her. She was standing by the window with her back facing me.

"I was but when you didn't show, I figured it was over," I said, outlining her shoulders. I tried to stop my urge to hold her, but I gave in to it and wrapped my arms around her waist.

"Like that's really what you want," she said. "We both know better." She put her hands on top of mine and pulled me in closer.

"That's what I want. Isn't that what I told you last night? If we keep this up, Pam, it's not going to work. Damion will find out." I kissed her neck in several spots.

"Damion should know after all the shit he put me through that I'm probably seeing somebody."

"Maybe you're right, but I tell you one thing, he doesn't think that somebody is me. You best believe that, 'cause if he did, my ass wouldn't be standing here."

"Damion fucked me over, and he's getting what he deserves."

"Pam, he may have fucked you over, but he didn't do shit to me." I pulled away from her, and she turned to face me. "I'm starting to believe this is all about getting the brother where it hurts. Sleeping with his best friend is the ultimate betrayal. Short of having my baby."

"I'd love to have your baby."

"Come on, Pam. Now, you're talking crazy. I got one baby mama drama; I don't need two. Besides, I did want to at least live to see thirty." She turned to face me. Her look said something different than I wanted to see. "You're not, are you? Are you?"

"No, unfortunately. My test came back negative."

"I thought you were on the pill?"

"I was until I stopped using it. I want to have your baby."

"Girl, you are crazy. That's some Reesey shit right there. We can't do this no more."

"Yes, we can, and we will. If you stop seeing me, Porter, I'm going to tell Damion why he hasn't been getting any."

"Why would you do that?"

"Because I can't deal with him without you, that's why. You can't leave me just like that. Not when you get tired and start feeling guilty. Fuck him. He wasn't feeling guilty when he took me from you."

"Now you're going way back to high school. Besides, we had already broken up."

"No, we hadn't. He came on to me way before you and me broke up. He was the one who told me about you and Reesey. I knew before you even told me."

"I don't even care about that, Pam. That was high school."

"I'm in love with you. Don't leave me." She wrapped her arms around my neck and pressed her lips against mine. "Don't leave me, baby."

I needed to get out of my little box and get some fresh air because I needed oxygen to think, so Pam and I took the short ride to Belle Isle. Before we left the apartment, I gave her one of my knit hats and a large jacket for a disguise.

We sat in the car along the water's edge, reminiscing about the good old days, back when we didn't have to sneak. I wasn't pressuring her to leave Damion, and she wasn't trying to make me stay with her. We were both simply enjoying the moment. She leaned into me and starting kissing me, then a few minutes later she pulled back.

"What's wrong?" I asked.

"I think that was Hoffa in that Navigator that just passed."

"Hoffa don't have a Navigator. Don't worry about that."

"Not driving, on the passenger side. Didn't you see that truck slow up?" she asked.

"I wasn't paying it any mind."

"Do you think we're crazy?" Her voice was mixed with sighs.

"Yep, I know we are."

"I wish I could help it. Now I know how people feel who are addicted to crack."

"You calling me crack?"

"I'm calling you addictive."

"So are you, baby." I kissed her forehead then started the car and pulled off. I didn't think that was Hoffa in the Navigator, but just in case, we didn't need to still be standing there. Even if Pam had on a knit hat, it's like Johnnie Cochran said during the O.J. trial, a knit hat isn't much of a disguise, it's just a person in a knit hat. Pam and I had gone through great pains to keep everything on the down low. She'd usually keep the car parked in her garage at work, a different structure than Damion knew about, and she'd either take the bus to my house or have her girlfriend who lived in Alden Park Towers drop her at the restaurant that was walking distance from my place. Whatever she did, it wasn't consistent. It would be nearly impossible for Damion to backtrack Pam's steps, she made sure of that. Belle Isle was a slipup and I had myself to blame if anyone did see us, but I doubted if anyone had.

26

I went by The Perfect Touch because it would look strange if I didn't. Especially since Damion had already called me out on how long it had been since I had stopped by. Still, I didn't like being there, playing Madden '99 while I listened to Damion rub it in about Barry Sanders' retirement. It was like déjà vu, only this time Damion was the one who needed to pay more attention to his home, and I definitely didn't want to be the one to break it to him. I didn't stay long, and I purposely lost the game.

"You coming over this Saturday to play cards?"

"This Saturday? On Christmas? I'm not sure, man. I got a date," I lied.

"Who you seeing now, still the teacher?"

"Nah, a new one. It's nothing serious. Nothing to even talk about."

"Man, something wrong?" Damion asked. "I can't remember the last time you came by the house. Is it about Barry or what? You know I'm not going to hold you to that thousand dollars."

"Oh, I'm not worried about that."

"Come on by. Bring your girl if you want. She can keep Pam company."

"I might."

"Yeah, alright," he said, looking at me skeptically.

———

Hoffa was sitting across from me acting real strange—chewing on his toothpick, keeping his eyes glued to me, and being quieter than usual. Not one joke had escaped his mouth in the hour since I had arrived.

Damion's house was decorated nicely. He and Pam had a real tree up and underneath there were plenty of gifts—mostly toys for the kids. You could hear a pin drop inside the house. No rap music was playing. The kids were over Pam's sister's house. They had left right before I arrived at 8:00 P.M.

"What you do last Thursday, man?" Hoffa asked me.

"What I do last Thursday?" I repeated the question as if I didn't understand it, or maybe I hoped it would change or I wondered if it was a trick. I wasn't sure. "Nothing."

"Nothing?" Hoffa questioned.

"He said nothing!" Damion said, irritated because he was losing. "Pick up your damn book, shit." Damion didn't wait for Hoffa to pick it up, instead he gathered Hoffa's book of cards and threw it over with Hoffa's other two.

"I understand he said nothing, but I think he did something. What Pam do last Thursday?"

"Pam!" Damion yelled for her, then turned to Hoffa, "You getting on my damn nerves. Can't even play a game of fuckin' spades. Pam, come down here!"

I heard feet on the staircase. "Yes," she said, walking into the dining room.

I kept my eyes on my hand, rearranging them again. Something didn't feel right.

"Hoffa wants to know what you did last Thursday."

"Why Hoffa want to know shit? What did you do?" she asked Hoffa.

"I was at Belle Isle."

Out the corner of my eye, I saw the expression on Pam's face change slightly, but she played it off nicely. "Probably getting high."

"Damn, how you know?" Hoffa asked with laughter.

"I know you," she said to Hoffa. "And I know you didn't call me down for that," she said to Damion.

"Nah," Damion said, throwing out a joker.

"Why you lead with a joker, man?" I asked.

"Because jokers are wild, just like the two of y'all. You gonna fuck my wife?" he asked with a psychotic smile on his face. He leaned back in the chair so far I thought the back legs were going to snap before he had a chance to set it down. "She ain't even fuckin' her husband but she gonna fuck my best friend. Or should I say the man who I thought was my best friend."

"What the fuck you talking about, man?" I asked, looking bewildered.

"What the fuck am I talking about? Uh, I don't know. Hoffa, what the fuck am I talking about?"

"I guess you talking about the fact that they were down at Belle Isle kissing in the car you hooked him up with."

"You don't know what the fuck you're talking about," Pam said to Hoffa. "You lying bastard. He's lying, Damion."

"Shut up," Damion said, holding his fist up to her face.

"Get your fist out her face. I'm not going to let you hit her," I said.

"Woo, this motherfucka right here got some nerve," he said to Hoffa before he turned to face me. "I mean you really got some nerve. If I didn't know better," he said as he leaned into my face, "I'd swear you were the husband, and I was just some punk nigga, but I know better." He grabbed me by the collar and pulled me on to the table. "Merry Christmas, nigga."

I heard Pam scream out in horror as Damion, Hoffa, and Damion's other boy started beating me. I couldn't throw any return punches because they had me pinned against the table. This was probably the end for me. "Richard," I yelled out.

"Who the hell is Richard?" I heard one of them say before everything went completely dark.

27

H ey," my brother said to me. He hadn't changed. Hadn't gotten any older. "You not dead. Don't worry."

"I'm not worried, Richard."

"You could be dead," he said firmly, "but God isn't ready for you. You still have so much to learn. You need to learn how to love God the Father and accept that Jesus died for our sins."

"I do love God. I love Him. I accept Jesus as my Savior."

"Then live like you do. He's bigger than your life, than anybody's life. You need to love Him before it's taken."

Richard started walking away.

"Don't leave me, Richard."

"I've got to leave you because you're not dead, and you better be praising Him because you're not. What if you were dead? We wouldn't see each other. You know we wouldn't see each other if you were dead. Not the way you've been living. Love Him, brother."

———

I felt a chill go through my body while hundreds of angels fluttered around me.

Suddenly, a large hole opened above me, and there was bright light and a massive presence. The angels continued around me like they were mending me, making me whole again and then all of them went into the opening one by one and after they all entered, it quickly closed.

I opened my eyes to blurred vision, figures standing over me that I could not bring to focus because the light was stinging my eyes.

My back rose slowly with the bed and I heard a voice ask, "Are you thirsty?"

My brain said, "Yes. Can I have some water?" but no one could understand my words.

"What, Porter? What did you say? Did you understand him? Give him a glass of water," one of the voices said.

"Here, Porter. Do you want water?" a different voice asked.

My hand reached out for it. I felt the glass slip through my fingers. I heard it crash, and I heard loud noises that were rattling my brain. I was so sleepy. I just wanted to rest forever.

"Let's leave and let him rest. Porter, this is your mother and father and Pam. I don't know if you can see or hear us. You're in the hospital. It was a terrible accident. You were carjacked on Seven Mile. I guess you wouldn't get out of the car, and they pulled you out. I don't know exactly. You're going to be fine though, but you have a concussion. Try to rest, and we'll come back tomorrow." I heard footsteps, and then I heard my mother say, "Now tell me again what happened, and how it was that you were able to call the police? You and Damion just happened to be driving by?"

"Uh-uh!" I mumbled, trying to grab Pam back inside. I didn't want her telling my parents anything. Mom was too smart to be lied to. She'd watched *Perry Mason* and *Columbo* for too many years and always knew who did it before anyone else could figure it out.

———

Pam came back early the next morning.

My vision was better, but I was irritable and I didn't want to talk a lot or hear much talking either. She was trying to convince me to file criminal charges against Damion, Hoffa, and the third guy. She wanted me to press attempted-murder charges and robbery since they stole my car. Technically, Damion took everything back that belonged to him. He may have done it forcefully, but that's exactly what he did. The car I paid him ten thousand dollars for and drove barely five months, he still had title to. Of course, Pam was his too. I realize that now that I'm lying here with my face swollen and my ass beat.

"Pam," I said, struggling to get the words out, "it's over. Go home to your family. I'm not your husband and never will be."

"I'm sorry," she said as tears filled her eyes. "I'm so sorry."

"Don't be sorry, be gone," I said as I became irritated with her tears. "Pam, leave and don't come back. Being around you could get me killed.

Not that I'm afraid to die, but I got to do some things first. Like find God. Find my own woman. Have my own family. Things like that. You feel me?"

"I feel you." Her throat crackled.

"You know what I'm saying?"

She cleared her throat. "You saying what you know."

PART FOUR

Winona and Porter

28

It was January. Hard to believe that it was the year 2000—the new millennium. This time next year was the North American International Auto Show my company was preparing for. I was working hard at the office, trying to prove to Tyler that I could design the perfect concept car for Daimler Chrysler, but lately he had seemed to dismiss my designs and concentrate more on the rest of the team. It was a minority company, but I felt like the token. Not that I expected special treatment, but equal would have been nice.

For New Year's, I made a resolution to deal with my issues a little better. I couldn't go on pretending to be well because I knew my time was nearing. Sosha never missed a week calling Keith. The last time she spoke to him, though, he was coughing real badly. I guess he was getting sick. Next it would be me.

I figured that I may need counseling, a support group or at least someone to confide in, most likely Gina. I wasn't sure what it was going to be, but it needed to be something because I was tired of these mood swings, and I was having one at the moment.

It was Friday and Gina called a little after 7:00 P.M. saying she was coming over, but I didn't feel like being bothered, which was the very reason I sent Sosha off to her grandparents and let Carlton use my car so he could drive to the golf dome—anything to be by myself. Still, I couldn't turn Gina away. She wouldn't do that to me. I could remember a time when I couldn't stand to be alone, but that time was becoming barely a memory. Now I wish I were alone. Wish I didn't have kids to contend with daily. I wish it were just my dog and me and the Lifetime channel.

I stood at the entrance to the living room and watched Samson jump on to my brand-new sofa, curl up, and shut his eyes. If one of the kids were sitting there, I'd tell them to go to the den, but since it was Samson and he never gave me any trouble, I'd let him sleep in his big ball. I loved that puppy, even though he wasn't a puppy anymore. Nearly three years old, but he still loved me back the same as he did when he was three months old and we picked him up from the breeder. He's Sosha's dog, but I'm usually the one who feeds him. I'm usually the one who ends up taking him for a walk. To Samson, I'm his master not Sosha. He knows this is my household and that I'm sick. I can tell by the way he sniffs me and whines, because he knows I'm dying.

The doorbell snapped me out of my I-wish-I-were-dreaming stage. I wish this shit that is going on in my life right now wasn't really happening. *And,* I wish Gina wasn't at my door. She wanted to see my house for the first time in the almost seven months since we've lived here, but I believe the real reason she wanted to come over was because Mark was out of town on business, which always made Gina feel nervous and insecure. I think deep down she was afraid that Mark would do what her first husband did after work one day and just not come back.

I opened the door and smiled at her while she stood beside an exotic tree plant that was a little more than her height of five-five. She picked it up by its base, rocking sideways as she came through the door.

"This is your housewarming gift," she said as she set it down in my foyer and dusted off her gloved hands. "And you better like it because it was special-ordered from a ritzy plant shop in Birmingham. I don't even want to tell you how much I paid for it. Do you want to know?"

"No, because I don't want to feel bad after I already told you not to buy me anything."

"I had to buy you something since I'm coming over to see your new house for the first time. Sorry it took me so long, but I'm not an executive and I work twice as hard as you do, which means I have very little time to socialize."

"Yeah, right. The only reason you work that hard is because you want to, not because you have to."

She walked around the foyer looking up through the mahogany staircase. "This place is big."

"I need all the space I can get with two kids. You'll see when you have some."

"Where are those kids of yours, anyway? I want to see them. It's been so long."

"They're not here right now, but their pictures are on the mantel."

Gina walked into the living room and over to the mantel, studying the photos carefully. Her presence disturbed Samson, who jumped off the sofa and ran upstairs, probably heading for my bed. She turned and looked back at me as I was walking into the room. "They're not here, right?" I nodded. "It's a shame how much Carlton looks like Derwin."

"Are you calling my son ugly?" I stood beside her with my hands on my hips, waiting for a reply.

"No, I'm not saying that."

"You implied it. You never hid the fact that you thought Derwin was ugly."

"That's true I didn't, and Carlton favors Derwin, but he's not ugly. You can tell he's his son, but thank God they're not identical. Sosha is going to be a little hot mama, isn't she? She is so pretty, but you all don't favor at all. The one time I did see Keith I didn't remember him being all that attractive to produce Sosha. Tell the truth, is Sosha Keith's?"

"Girl, please. Of course. Keith just let himself go, but I saw some earlier photos of him as a child and he was very attractive. His family, especially his mother, is real pretty."

"Well, girl, what do you want to do for the rest of the night? I'm yours. You want to order a pizza, watch a movie, go shopping, what?" She took off her cashmere three-quarter-length coat, removed her tam, and handed both of them to me.

I walked to the entrance closet to hang up her coat. "We eat so much pizza in this house it might as well be Pizza Hut."

"Do you want to go out and eat?" she asked.

"Not really. I'm not hungry."

"Don't tell me you're on a diet, or are you just back to your strange eating habits? I see you've dropped a few pounds. Have you been working out?"

"No. Do I look skinny?" I walked back into the living room and paraded in front of her.

"No, you just look like you may have lost a few pounds."

"Maybe. I'm letting this job get to me." That's what I was hoping it was. I didn't want to think I was wasting away.

Gina let out a loud sigh and collapsed on the sofa. "I don't need to eat anyway with my big butt. If only my body could be as slim as my hands, I'd be on to something. These hands don't even look like they belong to me." She studied her hands and then quickly disregarded them. "Mark said something about my weight the other day. He tried to say it in a joking manner but I know he was serious. He said, 'baby, you sure you're not pregnant because that ass is sure spreading.' Girl, I was so pissed."

I sat on the sofa, leaving one cushion between the two of us.

"I wouldn't worry about it," I said.

"I have to. You've seen the women in my family. Name one that's not big. Oh, girl, before I forget, guess who I saw at Rite Aid? Do you remember Dennis Randall?" I shook my head. The name sounded familiar but I couldn't place the face. "Dennis Randall. Remember him? I think that he went to U of D. No, he went to Cass and ended up getting kicked out his sophomore year and then he went to Mumford not U of D. Remember the pretty boy who I had a big crush on freshman year. Remember? He used to throw parties with a bunch of other guys. I can't remember the name of their club, but he was real popular and he had two older brothers who were popular too. He knew Derwin."

"I think I remember him. Straight hair?"

"Yeah. Dark-skinned brother with hair that looked painted on. Girl," she said, looking around the room like she was about to kick out something too heavy for others' ears, "he looks like he's dying of AIDS. Swear to God." I was speechless. My heart began beating so fast my mind could barely keep up. "He was filling some kind of prescription. Walking with a cane. He had a big knit hat over his head and a heavy coat and scarf. Okay, I know it's January but today it wasn't exactly freezing outside, and with all that stuff on, he still looked like a skeleton."

"He could have cancer," I said, rolling my eyes.

"He could, but I doubt it. Besides that, I always thought there was something about him that spelled gay. Fine as he was, I just always thought that. He had a guy with him who was helping him because he was too frail to probably go anywhere by himself. He looked like he was on his deathbed. I was surprised that he recognized me because I don't think I look anything like I did in high school. Anyway, he'll probably be dead before the month is up. We'll probably read his obituary in the newspaper."

"Mmm. That's sad." She continued talking but my conscience was speaking louder than her mouth, and I could only follow one so I choose my thoughts over her opinions. AIDS, that's what I'd eventually end up with. I didn't know if I was doing the right thing by not taking medication. I went to three different specialists before I found one who agreed that I didn't need treatment. The other two preferred early intervention. They felt it would increase my life in the long run, but my doctor in Dallas, Dr. Greenleaf, said he'd rather wait until I became ill to start treatment so my body wouldn't become resistant to the drugs through prolonged use.

Now, I have this brand-new doctor, Dr. Gant, and I was thinking about switching. He has me come into his office once a month. Dr. Greenleaf only had me coming in once every three months. Dr. Gant constantly checks my blood levels, trying to convince me that I need to get on medication. It didn't matter what he or any of them said; I know I'm not taking medication regardless. Medicine meant I had *it*. I still hadn't convinced myself of that yet. Sometimes I know I have it. Those are the times I don't feel like being bothered—like today.

"That is sad but it's a fact. Could you imagine being Magic Johnson's wife right now? Could you imagine being married and finding out your husband has AIDS?" Gina asked, snapping me out of my daze.

"Magic doesn't have AIDS. He's HIV-positive."

"Same thing."

"No, it's not, Gina. There's a big difference between AIDS and HIV."

"I don't know. I'm not an expert on it, are you?" she asked sarcastically.

I hesitated. "No, but with all the public service announcements, I feel like one. Can we change the subject?"

"It is getting a little depressing. So how are you and your boss doing? What's his name, Tyler? How's Mr. Roundship? Has he asked you out yet?"

"No. Why do you keep asking me that?"

"Because the man likes you."

"The man likes golfing with my son. He likes joking around with the white boys at work. He doesn't like me."

"I think Mark's cheating on me," she slid in.

"Gina, don't start. You have no proof of that other than what your ex did. Stop doing that to Mark. You have a good man."

"He may be a good man, but I don't trust him. I'm probably going to eat this whole weekend worried about it."

"Worrying isn't going to change anything, believe me."

"Do you mind if I stay here tonight? I don't want to be alone."

"No problem, Gina." I had to say that because that's what she would have said. When I was going through my thing or two with Derwin and then Keith, she always listened. She was a better friend to me than I was capable of being to her, but tonight I could pretend to care when in actuality I gave a shit less. I wish that's all I had to worry about, whether my husband—something I never had—was cheating on me. She didn't know how good she had it.

It seemed kind of like the old times when Gina would sleep over and we'd stay up all night gossiping. Only this was much better because I didn't have to worry about my father embarrassing me with all his loud talking, cussing, and complaining. I didn't have to worry about my mother coming in saying, "Lights out. You ladies go to bed now." I don't know why my parents irked me more than they did my other siblings. Maybe because I was the youngest and I was more sensitive to everything. At one time I was Dad's favorite—until a simple mistake. Okay, maybe it's wasn't simple, but a mistake nonetheless cost me a father.

I'd be glad when the next day came so Gina could leave my house and go back to wait on her husband's phone call.

29

Porter

I heard it again. I was listening to the radio while I rode northbound on the Lodge freeway heading toward Northland Mall to go to Target. This was the second time in less than an hour that The New Millennium Comedy tour, starring Hoffa and Earl T was being advertised on 103.9.

It was just like Hoffa planned, a tour of the black college campuses. The first show was close to home at Central State University in Wilberforce, Ohio, starting next month, February 5.

I guess Hoffa was able to run his idea by Damion himself. Especially after Hoffa made sure he really did rule me, the middleman, out, but I guess I should be thankful they spared my life.

I couldn't remember exactly what I needed from Target, probably something for my apartment. I'd think of it eventually. Sometimes, I just had to go about my day and wait for my mind to catch up with my body. It always did eventually. I had been out of the hospital for a little more than two weeks, but the headaches still came regularly. All of the swelling on my face went down and my dizziness seemed to have stopped.

When I pulled into Target's parking lot, I remembered I needed to buy some basic household items like toilet tissue and laundry detergent. It was crowded like I knew it would be on a Saturday afternoon. I pushed the cart around for almost an hour, looking at things, wondering if I already had them at my place or whether or not I needed them. That's when my cart bumped into Adrienne's. "Excuse me," I said to her. I looked into her face and noticed it was carrying a natural glow. Her skin had cleared up and her braces were off. This was the first time I really looked at her features. She was actually kinda cute.

"Oh, hello, Porter," she said, barely looking in my direction as she maneuvered her cart around mine. That's when I noticed a man walking down the aisle with some laundry detergent in his hand, smiling. I kept pushing my cart down the aisle, but as I was turning, I looked down it. The man had stopped at Adrienne's cart and placed the detergent inside. "What else do we need?" she asked him.

"Whatever you want? Whatever you think we need, honey." he said. I smiled. Maybe that psychic of hers was right. Maybe she would be married soon. There's somebody out here for everyone, but I'm tired of playing the waiting game.

I got to thinking about that psychic again. The things he told me, no one could guess, and no one else other than my family knew. So what was it about this woman I was going to save? Maybe I needed to go back to the psychic. I couldn't really remember which apartment building it was. I started to walk back and ask Adrienne for the address, but I shrugged it off. I still didn't want to mess around with fortune telling. What was going to happen would happen. I don't think I need to know in advance.

30

Winona

"Mom!" Sosha yelled at the top of her lungs from her room. "I see a mouse. Come get it, Mommy! Come get it, come get it!" I heard her little feet running in place on the floor above me. The kids were stressing me out. Sosha because she should have stayed over her grandparents the entire weekend since she loved them so much. I thought after Gina left this morning, I could have a day of peace, but Sosha had to call crying she missed Samson and me.

"Mommy," she said through the ugly cry, the one that made her sound like a cow, "come get it!" she screamed.

"Sosha, it's smaller than you. It's not going to do anything. I put poison down; it'll die eventually.

"Take me back over Grandma's house."

"Sosha, go in Carlton's room."

"Take me over Grandma's!" Sosha continued screaming while she ran in place, still acting like a baby.

As soon as she turned ten two weeks ago on January 10, her period came. Not the day before or the day after but on her birthday. "Take it back!" she yelled when she saw the blood. "It hurts." I tried to keep from laughing, but I howled because it was so funny. Not that my baby was in pain, but it was the way she said it. She thought she was dying, and I thought ten was too young for her to start her menstrual cycle. Mine didn't come until I was twelve. Besides that, she was still such a little baby and a menstrual cycle signaled womanhood. After reality set in that my little girl was going to be a woman, I locked myself in my room that evening and pictured her dating, making some of the same foolish mistakes I did. Only she'd be exposed to more men than I was because she's going to be such a beautiful young woman. I don't know if that's good or bad. Maybe the men will treat her better or maybe her looks will wear off in their eyes and they'll eventually treat her the same way they did me.

I walked upstairs to see about the mouse. When I opened Sosha's door, she was balled up on her bed, shaking and pointing underneath the radiator.

"I'm sure it's gone now," I said.

"It's under there, Mommy. Chewing. Listen."

I stood silent. Listening to the rattle coming from the radiator.

"Maybe it's the heat knocking against the pipes."

"It's the mouse! There it goes!" she shouted as something scurried from the baseboard and went into the closet, causing me to jump.

"You want to come in the room with me?" I asked.

She nodded and flew off the bed with her comforter. I tried to relax in my bedroom on my bed with Sosha hugging my waist while she watched television.

She fell asleep after a couple of hours of staring at the tube. I turned the radio to Matchmaker in the midst of Earth Wind & Fire's "Reasons." Deep down I was hoping that after the music stopped playing I'd hear a man to whom I wanted to write. The first caller went by the code name Lovable. His voice was deep and sexy enough for me to imagine him saying that he wanted to make love to me. After he started describing himself, I became even more interested. I took my pen and paper out of my desk drawer to take down the station's address, but quickly threw it back inside because the more he started talking the more I detected lies. He wanted the listeners to believe that he played for the Detroit Lions, but then it went from he played for the Detroit Lions to he was in the Lions camp to his best friend was a Lion. Then he had four kids no, I'm sorry, five. He had so many that I guess he lost count. His five and my two, that's half a class. No, thank you.

When Nikki ended the call with him, she provided listeners with the telephone number to the station and invited the ladies to call. "Yes, I'm talking to you, young lady, the one sitting at home with rollers in your hair on a Saturday night and nowhere to go, but if you had that special someone, could you imagine what your night would be like?"

I let out a deep sigh, picked up my cellular, and walked into my bathroom. I locked the door and promised not to hang up this time.

"Nikki Taylor's Matchmaker," a man said. "Are you calling to be matched up?"

"Yes," I said with a trembling voice.

He told me that Nikki had one caller ahead of me. I sat on the closed toilet lid, tapping my bare feet while I examined my freshly painted French pedicure. He started asking me questions. Asking for my code name and my real name. I didn't have a code name, but I said Sincerely out of the blue. He asked for my address and phone number. I was giving up a lot of information to a stranger. He explained that when they received letters from male listeners who wanted to meet me, they would forward those on to me. The rest would be up to me.

"You're going to be on the air in five, four, three, two, one."

"Sincerely," Nikki said, "how are you this evening?"

"I'm fine."

"You sound nervous. Are you nervous?"

"Yes."

"Don't be nervous, because you are not the first one to do this and you won't be the last. So, Sincerely, tell us about yourself."

31

Porter

It was February and cold outside, but hot inside the church, a combination of the crowd of almost a thousand and a lack of functioning central air. I removed my suit jacket and rolled up the sleeves to my white shirt. I came to the church on Sunday for early-morning service. I came alone and wore a suit for the first time since my high school graduation. I was here because Zeander invited me to his church to hear the bishop's sermon, "Taking Control of Your Life." Even though I didn't see Zeander, I knew he was there because he was always in church; it was his second home. He attended both Sunday services 8:00 A.M. and 11:00 A.M. and went to Thursday night Bible study and early-morning prayer every day he wasn't working. I only came because I promised him I would and because I felt that I needed to hear how I could take control of my life since it had been so out of control lately.

Ever since the accident, I hadn't felt the same. My head bothered me a lot, especially in the last week. Probably because I knew Reesey was due to give birth any day. Even though it had been almost two full months since I left the hospital, there was still a constant pounding. I prayed for a healing but so far things inside my head remained the same.

I sat in the second to the last row of the balcony on the end next to a large woman who used the church bulletin as a fan and her hands to wipe the big sweat bullets dripping from her forehead. I could remain incognito all the way up there, away from those with two Bibles (King James and Amplified) in their possession, fat highlighters to soak up the text, and notebooks to jot down the bishop's every word.

It took me several minutes to locate scripture. I would listen to the bishop and try to follow along as fast as I could, but I couldn't keep up.

The part that made me the most uncomfortable was when he had us turn to our neighbor and say things like, "I'm taking control." This was happening every ten or fifteen minutes.

"The devil thinks he has my mind made up, but I'm taking control," I said to several people around me.

The bishop stood gripping a cordless microphone. "Some of you need to be loosed. Loosed from anger. Whatever it is that's got you so bitter. Let it go. Turn to your neighbor and say, 'I'm letting it go.' "

"I'm letting it go," I said to the woman beside me and the man behind me and the one beside him.

"Whatever it is, I'm letting it go," the bishop said.

"Whatever it is, I'm letting it go," I repeated.

"Please turn to Leviticus 20, verse 10. Leviticus 20:10 says, 'And the man that committeth adultery with another man's wife, even he that committeth adultery with his neighbor's wife, the adulterer and the adulteress shall surely be put to death.' You're playing with fire and sooner or later you're going to get burned. Turn to your neighbor and say, 'I'm putting the matches down.' "

"I'm putting the matches down," I dragged out.

"Loose yourself from temptation. A woman on the job told you nobody has to know. I know you're married. I know you've got children, but don't nobody but you and me need to know. What about God? Does He not know? Loosed. Loosed from addiction. It's people sitting at home, making excuses of why they don't want to come to church. Talking about the saints. Saying that Christians got too many problems. Looking at you like you have two heads when you start to preach the Word. And they're right. Everybody in here has a problem, and everybody in here knows the solution. At least they should. It ain't no forty ounce. It's not cocaine. It's not taking your mortgage and your car note and your grocery money and going down to the Mirage to play the slot machine either. It's not another woman's husband. No other man's wife. It's not pornography. And if that's what you think it is, you need to be loosed."

I watched as hundreds of people from below jumped to their feet and raised their hands toward the ceiling. "Don't think because you're in here shouting at the top of your lungs that you're saved. Not if you're a sanctified sinner. Turn to Matthew 7, verse 15. I'm going to read this from the Amplified version: 'Beware of false prophets who come to you dressed as sheep, but inside they are devouring wolves.' You think God don't see you out partying on Saturday. You're hoeing on Saturday and hallelujahing on Sunday. Some of you been carrying around secrets for years. Now the secret has become bigger than your own life. I'm not talking about choosing to stay private about what you do in your life. I'm talking about secrets that could destroy lives and families."

During the middle of the bishop's sermon, I left quietly because all this was hitting too close to home.

———

I walked through the parking lot looking for the Mercedes CLK. Sometimes that happened. I'd forget about things and it took a while for me to remember that things weren't the way my mind was telling me. I didn't drive a CLK anymore. I was driving my mother's old BMW, which my father gave me on loan after his short-lived marriage died. So that's what I needed to start looking for, Mom's white convertible BMW 323.

———

As I drove, I thought about what the bishop was saying for a quick second. Long enough to discard almost every word. If Pam and Damion's marriage did break up, I wasn't completely to blame. If Damion could have kept his dick in his pants, none of this would have happened. I wouldn't have had Pam crying on my shoulder. I wouldn't have been weak to her request and to my fantasies. It would have stayed as only a thought in my head. I didn't know if they were still together. I didn't have anyone to ask. Hoffa helped beat my ass so I wouldn't exactly say we were on speaking terms. Even if Pam did try to call me, my cell and home phone were both new numbers; so was my pager. I didn't know. I always was cautious and felt like I had to watch my back just from the Detroit element always lingering, but never from people I knew. Now, I'm really paranoid. I'm not sure if Damion meant to kill me and didn't or if he meant to keep me alive. I kept thinking one day he might finish the job, him or one of his boys.

The faint ring of my cellular was coming through the center car console. I raised it and started rambling through my CDs until I had the small flip phone in my grasp. "This Porter."

"Reesey's mother called and said she had a girl. Seven pounds, eight ounces," Mom said over running water. "Reesey named the baby Portia. She was born at 5:58 A.M."

"So are you going down there?" I asked.

"That's your responsibility. You need to go just in case that girl isn't lying. I can't see her doing it twice unless she's really off. Go there and tell me if I'm a grandmother for real this time."

"Guess where I'm pulling up to?"

"I'm not in to guessing games. Where are you, Porter?"

"Outside Grandma's old house. Well, it's not a house anymore." Mom didn't respond, but I knew she was still there. It was only fair that she be forced to think about what happened even after nineteen years. I had to think about it every day for the rest of my life so she needed to feel bad for her part for at least one day, and Dad needed to feel bad for his part too. Neither one of them were around when we needed them. My brother and I were just like orphans, only we knew who are parents were. Instead of leaving us on a church step or hospital admittance, they left us with relatives while they went around pretending to be single. Living their lives while they destroyed ours. One day, I might let my parents know exactly how I felt growing up. I might have to tell them that because of my childhood I feel like I'm going to be fucked up for life. If it mattered any I'd do it today, but since my brother's not coming back anyway my mother might as well go on pretending that she did the best she could.

"You don't need to be there. Why don't you go to the hospital, Porter? Think about life instead of death." She hung up the phone because she was too afraid I might say something she didn't want to hear.

I sat in the car for a while longer until seven digits popped into my head that I decided to call. I didn't know to whom they belonged. I was starting to have problems with my long-term memory. Some things that happened before the beating were just a blur.

"Hello," a woman's voice said.

"Hello, who is this?" I asked.

"Who is this?" she asked back with attitude.

"Porter."

"Boo. Boo, I was wondering when you were going to call me."

"Who is this?"

"You called me. You didn't know you called Vanity?"

"Who? I don't know a Vanity."

"Jade, boo."

The minute I heard that name, all the memories of him came flooding back. We talked long enough for me to find out he wasn't doing anything. I probably thought about him subconsciously because he only lived a few blocks from where I was.

I invited him to go to the hospital with me to see my baby. Even though Jade knew Reesey, she would never in a million years recognize this Jade renamed Vanity, and Reesey would be so jealous of her body, which was why I wanted to take Vanity along.

———

I allowed Vanity to walk ahead of me so I could watch him sashay down the hospital halls. I shook my head because he was overdoing his femininity. Women didn't walk, talk, or act the way Jade did, but I didn't say anything because sometimes I had a tendency when I got started to fly off the handle, even more now after my head injury than before, so I had to teach myself how to remain silent all over again.

I was in the hospital, staring at the babies behind the glass, wishing one of them belonged to me, even though I didn't have a wife, and no business wanting a child, but I did. I wanted a baby bad. Boy or girl, I was going to be a good daddy and prove the world wrong about black men.

I smiled as I looked at the baby with the pink hat on her head. Felt joy in my heart. Then I remembered that I did the same thing with the other one, and look what happened.

"Do you want to go inside and hold the baby?" a nurse asked. "Parents can go in." I walked inside the nursery and over to the baby. A sticker with the name Portia Washington was attached to the basinet.

Jade stayed behind the glass smiling with envy at my little one.

I looked down at the baby and I knew. I could tell from her stretch, from the wiggle of her tiny nose, and those fat cheeks—this was my baby. I held her as I sat in a rocking chair. I had the baby, but I didn't want the mama.

"Would you like us to take a picture? We have a Polaroid."

I nodded and smiled.

"Say cheese!" the nurse said.

"Cheese." I put a wide grin on my face. The lights from the flash disturbed me. I stood and quickly handed my baby over to one of the nurses. I took a few steps forward, toward the door, but felt my feet sliding from underneath me.

———

"Good thing you were already in the hospital when you passed out," the doctor said as he looked down at me. I was tucked tightly under a bedsheet, trying to figure out why I kept having dizzy spells and blacking out, one time while I was at work. Luckily, I wasn't responding to a fire, I was just picking up a few things from E&J Market to take back to the firehouse. Still, the department sent me home until I received clearance from my doctor saying that I could return, which took nearly a month.

"This seems like it's more than a concussion," I said, struggling to get the first few words out.

"We're going to transfer you to your own hospital within the hour, but I've already consulted with your doctor and recommended an MRI."

"What's an MRI? You mean like a scan?"

"Yes, a scan. With that, any problem that may be going on inside of your head will be identified."

"What do you think the problem is?"

"In my opinion it's a subdural hematoma."

"Excuse me for my ignorance, but what is that?"

"A tearing of blood vessels in your brain."

"That doesn't sound too good."

"Well, that's why I'm suggesting an MRI, because it's not that good but some forms are better than others. It's possible that you have a chronic subdural hematoma. In that case, a surgeon can operate, drain the blood, and you should be fine."

"So I'm going to need surgery?"

"More than likely you may."

"Be straight with me, doc. What is the worse that can happen? I'm a firefighter; I can handle it. What's the worse?"

"Assuming it's the chronic form and not the acute one, then permanent brain damage is about the worse that could happen."

"Oh, is that all, " I said sarcastically. "I thought I had something to worry about. Just permanent brain damage, huh? So, I'll be like a vegetable. I mean that's the worse, right?"

"But with surgery, you wouldn't have to worry about that."

"And if it's the acute form?"

"Considering the time frame, I don't believe it's the acute form. Usually the symptoms occur very soon after the head injury."

"But if it is?" I asked.

"Acute hematoma can be fatal. Either way, I wouldn't recommend you going back to work for a while, and you'll probably need someone looking after you. You're married, right?"

"It's just me, myself, and I."

"She said she was your wife?"

"Who said?" The doctor and I looked over at Jade who was standing near the entrance smiling and waving. "That's not my wife. He's a friend."

"He?" the doctor asked, puzzled.

"I mean she. Doc, I can't miss work. I want to go back to work as soon as possible. I don't like sitting around."

"I'm not your doctor, but if I were, I'd have you out for at least three to six months."

"Like a vegetable."

An orderly stood at the entrance to the room with a wheelchair. He looked at the doctor for permission to enter, and at the doctor's request he wheeled the chair in and over to my bed with his head turned in Jade's direction.

"I guess they're ready to take you to your hospital now," the doctor said as he pulled the metal bar down on my bed, and assisted me from the bed into the wheelchair.

"Doc, remember you said it was a good thing I was already at the hospital?"

"Yes."

"Why was I here?"

I saw the Adam's apple in his throat move. "You were in the nursery. I believe you were visiting your baby."

I didn't say another word because I didn't know what the hell he was talking about.

32

Winona

I was sitting at the kitchen table taking off my Via Spaga spike-heeled boots that were probably too jazzy for the office, but, oh well, I wore them anyway, along with my brown Donna Karan pantsuit and my cashmere coat. In a couple more months, I'd have to store all my winter clothes and start shopping for some spring clothes. I loved winter clothes the most. I could really hook up some suits and boots. I looked like I had just stepped from the pages of *Vogue*. Too bad my day didn't go as good as I looked. It seemed like the meetings were coming more regularly and we were getting farther away from any type of concept and no closer to a car. Besides that, Jonathan, one of the car designers, was irritating me with all of his idiotic ideas. I wish we didn't have to be divided into two-person teams like his dumb-ass suggestion.

We were all one big team, which was hard enough on me since I was the only black outside of Tyler, and the only female. Then, Jonathan shoots up his hand at the last meeting and comes up with a brainchild of an idea, suggesting we scale down to smaller focus groups to help with our creative process. You could tell he didn't take the time to really think it out. He just wanted to add something because Tyler made it clear that he appreciated participation at meetings.

I rolled my eyes the minute I heard Jonathan speak, and I didn't care who saw me. Unfortunately, Tyler was looking right at me, but he sort of grinned, and I had no idea what that meant.

I watched Sosha storm into the house, swinging her book bag and fat braids as she headed for the stairs. Carlton was following closely.

"Can we call Daddy today?" she asked right before her foot hit the first step.

"Later on," I said, rubbing my temples. In the car on my way back from picking them up from their grandparents, Carlton was trying to talk about the car he wanted me to buy him—a PT Cruiser. I cut him off in mid-sentence. I had already decided to buy him a new car for his seventeenth birthday, but I was keeping it as a surprise. July would be here before I could blink. He only had five months to wait, but if he didn't shut up, I'd give him a car all right. One run by batteries and a remote control.

"Mom," Carlton said as he walked over to me and shrugged, "I'm not trying to get on your nerves."

"Yes, you are Carlton. Yes, you are. Because if you weren't you wouldn't be standing here. You didn't ask me how my day was. All you started doing was negotiating for a car."

"I was just going to tell you what Grandma and Granddad said."

I sighed. "What did they say?"

"They said if you got the car they'd pay for the insurance."

"Do you know how old I was when they bought me a car?" He didn't respond because he already knew the answer. "They never got me one. They never even allowed me to drive one of theirs. I was in college before I got my driver's license. Something I should have gotten at sixteen. Now they want to play nice, do for you what they never did for me. Boy, you don't know how good you got it. Now get on out my face."

Carlton stormed up the stairs, slamming his door so hard I swore it had to be hanging off the hinges. "Don't try me, boy!" I yelled to him. I had a real bad day. It started when I walked in and Tyler said I was stepping too far ahead of myself. "Why, because I have ideas?" I asked him.

"No, because you're making the guys a little nervous." He meant the white guys. The kind of white guys who found it hard to believe that a black woman was holding such a high-powered position. I'm sure they think I'm part of the same diversity initiative of which Bradley is a part. It's amazing how a company like Bradley that's considered fifty-one percent minority has only one minority outside of Tyler on this project—me. Supposedly, it looks a lot different at the Chicago head-quarters, but I wasn't sure about that. I wasn't sure about Bradley or this position anymore. It felt real temporary.

The phone rang half a dozen times before either one of my kids thought about answering.

"Mommy," Sosha yelled, "it's Gina."

"Tell her I'm busy," I yelled back.

A few seconds later Sosha responded with, "She said no you're not, pick up the phone, and stop acting funky. That's what she said, Mommy, not me."

I guess Gina knew me a little too well. I took a deep breath and walked over to the wall phone. "Hello, Gina. How are you doing this evening?" I asked in the friendliest voice I could fake.

"I've been meaning to call you. I heard you on Matchmaker the other night. That was you, wasn't it?"

"Maybe."

"It was. I know your voice. So, have you gotten any responses yet?"

"That was about a week ago. I called the station back the next day and told them I changed my mind and not to forward any of the responses."

"Winona, why? You should try to meet somebody. Even if it is through a radio show."

"After I realized how stupid the whole thing was I just didn't want to be bothered."

"Why was it stupid, Winona?"

"Because it's meeting someone blindly."

"So what? I have a friend at work who met her husband through the paper."

"Is she white?"

"Yes. What's that have to do with anything?"

"They can do that. We can't. I don't know why that is, but it is."

"I'm sure black people have done it too."

"I haven't known any to, have you?"

"You're making excuses. I'm going to have Mark introduce you to one of his coworkers. He's recently divorced, but he's a real good catch."

"I don't want to meet a man who is recently divorced. There are all kind of problems right there."

"Well, what kind of man do you want?"

"I don't want one at all."

"So you want a woman?"

"Why is it that if a woman doesn't want a man that means she's a lesbian? How many times do I have to tell you there aren't any more Marks left. I'm learning to be content alone."

"It's only natural to want a man if you're a woman."

"Well, Gina, my relationships with men haven't been natural."

"I wonder why that is. Let's look at the men you've chosen and start from there."

"Hello, Gina. Can you hear me?" I asked, shaking the handset to the wall phone and pretending to have trouble on the line. "I think my cordless is going dead. I'll call you back later, bye-bye."

"Mommy," Sosha shouted as she ran down the stairs, "let's call Daddy now."

I rolled my eyes. Every time I had to dial those eleven digits, my insides felt like they were coming out. "All right. All right." I stood by the wall phone, looking down at her, hoping that the phone would keep ringing like it was so I could hang up, but just as I started to, a woman answered.

"Who is this?" the woman asked before I had a chance to hand Sosha the phone.

"This is Winona. I was calling for my daughter."

"Winona! You're the bitch that gave Keith AIDS. You have a lot of nerve calling here. He's dead," she barked.

"What?" I asked, confused. I covered the phone. "Sosha, he's still in the hospital."

"Still? Can we call the hospital?"

"No, go upstairs. Go right now. I'll be up there." I watched Sosha run upstairs.

"Hello!" the woman screamed. "I said, he's dead, but I don't understand how he's dead and you're still alive when you're the bitch that gave it to him."

"No, I didn't give him shit," I whispered as I stretched the phone to the steps and looked around. "Let's get this straight. He gave it to me. He went both ways."

"You're a lie and the truth ain't in you."

"You can believe whatever you want to believe. When did he die?"

"I'm not telling *you*."

"I have a child by him so I have a right to know."

"Um, too bad."

I heard a dial tone. "Hello. Hello." My fingers started rapidly pressing the buttons on the phone. She didn't have to tell me anything. I could find out from his parents. "Mrs. Kemp," I said after she answered.

"Winona," she said with little life in her voice. "Do you know about Keith?"

"Is it true?"

"Yes, it's true. Keith died last night. He battled it for as long as he could. He just couldn't hang on any longer. That car hit him head-on. He was in a coma for a while, but his internal injuries were just too severe."

"A car hit him?"

"Yes. Keith had been drinking. You know how he liked to drink."

"He died in a car accident? Are you sure?"

"Of course I'm sure. How did you think he died?"

"I didn't know. His girlfriend wouldn't tell me much."

"Don't even mention her. She's trash. She fed Keith drugs and alcohol."

"I'm sorry, Mrs. Kemp."

"Are you going to let the kids come to the funeral?"

"When is it?"

"This weekend. You have to let the kids come. I'll pay for their airfare and pick them up from the airport. They have to show their last respects to their father."

"Of course they can come."

"Are you coming?" she asked.

I paused. I couldn't. Not even to show my last respects, because I had none for him.

After I ended the conversation with Mrs. Kemp, I walked upstairs preparing myself to hear Sosha's cries. I was numb about Keith's death, wondering how he ended up the way he did—lost, when he came from such a good family. I don't know what happened or if anything has to happen for a child to turn out bad. Like I've always heard, every family has a black sheep, and some have herds. When I met Keith, I knew he smoked marijuana from time to time and liked to drink beer but no hard liquor. After we split, I could tell his life went down. I'm not saying it's because we split, but that's when I noticed it.

The television was blaring through Carlton's closed door.

I could see Sosha sitting at her desk doing homework. I never had to remind her to do her schoolwork; it was her passion, like sketching cars was mine.

I didn't know which room to enter first. It would probably make more sense to tell Carlton since he was the oldest, and he could help me tell Sosha, but since Carlton and Keith were never close and I knew, even though Carlton didn't, that Keith wasn't his real father, I felt more compelled to go to Sosha, but I followed what I felt was proper protocol and knocked on Carlton's door.

"Carlton, open the door. It's important." He lowered the volume to the television, but as I stood waiting, I didn't hear any movement from inside his room. "Carlton, did you hear what I said? I need to talk to you." It didn't take long before his door opened, revealing his long face frowning at me. "I have some bad news, Carlton," I said as I walked into his room, closing the door behind me.

"What kind of bad news?"

"It's about," I cleared my throat, "your father."

"What about him?"

I cleared my throat once more. "He was involved in a car accident and he didn't make it."

"So he's dead?" I nodded. "Okay."

"That's all you have to say is okay?" I asked.

"I don't care like you don't care."

"How do you know I don't care?"

He gave me a look like I was slow. "Because I'm not stupid like Sosha. It was pretty obvious that you couldn't stand that man."

"That *man* was your father."

"Was he? Didn't seem like it."

"Well he was," I said, slamming the door behind me.

"Mommy," Sosha said, running out into the hallway, "come help me study for my science test. If I get anything less than an A on this test, I'll die. You don't want me to die do you, Mommy?" I looked down at her and started crying. "What's wrong, Mommy? I'm not really going to die."

"Sosha, let's go to my room."

I took her hand, mentally rehearsing how I was going to tell her that her daddy was in a better place. How we all had to die eventually and when we die we go to heaven and get to live with God and the angels. I was going to tell her that she could still talk to her daddy, just not over the phone.

33

Porter

I was lying flat on my back with my head pointing toward the ceiling. I kept my eyes steady on the lights above me. There was a possibility that this would be the last time I saw light, artificial or otherwise, so I wanted to remember how good it felt even in this sterile environment.

The doctor who saw me right after I collapsed in the hospital was right. I had a hematoma and had to get it removed. Three weeks after collapsing, I was back for surgery. For some reason, I couldn't escape that place.

"Are you okay?" one of the nurses asked.

"Not considering the circumstances."

She smiled quickly, probably out of pity.

The surgeon would have to drill burr holes into my skull then open a section to remove the large hematoma, so I wouldn't say I was okay. Besides that I didn't want to be put to sleep, that's the way my dad's sister, Eartha, died.

"Everything's going to be fine," she said. I'm sure that's what they're trained to say. I knew I'd find myself in a hospital eventually, but I thought it would be from smoke inhalation or first-degree burns. Never would I have thought my brain would be bleeding. "In just a few minutes I'm going to start counting, and I want you to repeat each number I say. Okay?" She stepped aside, allowing a short, thin white man to step in front of her.

He picked up a large needle and squirted fluid out of it a few times before aiming it into my vein. "Don't be alarmed. It's going to sting a little and you'll feel pressure," he said.

"I'm a big boy. I can handle it." I flinched when the long, thin needle pierced my skin.

"Porter, I'm going to start counting," the nurse said. "Repeat after me. One."

"One," I said.

"Two."

"Two," I said.

"Three."

"Three."

"Four."

"Fo..."

According to the surgeon, the operation was a success. They were able to remove the hematoma, but now I was on phenytoin, an anticonvulsant drug that was supposed to help prevent seizures. I still had to suffer the effects of memory loss, attention problems, and anxiety for some time, possibly as long as six months, and another blow to the head, even a fall in which my head was hit severely, could kill me. The problem was the doctors were acting like maybe I wouldn't be able to go back to work for another eight to twelve weeks. Everything depended on my progress. I was willing to sit out for a month at the most, but after that I was going to show progress, even if I had to fake it.

I'd been in the hospital for a week and was due to be released on Wednesday, just a couple of days away.

The phone started ringing. Every time the phone rang in the hospital room, I'd look over hoping there was Caller ID. Didn't matter who it was, because there wasn't anyone I wanted to talk to. I only wanted to talk to God and my brother, but I wasn't sure if either wanted to hear from me.

The phone wouldn't stop ringing. Usually my nurse would answer it for me and say I was sleeping, but she had stepped out of the room so I set the Bible down on my lap and picked up the phone. "Hello," I said.

"Did you mean what you said yesterday?"

"Jade, what did I say?"

"Porter, please call me Vanity. Did you mean it?" he screamed.

"I can't even remember talking to you yesterday. What did I say?"

"You said you never wanted to see me again. You screamed it to the top of your lungs and started pointing your finger toward the door telling me to take my queer ass home. Then when the nurse came you said, 'that's a man. Did you know that was a man?' "

"I didn't say all that."

"Yes, you did. Did you mean it?" I started rubbing my temples. "Did you, boo?"

"Yeah, I meant it! If I said it, I meant it! Damn! I'm in the hospital trying to recover and all you can do is bug me with that shit. I don't want to ever see you again. My brother told me not to deal with you. You not right, and you ain't never going to be right."

"Your brother is dead."

"And so are you!" I shouted. "You killed yourself when you changed your sex." I lowered my voice. "Just don't call me no more, okay?"

"Do you mean it? Don't say it if you don't mean it."

"I mean it."

"Okay. Always remember that I love you."

I slammed the phone down. I was tired of hearing that bullshit.

34

Winona

It was the middle of May. I had almost been in Detroit for one full year for all it had been worth. I had to sneak and go to the hospital once a month, praying each time that I entered the Detroit Medical Center I didn't see anyone I knew. Then I had to plead with Dr. Gant to wait before putting me on the medication. "Give me a few more months of testing to see if the results are consistent. If they are, I promise I'll take the medication without question." My personal life was my kids and listening to that stupid Matchmaker show. That's all I had. That's all I was ever going to have.

Sosha was getting better with handling the death of her father. She cried for the whole day when I told her, but when she came back from the funeral nearly three months ago, she seemed to be at peace. She showed me the obituary and told me about her cousins who were there from California whom she had never met. She was taking it better than I had expected. Carlton, on the other hand, didn't say one word about the funeral. Other than stressing how glad he was to be back. They only stayed two days. Before Sosha walked upstairs to go to her room that first night back, she hugged me real tight and told me she never wanted me to die. Ever.

"We all have to die sooner or later, Sosha."

"Not you. Never you."

Carlton was sitting at the breakfast table watching me straighten the kitchen. "Are you going golfing this morning?" I asked.

He shook his head. "This afternoon."

"Is Mr. Roundship back from Chicago?"

"Yep. Why do you call him Mr. Roundship? I call him Tyler."

"So do I, but he's an adult and I've already told you that you should call him Mr. Roundship."

"Please, when we're out on the course, he's the kid, and I'm the adult so he better respect me because I show no mercy."

"I guess you like golfing with him. Maybe he can be a role model for you."

"I like golfing. Don't matter who it's with, but I wouldn't exactly call him a role model. He thinks he's some big corporate hotshot. His ego is bigger than the state of Texas, and I love when I beat him and burst it. Hey, did I tell you that the last time we golfed, he was asking about you?"

"Asking about me in what way?" I asked.

"What you like to do and who you're seeing."

"He was asking all that?"

"Yeah. I think he might like you."

"What did you tell him?"

"I told him that you weren't seeing anybody, but that you were looking because you called the Matchmaker show."

"Why did you tell him that?" I took the dishes out of the sink and threw them into the dishwasher.

"Because I heard you on the radio."

"I wasn't on the radio."

"Mom, I know your voice."

"Even still, that was a long time ago—" I looked at Carlton like he was insane—"why would you tell him that? I'll never be able to look at that man the same again."

"Chill out, Mom. It's not that deep. He was surprised that you were that desperate."

"Desperate?"

"I mean, he didn't say desperate. That's just what I'm saying."

"I don't want to talk about this anymore."

"Cool." He walked over to the refrigerator and opened one of the side-by-sides.

"Besides, why is he worried about it?"

"I doubt if he's worried. You need to go grocery shopping," he said as he closed the refrigerator door. "We're out of milk."

"No we're not, it's on the counter." I took out my Hungry Jack instant pancake mix and started preparing breakfast.

"Mommy," Sosha said as she walked down the stairs holding her pink neon cordless phone, "some man is on the line for you."

"This early," I said.

"That's him," Carlton said. "He said he was going to call you and ask you out for breakfast."

"Shut up," I mouthed to Carlton. "Who's calling?" I asked Sosha. "Ask who's calling."

"Who's calling?" Sosha said into the phone. She covered the mouthpiece with her hand. "Tyler," she whispered back to me.

My eyes enlarged. I wiped my wet hands on my sweatpants and reached for the phone. "Hello."

"Hey. How are you?" Tyler asked.

"Hey. I'm fine. How are you doing? How was your trip?"

"My trip was all business, real short. I was back Friday before midnight."

"You called to speak to Carlton, right?"

"No, I called to speak to you to see if you wanted to go out for breakfast."

"I'm already cooking breakfast, but you're welcome to come over."

"By the time I get over there, I'm sure it'll be cold. What about this? Carlton, Craig, and I are playing at Rackham this afternoon. Would you like to finish off our foursome?"

"I already told you, I don't golf."

"You don't have to golf. You can ride along in the cart. It's very relaxing on the course."

"Let me think about it." I watched both the kids stare into my mouth.

"Afterward, we can drop Carlton off and I can take you out on my boat."

"You have a boat? Must be nice."

"It's just a little thirty-two footer."

"That's a pretty nice size."

"It's okay, but I'm getting a yacht real soon."

"Must be nice."

"You'll see how nice it is."

"I will? How is that?"

"Don't you want to go out on it and relax? You can't be all work, Ms. Fairchild."

"If we're going to go out on the boat, I want you to take me out. I want to cruise the Detroit River."

"We can do that, but I really want you to go golfing with us. Do you have a set of clubs?"

"I have a set of clubs, but I can't go. I have Sosha."

"Can't you find a baby-sitter? Learn to live a little, Ms. Fairchild. Stop shutting yourself out."

————

My head was still. Eyes on the ball. I pulled back on the club the way Tyler showed me. "You're pulling up," Tyler said when I started to complete my swing, causing me to dig a hole in the green instead. "Let me show you." He stood close behind me, but with enough distance so I couldn't feel anything I wasn't supposed to. His arms outlined mine as he pulled my arms up and sideways and then down in one quick sweeping motion.

"I knew this was going to take all day," Carlton said in a huff. "Let me show you how the pros do it." Carlton took out his driver and with ease and precision drove the ball far into the fairway.

"I'm telling you, you've got yourself a prodigy," Tyler said to me.

"Why don't the three of you play?" I asked, observing Carlton and Craig grow impatient. "I'll watch. I don't mind. You know I can't keep up with you guys."

"You sure can't," Carlton said as he swung his golf bag over his shoulder and proceeded to walk down the fairway.

"What am I going to do with him?" I asked.

"You're looking at the next Tiger Woods right there," Tyler said as we watched Carlton take his long strides.

"So I've been told," I said.

They played nine holes instead of eighteen because after the sixth hole the sun starting making me feel dizzy, but I didn't say anything until around the eighth hole. My headache started to bother me so badly that I left them at the beginning of the ninth hole and went to the rest room to take two Tylenol. Within ten minutes, I felt much better but everyone was ready to go then, especially Carlton and Craig who felt put out by my presence.

————

"Have fun on the boat," Carlton said to us after we dropped him off at the house.

I was riding in the passenger seat of Tyler's Mercedes 600 SL. He slid in an Art Porter CD and I started to relax a little until he took my hand. I looked over at him. "I could never say this at work, and I really shouldn't say it now, but I'll put myself out there. I'm very attracted to you. Am I wrong to say that or is the feeling mutual?" he asked.

"It's mutual." I didn't know what else to say. I was attracted to him. He was a very attractive older man with lots of money and power. What woman wouldn't be?

"I just wanted to make sure." He continued holding my hand, gently circling his thumb inside of my palm.

———

I timed how long it took Tyler to speak as we cruised along the Detroit River. After thirteen minutes he asked, "Would you like some wine?"

"No thank you. My head's starting to pound." He turned off the engine. "Why are we stopping?"

"Maybe you'll feel better after you lie down. I have a bed downstairs."

"I don't know, Tyler. I don't think so."

"Come on. We're two adults. What do you think's going to happen?"

I followed him, holding his hand, knowing that if the rumors were true, and I didn't go through with this, my career with Bradley was surely over. I heard about all the women Tyler had in Chicago. Several of them had worked or were working for the company. *We could use a condom,* I thought.

"Take off your clothes," he said as he stood looking down at me.

"Excuse me? Tyler, it's not that kind of party. "

"It's going to be fine. Trust me." He started getting undressed, stripping down to his boxers and stepping out of them to prove just how ready he was for the party to begin. "Take off your clothes," he repeated as he rubbed the forest of hair covering his chest. I couldn't stand a hairy chest. Couldn't stand to feel it rubbing against my skin. He unbuttoned the first button to my short-sleeve knit shirt."We're both attracted to each other." He continued unbuttoning my shirt until my black Victoria's Secret bra was exposed. I felt awkward standing in front of his naked body. I felt even more awkward as he raised my skirt and pulled down my panties."Step out of them." For some reason I did, but I walked away from him. There weren't too many places to go, but I found a corner to stand in. He licked his lips like I was a piece of meat he was about to devour. "Your body looks even better than I imagined."

"I'm sorry, but I can't do this." I picked up my panties from the floor and slipped them back on.

"Woo woo, we can do this, and we will. Don't play, okay."

"We can't, Tyler. We really can't. Don't make me say it," I said, looking away from him.

"What?" he asked.

I didn't want to tell him, but I had to. I had to say it or else he might force himself on me. I closed my eyes and said, "I'm HIV-positive."

"Say what? I hope you're kidding. Please tell me you're kidding."

"I'm not kidding," I said after opening my eyes and looking directly in his face.

"And your diseased ass was going to fuck me? What you trying to do, spread your shit?" He peered down his narrow nose contemptuously.

"I wasn't going to have sex with you," I said

"So why are you standing here naked?"

"Because you took off my clothes."

"You've heard of the word *no,* haven't you?"

"Okay, this was a mistake," I said.

I looked up at him, widening my eyes innocently. He was looking down at me, appearing upset at first, but then he seemed to calm down. His eyes ranged freely up and down my body while he stroked his penis. "I got condoms."

"What?" My jaw dropped.

"I got condoms. I really wasn't going to use one at first. I was willing to risk it, but now that I know, I'll just use a condom."

"Did you hear what I said?"

"Shit, all the unprotected sex I've had, I'll just use a condom. That's what they preach, right, having safe sex, because you never know who has it. Shit, I might and not know it. So that's what we're going to have, safe sex."

————

The noise of the phone ringing woke me from a horrifying nightmare in which I was a bridesmaid in Derwin's wedding.

No one should have been calling this late unless it was Gina calling me back, but I seriously doubted. We had talked for nearly two hours as I filled her in on my horrifying afternoon, skipping over the part of my HIV confession. I told her everything else, and she told me to expect retaliation.

"Hello," I said. "Who is this?"

"Tyler."

I sat up. "Yes."

"You played me today."

"What do you mean I played you?"

"You sprung too many fucking surprises on me. Heat of the moment

I almost fucked you. Thank God I changed my mind."

"You changed your mind? I was the one who said no."

"Like I said, it's a good thing *I* changed my mind. Now, even though I know there aren't any policies about employees working with AIDS."

"I don't have AIDS, I'm HIV-positive."

"Either way, I find you to be dangerous."

"To whom?"

"To me. I'm not in the habit of sitting up every day looking at a fine woman I can't have."

"What are you saying?"

"I don't know what I'm saying yet. I need to think about it. Take care of yourself, and I'll see you on Monday."

35

Porter

I'd been out of the hospital for almost three months and it seemed like I was starting to return to my normal self. Most of my memory was back, but I was still having a little problem with my short-term memory. I stopped taking phenytoin after the first week. I was glad about that because I didn't want to be restricted to taking medication three times a day for the rest of my life. I suppose a better word was *thankful*. I was starting to realize just how thankful I should be for all that I did have, but now I had to do what my brother said and I had to start praising God.

I went back to the church, this time without an invitation and without knowing the topic of the bishop's sermon. I sat in the church sanctuary a few rows from the pulpit. This time I came before praise and worship started. I stood and gave praise to God for what He'd already given me.

Then the moment came near the end of service when the bishop invited all those who wanted to accept Jesus as their savior to come join him at the front. "If my message today has reached you in any way. If you need to be delivered, if you need more than the world, if you need to be made whole, please come to the front."

I looked around, watching the people pour down from the balcony. There were at least one hundred people filling the front of the church with more coming. The bishop began laying hands on them. Something was pushing me. My inner voice said, "Go, Porter. It's your turn. Don't be afraid." I took one step forward.

"Excuse me," a woman said as she pushed passed me in the pew and rushed down the aisle to wait in the crowd with the others.

I didn't move after that. Even after the bishop said, "Jesus will wash away your sins." I had so many. Too many. I didn't want to leave the church though. I needed to be in that place, preparing for the day when I would be able to accept Jesus into my life and live right.

36

Winona

When I got to work, I did something I never do. I fixed myself a cup of coffee, black without sugar or cream. I needed to be wide awake and perky when I entered Tyler's office to feel him out.

I walked slowly down the hallway. The palms of my hands were becoming sweaty and I felt butterflies in my stomach as I came closer to his office and his open door.

He was rocking in his leather chair, stroking the phone cord as he whispered into the receiver.

I stood in the doorway with my arms folded, wondering when or if he was going to acknowledge my presence.

"Hold on for a second," he said to the person on the other end of the phone. "You need something?" he asked.

"I can wait."

He motioned for me to enter. I walked over to his desk and sat in front of him.

"Okay, I'm back. Where was I? I want to take you out tonight. I can fly to Chicago and be there by seven. No, I haven't been in Detroit long enough to have a woman but I've been out with a few, and the ones I've dated seem like a real trip," he said as he stared in my direction.

I looked down at my watch to break his stare.

"I'll come back," I said.

He held up one finger. "Listen, Mom, I'll be at your house later on. I'm going to head to the airport in a few hours. See you soon. I love you." He hung up the phone. "What can I help you with?"

"I need to know the status of the project. I've been hearing things."

"Things like what?" he asked as he stood and walked over to the door to close it then walked back to his desk and sat down.

"Things like I'm reassigned to something that has little if anything at all to do with the auto show. Is that rumor or what?"

"It's or what."

"So it's true?" I asked.

"Didn't you get my email?"

"What email?"

"The one marked confidential," he said.

"When did you send it?"

"Hold on for a second." He swiveled his chair to face his computer screen, which displayed his Lotus Notes, clicked on his mouse before he turned back to face me. "It should be in your in box when you go back to your office. Everything in there is negotiable."

"And what are we negotiating?"

"Look, Winona, you really don't have experience. I was helping a friend of a friend of a friend out by hiring you. I thought things could work out."

"You thought what kind of things could work out? Stop talking in riddles and say it."

He shook his head. "It doesn't matter anymore. Your pay will stay the same because you're under contract, but effective Monday your job title and duties will change."

"To what?"

"Executive assistant."

"You're demoting me?" My eyes bulged from their sockets. "You want me to quit, don't you?"

"No, I don't want you to quit."

"Whose assistant will I be?"

"Jonathan's."

"Like I said, you want me to quit."

"Winona, I don't want you to quit, but who do you think you are?" He turned up his nose while he looked over at me. "Do you know who I am?" He straightened his tailored tie. He always bragged he had all of his ties imported from Italy. Well, at that moment I wanted to walk up behind him, take his tailored tie, and strangle him with it. "I'm the boss and you could have had me. I took you on my damn boat and rode you around the Detroit River, and for what thanks? Leaving me hard and dry, and with the shit you told me. Don't do that to any other man or you might find yourself in the river next time."

"When I first met you, you said you didn't consider yourself anyone's boss. Remember that?"

"I took that straight from a manager's seminar. I am the boss of everyone up in here."

I shook my head and smiled. Not because I was happy, but because I was furious. I wanted to cry, but couldn't. My voice began to quiver as I spoke. "I can't believe you're like this. I should take my complaints to corporate. I used to work for Chrysler. They don't condone this."

"Well, baby, this ain't Chrysler, and what complaints do you have? Oh, that you're not qualified to build them a model so I did what I had to do and demoted your ass back down to what you are qualified to do, which is assist someone who is? Is that what you're going to tell them? I can't jeopardize a big contract on an amateur, especially when it's not completely firmed up yet."

"How can I get out of my contract?"

"You can't. If you quit you're not going to get paid and you'll owe us twenty-five thousand dollars from the relocation package, which I will legally pursue you for. So you might as well stay here for the next year and get paid for not doing shit."

"I knew this wasn't going to work out."

"It could've. If you would've played your cards better instead of exposing your trump. Now, if you could please excuse me, I've got work to do before I cut out of here. Make sure you're out of your office first thing Monday. There'll be a small cubicle with your name on it right outside of Jonathan's office."

"All I want are my sketches. I can get work. Just give me my designs."

"Your designs?" He laughed. "Read your contract. Those designs are the property of Bradley Automotive. I'm sorry, I wish I could stay and chat but, uh, I got a plane to catch."

———

I barricaded myself in the bedroom, throwing anything that wouldn't break against the wall.

"Mommy, what's wrong?" Sosha shouted as she banged on my locked door.

"I'm having a nervous breakdown, Sosha. Please leave me alone."

"Do you want me to call Grandma?"

"Not unless you want me to kill myself."

"What happened, Mommy?"

"Nothing, Sosha. Just leave me alone!"

"Mom," Carlton said, trying to sound like someone's father. He started banging on the door. "Open the door right now, Mom."

"Carlton, leave me alone. Both of you just leave me alone. I'm in the middle of something.

"You must think I'm a fool," I yelled to the air. "Do you really think I gave you my best designs? I still have designs. My mother always told me to save your best for last. Fuck you, Tyler." I took off my pumps and threw them against the closed door.

After I had thrown all my books, shoes, pillows, and clothes, I collapsed on the floor and started softly banging my head against the hardwood. The tears came soon after. How could I think I was worthy of something this big? After I left the office, I went over to the Tech Center to find Jennifer, but she was in Germany on business. Her secretary said she'd be checking her messages daily, but I didn't even leave one. How could someone who put me in this mess now rescue me from it? I was still going to let her know how Tyler was because I'm sure she didn't realize. I had until next year, the summer of 2001, to figure out what the hell I was going to do, and as of now, I didn't have one clue.

"Mom, Gina's on the phone for you," Carlton yelled out.

"I didn't hear the phone ring. Did you call her?"

"Yes, I did."

"Why? Did I tell you to do that?"

"Just pick up the phone."

"Tell her I'll call her back."

"She said if you don't pick up the phone she's coming over."

I crawled over to my nightstand and removed the phone from its cradle. "Hello," I said sternly as I picked myself up from the ground. I stood in front of the mirror on my nightstand, looking at my raccoon eyes and tangled hair.

"Girl, what's the problem?" Gina asked.

"Carlton, hang up the phone." I heard a click, followed by another sound that let me know he was trying to be slick and stay on the line to eavesdrop. "Carlton, hang up the damn phone!" This time he slammed the phone down.

"What happened today at work?" Gina asked.

"You wouldn't believe it if I told you. Let's just say, I got a new position."

"Another promotion?"

"Not quite. More like a demotion. I got my old job back and when the contract is over next June, I'm getting the boot."

"You know why that happened, don't you?"

"Of course I do, I'm not stupid, and besides Tyler made it more than clear."

"Well, girl, that means you've got a sexual harassment lawsuit."

"Not really because I willingly went out with him."

"Yeah, and, so, he's demoting you because you wouldn't sleep with him. He can't do that."

"I can't prove that's the reason why I was demoted. Besides, I was reading back over this joke of a contract and it says right here in section five that an employee of Bradley can be reassigned to a job classification that is above or below his current position without notice or reason. There's so much fine print and mumbo-jumbo throughout these five pages that I have no idea why I even signed on the dotted line."

"You have to call Jennifer."

"I already did. She's in Germany for a month."

"Well, when she comes back you have to call her again. She's going to have to make this right, and you know she will."

I didn't have to call Jennifer because she called me after she heard that I had suddenly taken ill and had been out of the office for two weeks. I convinced my doctor to sign my disability papers, and since it wasn't necessary for me to disclose to my employer what was wrong with me, I could take my vacation in peace, even though I didn't have any peace because I had worried so much I was covered in hives and now I had a genuine reason to stay out.

"I feel so bad," Jennifer said through the phone.

"Don't," I said, wiggling my toes as I ate vanilla ice cream and flipped the television stations with my remote. "I knew it was too good to be true. I should have read what I was signing more carefully."

"Don't worry. I'm consulting with the Office of General Counsel about Bradley as we speak. The company is a fraud, and we're severing the small ties we did have with them immediately."

"What do you mean a fraud?"

"There are some companies who will pretend to be minority based to get major contracts awarded to them. Bradley was supposed to be a part of our diversity initiative to expand our minority supplier base. However, a Bradley competitor, who is going to get the contract, kindly pointed out that Bradley isn't a true minority company. Tyler's just a figurehead. I'm sure he's getting paid a pretty penny, but he doesn't have ownership. They'll probably be sending out pink slips to everyone next week."

"Jennifer, you know I'm not the type to ask for favors but I feel that you owe me one. I need a job."

"I'll get you one. Don't worry."

37

Porter

Mr. Fortier opened his door as I walked by holding my Bible. "How was service today?" he asked.

"Wonderful sermon." I had been attending church regularly, and this Sunday I finally went up for altar call to accept Jesus Christ as my Lord and Savior. A young male counselor took me in the back and read some scripture. He explained to me that I would face many challenges, and he explained how the devil would start attacking me. I was honest with him. I told him that I had a weakness for women, and even though I hadn't had sex in several months, the thought crossed my mind constantly. He told me to pray for strength, self-control, and patience. "Yeah, Mr. Fortier, you should have been there."

"Maybe you can pass along a word to me, son."

"I doubted if I could pass one on to you, but you could probably pass something to me, Mr. Fortier."

"I can try. Come on in."

He stepped aside from his door as I entered his spacious apartment. I didn't expect his place to be so decked out, considering he wore the same pair of no-name black sneakers and what looked to be the same tan pants and plaid shirt.

"Nice place," I said.

"I haven't changed anything since my wife died. She had good taste. Real good taste. She married me, didn't she? So, have a seat."

I sat in a leather chair that he said his wife bought at an Art Van clearance sale for only two hundred dollars.

"Do you want anything to drink?"

"No, thanks. Do you drink, Mr. Fortier?"

"I meant something like water or juice. Not alcohol. You don't drink, do you, son?"

"Sometimes, but no thanks. I don't need anything."

"So, what's troubling you, son?"

"Nothing, really."

"Something is or you wouldn't have asked me for a word. Besides, I knew there was something going on even before you went into the hospital."

"How's that?"

"Watching, observing, and listening. That's all you have to do to find out anything you want to know. I haven't seen that fair-skinned lady come by to visit you anymore. She seemed like she'd make a nice wife, if she wasn't already married." He cleared his throat. "She was married, wasn't she?"

"Yes, Mr. Fortier, she was," I said shamefully.

"I guess her husband found out and that's how you had your accident. What kind of word you need, son? You crash yet?"

"What?"

"Have you hit the bottom step like all young people do sooner or later? I've watched you tumbling, but sometimes you have to let the person fall and hit the bottom step."

"I guess I'm still waiting to crash."

"Don't wait for the crash. Brace yourself. You not on drugs, are you?"

"No, sir."

"That's a good thing, then you definitely don't have to wait for the crash. You have a plan, son? Priorities? Do you know what you want out of life?"

"I know some of the things I want, not all."

"Why don't you talk about those things? That's if you feel like it. I know you keep to yourself most of the time."

"I was reading in the Bible about how God created Eve from Adam's rib. I want that. I need that."

"A woman?" He frowned. "You think so? You think a woman's going to make you better? You ever heard the saying, if you can't come correct, don't come at all?"

"Yeah, I heard it. I plan on coming correct. I can't help what I need. I want a soul mate." I shrugged and then sighed. "I just don't know if that's in God's plan for me."

"I'm sure with continued prayer, your soul mate will come."

"I don't know, Mr. Fortier," I said, dragging my voice. "I've done a lot of dirt to women. It's just been sex, and I've had a lot of it." I dropped my head down into my hand and started shaking my head. "I cheated on my first girlfriend with Reesey. Then I stayed with Reesey for twelve years, and I cheated on her damn near the entire time, but I'd mentally block it out like it never really happened, even convincing myself I was faithful because whenever I was with another woman, I never let out my emotions. Then when I finally decided to settle down, stop trying to do the same thing my boys were doing, she gets pregnant by another man. So what I do? I go right back out there doing the same thing over again but worse, I sleep with my best friend's wife and end up in the hospital beat nearly to death—what goes around comes around I guess."

"Didn't you say you were saved?" I looked at him, but remained quiet. "I mean, if you're truly saved, you have to let go of the person you were out in the world. That's if you're truly saved. I understand you want a woman—a soul mate. You don't need that right now. You're a man so there's nothing wrong with desiring to have a woman. You want a word, right, son? Find yourself, and after you become whole, God can take your rib and bring you the woman you want so badly. Not before, because if he took your rib before you were whole, you wouldn't survive."

I walked back to my studio after Mr. Fortier finished his lecture. I opened the door and looked around. It was a small, lonely space that I was living in.

I shut the door behind me and walked over to my saxophone, removing it from the case. It had been a long time since my lips kissed the brass, but there were two things I'd never forget to do. One was playing the saxophone, the other was playing the drums. I had gotten out of doing both, but I was going to start again. Soon.

My cell phone started to ring right as I blew the first note.

"Yeah," I said, rushed.

"Porter, don't hang up," Jade said. Last time I saw him he was at Northland mall about a week and a half ago. He was with some thug-lookin' dude. The dude was a big guy, sloppy big, around my height. He was iced out. Looked like the doper type. I walked right by them and didn't speak. "When I saw you I almost cried because it brought back memories of how much I love you."

"Who was that dude you were with?" I asked.

"Chester. Nobody."

"He was somebody, because he was holding on to your hand real tight. Did you tell him what you really are?"

"No. Don't start that, okay."

"That's dangerous. What does he do for a living, sling dope?"

"It doesn't matter. I'm not seeing him anymore. I'm getting ready to move to Chicago to be with my mama. I already have a catering job lined up. I'm tired of Detroit people, but I will miss you. Will you miss me?"

"Yeah, Vanity, I'll miss you."

"You got my name right for once. Are you gonna come visit?"

"I can't promise you all that, but take care of yourself, okay?"

"You too. Oh, and hey, you gonna make some woman real happy one day."

"I hope you find what you're looking for out of life, Vanity."

"Oh, I'm fine. Vanity will always be alright, you heard me? But, you, Porter, I hope you find what you're looking for. I'm sorry I could never help you with whatever your problem is."

"Take care." I hung up the phone before the final good-bye. He was the last person from my past, outside of my parents, I still communicated with. Now I felt like I could start fresh.

38

July had finally arrived. It felt like a new beginning because I was assigned to a new job with a new boss, Angel Templeton, who I respected, and not just because she was a female and black but because she had her stuff together. She was married. Had three kids. One had just finished his first year at Howard University. The other two were twin girls in their sophomore year at Cranbrook Academy, a prestigious high school in Birmingham, Michigan that looked and was run like a college, with dorms for the students. Her husband was a VP at Dunn & Associates Advertising, one of the largest advertising firms in the Midwest. They lived in what looked to be a million-dollar house in the Bloomfield Hills subdivision, Wabeek. I didn't look up to her because the back of her house faced water or for the other material things that she had, but more from the way in which she carried herself with all that she did have. I wasn't sure if I had been given her life whether or not I would have been able to carry it off so well. I had a way of messing most everything up, even blessings.

I watched her as she approached me. We both had on our smiles. "Winona, sometime this week I want to further discuss your concept design of the GXT. I'll tell you what I'm thinking later." Angel had already taken an interest in my designs and my portfolio. She asked if it was okay to copy the image of the GXT so she could show a few people, and of course I told her it was.

I booted up my computer and let out a long sigh because I was starting to feel okay about things. I nearly leaped from my seat when my office phone rang because it was so loud. I looked down at the display assuming it was an interoffice call, but it was on one of my outside lines.

On the third ring I answered, "Engineering. This is Winona."

"Winona, I quit," Gina said, laughing. "That B came up to me one last time, talking mess about the length of my phone call with my husband, and I told her I didn't have to take her shit. The woman made me cuss I was so mad, and I walked out."

"Girl, good for you. You didn't need that job anyway."

"Let's meet for dinner to celebrate."

———————

Gina and I decided to meet at The Soul Station. I'd never been before, but I'd heard about their side dishes and I was in the mood for some corn-bread dressing and candied sweet potatoes. I wasn't, however, in the mood for the after-work traffic that was jamming I-75 south. It would taper off after the Eight Mile exit and I'd be able to fly the rest of the way downtown.

"Ribbon in the Sky" played on 103.9, and that song took me way back. I think I was a junior in high school. Derwin had just broken up with another one of his girlfriends, and he needed to see me so he could cry on my shoulder about some other girl. He wanted me to console him. Tell him how stupid the girl was for giving up someone like him. I remember sitting in his convertible Mustang in some abandoned lot off East Jefferson looking across the Detroit River at the Canadian Club sign. The radio station was turned to WJLB 97.9 and "Ribbon in the Sky" was on. For that one moment I knew I was stupid. I knew I could do better, but I didn't know how to do better so I did what I had always done and let the seat go all the way back and watched the windows fog up with our passion.

———————

I was sitting at the booth finishing my glass of water because I had made it to the restaurant before Gina. After waiting for twenty minutes for her to arrive, I couldn't wait another second because I was starving and tired, a lethal combination, so I called her on her cell phone. "Where are you?" I asked after she answered. I was looking straight ahead at a very handsome, dark skin, baldhead brother who appeared to be checking me out. He sort of looked familiar.

"I'm at Soul's Kitchen. Where are you?" she asked.

"Soul's who? You said Soul Station not Soul's Kitchen."

"No, I didn't. I distinctly remember saying Soul's Kitchen because that's closer to both of us. Come on, I'll wait for you. It's on the way to your house, anyway."

"Girl, I'm about to order takeout and call it a day. Are you still going with me tomorrow?"

"Yeah, to pick up Carlton's car, right? I'll be there."

39

Porter

I'll get this order," I said to Tanisha as I moved her aside and watched the pretty lady stand in line with her head tilted up toward the menu board.

"Why, so you can try to mack?" Tanisha asked with her lips puckered.

I ignored her. "Welcome to the Soul Station. May I take your order?" I asked the woman. She was still browsing the menu so she hadn't yet established eye contact.

"Honey, you don't know what you want? 'Cause I know what I want," the woman behind her said.

"This is my first time here," the pretty woman said.

"Um, maybe you need to step aside so you can take your time looking," the other woman said.

"Do you need some help with the menu?" I asked.

"I guess," she said, still looking over my head. When the pretty woman stepped aside to let the other lady order, I did too.

"Okay, you gonna help her, so who's gonna help me?" the other lady asked loudly.

"Tanisha, help this woman," I said.

Tanisha smacked her lips and rolled her eyes. "Welcome to the Soul Station. *May I help you?*" Tanisha asked with deliberate attitude.

I leaned on the counter and waited for the pretty woman to speak.

"Have you ever tried the Side Splash?" I asked, standing up straight again.

"What's the Side Splash?" she asked, finally making eye contact with me. I hesitated when our eyes locked. I knew her from somewhere, but I couldn't remember where, and for the first time in several weeks, I forgot what I was thinking. "What's the Side Splash?" she repeated.

"Tanisha, what's the Side Splash?" I asked.

"What? Don't you know?" Tanisha asked, rolling her eyes. It's a sampling of all our sides along with corn bread and a dessert item."

"That's what it is," I said to the pretty woman.

"Okay, I want that."

"Anything else?" I asked.

"No, that's it."

"One Side Splash to go, please," I yelled into the kitchen through the cutout. "Your name?" I asked as I turned to face her.

"Winona."

I knew that name. I had heard it before. She had told me that name before. "Do we know each other?" I asked.

"No," she said, focusing in on my eyes. "At least I don't think so."

"Your food should be ready in a couple of minutes." I watched her drift away. First toward the tiny waiting area that was standing room only, then out the door. I wanted to go after her and introduce myself, tell her how fine she was. How much of a lady she seemed to be, but then I thought about what the bishop said to the single men at the service on Sunday: "Stop trying to holla at a woman. Every time you see a woman who looks halfway right, you tell your boys, 'hold on, let me go holla at this one.' What makes you think a woman wants to hear your noise? Stop going to the clubs trying to meet your wife or whatever you plan on calling her for the night. Stop coming to church after you've worn out your welcome at all the clubs in the city and try to turn our church home into your next hangout."

"Porter, pick up line one," Tanisha said.

"Who is it?" I asked.

"Reesey."

"Tell her I'm busy."

"She said it was important."

I walked over to the phone that was off to the side near the cash register, took a deep breath, and counted to ten because I could feel sharp pains slicing through my head.

"This Porter."

"Porter, listen, what you doing this weekend?"

"What's up, Reesey?"

"Can you keep your baby?"

"For the whole weekend? I just kept her. What's the deal?"

"You know I told you I'm moving."

"No, you didn't say nothin' about moving."

"I didn't? Yeah, I'm moving into a brand-new condo in Royal Oak."

"That's nice."

"Well, that's why I need you to keep the baby."

"I'm working this weekend."

"Can your mama keep her?" she asked.

"Can yours?"

"She's helping me move, Porter."

"So you bought a condo? What you do, hit the Lotto?"

"Actually, no, but, that's neither here nor there. If you can't keep her, I'll find somebody else. When did you go back to work?"

"Tomorrow's my first day back."

"Isn't that kind of soon?"

"I've been off almost five months and had to fight like hell to convince the department I was ready to come back, so it's not too soon at all. It's not soon enough."

"I'll find somebody. Don't worry about it. Which I'm sure you won't anyway."

"What's that supposed to mean? I take care of my baby."

"I didn't say anything about you taking care of your baby."

"How's Porter—I mean Dean. How's he doing?"

"He's doing good."

"That's good. So, you must be moving in with your other baby's daddy, right?"

"Right."

"I figured that. You can tell me that. Ain't no love lost."

"Bye, Porter."

I hung up the phone and thought about how ironic the situation was that I had been in. One day after my operation, Reesey came to the hospital to visit. She was in a good mood because she was finally wearing a large diamond ring on her wedding finger. She was engaged and it was finally confession time. She told me that Porter wasn't mine. Like I didn't already know, but this was the first time she admitted it. Ironically, he wasn't her boss' child either. She had never even had sex with her boss, and I believed her because she was telling the truth about everything else. The baby's father was Dean Phelps, a bench warmer for the Pistons. He was a biracial dude, taller version of David Justice but with blue eyes. Now I've got my name back and the baby has his daddy's name, the way it's supposed to be. Dean makes a lot more than I do, but he's no starter, and doesn't have endorsements, so he still has reason to worry. Until a man can be like Mike and roll with some serious millions, Reesey won't ever be satisfied and will always be subject to cheat. I'm glad that's his worry now and not mine.

I got to thinking about the situation and how convinced I was that Pam had told the truth. It sounded just like the truth coming from her, but come to find out Reesey had never gone around telling one person that the baby she was carrying belonged to her boss Jack. She said she wasn't stupid, and even if the baby had been Jack's, she said she'd never tell her business like that when she knew all those girls at the job hated her. I never told her where I got the information from but Reesey left me with these words. "Some people will wait a lifetime to get revenge when they feel they've been wronged." That's the deepest thing I'd ever heard her say, and I think she was right.

The fact was Pam didn't know if Reesey had cheated. She just took a look at that baby and just like my mother and a lot of other people, assumed the baby was mixed. She probably saw how much favor Jack was throwing Reesey and made up her own story. It got me to wondering all sorts of things, like whether Damion had a child out of wedlock living across town. I was his boy, he'd of told me. That was probably something else Pam made up so it would seem like we were both in the same boat. I'd never know for sure, and besides, it didn't matter now.

40

Winona

Carlton had no idea that today for his seventeenth birthday, I was surprising him with a brand-new PT Cruiser. He deserved it, for putting up with me for one thing, and especially after I received his last report card of the year filled with A's and B's and only one C in trigonometry, instead of the usual C's and D's. He seemed to be taking his classes more seriously ever since he met his new girlfriend, Jill, who was book smart and a good golfer—almost as good as him.

I drove the new car down Eight Mile with the large red bow that was strapped to the roof flapping in the wind.

Gina was following directly behind me.

I pulled into the garage beside my car and Gina pulled up behind my car, which would give Carlton room to pull out the Cruiser when it was time to pick up Sosha from my parents. Of course, I was certain, he'd want to drive it immediately. Carlton was golfing at Rackham with Jill. Eighteen holes with a noon tee time and it was only a quarter after one so we had plenty of time.

Gina and I walked into the house from the garage. I set the Sanders' cake box down on the kitchen table, threw the trick candles on top and set the car keys beside them. We headed upstairs to prepare Cartlon's room with the other small gifts I had bought for him. I was going to pretend that once again he was out of luck when it came to getting a new car. Then at the last possible moment, after Carlton had given up any hopes, I was going to tell him the keys were somewhere in his dirty closet that I'd been begging him to clean. I bet he'd clean it then.

I had specifically told Carlton I was working late, when in actuality I left at eleven.

When I reached the top step, I heard jazz music coming from my room. I also heard a man's voice cry out, "Whose pussy is this?" That wasn't a man. It was Carlton. I looked over at Gina. If I had a gun in the house I know at least two people who'd be dead, and Gina and I wouldn't be among them.

"What in the hell is going on in here?" I asked as I pushed my angry presence through the door. Carlton was pumping his skinny naked body over some plump girl. The girl's eyes shot out like darts when she saw me. She pushed Carlton off of her and scrambled to get dressed. "In my bed, Carlton! In any bed. I don't appreciate this at all, but in my bed, I really don't."

"Mom, I can explain."

"Can you? You think so?" I asked. My heart was hammering.

"Sure I can. This is my girlfriend, Monica."

She smiled at me quickly as she jumped into her jeans, flopping her large breasts around in the air.

I looked over at Gina who was trying to cover up her laughter, but I couldn't find anything funny.

"Spare me the introduction. I want both of you to finish getting dressed then I want to talk to both of you individually downstairs. Starting with you, young lady."

"I really need to get home."

"You didn't really need to get home a couple of minutes ago when you were screaming out my son's name. Downstairs!" I ordered her. I don't know how I was ever going to get that image out of my head. My son. Firstborn. Humping in my bed. I paced the den before settling in front of the fireplace.

Monica came down, still fidgeting with her clothes. She tried to avoid any eye contact with me, but I chased her roaming eyes from side to side until they agreed to meet with mine.

Gina was sitting over in one of the love seats, listening.

"How long have you known my son? It couldn't be too long because I've never seen your face before."

"No, ma'am. Hasn't been that long."

"This is no time to be polite, because what I just caught the two of you doing in my bed wasn't polite."

"I didn't know that was your bed. He told me it was his room."

"Does that look like a teenage boy's room to you?"

"No, ma'am."

"You did know this was my house, or did you think it was his too?"

"Well, it is his house too. He lives here."

"Don't get smart," I snapped.

"Yes, ma'am."

"Don't yes and no, ma'am, me either. I'm going to make this short, sweet, and to the point. I hope the two of you used protection."

"We didn't do anything."

"They didn't do anything," I said, smiling over at Gina. "So I guess my eyes were playing tricks on me? I guess I didn't see my son's naked body moving up and down on top of yours. Is that what you're saying?"

"Yes, ma'am."

"I know what I saw. I also know what I didn't see, and I didn't see a rubber on my son's penis when he jumped off you. Are you on the pill?"

"Yes, ma'am."

"Good, because my son is going to college. And he's not going to be a daddy at seventeen years old. I don't care what he does after he graduates from college, but before then, it's my business. Aren't you afraid of getting a disease?"

"No, ma'am."

"Well you should be. You young girls are so stupid. He's not thinking about you. He's not thinking anything about you. Can't you see that? How can you not see that?" I spoke to her the way I wished someone had spoken to me years ago. "I want your parents' number because they will know about this. I don't want you coming over my house, and I don't want him going over yours. I'm breaking up with you for him. Do you understand?"

"But I love him," she cried.

"How old are you?"

"Fifteen."

"Fifteen? At fifteen you don't love anybody, barely yourself. Why else would you give up your gift to a young boy who doesn't know what to do with it? Or maybe you had already given it away to some other young man."

"I love your son."

I heard Carlton's feet tumbling down the stairs. He stood at the entranceway to the den with his head hanging low. "Carlton, I want you to be honest with this girl and tell her you don't love her. Tell her that you already have a girlfriend named Jill, who's a good girl and wouldn't be caught fucking in your mama's bed."

"But I do love Monica. I love them both."

"What do you mean you love us both?" Monica asked.

"Calm down," Carlton pleaded.

"Calm down? You had me break up with Jacob and now you're going to tell me to calm down. No way." She stood and stormed toward the door.

"Wait, young lady," I said. "I'll take you home."

"I don't need anyone to take me home. I just live around the block."

When she walked out the door, I turned toward Carlton and said, "I don't want you seeing her anymore."

"Why not?"

"Why not?" I asked Gina then turned toward my son. "You're smart. You got a good report card, so figure it out. And fool, you didn't even use protection." I smacked him upside his head. "I'm so disgusted with you. Don't you know this girl could trap you with a baby."

"Is that what you did?"

"What?"

"You had me young. Did you trap him?"

"No. K-Keith and I wanted you," I said, stuttering.

"Mom, come on, stop lying about it. I already know Keith's not my real dad. I know what happened. I know my father stood you up on your wedding day. You probably think I'm just like him. Well, if I did get a girl pregnant, I'd take care of my baby, and I sure as hell wouldn't be a punk and leave her standing at no altar."

How could he know about all of that after I was so careful to hide it from him? I looked over at Gina. Our eyes locked with confusion.

Carlton was waiting for a response, but I was dumbfounded out of one. I walked into the kitchen, pacing the linoleum tile twice before I re-entered the den. "Happy birthday," I said as I handed him his set of car keys.

"Mom, I know you probably didn't tell me because you didn't want me to think my father didn't want me, but it doesn't matter."

"Who told you about your father?"

"Does it matter? It's true, isn't it?"

"Tell me who told you, because it does matter."

"Your father told me about my father."

"My father? No, I don't believe you."

"Well he did, and he said I look just like him."

"I don't believe you, Carlton. You're trying to pick something out of me, but there's nothing to pick out."

"I already know all I need to know. I know I'm six-two and Keith was all of five-six. I'm light. Keith's dark. I know, Mom. I also know that my father grew up on this street, right across from this house."

"Alright, so you know. So what? That doesn't change anything about the stunt you tried to pull this afternoon. We'll discuss your father at a later time."

"I don't want to know anything about him. I know I messed up today, but don't worry, it won't happen again. I won't disappoint you. I promise."

"Too late for promises because you already have. What were you thinking? You had sex with that girl in my bed. I don't care if you do know about your father," I said, snapping into some zone that I couldn't even recognize. "Don't think you're going to talk your way out of this one, boy. You're grounded, and I have half a mind to take back this car. You're just like your no-good father, leading girls on and using them."

He ran past me into the kitchen and through the door to the garage. I didn't move immediately, not until I heard the garage door open and realized he was going to drive off.

"We better go after him. He seemed upset. I don't want him running into anything," Gina said.

Gina and I both picked up our purses and headed for the garage as Carlton tore down the driveway almost scraping the side of Gina's car. By the time we got in her car and pulled out of the driveway, he had quite a lead on us. We spotted the tail end of his car several cars ahead. He made a left turn on to Livernois at a red light.

We stopped at the red light, waiting what seemed like eternity before it finally turned green.

"No telling how long he's kept all that inside about Derwin," Gina said.

"I can't believe my father did that. Why would he do that? That's not his place."

Carlton was still a ways ahead of us, and it seemed like we were getting stuck by almost every light. We saw the last of him when he turned on to the Lodge freeway. I panicked then because he wasn't experienced enough to take the expressway.

41

Porter

An alert came through the printer at 2:00 P.M. There had been a roll-over accident involving a tanker truck and several cars on the Lodge freeway near downtown. The tanker had overturned and exploded and several gallons of fuel had escaped. Flaming fuel rolled down manholes, blasting off the covers. The entire freeway had been shut down in both directions.

We were one of twenty-six fire companies called to the scene, including Hazmat, the hazardous material team, which didn't assist at all because they weren't equipped to.

"We have a teenage boy trapped in his car. It's too dangerous to go down," the captain said. "The rest of the people got out and ran to safety, but the truck driver most likely is dead."

"Which car is the boy in?" I asked.

"That's my son, Carlton. Today is his seventeenth birthday and I bought him that PT Cruiser. Please save my son. Please save him. If he dies because of me, I won't be able to live with myself," a woman pleaded.

I looked at her twice. The first time because she was the lady I saw at the restaurant the day before. The one to whom I was so attracted. The one I wanted to say something to but couldn't or didn't. I looked at her the second time but focused on her eyes. I saw my mother's eyes, pleading with the firefighter to go into my grandmother's house that was burning to a crisp. I heard those same screams all over again.

"I'm going in," I said. There were firefighters on both sides of the freeway spouting out water from their hoses on to the freeway as I ran down the steep slope.

"Porter, you're walking on dynamite," Conrad said. "Hazmat will get it under control."

"What are they waiting on?" I yelled. I made my way down and on to the freeway, across three lanes of fuel, and realized I had forgotten to take a tool. My head started spinning. The last thing I needed was another blackout. I hadn't had one in more than a month, but something was wrong because I was struggling to gain composure, and I slipped on the slick concrete and fell to the ground landing on my butt. "Okay, Lord, You've got me out of a bunch of mess in the past. I know if it's my time, it's my time." I saw a sparkle come from the tanker truck. "But I can't believe it's my time!" I shouted as I reached the mangled car that was flipped over and resting on the passenger side. "Father, You are my refuge and my fortress. No evil shall befall me, no accident shall overtake me, nor any plague or calamity come near me." But then I thought about what the bishop had said the first time I attended church, and maybe I was surely dead. I struggled with the car door, trying to open it. "Can you hear me?" I asked Carlton.

"Yes," he replied.

"Can you open the door?"

"No, I'm stuck in the seat belt."

"Okay, hold on. Do you have a free hand?"

"Yes, but I'm afraid to move."

"You have to move. We're out of time. Try to open the door."

I waited for the boy, looking around the car to see if there was any way I could gain entrance. I needed something to break the glass, but I didn't have time to go back. "Lord, come on. Jesus, please. Richard, I need help."

I heard the door come ajar. That's when I snatched it open and leaned into the car and pulled out Carlton.

"Are you hurt?" I asked as I saw a flame streaking down from the gas line heading into the path of the tanker.

"Not really."

"Good. Run as fast as you can in my direction." We ran. Not up the slope but down the freeway in the opposite direction of the truck and the fuel. Everyone was running.

"Pray that that flame doesn't reach that tanker," I shouted to Carlton.

"I'm praying."

We ran up the West Grand Boulevard exit, and collapsed on the grassy median.

"Do you think the truck exploded?" Carlton asked as he was catching his breath.

"If it did, we'd have seen it, felt it, heard it."

We stayed on the grass, neither one of us moving. We needed to catch our breath and thank God.

The captain's car pulled up and Carlton's mother jumped out of the backseat, running to her son to embrace him.

"Thank you so much for saving my son's life," she said.

"I was just doing my job," I said.

"You were doing more than just your job. You were doing more than you had to by risking your life. Thank you for having this job," she said. "How can I say thank you enough? Please let me do something to show my appreciation." I stared at her, and she didn't even know why. This was some sort of fate. I remembered now where I'd seen her the first time. It was at the gym. Then at my parents' restaurant, now I had saved her son. I couldn't help but think briefly about what the psychic said, but I threw that out of my head instantly because I couldn't mix God up with that other stuff. This was a work of God. "Will you let me cook you dinner to show my appreciation?"

"It's not necessary," I said, praying she'd insist.

"I know it's not, but please let me."

"Well, if you insist," I said, knowing there wasn't any way I was turning down that invitation.

"I do. I insist."

42

Winona

It had been almost a month since the accident, and not only had neither Carlton nor I discussed the events leading up to it, we never even hinted around the subject of his father. There was no one for me to talk to. I'd already consulted Gina, who for the first time was no help. I couldn't agree with her assessment. I refused to simply let it alone. Let Carlton forget about his father, not now that he knew his father wasn't Keith. I felt I was the one responsible for keeping them apart for all of those years, so it was up to me to find Derwin. If Carlton had died in that accident, where would that have left me? I wouldn't even be able to call his father and tell him that the son he never met was dead.

"Carlton, do you have a minute?" I asked after knocking on his bedroom door.

"No, Mom," he said through the door.

I knocked a few more times but much louder.

He snatched the door open and stood in front of me tucking his short-sleeve shirt into his dress pants.

"Where are you going?" I asked.

"Out with some friends."

"Carlton, sooner or later we need to talk about your father."

"Sooner or later maybe, but not now. Can I use your car?" I hesitated before handing over the keys. Even though he claimed the accident was the fault of the truck driver's and not his, I was still cautious about letting him drive. "When is my car going to be out of the shop?" He ran down the steps, heading for the front door.

"I'm not sure. The passenger side is smashed in. I'm expecting them to total it, but who knows." I followed him.

"I'd rather get that Liberty that's coming out anyway." He was halfway out the door.

"Don't stay out all night," I said.

He slammed the door rather than reply.

"Mommy," Sosha screamed from her room, "since Carlton is gone with your car, can we order a pizza and watch a TVD?"

"You mean a DVD, don't you?"

"Yeah, a DVD. Can we have a girls' night out and invite Grandma?"

"You're always with Grandma. Why can't it just be us?"

"It can, Mommy."

———

It was a quarter to five. I was at work sitting at my cubicle, looking through my Franklin Planner. "Is that today?" I asked myself, because if it wasn't under my things to do, it wasn't going to be done. "It is today," I rested my finger over the read ink that read, RED LOBSTER FOR CARLTON AND DAD'S B-DAY. We were supposed to go to Red Lobster on Carlton's birthday, but due to the circumstances, we decided to postpone it until the following month and celebrate it along with Dad's. Of course, I never told my parents exactly what happened. I never told them Carlton was in a near-fatal accident, because I didn't want Dad turning it around and making me out to be an unfit mother. I just said Carlton was upset because the car order was delayed. I also never asked Dad why he told Carlton about Derwin.

My office phone was ringing. I waited longer than usual to answer because I was still programmed into thinking Beth Anne was going to pick up, but those perks were over. No more executive assistant and no more office. My band level went from a 96 to a 93. My ninety-seven-thousand-dollar income was reduced to sixty-two thousand. But I was determined to keep my head up. At least I had a job, and to most folks a good-paying one.

"Winona Fairchild," I said after picking up the receiver. There was silence. I was almost ready to hang up when the man on the other end said, "Winona?"

"Yes." Duh, I had just answered Winona Fairchild, so it was obvious I was Winona.

"Do you know who this is?"

"No, I don't."

"It's Porter. Porter Washington."

My mind was still empty.

"I guess you forgot my name. I'm the firefighter."

"Oh yes, the one who saved my son. I'm so glad you called me. I was meaning to call you but I lost your number. I know that sounds like a line."

"It does, but I know it's not one because after you wrote my number down on your business card you handed it back to me."

"Did I really? I was so out of it that day."

"Understandably so, but when a beautiful woman commits to dinner, I will take her up on it."

I smiled. If I didn't know any better I might think the youngster was coming on to me, but I knew better.

"I promised you dinner and I keep my promises. How about this Saturday?"

"This Saturday is perfect because I'm off this weekend."

"Great. What do you want me to cook?"

"Surprise me."

————————

Gina and I walked into Red Lobster at a quarter after six. I had called and asked her to come with me for moral support, and she agreed. She knew how strained my relationship was with my father, but she didn't understand, because to an outsider, my dad was great. He only treated his kids—mainly me—like shit.

My family was seated at a large table in the back of the restaurant. Everyone was there, including my older sister, Colleen, and her boyfriend of eighteen years, Thomas. My brother, Trent, still looked the same, only his hair was starting to thin out like my father's. He brought along his wife, Felda. They didn't have any children to bring. Val and Bo came, and even their two grown children, Bo Jr. and Raven. Of course, both of my children were present and my parents.

Three large salad bowls were on the table, along with enough biscuits to feed a starving country.

When I walked over to the table, a few members of my family smiled. The rest, including my father, didn't look at me at all, but all of them greeted Gina.

"Don't forget, Gina, I'm coming this Saturday. Me and Fatty over there," Val said as she pointed to Raven who looked like she was about to drop a baby any day.

"How far along are you, sweetie?" I asked.

"Six months, but I'm having twins so that's why I'm so big."

"Hi, Mommy. Hi, Gina," Sosha said as she blew kisses.

"Hi, baby," I said.

"Hey, munchkin," Gina said.

There were no seats left so Gina and I stood until the waiter brought over two chairs and reset the table to include two more place settings.

I sat next to Colleen and across from Trent. Somehow all of my siblings managed to stay with their mates. It made me question my past relationships. Perhaps, I never found a decent man or one who truly cared for me because there was something around me or inside of me that repelled the good ones. Not only men, people in general. Gina was my only friend. We managed to hang on to each other for twenty-seven years by no initiative of mine. She was a good person. I don't know how I lucked up and found such a good friend.

Looking around that table made me feel empty. Everyone had someone in his or her life but me. Aside from my kids, I was alone, as I had always been.

"Is everyone ready to order?" the waiter asked in a cheery voice.

I hadn't even looked at my menu, but as many times as I'd been to Red Lobster over the years I didn't need to. "I'll have the Lobster Feast," I said to the waiter as I handed him my menu.

"Why does she always have to pick the most expensive thing on the menu?" Dad asked.

"And she won't eat it all," Val replied.

"I'm not ten. I eat all of my food now and I also pay for my own meals, so I'd appreciate it if the side comments stopped."

"Do you pay for your children's meals too?" Dad asked.

"Of course, Dad. Did you think you were going to come out of your own pocket on your birthday?" I asked sarcastically.

Everyone started rolling their eyes.

"I'm going to have what Winona's having," Mom said.

"You don't come to Red Lobster and spend thirty dollars on one meal," Dad said.

"Why don't you?" I asked.

"Because you don't. This isn't a five-star restaurant."

"You don't like the choice of restaurant, Dad? What, are you calling us cheap? If so, we get it honest, but I'm not that cheap because I'm paying for everybody's," I said.

Suddenly orders started upgrading.

"You in such a giving mood, why don't you give me back the fifteen thousand you stole from me before you left town," Dad said after the waiter walked away. The mood quickly changed. A nervous quiet fell over everyone but me.

"I can't believe you said that in front of my children."

"I can't believe a child of mine would do that to me."

I stood.

"Where are you going?" Val questioned. "I know you're not leaving before the check comes."

"Don't worry, I'll leave an imprint of my card at the register." My voice quivered.

"Oh, good," Val said, reaching for the basket of biscuits.

"Sosha and Carlton, wait outside with Gina please."

"No way," Carlton shouted. "This is for my birthday, and I love Red Lobster. Why do we have to leave?"

"Carlton and Sosha, go with Gina," I said calmly.

"Mommy," Sosha said, "why we gotta go? I didn't even get to finish my salad."

"In the damn car!" I shouted to them, and watched them scramble out of their seats and march through the restaurant.

I took a deep breath after the three of them left the table. I didn't feel like arguing. No sense anymore, so I remained calm. "Fifteen thousand was a lot of money, and I'm sorry for what I did back then, but as I recall the story ended with the cancellation of the honeymoon, return of the ring, the dress, and the veil, and a partial refund on the reception hall. When it was all said and done there was about seven thousand dollars worth of items that couldn't be taken off your credit card." I removed my checkbook from my purse and scribbled out a check for seven thousand dollars. "Here's your money." I handed the check to Colleen who passed it down. "Mom already told me that you settled with the credit card company for half that, but just keep the rest, because I also owe you for college, and I guess every other mistake I ever made in life that cost you some money, but just like I made mistakes, Dad, so did you, and your latest one was telling my son who his father was before I was ready for him to know. I guess you thought it was okay to mess up your kids, but don't fuck with mine."

"Who's messed up?" I heard Val ask while I was walking away. "Speak for yourself. Don't forget to leave the imprint at the register," she yelled out.

43

I felt bad the way I left the restaurant a few days before. I was always messing up something. This time it was a family birthday celebration. As hard as it is for me to finally admit it, I'm beginning to realize that this was the end of my relationship with my father. I couldn't mentally deal with him and everything else I was going through. It was too much stress involved. I can't stand being in the same room with him. That's why if Mom wants to see the kids either she can come over to my house and visit or Carlton can drive Sosha over there. I'm done going that way.

"You know I'm having that man over for dinner, and I expect you to stay here for it," I said as I trailed Carlton who was walking out of the kitchen carrying his Air Jordans. He walked into the den and sat down at the love seat to put on his gym shoes.

"What man?" Carlton asked, checking his watch. He was obviously waiting on someone because after he looked at the time he looked out the window.

"The fireman who saved your life, Carlton."

"So, what's that got to do with me? Have fun. I'm sure the two of you will hit if off just fine."

"Carlton, that man saved your life. He's not coming over here for me."

"I already thanked him. I saw how he was looking at you. Believe me, I'm sure he'd rather me not be here. That's the best thank-you I can give him."

"Carlton, please. He's too young for me." Carlton shrugged. "I've decided I'm still going to try to find your father." He started humming. "I'm sure you want to meet him." His hums became louder.

"I don't care if I meet him. There are a lot of kids who don't know their father."

"That won't be you. I'm going to make sure you meet him."

"Whatever you want, Mom." I heard the doorbell ring. "I got to go." He ran to answer the door. Seconds later I heard it slam.

I walked over to the window and looked outside at him laughing with his male friend. Two young girls were waiting for them in the car.

Last week, I decided that if I could find at least one of Derwin's high school friends, maybe he would know how to get in touch with Derwin who was the type to keep in touch with his close friends, so I went on Classmates.com and searched for all of them, including Derwin. I put in the year of graduation and looked for Duane Adams, Mitchell Armstrong, Derwin Clouds, and Steven Towers. The only one listed was Duane Adams so I sent him an email and waited for a response. A couple of days later he sent me an email back saying he hadn't heard from Derwin in more than ten years but Mitchell Armstrong probably would know how to reach him and he gave me Mitchell's phone number. Then he said, P.S. Say hi to Sylvia for me. I had no idea who Sylvia was unless he was talking about Sylvia Banks. In that case he probably thought I was Wanda Childs, Derwin's cheerleader girlfriend from high school. Oh, well, I still got the info I needed, which was all that mattered.

I walked downstairs into the kitchen, and while the roast was cooking in the oven, I took a moment to rehearse what I would say if Mitchell answered the phone. "Hi, is this Mitchell? Mitchell Armstrong from Cass? Hey, this is Winona Fairchild. Remember me?" He'd probably say hell no and slam the phone down. He was part of that same, "my daddy's a doctor" clique, the one Derwin pretended not to belong to when he was around me. *Might as well get this over with,* I thought as I dialed the number. The phone rang five times before a woman finally answered. "Hello," I said. "May I speak with Mr. Armstrong, please?"

"He isn't in. Who's calling?"

"Winona. I went to high school with him." I wanted to explain because I didn't want his wife thinking I was disrespecting her household. I know how women can be.

"Winona, what's your last name?"

"Fairchild."

"From Cass Tech? Hey, girl, this is Beverly. Beverly Spader. Beverly Armstrong now. Did you run into Mitch? Girl, I heard you moved away some years ago. So how are you doing?"

"I'm fine. How's everything going? So you and Mitch got married, huh?"

"Yeah, and we moved into his parents' house after his father died in '95. Then the next year his mom passed away. SO GIRL, HOW YOU DOING?" she shouted.

"Fine. Just fine." Beverly and I never were the best of friends, but we weren't enemies either. The only thing I remembered about her was she liked to run her mouth.

"I'm glad you called. Let me have your number, I'll make sure Mitch calls you. I didn't know the two of you were tight."

"Actually, we weren't. I'm trying to reach Derwin. I was tight with him."

"You were? Derwin Clouds, right?"

"Mmm-hmm."

"I didn't even know you knew each other. Mitch has his number. Knows it by heart as much as they talk. You know he's been married and divorced three times?"

"Divorced? Who, Derwin?"

"Mmm-hmm. After eight years of marriage with the last one and two adopted kids, they decided to go their separate ways. She took the kids and moved back to California where she's from."

"Adopted children?"

"Yeah, adopted. They could never conceive. Mitchell and I decided that it was Derwin because none of his three wives had children by him. He married one girl straight out of college. That marriage only lasted a year. Listen to me telling all the man's business. Don't tell him I told you any of this stuff, okay?"

"Don't worry. I won't. So did he ever go pro?"

"Girl, you know he didn't. He's a dermatologist just like his father was."

"Do you think you can find his number?"

"Hold on for a minute and let me look." While I was waiting for her to return to the phone, I fished around in one of the kitchen drawers for a pen and some paper. "I couldn't find it, but Mitch knows it," she said as she returned. "I know it starts with 866—"

"What state has an 866 area code?"

"That isn't an area code. You know Detroit's area code is 313."

"Derwin lives in Detroit?"

"Yeah. Where else would he be? You know he always thought he ran this city. Thought he was mayor. He even tried to run, but didn't get passed the campaign fundraiser party. He's still the same Derwin."

"He's always lived here? I thought his parents sold their house to move closer to him?"

"They sold their house because his father has Alzheimer's so they put him in a home, and Derwin's mother went to live with Derwin's family who was supposed to move to California but like I said he's divorced for the third time."

"So you mean to tell me that Derwin lives in Detroit?"

"He sure does, right down in Indian Village in one of those big homes that he's trying to sell now because it's only him. His mother ended up renting at one of those new luxury senior citizen apartments."

"I don't believe this." All of a sudden, I heard the doorbell ringing. I ignored it. I couldn't stop my conversation now that it was really getting good. "So do you all see him?"

"My husband does, even though I told Mitch to stay away from him. I don't want Mitch getting any ideas. Thinking he'd rather be divorced, if you know what I mean. We have three kids and if that fool tries to leave me I might have to kill him."

"How old are your kids?"

"Monica is my oldest. I had her before I married Mitchell; she's fifteen. The twins, Mitchell and Michael are nine."

"Oh my God, your daughter's name is Monica? I think my son used to date your daughter."

"What's your son's name?"

"Carlton."

"I know a Carlton used to come over and visit Monica from time to time. It's probably the same one."

"I'm sure it is. Has to be."

"Is he tall and skinny and can golf real well?"

"That would be him. Does he look like anybody you know?"

"Well, now that you mention it, my husband always said that he looks like Derwin." I let the phone go silent. "Is that Derwin's child? Oh, my God. My daughter was dating Derwin's child. No wonder Mitch liked him so much. I can't wait to tell Mitch, Derwin has a son. I didn't know the two of you knew each other like that. You certainly kept it on the down low."

That's because he was lowdown. "I'd rather you not tell Mitch, but if you do, tell him not to say anything to Derwin. I want to be the one to tell him."

"You mean Derwin doesn't know after all these years?"

"Long story, but he knows."

"Is that your doorbell I keep hearing?"

"Yes," I said, rushing off the phone. "I'm expecting company. I'll call you tomorrow."

"Please do. Maybe we can do lunch one day."

44

Porter

Four rings, still no answer. I didn't want to knock, even though I could see part of Winona's head. It looked like she might have been on the phone. I saw her get up from the kitchen table and then disappear. A few minutes later, she started walking toward the door in a long, fitted dress that hugged her curves nicely.

When she opened the door, I sensed that her mind was a million miles away, preoccupied with something serious as her eyes roamed passed me.

"Wow," I said, in response to her beauty.

"Wow what?"

"Whatever you're cooking smells really good." She smiled, but still didn't look directly at me. I stepped through the door and looked around. "Is your husband home?"

"My who? I'm not married."

"Are you sure?"

"I'm pretty positive."

"Nice house." I looked around. It was a big house with not enough furniture to fill it, but what she had was nice enough. More than what I had.

"Please follow me," she said.

I followed her into the dining room. She had the table set for three, and jazz was playing in the background.

"Is that 103.9 jazz hour?" I asked.

"Sure is," she said as she walked over to the portable radio sitting on one of her extra chairs, which was pulled against the wall, and turned up the volume.

"I love the jazz hour."

"I love this station, especially the morning show," she said. "It gets me to work on time and helps me wake up while I'm on my way."

"What about Matchmaker?" I asked. "Do you ever listen to that?"

"No. Never," she responded quickly.

"Me either." We both sat at the dining room table.

We both looked at each other and started to laugh. "I was on the air once but then I called them back the next day and told them I changed my mind," Winoma said.

"I probably heard you. I listen to the show whenever I can. It's interesting."

"Would you ever write in or call?" she asked.

"I used to say never, but after knowing you called I guess I should never say never, huh? Do you want to know something?"

"What?"

"I met you twice before, once at Gold's gym. I helped you work out, and then the second time I saw you at my mother's restaurant, The Soul Station. Both times, I wanted to ask you out."

"It's a small world. See, we didn't even need Matchmaker." Her eyes enlarged slightly. "I mean. Why did I say that? This isn't a date. This is a dinner. A thank-you dinner."

"Then where's your son? Shouldn't he be here since it was his life I saved?"

"He was supposed to be here. You see the table is set for three, but he had a date. I tried to make him cancel, but you know how teenage boys are. You can probably remember being one."

"What are you trying to say, I'm young? Am I too young?"

"Too young for what?"

"Not for what, for whom? Am I too young for you?"

She cleared her throat. "For me? The roast must be ready." She stood and so did I. It was my intention to steal a kiss. I wanted to catch her so far off guard that she'd have to stop playing that innocent role because I could tell by those curves she wasn't innocent. I looked down at her as she looked up at me, but as I moved my face toward hers, she scurried sideways. "I've got to check on the roast." She disappeared into the kitchen.

"The hell with the roast. I don't even like roast," I said underneath my breath. *What am I doing?* I thought. *Why am I doing the same old thing? Don't come on a lady like that. Man, what's wrong with you?* Being a Christian was a struggle, and I was too new in it.

"I hope you like roast," she yelled from the kitchen.

"Oh yeah, it's my second favorite dish."

"Oh, what's your first?" she yelled back.

"Everything else," I whispered.

"What did you say?"

"Turkey and dressing."

"I started to make turkey and dressing."

I heard a crash in the kitchen so I ran in to assist. The roast was lying on the floor. Bits of grease had splattered on to her dress.

"I don't believe I did that."

"No big deal. We can go out to eat."

"But I made you dinner. You don't understand. I made this, and I don't cook every day. I feel so bad."

"Don't. I don't even like roast. You better get out of that dress before you hurt yourself."

"I thought you said it was your second favorite dish." She walked over to the kitchen sink, ran water over a dishrag, and removed a roll of paper towel from the counter.

"Yeah, but you didn't hear what I said after that: next to everything else."

"Okay, let's go out." She stooped to clean up the mess.

"Let me help you."

"No, I'll clean it. I made it." She hiked up her dress and kneeled down to wipe up the grease. "Where do you want to go for dinner?"

"You better be careful. That dress is too nice to mess up, and you're really wearing it."

She looked up at me and smiled. "That's so sweet of you to say."

"All I said was the truth." I wasn't used to paying compliments, but I thought I needed to try something different since I was already feeling something different with her. "We can go to my parents' restaurant."

"Okay, let's do that, because I really did love those sides." Besides, it's such a nice day. We should get out."

————

"Hello. How is everyone at Ladder Number 12?" Mom asked, making reference to the number above the booth. "You two make such a lovely couple, but I guess you hear that all the time, don't you? Or is this your first date?"

"Yes, it is," I said, watching my mother pretend not to know me.

"Well, then, it's on the house. It's not a blind date, is it?" Mom asked.

"No, it's not," I said.

"You two look so good together. And young man, you remind me so much of my son. Be sure to go by the wall on your way out and take a look at his picture. Honey, they look like twins. It will scare you."

"Which one? I saw the picture on my way in and there are two boys on it, not one," I said, watching Mom stare me down.

"That's right, there are and they do favor but I'm talking about the one standing next to his father."

Mom and I locked eyes until Winona said, "This is a wonderful restaurant, and you have the best sides."

Mom turned her attention toward Winona. "If I were you, I'd make my son take you out tomorrow because he's getting a cheap date since he doesn't have to pay for this one."

"Should I?"

"You better. Never let men shortchange you. They'll take the money they saved and spend it on another woman. You better believe that. " Mom laughed and Winona's laugh followed. What was frightening me was the fact that Mom seemed to like Winona. She was doing things to make it obvious, like picking Winona's hand off the table and examining her French manicure and complimenting her on her outfit, which I couldn't stop looking at either.

"Who does your hair? That has to be the best weave I've ever seen." Winona's eyes enlarged. "Don't worry, my son doesn't have anything against a weave. I've worn one for nearly ten years."

Winona started stroking her long locks. "But it's all mine."

My mother drew back. "All that hair?" Mom looked over at me with puckered lips.

"Almost anyone can grow their hair long. My hairdresser says that hair grows at a rate of a half-inch a month more or less. Mine usually grows an inch a month. But it really didn't start growing like this until after I had my first child."

I used my hand like a saw and was cutting across my neck, motioning Winona not to say another word.

"Your first child?" Mom asked, looking over at me. "What are you doing? Why are you doing that with your hand?"

"It's a dance." I repeated the motion more rapidly to make it appear as if I were dancing. I stopped after Mom looked away and shook my head slightly while I looked at Winona, trying to let her know to change the subject.

"So tell me more about your children," Mom said, plopping down on the cushion next to Winona.

"I have two children, Carlton is seventeen and Sosha is ten."

"So, if you have a seventeen-year-old, how old are you? If you don't mind me asking."

"No, I don't mind, I'm thirty-seven—actually, I'm thirty-eight, I just turned thirty-eight two months ago."

"Oh, a Gemini. Right?" Winona nodded. "The twin. Y'all have two personalities. I dated a Gemini man. He was good in bed, but not worth a quarter out of it."

"Mom, can you stop talking about the zodiac?"

"Oh, that's right," Mom said, puckering her lips, "you saved. I forgot. Anyway, honey, as long as you're younger than me, I don't have a problem with it. It's only when those women my age want to push up on my son that I get upset."

Winona smiled. "I don't mean to interrupt our conversation, but can we eat?"

My mother burst out in laughter. "I like you. I like her," she said to me, like she was telling me not to mess up. Mom left us, promising to return with a sampler plate of some of her favorite dishes.

"I really like your mother. I admire her for owning her own business." Winona's bright eyes were looking around the place.

"What do you think about me?"

"I'm thinking a lot of things."

"Name one."

"You're a wonderful man for saving my son."

"Can I tell you something?" She nodded. "Don't take this the wrong way, but I can't believe you don't have a man. You're too sexy to be by yourself."

"Really?"

"Yes, really. I'm sure you've heard that before." She shook her head. "Well some men play games. A lot of them do. If they never told you that, it doesn't mean they weren't thinking it. So, what do you think about me?"

"You're attractive."

"You think so? Am I your type."

"I don't know you yet."

"Physically speaking, am I?"

"Mmm-hmm."

"We'd make some good-looking babies together, don't you think?" I didn't know what possessed me to say that but she got a laugh out of it.

"I'm done in that department."

"Why? Did you tie your tubes?"

"Why are we talking about tubes and babies? This is our first date, and it's not actually a date."

"It's a date, but it doesn't feel like a first date. It feels like I've known you for a while. I feel comfortable around you, and like my mother said, I'm getting off cheap so I want to see you again tomorrow and take you somewhere that I have to pay for." She didn't respond. "Is that okay with you?" She nodded. My mother returned with the family-size platter, and then she sat back down next to Winona, and we all ate and laughed the night away.

———

I walked Winona to the door and stood in front of it with my hands in my pockets, waiting for something to happen, something I'd be able to think about all night and into the morning. She already told me on the ride to her home that she was tired so I didn't expect to be invited in, but I did think a kiss would be nice so I took one before she had a chance to duck out of the way. When my lips met hers, she didn't resist. My hands came out of my pockets and surrounded her waist. I pulled her in to me. I felt myself becoming excited. We stood on the porch kissing for several minutes before she pulled away from me. "My son's inside. At least he better be by now."

"I'm leaving. Just one more."

"You're saved, remember?" she asked.

"I'm also a man, remember?"

"One more," she said, putting up a finger.

We started back where we left off, and I felt the firecrackers go off inside of me. As corny as it sounded, I knew this was it. She was the one. I never kissed a woman on the first date. The only women I've ever kissed were Pam and Reesey. Kissing was too intimate to waste on a fling, but I could tell from the sparkle in her eyes she wasn't a fling.

Winona pulled away from me again, whispered in my ear that she enjoyed the evening, and started fumbling through her purse looking for her door key. "How old are you?" she asked, like she was looking for a reason not to like me, and then she went back to searching for her key. "I know you're probably too young for me."

"Do I look like a boy or a man?" I watched her eyes peruse my whole body, from the top of my baldhead to the laces on my Mauri shoes.

"How old of a man are you?"

"Old enough."

"No. You're a baby," she said as she pulled out the keys from her purse. "Nothing but a baby."

"You're going to be the baby. Not me. I guarantee that." I waited for her to open the door, and then I gave her a quick smack on the lips. "I'll see you tomorrow, that's if you let me." I watched her look down at my feet. "Big, aren't they?" Her eyes started crawling up my legs, skipping over my crotch, straight to my face.

"Do you really want to see me tomorrow?" she asked.

"I think I want to see you every day, but I'll let you know for sure tomorrow."

"Just call me tomorrow."

I nodded. I waited for her to open the door and go inside. Now it was my turn to sigh because I really didn't want to mess this up, and I knew me. Anything was possible.

———

I thought it was too early to call her, but it wasn't too early to think about calling.

The night before, after I got home, we talked on the phone for more than an hour. When she started to get sleepy, her voice changed. Got deeper. Sexier. We started making sexual references, but she stopped before either of us took it too far. I wondered if I was this excited because she was new or someone special. I wondered whether I was whole enough for God to have taken my rib, but I had asked two questions I couldn't yet answer. She could be my rib, even if it had only been one day. She could be my rib. I simply had to be patient with her. Get to know her before I hopped in the bed, but it had been so long since I had sex, almost a year, and I wasn't sure if I could hold out.

"Good morning," I said after Winona answered the phone.

"Good morning."

"You don't sound like you're asleep."

"Nope," she said, "I'm drinking cranberry juice and watching *Love Jones*."

"Why are you watching that without me? That's one of my favorite movies. What part are you on?"

"Darius just put an omelet on a plate for Nina and it looks so good. I wish a man would cook me breakfast. Hint hint."

"I can do that, but I wish a woman would—"

"We can go to IHOP," she interrupted.

I laughed. "I was going to say, let me know what she wants for breakfast."

"A cheese omelet of course. Just like in the movie."

"Done. Do you want me to come get you?"

"No. I wouldn't expect you to drive all the way over here and then back to your place just to cook me a cheese omelet. I can come to you."

I gave her my address and the directions. She said she knew the building well because her girlfriend Gina used to live in the building next door a long time ago.

After our conversation ended, I realized I didn't have any eggs, milk, or cheese in my kitchen. I could've run to the grocery store to get some, but I was afraid that I might miss her. I tried catching her at home before she left but her daughter answered instead.

"My mommy isn't home. Who's calling?"

"I'll call her back."

"Wait a minute! I asked who was calling. Who is this?"

"My name is Porter."

"Are you my mommy's boyfriend?"

"Did she say she had a boyfriend named Porter?"

Sosha giggled and hung up the phone.

I smiled while I dialed Winona's cell number. A recording said the person I was trying to reach was out of the service area. We were going to have to go to IHOP or either I'd have to wait until she got to my place and we could go to the grocery store together.

I walked out of my studio and then back in so I could see what Winona would see for the first time. I must have done this six or seven times and each time I found something I needed to pick up or move in a different direction. On my eighth trip out, I stumbled into her.

"Leaving?" she asked.

"No, I was going out into the hallway." I stood blocking the open doorway.

"Can I go inside?" she asked.

"Sure." I stepped out of her way and watched her float by me. She stood near the entranceway looking around. "I'm not trying to get out of fixing you breakfast, but I don't have any of the key ingredients. I meant to go grocery shopping, but I forgot. I have a problem with my memory sometimes."

"Yeah, a lot of men do."

"No, I'm serious."

"I'm sure you are."

"We can go to the grocery store together."

"Let's just go to IHOP," she said.

We stood in the short line at the IHOP in Ferndale, Michigan, before a tired old waitress finally came by with two menus, waving her hand for us to follow her. She put us in a back booth, behind a larger one that had four small kids. Two of them were sitting on their knees turned facing my direction. The little girl took her small fist and grabbed hold to Winona's hair and yanked it as hard as she could. I saw the hand coming, but I couldn't say anything fast enough to prevent it from happening.

"Get your kid off me!" Winona screamed while her head was being yanked back.

"Donetta, leave that lady's hair alone!" the mother yelled as she smacked the little girl's hand so hard it turned her brown skin red. The little girl started screaming after she let Winona's hair go.

"Oh, my God!" Winona said, shaking her head and untangling the mess the child made with the long strands. Winona sighed, then closed her eyes and opened them again as if to start over.

"Are you okay?" I asked.

"I'm fine. Oh, my God." She placed her hand over her forehead. "My head is killing me, but I'm okay." She took a deep breath and did the thing with her eyes again and then she seemed much better.

"Tell that lady you're sorry!" the woman yelled to the little girl.

"I'm saw," the little girl said, sucking on a sausage.

Winona threw up one hand and without turning to face the family, said, "Don't even worry about it."

"Do you ever think about cutting it?" I asked.

"Cutting what?"

"Your hair. Maybe wearing it shoulder-length or shorter."

She turned up her nose. "My hair used to be just a little below my shoulders, but then I decided to let it grow out. Why, you don't like long hair?"

I shrugged. "I used to. That used to be all I was into when I was younger, but now, how long a woman's hair is doesn't really matter. I'm not telling you to cut your hair. I was just wondering if you ever thought about it."

"I've thought about it, and one day I probably will change up and cut it, but I didn't let it grow out for a man and I'm not about to cut it for one either," she said with slight attitude.

"Oh, I wasn't implying that you should cut your hair for me. I'm sorry if you took it that way. I think your hair is pretty, and it's yours to do whatever you want with."

Stacy walked in with two of her girlfriends. They were dressed in short skirts, high-heeled sandals, and low-cut form-fitting tops. I was praying she didn't see me, or if she did she would keep her distance.

"They're pretty, aren't they?" Winona asked as she watched my eyes roam in Stacy's direction.

"I wasn't checking them out in that way. I was looking at them thinking how much better you look."

"That is the best line I have ever heard."

"It's not a line. It's the truth. You're beautiful."

"Well, I was simply stating a fact. They're pretty."

"You like women?" I asked.

"No," she said as if she were offended. "I'm just not the jealous type. You don't have to sneak a look. Look. Because if Michael Jordan or Denzel walks up in here, I'm going to do more than look—I'm gone."

"Don't neither one of them have anything on me."

She rolled her eyes but kept her mouth closed out of politeness.

I was trying to be a gentleman throughout breakfast, but it was hard because she was eating her food so seductively. Not like I was used to seeing a woman eat. Not like it was her last meal, but I could tell she was enjoying it. She licked her lips, and I had to move around in my seat to settle back down.

"Are you okay?" she asked.

"Yeah, my back hurts a little bit, that's all. Can I ask you a personal question? The other night, after our first date…" I paused.

"What were you wondering?" She looked directly into my eyes. "I haven't been with a man in six years."

"How did you know that's what I was wondering?"

She shrugged. "You sort of alluded to it last night on the phone."

"When you say you haven't been with a man, do you mean in a relationship or do you mean sexually?"

"Both."

"Damn, how does that feel?"

She shrugged again. "It was hard the first couple of years, but the next year was so easy. I felt so good. I thought I could go on like that forever, but then the fourth year came and it got a little complicated. By the fifth year, I was ready to do whatever with whoever."

"How do you deal with that?"

"I pray every night for patience and strength."

"You don't masturbate?"

"No, I pray."

"Before or after you masturbate?"

"Not funny. I pray, and that's all I need to do."

"You want me to believe that someone who hasn't had sex in the past six years just prays and the desire is gone?"

"I'm going to be honest. In the beginning, okay, I used to masturbate, but I got tired of it and stopped that after the first year."

"Why didn't you get a sex partner?"

"A sex partner? You mean someone who you have sex with and that's all you do? No commitment. No relationship. Nothing but sex."

"Yeah. No strings."

She raised her eyebrows and looked away from me, then back toward me. "Even when I was your age, I wasn't like that."

"Don't start with the age."

"Seriously, I have only been with two men my entire life. I know that sex is sacred. No more sheets."

"What?"

"Juanita Bynum. Have you ever heard of her?" I shook my head. "She's a prophetess. She talks about…forget it. It's too long to go into."

"You seem spiritual."

"I try to be, even though I don't go to church."

"You don't have to go to church to be spiritual."

"I guess you're right, but I still want to go." She cut a piece of her cheese omelet then dropped her fork and knife on the plate. "I'm stuffed."

I looked into her eyes like it was already tomorrow and she had gone away from me too soon. Those were the eyes that I wanted to remember. The innocent eyes of a woman who had lived ten years more than me, but was the next closest thing to a virgin that I knew. Six years. It was going on eleven months for me, and I felt like I was about to explode.

45

Winona

It was almost three o'clock on Saturday when Porter called me from his cell phone and said, "Put on some jeans, a T-shirt, and pull your hair back, I'm coming to get you." I had told him the night before that I wanted to have fun before the summer was over. It was already the end of August, and I hadn't done anything to really let my hair down. I wanted a convertible and a long stretch of empty highway so I could speed down it. I wanted to be free and Porter said, "I know just what you need."

Almost an hour had passed so I called his cell to see what was taking him so long, but I was switched to his Sprint PCS voice mail. Before long, I started pacing my Reeboks across my Oriental rug in the foyer, and doing patty cake against my Levis. As usual Sosha was over her grand-parents' and Carlton was out with one of his new girlfriends, not Jill. She'd broke up with him the day after his birthday, despite his accident, which led me to believe that Jill had found out about Monica. Even if Carlton wouldn't admit it to me, I know that's what happened.

Finally, I heard the doorbell ring. Even though I felt like running to answer it, I decided to take my time. Porter and I had only been dating for a few weeks but I was starting to get attached already, partly because we spoke on the phone every day, three and four times a day. He sent me emails and took me to the firehouse to meet his coworkers. We went places. He didn't seem to be ashamed of me. I guess he liked me.

I checked my hair and lipstick in the large mirror hanging on the wall, and then I walked calmly to the front door to open it.

Porter was standing on my porch holding a helmet and grinning. "You ready to take a ride on the back of my motorcycle?" he asked.

"You have a motorcycle? When did you get it?"

"Today."

"Today, Porter?" I glanced over at the silver bike that looked like it belonged in the space age. "It's nice. It looks like it can go real fast."

"It can, which means you'll have to really hold on to me tight. Can you do that?" he asked, handing me the helmet he was holding.

"I guess I have to."

"Don't you want to?"

I smiled. "You know I do."

"I don't know anything. Only what you tell me, and you don't say much."

———

We rode down Woodward Avenue heading south toward downtown, taking a detour down a side street to connect with I-75. A traffic light caught us right before we had a chance to zoom on to the entrance ramp.

"Have you been riding long?" I whispered into his ear.

"Not really. Actually, the guy who sold me the bike took me out for about thirty minutes today to teach me."

"Just today, honey? You mean you've never ridden a motorcycle before?"

"No."

"Aren't you supposed to have a license to ride a motorcycle?"

"Yeah, but I need to learn how to ride it before I go to the Secretary of State to get my license."

I wrinkled my brows. I wanted to be carefree but Porter was taking my fantasy to a whole 'nother level.

The light turned green and he accelerated on to the expressway ramp. I was nervous as I pictured my demise. But then I realized I had nothing to fear but death, which was already growing inside of me. For that moment, I realized no one is safe. A freak accident in a matter of seconds could kill both of us on this expressway and that would have nothing to do with my disease. That's what happened to Keith. I held on to Porter tighter while a rush fell over me. Suddenly, I felt free. As corny as it sounded, I wanted to pull off my helmet and let my hair blow in the wind.

We rode down the expressway, exiting on Bagley, then rode East Jefferson to Belle Isle. When he turned on to Belle Isle bridge and took it across to the park, I started having flashbacks from high school. I couldn't remember how many times I had been in this park. Down some dark path, pinned up in a car with Derwin doing whatever he wanted, whatever we could do in a convertible Mustang. I didn't like the reminder, nor did I understand why something that happened so long ago was still so fresh in my head. Maybe because the book was never finished between Derwin and me, only a few chapters had been started and we never made it to the turning point. I have his son and he knows he has a son, but he hasn't tried to reach out to find him, which hurts because somehow I thought he was better than that. Not that he ever gave me reason to.

Porter pulled into a lot near the Detroit River and parked in one of the few empty parking spaces. I was the first to hop off the bike and stretch, removing my helmet to shake my hair loose.

"What are they staring at?" Porter asked as he watched a Ford Expedition with three guys eyeing me. "I don't like the way they're looking at you."

"Don't worry about it." I waved off his concerns. "We can go somewhere else if you like." I threw that out because I didn't want to be there in the first place.

"You want to go somewhere else?"

"Well, we could go to Canada. We can take the tunnel and we'll be there in ten minutes. I know a real nice park over there called the Queen Elizabeth."

So that's what we did. We rode under the tunnel and then waited in a long line of automobiles that were pulling up to the customs' gate. When we reached the gate, a male customs' agent asked for our citizenship and for the purpose for our visit. After we told him we were going to the park and then to dinner, he asked if we were concealing any weapons or drugs. He let us go after we answered no to both questions. We then rode past a black Suburban that had been pulled over and was being searched by a few officers and a German shepard.

I remembered right where the park was located, and I directed him to it. Porter parked his bike between a minivan and an Accord. We walked hand in hand among the flowerbeds, watching the black squirrels scurry up tree trunks. After passing a few park benches, we decided to sit and take in the scenery. We were quiet for several minutes. Even though my mouth wasn't speaking, my mind was. There was something about Porter that was special. I felt so comfortable around him, almost too comfortable, almost comfortable enough to tell him my secret, but I wasn't crazy.

He cleared his throat. "It's a lot about me that you don't know, that I want you to know," he said, stroking the palm of my hand with his. "I want you to know everything about me in time." There was silence again. I remember a time when I wouldn't be able to wait for him to open up. I was always in such a rush. For what, I had no idea. I would have pressed him and pressed him until he eventually told me, but I wasn't in a position to do that now, because when people start sharing themselves, they expect the other person to reciprocate. There weren't a lot of things I wanted him to know about me, but there was the one thing he needed to know. I couldn't say if I would ever tell him. Even in time. I think I wanted to ride this one out for as long as I could and end it right before anything got too serious. There were so many ways I could make him disappear and he wouldn't be the wiser.

———

After five weeks, Porter and I were still going strong. Seeing each other on every one of his off days and not missing a day talking to each other over the phone.

"Where have you been for the last few weeks?" Gina asked through the phone line.

"I've been here," I said, as I sat on my bed filing my nails.

"You have not, you lying heifer. Where have you been, and who have you been with?"

I rolled my eyes. Should I tell her? Should I tell her I've been spending every day and a few sexless but passionate evenings with Porter, a fine brother, ten years my junior. Hell no, because she'd think I was crazy. "Guess who lives in Detroit?"

"Who?"

"Derwin."

"Don't tell me you've been with Derwin."

"No, I haven't been with Derwin, but remember Beverly Spader?"

"Beverly, class snob Beverly?"

"Was she class snob? How could they vote her class snob as much as she ran her mouth?"

"But what was she running her mouth about? Nothing but herself. So what about her?"

"She married Mitch Armstrong. You remember him?"

"Of course I remember Mitch. He was my boyfriend junior year, remember?"

"That's right, well they're married and she's the one who told me about Derwin."

"That still doesn't explain where you've been, and don't lie to me, because I already know you have a little boyfriend."

"What do you mean by that?"

"Exactly what I said. Go on and tell me about him."

"Gina, there's nothing to tell." My other line beeped. "Hold on."

"Hurry up."

"Hello."

"Hey, girl, this is Beverly."

"Oh, hey, Beverly. Girl, I'm on the other line, but I'll call you right back."

"When are we getting together for lunch?"

"I don't know. My schedule is so hectic these days," I said.

"Let me have your number at the office. I've already got something to write with." I rambled off my digits and prayed that she'd transpose one of them. "You must work in the Tech Center. I recognize the exchange. My sister works there."

"Who's your sister?"

"Just a little peon. You don't know her."

"Girl, nobody at the Tech Center is a peon."

"That's true, even the janitors get paid."

"You mean maintenance engineers," I said. We both laughed.

"Before I let you go. Guess who's coming to dinner tomorrow night?"

"Derwin?"

"Bingo. Do you want to come? I'd love to see him shit in his pants."

"I've got plans, but I do still want his number. I've been meaning to call you. Do you have it?"

"No, I've been trying to wait until I can catch it on Caller ID. If I tell Mitch about you, he will surely tell Derwin. I know you don't want that, and we women have to stick together the same way the men do."

"I hear you." Gina clicked off the other line and called right back.

"I'll let you get that, but I'll call you one day next week to do lunch."

I clicked over to answer the line. "Sorry about that, I'm back."

"Back from where?" Porter asked.

"Oh, hi, Porter. I thought you were my girlfriend."

"As long as it was a girlfriend and not a boyfriend, I'm okay with that."

"You're such a charmer."

"Hey, listen, do you want to go to the African-American Art Museum for a poetry reading tonight?"

"Tonight?"

"Yes, tonight. Why, do you have other plans?"

"No, Porter, but we have been spending almost every night together for the past few weeks."

"No, we haven't spent one night together, but we've seen each other on every one of my off days for the past few months, but who's counting?"

"We're going to have to slow this down."

"Life's too short to slow down something that feels this good. You know what I mean?" he asked.

I smiled. "I feel you."

"What did you say?"

"I feel you," I repeated to his silence. "Is everything okay?"

"Yeah, I was just thinking about something. Anyway, you might want to bring along your friend because we won't be able to spend too much time together."

"Really, why come?"

"Why come? Now, I thought I had myself an educated woman until you said that."

"That's how Sosha used to talk when she was little. Why come, Mommy? Why come I can't have no candy before dinner? Why come I can't suck my thumb?"

"I bet you're a good mommy."

"I'm all right."

"You're more than all right, baby."

"Tell me about tonight."

"I'm part of the entertainment so I won't be able to spend too much time with you until afterward."

"You read poetry?"

"No, I play the saxophone and the drums."

"Why didn't you tell me?"

"I was planning on telling you about that and a lot of other things. It's the first time I played with this group and the first time I've played my saxophone in more than a year."

"I bet you're really talented. See, you can spend every day with a person and still not know him."

"It's because I want it to be about us not me when we're together."

"But you are half of us."

"That's true. I can't argue with that. So, you're coming, right?"

"I'll be there."

Instead of riding with Gina and Mark, feeling like a third wheel as usual, I drove to the museum by myself and arranged to meet them outside. I parked on Farnsworth and walked to the center of the circular building.

This was not the building I remembered years ago. It was a lot larger and a lot more state of the art.

I wobbled on one of my two-inch heels while I waited for Gina and her husband to arrive. Late September in Detroit and it was already starting to get chilly. I was freezing. Served me right for not carrying a jacket or sweater or something, but only old people do that, and I didn't want to seem or act old. I wish I had brought something, though, because my face felt like one big ice cube. When my nose started to run, I walked inside and waited in the rotunda near a large podium, shielding myself from onlookers while I slid my pocket-sized mirror and a tissue from my clutch purse and wiped my runny nose. I kept one eye on the main entrance, and my other eye on all of the fancy dressers. A few minutes later, I decided to walk back toward the entrance so I could catch Gina and Mark as they walked in. "Winona," I heard a voice say faintly in the crowd. It was Gina. I had passed them without realizing it.

I walked back toward the two of them. "Hello, Mark," I said. I made it a point to speak to him first because he was staring me down so hard.

"Winona, you look nice this evening," he said, emphasizing *this evening*.

"Why did you stress this evening? How do I look other evenings?"

"Stop being so damn sensitive," Gina said.

We walked through the rotunda, weaving in and out of several rooms that were surrounded by paintings and sculptures. Each room hosted a new poet.

Porter's band was performing in the 317-seat theater, which was packed to capacity. It was standing room only at the point we arrived. I walked in and saw Porter's head rise slightly. I doubted if he could see me through the dark crowd of people.

"Which one is he?" Gina asked.

"The one getting ready to blow the sax."

"I was afraid you were going to say that."

"Why?"

"Because I can't blame you for not calling me. He's truly fine."

I glanced over at Porter. He seemed to be in a zone as he jammed on that horn. The whole band did, and all of those around them listening. Then, as my head began to sway to the beat, I saw him. I saw who I thought was Derwin walk pass the front row. He was sipping from a glass of wine. I almost couldn't believe my eyes until I heard Gina say, "Is that Derwin?" She nudged me and repeated the question.

"I think so," I said nonchalantly. Derwin walked up the aisle and our eyes met. Then, without warning, I fled from the room into the comforts of the nearest ladies' rest room, barricading myself inside one of the stalls. He hadn't changed a bit. He was still tall and lanky, putting on what appeared to be only a few pounds, but his face looked almost exactly the same, slightly fuller but the same. His hair was still glossy, still short on the sides and a little higher on top. I believe he even had a diamond stud in his ear.

"Winona," Gina whispered as she entered the rest room, "are you in here?"

"Yes, Gina. Was that Derwin?"

"Yes. He's here with Mitchell."

"You saw Mitchell?"

"Mitchell saw me. We literally ran into each other while I was on my way to see about you. "

"You didn't tell him that I was in here, did you?" I heard nothing but silence. "Did you?" I repeated.

"Sorta. I wasn't thinking."

"You sure weren't. Thanks a lot. Well, I'm not leaving this bathroom. I'll stay in here all night if I have to."

"Winona, isn't this what you wanted?"

"No. I wanted to see him on my own terms when I wanted to see him. I wanted to surprise him for a change, not be surprised like I was eighteen years ago when he left me at the altar looking like a damn fool."

"You can't stay in here all night."

"Then go out there and tell them that I left, and come back in here and tell me when you think they've left."

"I have no way of knowing when they're going to leave. It's too crowded in here to follow two bodies around."

"Did they see me?"

"Yes, they both saw you."

"How do you know?"

"Because Mitchell asked me who was my fine girlfriend because Derwin wants to meet her."

"Derwin hasn't changed. Did you play it off like I was someone other than myself?"

"Hell no, I said that's Winona. Don't you remember her from high school?"

"What did Mitch say?"

"I'm not telling you."

"Tell me what he said."

"I'll tell you, but don't tell me ten years later that it hurt your feelings."

"I won't. Just tell me everything he said about me."

"All right. He said, and I quote, 'Ain't no way in the hell that's Winona, not the Winona I knew, unless she got plastic surgery.' "

"Fuck that fat motherfucka. Did you see his ugly ass? He might have been cute in high school, but he's fucked up now!"

"He sure is. Okay, come on out."

"I'll come out when I feel like it."

———

Somehow, I managed to sneak out of the rest room and out of the museum. I left before I wanted to, before I had a chance to see the rest of Porter's performance. I called him from my car when I thought he was probably done performing and looking around for me.

"Why aren't you at the museum?" Porter asked.

"I was there, but Gina got sick so I had to leave early."

"I thought you were coming by yourself and Gina was coming with her husband."

"I did. She did. But I left when she got sick because I was worried about her."

He laughed. "You don't have to lie."

"What do you mean?"

"I can tell when women are lying. Just don't start lying to me, not now that I'm getting so attached to you."

"Okay, I was lying. Carlton's father was there. I haven't seen him in about eighteen years, so I left. Don't ask me a bunch of questions about it because I don't want to talk about him."

"I don't either. I want you to come over. I want to make love to you. I want to show you what you've been missing for six years. I want to teach you whatever you may have forgotten."

46

Porter

We were lying side by side in my bed with nothing on except our underwear. She was spooning her body inside of mine, while I kissed her shoulder and caressed her arm. We had only been dating for a few weeks but I was ready to put a ring on her finger. This was it. I could feel it.

"I want to make love to you, Winona." I was thinking about the night before. How close we came to almost making love. I had a condom on and she licked the head of my penis two or three times but stopped. Then I stuck a little of me inside of her, but she wiggled free. Telling me what we were doing was wrong. "I don't want to be the one to make you backslide," she said. That's how close we came last night, and tonight I wanted us to do more than come close, I wanted us to both cum.

"It's too soon," she said, moving my arms from around her waist.

"How is it too soon?"

"It's too soon. Trust me."

"Well, how long am I supposed to wait?" I asked.

"Do you need a time frame?"

"I need an idea," I said as I started kissing her back.

"I can't give you one because I don't know. Just when it feels right, I guess. Does the church you attend think fornication is okay?" she asked sarcastically.

"Winona, of course not. Being celibate is a struggle for me. I can't do it. I mean, not with you I can't. I have no intentions of leaving you ever. I know having premarital sex is supposed to be wrong. It may be wrong, but I can't help it."

"I'll help you help it."

"What are you afraid of, Winona? You think I'm going to hurt you like the last man did and the one before that?"

"Why do you say that? How do you know any man hurt me?"

"Because that's what it always boils down to with women. They've been hurt. Now, I've got to pay for something some other man did to you."

"Maybe you're paying for something you did. You don't want to make love to me, Porter. You haven't even told me that you love me, so how can you make love to me?"

"I want to have sex. Does that sound better?"

"No, it sounds common. I want to be loved before I'm made love to, otherwise you can go out and have sex with anybody."

"Well, why are we laying here like this? You got your butt pushed so far up against me and we're both practically naked. This ain't nothing but teasing. How do you know I don't love you?" I sat up, pushing two pillows behind my back.

"You're the type that if you did, you would have told me by now."

"Shit, you don't know that. You don't know—" I paused before finishing my sentence. I was starting to snap into the other me. The one I had controlled so well up until now.

"What? Go ahead and say it." She sat up to face me. "I don't know you. Isn't that what you were about to say? So how can you love someone who doesn't even know you?"

"Easy. The same way I love my parents. They don't know me either. Don't nobody know me. Shit, I barely know myself."

"So how does someone who barely knows himself know that he loves me?"

"I know I've never felt this way before."

"So does that mean it's love?"

"It's something strong."

"Not necessarily love though, right?"

I sighed. "I love you," I said

"Why?"

"What, you need your ego stroked tonight, baby? Is that it?" I was becoming perturbed.

"No, I just want to know why."

"Let me show you." I reached out for her, putting my hands around her small waist to bring her body toward me.

"No, Porter."

"Damn, Winona. You're thirty-eight years old, not thirteen. Shit, you act like you ain't never done it before."

"But of course you know I have because I have two kids." She got out of my bed and started putting on her stockings. "Go ahead, finish your sentence. You thought I was going to be easy since I'm almost forty and have kids, huh?"

"Winona, stop. It doesn't have anything to do with your age or your kids. I'm just mad because you're going to pull away from me. I just know it."

"How do you know?"

"Because I can see it. I can see shit before it happens."

"Really?"

"Yes, really."

"So, you're a psychic now?"

"Hell no!"

"Well, that's what you said, you can see things before they happen. That's a psychic."

"Look!"

"Ooh, temper. I've never seen that side of you before."

I sighed. "Get back in the bed please."

"No. Take me home."

"I'm not taking you home. Come here." She inched her way over to me. "What's this?" I asked as I removed the fake lash that was hanging from her left eye and held it up to her face.

She covered her mouth. "I'm so embarrassed."

"You wear fake eyelashes? What else is fake? Are you sure you don't have any tracks up in that head of yours."

"No I don't," she said as she snatched the lash out of my hand. "So I'm not perfect—sorry. I'm sorry I'm not the cheerleader type." She snatched off the lash from her other eye.

"But you are. That's the funniest thing about it—you are and you don't even realize it."

"I'm not the cheerleader type and I'm definitely not perfect. Believe me. Don't try to change the subject. I want you to take me home."

"I won't touch you. You can put on a pair of my pajamas and just lay here with me. I don't want to be alone. Not tonight." She looked in my eyes, then wiggled out of her stockings and climbed back in the bed with me. I was hoping that she'd change her mind. Maybe when I woke up around three or four in the morning she'd be in the mood for love.

I made love to Winona last night. Only in my dreams, but it felt like real love that I was making. This was becoming too difficult for me because

I wasn't used to being with a woman who wasn't quick with dropping the panties, but I had to go along with Winona's program in order to see her. She stayed the whole night. She didn't want to at first. Worried about her kids. I was glad to see that because I couldn't be with the other type of woman—the kind that had kids but forgot she did. Still I convinced her that Carlton was in his senior year and he could certainly watch Sosha, and they didn't have to know she was spending the night with a man. All she had to do was call them and tell them she was with Gina, which she did. I thought that meant I was going to finally make love to her after almost two months, but what it meant was I had to take a cold shower around two in the morning. She let me feel on her. Kiss her. Kiss her neck all the way down to her healthy chest before telling me to stop. I didn't stop right away. I had to think about it for a second, but I stopped because I didn't want to lose her. She said, "We have plenty of time to make love."

"I could die tomorrow," I replied, and I could. There was something about her that seemed very secretive. She seemed like she was hiding something from me. I don't know whether it was another man or what. It was something. She was good at hiding things. Shit, she was hiding me. We had spent a lot of time together and I still hadn't been around her kids. I hadn't seen Carlton since the day I saved him and I never saw Sosha. I still hadn't met her best friend, Gina, or her parents.

———

"Hello," the little girl said as she opened the door.

"Who is it, Sosha?" Winona yelled.

"How come you're not over your grandmother's?" I asked.

"Because they had to go somewhere. How you know my grandma?"

"Who is it, Sosha?" Winona yelled again, much louder.

"Who are you?" Sosha asked.

"Porter."

"Porter," Sosha turned away from the door and yelled to Winona.

"Get away from the door," Winona said.

"You're here for my mama?" I nodded. "I know your voice from the telephone."

"Sosha, I said get away from the door," Winona shouted.

"Why? We're talking," Sosha yelled back. "You want to come in?" she asked.

"I better wait outside."

Sosha walked away from the door, but left a small crack and then she returned a second later. "My mama is mad and not at me because I didn't do anything. She said I had to close the door on you. She just doesn't want me to know you're her boyfriend," she whispered. "She said call her if you want to talk, but don't just come over." Sosha slammed the door in my face.

I stood there for a second, removed my cell phone from the belt clip, but before I could call Winona, she was calling me.

"Porter, I don't believe you. That was my daughter."

"I know. She's cute. She looks just like you."

"No, she doesn't. Porter, I wasn't ready for you to meet her. Why did you just come over without calling? I'm beginning to think you don't trust me."

"I came over because I was in the neighborhood and I wanted to see you. I want to take you out, " I said as I walked to my car and sat inside.

"I can't go out. I have Sosha."

"We can take Sosha. I want to start spending time with your children and meet your family and friends."

"Oh, you want to play daddy? No thanks."

"I'm not trying to play daddy. Okay, if it's too soon then we can go out and maybe Carlton will watch Sosha."

"Is that the kind of parent you think I am?"

"What's wrong with Carlton baby-sitting? He's not a baby. I remember when I was his age."

"I bet you do. It wasn't that long ago."

"Oh, now you're dogging me about the age thing again. What's with the mood swings?"

You don't know my daughter. She's going to be asking me questions all day. She already said that you're cute. Next, she's going to be telling my parents. Guarantee it."

"I'd like to meet your parents."

"Maybe a ten-year-old can't tell that you're ten years younger than me, but my parents will be able to."

"The age difference isn't a big deal. It's not like you're fifty. You're not even old." I paused and watched Carlton pull into the driveway. "Carlton is walking up to my car."

I saw Winona peek through the blinds above.

"Don't let your window down," she said.

"I can't be rude."

I put my cell on mute and let down my window.

"What's up, man?" Carlton asked. "You getting out or you leaving?"

"I thought I was getting out."

He nodded. "Cool."

We both looked up at Winona in the window. "She's pissed," I said.

"I don't think she wanted me to come over without calling."

"Let me give you a little advice, man to man. If you like my mother, I suggest you don't piss her off."

"What pisses her off?"

"Coming over uninvited. Calling a lot. Forgetting birthdays, anniversaries, things like that. Oh, not crying on a sad movie, couch potatoes, and a man who doesn't work. I could think of a lot more with time."

"Thanks for what you gave me so far."

"It's the least I can do since you saved my life and all."

I looked out my rearview mirror. "Is that your girl in the car?"

"One of 'em."

"Player, player," I said, giving him dap, but he left my fist hanging.

"I can be a player, but don't think you can. I won't stand for anyone dogging my mother."

"I'm not like that. I have a mother myself so I know exactly what you mean."

"Cool," he said, hitting his fist on top of mine. "Don't worry, I'll chill my mother out. My girl and I will take Sosha somewhere. You can come back in about ten minutes. Mom will be here by herself then."

"Good looking out. Appreciate it."

"No problem."

I drove around the neighborhood, down a few streets, concentrating on the time. Ten minutes seemed like an eternity. I had questions to ask Winona concerning last night. I didn't have a chance to ask about Carlton's father because I convinced myself I didn't want to know, but I needed to know more about that situation and she needed to know about Reesey and my daughter, Portia. I sure hoped Winona wasn't playing me, saying it was too soon for sex with me while she was rocking some other man's world.

I walked up to the door and rung the bell twice. Winona opened it, wearing another turn-me-on dress. This one was cut real low in the front.

"Is Sosha gone?" I asked as I stepped inside.

"Yes."

I grabbed her and started kissing on her neck. "We got the whole house to ourselves. Let's go upstairs and make love."

"No, Porter!"

"Okay, we don't have to go upstairs. We can do it right here in the foyer."

"Stop, Porter, you're talking crazy."

"Why am I talking crazy? I'm being real by telling you what I want. I can't keep having wet dreams about you. I'm about ready to explode.

Come on, baby." I took off my jacket and let it drop to the floor, pulled my sweater over my head, and then began to unbuckle my belt. "Let's make love like two dogs in heat."

"Porter, please. That's nasty. I thought you were a Christian."

I froze with my belt buckle in my hand. "I am a Christian."

"Well start acting like one."

"You sound like somebody's mama."

"I am somebody's mama."

"Not mine. I don't understand. When we talk on the phone at night like this, it's what you want to hear or at least that's what you say. So help me to understand you better."

"I don't want to have sex if I'm not married. Go on and laugh. Tell me I'm too old to think like that."

"No, you're not too old to think like that. I appreciate that. So let's get married."

"Porter, be serious."

"I am serious. I respect your values and your friendship, so let's do it. I can't keep having these desires for you and feeling guilty at the same time. Let's get married."

"Just like that, let's do it?"

"Yeah, just like that. We can."

She shook her head. "It's too soon."

"Whatever. You don't want to have sex until you get married yet you're turning down my proposal. Help me out here."

"We haven't known each other that long."

"How long is long enough. I was with the same girl since high school and that was too long. I've never felt so good in my life until I met you. Swear to God."

"Don't swear to God."

"I'm swearing to God because He knows I'm telling the truth. I feel like an adult. You make me feel that good."

"Don't you mean a child?"

"No, I mean an adult."

"I thought feeling like a child meant a person felt good," she said.

"Not for me."

47

Winona

The receptionist called me to the front because someone had sent me flowers.

"Are you Winona Fairchild?" the delivery man asked. "Project engineering manager. Is that you?"

"Yes. No, I'm not a manager anymore, but that's me," I said, puzzled.

"These are for you."

"They're for me?" I had never received flowers from a man, sad testimony, but the truth. I tore off the paper that was covering the dozen multicolored long-stemmed roses. I didn't see a card attached, but of course Porter sent them. I headed back to my cubicle with the glass vase in my hands. I picked up my office phone and dialed Porter on his cellular. "Porter, they're beautiful."

"What's beautiful?"

"The flowers you sent."

"Oh, you like them?"

"I love them, Porter."

"Only one problem. I didn't send the flowers, so who did?" I had the right to remain silent so I did. "Winona, who would be sending flowers to your office?" he asked in a tone I'd never heard before.

"I don't know. Calm down."

"Are you seeing another man? Is that why we haven't consummated this relationship?"

"Consummated the relationship? Why such a big word?"

" 'Cause I didn't want to say *fuck* over your business line."

"Porter, calm down. I'm not seeing anyone but you." I looked through the arrangement, spotting a small card between a few of the roses. I read it and nearly fainted.

It's time for us to bring our past to the present. Please call me,
Derwin. He wrote his home and his business numbers under his name.

"I have to go. I'll call you back." I hung up the phone in the middle
of Porter's trust speech. I studied the card and wondered if I should call
the number or if I should throw the card away. Carlton didn't seem to care
about meeting Derwin. He had taken to Porter over the last few weeks
after I decided to let Porter start spending time with the kids. They even
went golfing. Porter was in the beginning stages, but Carlton was patient
with teaching him the sport. I didn't know where our relationship was
going to end up, certainly not marriage. I was of the opinion that my son
needed to know his father, even if Derwin did take me down dark alleys
I didn't really want to walk through. Hopefully, he'd changed. I picked up
the phone and dialed without thinking any further. His answering
machine came on, and I realized I'd called his home number. Of course, he
wouldn't be at home on a Tuesday morning. If anything he was probably at
the office so I called there next.

"Dr. Clouds' dermatology. Would you like to make an appointment?"

"No, not at this time," I said. "I'd like to speak with Dr. Clouds
please."

"Whom shall I say is calling?"

"Winona Fairchild."

"One moment please."

I held for long enough to know I should hang up, but I couldn't. It
had been eighteen years since I talked to him last, I could certainly keep
holding for as long as it took him to come to the phone.

"Winona?" he asked.

"Hello, Derwin."

"Winona, I can't believe it's you on the other end of the phone. What
happened when you were down at the museum? You disappeared."

"Honestly, I didn't feel like talking to you."

"I understand," he said.

"But you look the same."

"That's what they tell me, but you don't. You look great. Time certainly
has been on your side. I'm sure you're married, right?"

"No, I'm not Derwin."

"You're not?" His voice perked up. "Did you get the flowers?"

"Yes, but how did you know where to send them?"

"Beverly told me you worked for Daimler Chrysler as an engineer. I
did some checking from that point. It wasn't too hard. I can't get over
how good you look."

"Is that why you sent me flowers?"

"No, Winona. Over the years I've thought a lot about you and our son. I want to meet him."

"I don't know, Derwin…"

"Look, I know a lot of years have passed and I should have been there for him, and for you, but I'm willing to help where I didn't for so long. I need a relationship with him. I'm starting to feel like my life will never be worth anything until I do right by the two of you. I'm assuming he's going to college soon and I know that's going to be expensive."

"He has a golf scholarship to the University of Michigan."

"That's wonderful, but I'm sure there are other things he needs."

"I'll ask him how he feels about meeting you. To be honest, the last time I brought it up, he didn't want to."

"I understand. It might take some time. Mitch tells me he looks just like me, and he's supposed to be one hell of a golfer. I never told you this but my uncle was a professional golfer."

"There were a lot of things you never told me."

"That's true. There were, but you know I was young and stupid then. You were good to me, Winona. I just wasn't ready. Maybe we can go out on a few dates or something like old times."

"No, not like old times," I said.

"No, no, no, of course not like old times."

"Derwin, I'll get back to you about Carlton after I've had a chance to talk to him."

"Please get back to me."

"I'm not making any promises—like you never did."

48

Porter

It was Sunday at 3:00 P.M. Reesey and I were walking out of Dayton Hudsons with three large shopping bags full of clothes that I charged on the one and only Visa card I kept, my Capital One. I made sure to pay the bill in full as soon as it arrived. I was finally completely out of debt, but if I continued to let Reesey play me, I'd be right back in it. I loved my baby, Portia, but I couldn't stand being around Reesey. Whenever I wanted to spend time with my daughter there was always some catch—some hoop Reesey made me jump through, some mountain she made me climb to the top of first. Today, it was taking her and the kids shopping. Like she didn't already have a man who could afford to do that and more. I know he was out of town a lot since it was basketball season, but damn, didn't he leave his checkbook behind?

I was almost pissed I came to the mall, but then I saw Winona. I didn't expect to see her strolling through Northland with some goofy-looking man and her two children. Carlton looked uncomfortable, but Winona and Sosha were both grinning, and so was the man they were with. I was holding the shopping bags in one hand, pushing the baby stroller with the other. I didn't want to stop because I knew Winona would have a million questions for me, like I had for her. Still, I couldn't stop staring in their direction, and Carlton saw me.

I read his lips. He told Winona, "There's Porter." Winona's eyes jumped over in my direction and stayed there.

"Hold up for a minute," I said to Reesey. I put the bags down on a seat. "I've got to go talk to a friend."

"Take your time," Reesey said as she sat next to the bags and the double stroller.

I walked in the direction of Winona's eyes, striding confidently with my hands in my pockets. "Hey, baby," I said, smacking her on the lips. Carlton grinned and Sosha laughed all over herself. Winona slashed her eyes so sharp I thought I was cut and bleeding. "How you doing, man? I'm Porter, Winona's man." I extended my hand to shake Winona's friend's. He shook it loosely. Carlton and Sosha walked away from us and into Otto's Popcorn. "I didn't expect to see you here," I said to Winona.

"Likewise," she said, eyeing Reesey.

"Nice-looking family you have," her friend said.

"No, that's not my family. That is my baby, but that's not my wife, because remember I already told you this is my woman right here." I put my arm around Winona's waist and pulled her in to me.

"I heard you, but I didn't hear Winona mention you when I asked her on the phone if she was with anyone. Honey, I could have sworn you said you weren't."

"I don't remember you asking that question. I think you asked if I was married."

"Maybe that was what I asked. Any way, I'm Derwin Clouds, Carlton's father."

"Oh, you're Carlton's father?" I asked, looking down at Winona. "You're Carlton's father." I wanted to ask him where the hell he'd been all these years, but I picked up the signal from Winona and let it alone. "Are we getting together tonight?" I asked Winona.

"We're going to be together the majority of this evening," Derwin said.

"I'm sorry, but I wasn't talking to you. Winona, are we seeing each other tonight?"

She wiggled her waist free from my grip. "Not tonight."

I stared at her, and even though her eyes were now avoiding mine, I didn't let up. Not tonight? "Why not tonight, Winona?" Derwin looked at me as if he was shocked I was pressing the issue. "Excuse me, man. Can we be alone for a minute?" I asked Derwin.

He looked over at Winona and walked away after she nodded. "I'll be in Otto's," he said.

"Yeah, you go there," I said to him. The minute he was out of our space, I let Winona have it. "What kind of shit is this? How you playin' me?"

"What are you talking about?"

"That's probably the joker who sent you those flowers, isn't it?"

"Yes, he did."

"So you seeing your baby daddy, now?"

"You seeing your baby mama?" she came back with quickly. "I didn't even know you had a baby."

"I was going to tell you."

"When? After we were married?" She laughed. "Yeah, right. You're no different."

"No different than who, that joker?"

"Any of the jokers."

"I'm different alright, and you'll see that when I don't leave. Is he Sosha's father too?"

"No, I already told you Sosha's father died."

"I'm seeing you tonight," I said firmly.

"No, you're not."

She tried to walk away, but I grabbed her wrist and pulled her back to me. "Don't walk away, okay? I need to see you tonight."

"You can't." She pried my hand from her wrist and walked away.

49

Winona

I was sitting in Gina's family room, flipping through the pages of our high school yearbook, wondering what happened to most of these people on the pages. I'd flip a page and see another face I recognized. Then I got to the page my picture was on and flinched. I was so pathetic-looking—I was ugly, and I was probably still ugly.

"Was Derwin trying to mack?" Gina asked with laughter.

"Girl, he was putting it on strong, trying to convince me we were a family. Now here my son is damn near grown and we're a family now. I started to say, nigga, please. Who does he take me for?"

"The same fool you used to be, I guess."

"Girl, I guess so. Then he started saying let's go back to my place and get to know each other all over again. He must still be using that stuff."

"He must be, and poor Porter had to see you with him."

I rolled my eyes. "He was with his little family. That's enough grounds for me to dismiss him right now. We're supposed to be tight, but he's hiding a baby from me. You can't be hiding something that important from someone." I stopped suddenly.

"What's wrong?"

"Nothing," I said, remembering that I was hiding something equally important from him and more detrimental.

"Girl, are you sure nothing's wrong?"

"Yeah." I snapped out of it and closed the yearbook.

"So how did you finally get Mr. Clouds to release you?

"After we dropped off the kids, I told him I had to stop by your house. I made it sound important. I told him I really wanted to see him again just to make him think I was interested, but I am so *not* attracted to him. I can't believe I ever was."

My cell phone started ringing. It was Porter and I didn't want to answer.

50

Porter

"Hello," Winona said in the midst of laughter. My mind was racing. I wanted to know where the hell she was because I was coming to pick her up wherever she was. And she had better tell me the truth.

"Winona? Nice to hear somebody's having a good time over there."

"Porter, hey, what's going on?"

"You tell me."

"I'm over Gina's."

"Yeah, right." When I went over Winona's house, Sosha told me that she left with Derwin so I immediately called Winona's cell. She must think I'm a fool to drop that lame story about being over Gina's. "Put her on the phone!"

"Gina, say something to Porter."

"Hello, Porter, I've heard a lot about you."

"That doesn't mean shit. Who else is there?" I asked.

"Her husband, Mark, is here, just not in the room with us."

"Who else?"

"No one else. Would you like to come over?"

"Yep."

"Come on, then."

She gave me the directions to Gina's house. It took me twenty minutes rather than the thirty-five minutes it normally takes to drive to Dearborn from the northwest side of Detroit because I was going more than seventy miles per hour. When I got there and rang the doorbell, some man answered the door smiling like he was a salesman. He introduced himself. Told me he was Gina's husband, which he said automatically made him Winona's best friend.

"Good, maybe you can help me out with something," I said. "Who's Derwin to Winona?"

"No one you need to be concerned with."

"Good, because I'm in love with Winona." He smiled, nodded, and patted my back like he could remember being where I was.

I followed him into their den. Winona and Gina were sitting on the floor with their backs against the love seat looking at a yearbook. Winona looked up at me when I walked into the room. "I see you've met Mark."

"Yes," I said, walking over to Winona. She stood and I gave her a long hug. "Were you mad at me today at the mall?"

"Porter, we can talk about this later." Winona was blushing.

"Why?" I asked

"I'm here with my friends. This is embarrassing."

"I already told Mark that I was in love with you."

"No, you didn't."

"Yeah, he did," Mark said.

Gina said, "Oh, isn't that sweet? We can leave you guys alone if you'd like."

"I think they're getting ready to leave, honey," Mark told Gina.

"We were?" Winona asked, trying to read my face. "You just got here."

"I know, but I just came to get you and to meet your friends, of course. Better late than never." I cut Winona a look.

———

I drove around for more than an hour. Seemed like we had circled the city twice I was driving so much, but I wasn't talking. Neither of us said a word. I was thinking how good it felt just being in Winona's presence. That's how you know you're in love. Well, that's how I know. If I could be happy with just being with a woman without doing anything or saying anything then that's love.

"I don't want you seeing that dude no more." I didn't look at her. Just kept looking straight ahead. "Did you hear me?"

"I heard you."

I looked over at her. "That's all you have to say?"

"You need gas. The needle's almost on empty."

I pulled into a Mobil station on Seven Mile and filled up the tank. While I was standing there freezing my ass off, I started getting real upset by the way she ignored my request.

I got back in the car, blowing into my bare hands to warm them. I turned up the heat full blast.

She took her hands, placing them over mine and began rubbing them. "I know what I'm getting you for Christmas," she said.

"We have two and a half months before Christmas but isn't that supposed to be a surprise?" I asked. She shook her head. "Good, then I know what I'm getting you too. What size is your ring finger?"

"Porter, stop playing."

"I'm not playing. What size is your ring finger?"

"A six."

"That's all I need to know. No, I take that back. I need to know one more thing. Are you in love with him?"

"With who?"

"Carlton's father."

"No, I'm not. Not anymore. But he is Carlton's father."

"So!" I yelled out. "Nigga ain't been around for seventeen years. He ain't Carlton's father. Carlton don't want nothin' to do with him."

"Look, Carlton doesn't know what he wants. He's only seventeen. Things could change five or ten years from now."

"Nothing's going to change. This isn't about Carlton. It's about us. That's exactly how the devil works."

"What are you talking about?"

"Now that I'm getting deeper into the Word, I can see how the devil works. He's trying to tear us apart. He's after me."

"Porter, I'm worried about you. You're talking kind of crazy. I hope you don't get too deep into *the Word*."

"Don't make fun of it. It's serious, Winona. All I need is a good woman by my side. A woman who has my back and I have hers. I'm not going to lie to you; I've been out there, but don't worry, I don't have AIDS or nothin' like that, because I always used protection, except with Reesey of course. I'm too paranoid about things like that not to, but I have been around, before I met you. I've been with some women—quite a few."

"Can you take me home?"

"What's wrong?"

"I'm just not feeling well."

"Did I say something? Oh, about being around. I just want to be honest with you, but I don't have a disease. I don't have AIDS."

"Okay. I heard you the first time. Just take me home."

"Did I say something wrong, baby?"

"No, I'm just tired," she said, dragging her voice.

"Can I take you to my house so you can rest there? After we make love that is."

"No, I told you I'm not doing anything before marriage."

"We're getting married, remember?"

"No we're not. It's too soon."

"Yes we are. And it's not too soon. We can plan to get engaged on Christmas. That's enough time."

"Christmas will be here before you know it."

51

Winona

It was one week before Christmas. I had all of my decorations up. I bought a live tree from Eastern Market. I had finished all of my shopping a few days earlier. The presents were wrapped and under the tree, and I was excited that I was off work until after the New Year.

Carlton yelled to me that the doctor's office was on the phone. It felt like a knife sliced through my chest. I ran into the kitchen and picked up the phone hanging on the wall. "I have it, Carlton."

"I'm on the other line," he said.

"Carlton, get off the phone!" He hung up quickly. "Hello," I spoke softly.

"Ms. Fairchild, this is your doctor's office. You missed your appointment yesterday. Did you forget?"

"Yes, I did," I lied.

"Well, we need you to come in."

"Why? Is anything wrong?"

"We just need you to come in so we can go over your most recent test results. Can you come in today?"

"Can't it wait? Is it that important? Why don't you just tell me what's wrong?"

"We're going to have to start you on medication. I think the rest of the details you'd rather come in for instead of have me state them over the phone." As soon as she said medication, I felt a tear escape my eye and I watched it hit the ceramic tile. "Do you think you could get here within the hour?"

"I'll try," I said in a whisper. I hung up the phone and stood frozen in the middle of the kitchen floor. The doorbell rang, startling me from my position. "Who is it? Please, Porter, I can't see you right now." I walked like a zombie to the front door, stopping at the doorway when I noticed it was Derwin coming by unannounced. "Yes," I said with attitude after I flung open the door.

"Were you busy? Did I catch you at a bad time?"

"You sure did. What do you want? Why would you come over here without calling first?"

"I've been calling. You haven't been returning my calls."

"Well, I'd say that's a hint. You remember those, don't you? You should, you used to throw them my way often."

"Winona, that was a long time ago. How many times do I have to tell you I've changed?"

"You don't seem like you've changed. Anyway, what is it that you want?"

"I thought I made it clear the last time I saw you that I wanted to spend time with you and my son, and your daughter of course. I've been thinking a lot about you. Can I come in?"

I looked at him. He was wearing a tired leather jacket and jeans that made his legs look like sticks. "No. I thought I made it clear the last time we saw each other that I wasn't interested."

"No, you didn't. Not at all. In fact, you said you were interested."

"Well, I lied. I'm not. What do you think, after eighteen years we can start over? What, do you want to make me your fourth wife? Or would it be your fifth? I can't remember. If you've been married all those times and not one has worked out, don't you think something's probably wrong with you?"

"Something is wrong with me. I left my son and a woman who loved me at the altar and thought I never would have to look back."

"Good-bye, Derwin. You won't find your redemption here." I slammed the door in his face. I had too many things to worry about, and his feelings weren't one of them.

———

"This is not the end of the world," Dr. Gant said as he sat across from me in the examining room, patting my knee.

"I don't want to go on medication. That means I'm sick. I don't want to have to take pills two and three times a day for the rest of my life. I just don't want to do that." He handed me a box of tissue. "Why do I have to do it?" I took a pink tissue from the box and blew my nose into it, removing another to wipe the tears.

"Your CD4 count is 181 and your viral load is 110,000. As a general rule, we begin treatment when a patient's CD4 is less than 350 and the viral load is greater than 30,000 to 55,000. In your case both are at levels that warrant treatment."

"Why did it change so quickly? I just had a test a couple months ago. I don't understand."

"That's why you need medication to stabilize yourself." There was a knock at the door. "I have someone I want you to meet," Dr. Gant said. "I haven't told her anything about your condition. I'll leave that up to you, but she is very open with the fact that she is HIV-positive. I think you should talk to her. Will you, or do you want me to tell her to go away?" The knocks started back again.

"I'll talk to her."

"Come in," Dr. Gant said to the door. A very attractive young woman walked into the room. "This is Kelly Townsend. Kelly, this is Winona."

"Nice to meet you, Winona."

"I'm going to leave the two of you alone for a few minutes." The doctor left me in the room with a box of Kleenex, my tears, and a stranger.

"You don't look like you have HIV," I said.

"You don't either. Do you?"

I nodded. "Yes I have HIV," I said as I lost myself in all of my emotions and began to cry uncontrollably. "Damn, this is so fucking inconvenient."

"Tell me about it."

She held her hands out toward mine, and I noticed her wedding ring. "You're married?" She nodded. "Does your husband have it too?"

"Yes, he does."

"I guess that makes it easier."

"We met after we had both been diagnosed."

"So you're on medication?" I asked.

"I wouldn't live with this disease and not be on it."

I shook my head. "I don't want to start taking pills. I don't want to have this disease."

"No one does."

"That's true. No one does," I said.

"Do you have a support system? Your family or friends?

"Never. I will never tell my family. I'll die today, but I'll never allow my father to tell me that I fucked up and I'm just getting what I deserve."

"You might be surprised by what he would say."

"You don't know my father." I stood, took one last tissue from the near-empty box, and wiped my face. I probably looked like Rudolph the

Red-Nosed Reindeer but at least it was the season for him. "Thank you, Kelly, for talking to me."

"I don't feel like I helped. I've been living with HIV for eight years. I've been on meds for six. It's not the end of the world. What else can we do but deal with it? We can't change it right now. The meds are so much better now than they were when they first came out."

"I made some bad choices. I was impatient and I made some bad choices. Do you know how good my life could be right now if I didn't have to deal with this disease? I have a man, the man of my dreams who wants to marry me. Am I supposed to tell him I'm HIV-positive?"

"Yes, you are. Even though you don't have to because blood tests are voluntary in the state of Michigan for a marriage license, but you know you should."

———

Christmas Day arrived. Porter slept over because the weather turned bad, dropping almost eight inches of snow overnight. He stayed downstairs in the den and curled up under a comforter while he slept on my Jennifer convertible sofa. He said he had to be here in the morning when I first woke up.

I smelled bacon cooking downstairs. The kids were already up opening their gifts. I dragged myself out of bed and put on my long satin-and-velvet robe, tying the belt tightly around my waist. I didn't bother to wash my face, brush my teeth, or take my hair out of the raggedy ponytail. I just walked downstairs as I was because I didn't care about anything. I'd been this way the whole week, trying to avoid Porter nearly every day. The day before was the first day I'd seen him since I left the hospital, and I kept my distance.

Everyone was happy, which made me more upset, but I tried my best to conceal how I really felt. Sosha found it necessary to show me every gift like I didn't know what I bought, but she still believed in Santa Claus so I had to act surprised right along with her. Carlton was satisfied with his three pair of Nikes, two pair of Timberlands, several FUBU and Karl Kani outfits, and five hundred dollars. I told myself I wasn't getting in debt this year like last, but I think I spent more this time. I didn't care because for all I knew it could be my last.

I dragged my body into the kitchen and plopped myself down in the breakfast nook. Porter must be in love with me because he told me I was looking beautiful and then put a plate in front of me with a cheese omelet, bacon, ham, and slices of cantaloupe.

"Are you ready for your gift?" I looked into his eyes and almost cried. He shouldn't want me, but how did I tell him that without telling him the truth. "You already know what it is."

"Not now, Porter. This should be the kids' day."

"You're right. I know a better time for it." He kissed me on the forehead.

52

Winona

It was New Year's Eve. Seven hours before midnight, but only one hour before my date with Porter began and for some reason, I couldn't make myself move. I was sitting on the sofa in my robe and slippers, purposely trying not to let one thought occupy my mind.

I was still avoiding Porter. It had been a week now. I lied to everyone, saying I had to rush out of town on business, but I drove to Canada and locked myself inside the Hilton hotel. I called everyone from my cell phone daily so they wouldn't get suspicious. Eventually I had to come back so I chose New Year's Eve, and just that quick Porter had plans for us.

Samson was lying on the living room floor with his head resting between his paws, staring in my direction as I sat impatiently on the sofa.

All I had left to do was get dressed. I had already taken a bath, applied my makeup, and styled my hair.

My outfit was upstairs lying across the bed, and my bedroom door was closed so Samson wouldn't run in my room and get happy with my things.

Carlton was with one of his girlfriends, and Sosha was over her grandparents'.

My eyelids felt heavy. Occasionally I'd feel a chill shoot through my body like I was coming down with the flu. I walked into the kitchen, removed a bottle of extra-strength Tylenol from the cabinet, and took two with a glass of water.

I saw Porter as he was pulling into the driveway. I ran upstairs into my bedroom and slipped into my outfit as fast as I could. The hardest part was putting on my panty hose. I needed to be quick, but I didn't want to get a run. The silk dress took less than a minute to slip on, but I couldn't do it alone. I needed Porter to zip me up.

When the doorbell rang a second time, I was heading downstairs, holding together the back of my dress.

Porter's smiling face greeted me from the foyer. I was lucky to have him. That's what I had to keep telling myself, but it didn't matter what I said to myself because I knew the end of the road was nearing for this relationship.

I opened the door, and he was standing there dressed in a black tuxedo, carrying a box of flowers with a red velvet bow draped around it.

I took the box from him without acknowledging his kindness.

"Do you need some help with your dress?" he asked.

"Yes, please," I said as I walked into the kitchen to replace the week-old roses he had bought me.

He followed me. "You have the prettiest back," he said as he kissed it, and started slipping my dress off my shoulders.

"You're supposed to be zipping up my dress not taking it off."

"That's true." He took my dress all the way off and turned me toward him. "It's time we made love, Winona. I love you and we're getting married." He removed the ring box from the inside of his tuxedo pocket. "I was going to take you out to dinner and propose to you the romantic way, but I need to make love to you once and for all before I explode."

"Marriage won't work between us. There's too much going on." I slipped back into my dress and walked away from him, into the den. He trailed behind me.

"You mean because of Reesey and the baby?" I shook my head. "Well what? There's nothing that you can say that's going to make me change my mind. I love you. I want to be with you. We can work anything out. What's going on? Are you sure it's not because of Reesey and the baby. It's not Derwin, is it?"

"No, it's not Reesey and the baby. It's not Derwin. Porter," I took a deep breath, "I'm HIV-positive." He stood in front of me stiff. The expression he was holding on to immediately fell and his face turned to stone. No more pleading. No more wondering. No more wanting. There was nothing on his face other than a blank look. He sat down slowly on the love seat. "You didn't think I'd say that, did you? Go on and say it. I know that you're pissed. Wasted all of this time with some HIV-positive bitch. Go ahead."

"I just. I-I just," he stuttered. "You don't have to lie about the reason. If you don't want to be with me, I guess you can just say that. Don't say you're HIV-positive when you're not because that's nothing to joke about."

"Oh, you think I don't know that, but it's not a lie."

"It is a lie. You're not HIV-positive. Look at you."

"Why, because I don't look sick? Come on now. You know better than that. How long have we known about HIV? Everyone should just about know that you don't have to be skinny and walking with a cane. You can look at Magic and see that. There are a lot of people walking around with the disease who don't look sick."

"I never saw you taking medication."

"I just started taking it."

"Are you real sick?"

"I'm HIV-positive."

"But you don't have AIDS?"

"No, I don't have AIDS. The doctors say that I don't have a lot of the HIV antibodies in me, but I still have it, and all I'm trying to do is hang in there to get my son and daughter through college. Hopefully, if I die after that I'll have enough money saved up along with life insurance polices to take care of them. Who knows? Maybe Carlton will be the next Tiger Woods after all and neither one of them will have to worry about a thing."

"How did you get it?" he asked, refusing to look up at me, focusing instead on his stylish patent-leather shoes.

"From Sosha's father."

"How long have you had it?"

"I'm not sure. I found out six years ago. So that's my situation, and I don't expect anyone to deal with it," I said quickly. "I thought because I didn't sleep with you I was doing the right thing, but I know the right thing would have been for me to say we can't sleep with each other and this is the reason why."

"Do either one of your kids have the disease?" he whispered.

"No, and neither one knows about this or needs to know. They couldn't handle this. My entire life has been nothing but one big lie. I guess I made God mad, and now I'm paying for it."

"I don't think you made God mad."

"I must have. Anyway, now I'm tired of lying. So I'm just going to slow up, take a deep breath, and no more lying. When I can gather the nerve, I'll tell my kids, but Carlton just found out about his father. I can't spring a lot on him too soon."

"Wow," he said, sighing. "I just don't know. I didn't expect for you to say that. I expected you to say that you had another man or something. I didn't expect this. I was prepared for the other man scenario, but not this. Wow." He took a deep breath. "I just need time to think."

"I understand. I just wanted to let you know," I said nonchalantly.

"I appreciate it. You know what I mean? I just need a little time. Not long. It just caught me off guard."

"Oh, believe me, I know, because when I first found out, I was really caught off guard," I said, laughing.

"You're silly. This isn't funny."

"No, really I was. I felt like why don't I just drive off this bridge. It had never seemed like a good idea before that day, but that day, it was the best idea I had come up with in a long time. At least that way, instead of having acquired immunodeficiency syndrome on my death certificate, it could say internal bleeding, head trauma, anything but AIDS. Then I convinced myself that it wasn't that bad. I could do this. I'll deal with this. Sometimes, I feel like I can deal with it. Other days, I know that I won't be able to, and I try to take myself back to the day before. The day before I knew I was sick. I was still sick but I just didn't know that I was. So sometimes when I really can't handle it, I pretend that I'm okay. I pretend it's the day before I got tested. The danger in that is it's a very comfortable way to be and I may just choose to forget the truth. Start sleeping with men, passing it on to them, the way it was passed on to me. I don't want a man showing up at my door with a shotgun because I gave him something that he didn't know I had. So this is where I am. I'm sorry I didn't tell you sooner, when we first met, but give me credit, I didn't sleep with you, even though I wanted to. Give me credit for not putting your ass in the same situation my ass is in. And well, maybe even give me credit for not making Reesey look so bad."

"Hell no," he said. "It's not your fault, okay. Don't even say that you're worse than her. Nah, I'm not giving you credit for that."

"She's not that bad. She had your child."

"Okay, she had my child. She's the mother of my child, and Portia really is mine, but you're better than her. You are better than her. All I'm saying is that I need time to think about this." He looked up at me.

"About what?"

"Just about what's going on. I need to talk to some medical experts."

"What are you thinking, we can be together? Go get tested. If you test HIV-positive, then maybe we can be together, but if you're not, there's no way we can be together."

"Okay, but there is a way, because like you threw out Magic's name. He's married to someone who doesn't have it. I'm sure there are other people married to people who don't have it. I just need time to think about it. That's all."

"That girl must have really hurt you because you should not still be sitting here."

"Forget about that girl. She never hurt me. Life hurt me. You leaving my life will kill me. This isn't about her. It's about the two of us. I'm not afraid of this disease."

"You should be."

"I don't mean it like that. What I mean is I'm a firefighter. Every day that I go to work I put my life on the line. Even when I'm not working, I can die. I just need to know the risks that are involved. I need to know how I can make love to you without getting it, and how we can make this work."

"Okay, there's only one problem."

"What's that?"

"You act as if it's your decision whether we're going to be together, and it's not. I don't care how comfortable you may feel with it or think you can feel with my disease, I don't feel comfortable with it. I don't deserve you. I didn't deserve this disease. I'm just tired of getting things that I don't deserve." I stood and walked to my front door. It was a short walk, but the longest one I'd ever taken. I opened it and stood there staring at him, asking him with my eyes to leave, begging him not to say another word about the two of us, and he didn't. He stood, swept the imaginary dust from his pants, breezed passed me, and did exactly what I needed for him to do: He walked out of my house without saying one word.

53

Porter

I made it to the end of her street before I turned around and drove back to her house. I stopped two houses before hers and tried to figure out what I was going to say. I was in love with her, but she already knew that. I'd told her that plenty of times. I didn't care if she had HIV, but then I'd be lying because I did care, but how could I be mad when she told me the truth before we made love? She gave me a choice, something she didn't have. My inner voice was telling me to let her have some space. It was telling me that she needed time to herself. Not to confuse her. Only I was the one confused. It was times like these that made me believe that my life really was a mistake. I was probably the one who was supposed to die and not my brother. Why else would my life turn out like this? The one time I started to feel alive, I get the wind knocked from under me. I was mad as hell. I felt like I got HIV. What did it all mean? I didn't know. How did this change things? I didn't know the answer to that either.

I pulled in her neighbor's driveway then pulled out and turned around, going in the opposite direction of Winona's house. The sad thing was I had nowhere to go and no one to talk to. For the first time, I didn't want to drive all the way downtown to Belle Isle just to stare at some water and listen to music. I started thinking about the what-if. What if I had HIV and not her? Would I have told her or would I have just slept with her and wore a rubber? Or slept with her and not wore a rubber? I know I would have told her before we slept together, and when I did tell her I would want her to understand, but most of all I wouldn't want her to leave. Maybe Winona just needed a little time to think. I could give her that. I could give her a week. Maybe even two. Three at the max, but I couldn't leave. I'm different, or at least I want to think I am. I'm not pulling a disappearing act.

————

I got to the church at 7:00 P.M. I knew it would be crowded for New Year's Eve. Even folks who didn't regularly attend church would be there. Doors opened at 8:00 P.M. but there was a crowd of hundreds filling the large lobby. This was where my inner voice brought me—took me straight from Winona's house to the house of worship. It told me to pray and believe in a miracle, and that's exactly what I was going to do.

54

Winona

The lights on the downtown buildings twinkled like stars. The whole city seemed to be ablaze during the charity preview for the 2001 North American International Auto Show being held at Cobo Hall this Friday evening in January.

There was so much excitement in the air along with butterflies in my stomach as I walked through the main floor among a crowd of people, most paying $350 each to be there. I passed by the circular display for the PT Cruiser, which read, PT CRUISER 2001 MOTOR TREND CAR OF THE YEAR.

As I proceeded farther, I noticed a black choir singing an introduction for Ford's concept car, the Forty-Nine. Tony Dorsett was in attendance, helping to unveil the Suzuki Heisman Edition Grand Vitara and XL-7.

My boss, Angel, and I drank Piper Sonoma Brut and traveled from one unveiling to the next. She stopped to speak briefly with Mark Snethkamp. He owns several successful Chrysler-Plymouth-Jeep dealerships in the area, and his family had been in the automobile business for years.

I was standing in front of the Jeep Liberty display as the press was snapping photos of Daimler Chrysler Group President and CEO, Dieter Zetsche, along with another man I didn't recognize while they unveiled the Liberty SUV.

I was anticipating the next unveiling of a concept vehicle based on my GXT sketches that was renamed the X-Fire.

I stood beside a sheeted mound of steel with theatrical lighting beating over me. I saw flashes of tiny circles and a gray mass sweep by.

"Is it time?" I whispered to Angel, who was standing beside me. I was ready to watch my design get revealed to the world.

———

I woke up in a hospital bed with tubes stuck in my veins. My vision was blurred but I saw shadows standing over me. "What happened?" I whispered to Gina.

"You collapsed at the auto show and you were rushed to Detroit Medical Center by ambulance."

"Collapsed?" I questioned. "I forgot to take my medicine. It was so hot in there; I hope I'm alright."

"Kids, wait outside," Gina said. I didn't even see the kids. "Winona, are you okay?"

"Not really." I looked away from her. "I'm sick, Gina."

"Sick how?"

"Will you still be my friend?"

"Of course I will. Please, you know better than to ask me that foolish question."

I looked up at her. I was more afraid to tell her than I was when I told Tyler and even Porter. "I'm H I—" I saw her eyes well up with water before I could get the third letter all the way out—"V-positive."

"Oh, girl." A tear bounced on to the floor. "Why didn't you tell me?"

"I didn't want you to worry. Am I going to die?"

"No, you're not going to die. The doctor wouldn't say much to me, just that you fainted and seemed to be suffering from dehydration and exhaustion."

"Oh, I thought it was ending just like that. Silly me, I guess it doesn't work like that."

"Try not to talk so much. Get some rest. I'll watch the kids for you."

"Don't tell them, Gina. Don't tell my kids or my parents. Promise me."

"It's probably more stressful for you to keep all of this inside, babe. You've got to let it out and let the people who love you take care of you and support you. You need to tell your family. Maybe not the kids right away, but the rest of your family, and sooner or later your kids too."

"I'm the same person, Gina. I just want to be treated that way."

"I'm not going to treat you any different."

"I hope you don't. Promise me you won't."

"I won't, Winona. You know me. You know I won't. You should know if you don't."

"Everybody's not like you, especially folks in my family, and Carlton and Sosha don't need to know. Trust me."

55

Porter

I hadn't made it out of my bed in more than a week and hadn't been to work in almost three weeks. I wasn't answering the phone for anybody. I lied to the doctor and said I was having sharp pains in my head so he could put me on a medical leave. I found comfort in staring at the ceiling of my tiny studio and making images appear from the white paint.

I leaned over the side of the bed to turn off my answering machine after I heard Reesey's voice blaring through. "Porter, I need you to watch Portia today. It's an emergency. If it wasn't I wouldn't even ask." No sooner than I erased her message, the phone was ringing again. I picked it up because I thought it was Reesey calling right back.

"What time do you need me to pick her up?"

"Hello," the woman's voice said. "Porter, this is Gina, Winona's friend."

I cleared my throat. "Oh, hey, yeah, I'm sorry. I thought you were someone else." There was silence for a good minute. "Is everything okay?"

"I don't know if I should be calling you, but I know that she told you about, you know, her disease."

"Yes, I know. I want to be there for her, but she won't let me."

"I know Winona. She wants you to be there, but she'll never let you know that. I know you don't know this, but she's in the hospital."

"The hospital! For what?" I jumped out of the bed, stumbling over a pile of dirty clothes on the floor.

"Calm down. She's going to be all right. She was at the auto show and she collapsed."

I opened my eyes as wide as they could go, trying to imagine my

Winona falling out at the auto show on one of the most important days of her life. "What happened?"

"The doctor won't tell me much."

"I want to see her."

"She's at Detroit Medical Center and she's going to be there for another week. I'd give it a few days if I were you and then I'd go."

———

Reesey was standing at the front door of her new condominium in Royal Oak wearing a beaded dress with her small breasts hanging out of it and her tight stomach exposed. She called me back about an hour after leaving the message. Her emergency was a banquet she had to go to with her man, and the baby-sitter got sick at the last minute.

"I look good, don't I? Told you I was going to lose the weight. I finally did it this time. Do you want to come in?" I shook my head. "Do you speak or what?" she asked as she pulled a full-length mink coat from the entry closet and draped it around her.

A tall, light-skinned man walked down the stairs with my daughter in his arms. I assumed it was Dean. Not like I got to see him on TV that much. The cameras don't really point toward the bench too often. He handed Portia to Reesey, said, "hey" to me and walked into another room. I was waiting for her to tell me for the umpteenth time that he played for the Pistons.

"He plays for the Pistons."

"Right, I know. How long do you want me to keep Portia?" I asked as I took my daughter from Reesey.

"A couple of nights would be nice, if that's not too much to ask. After all she's your baby too."

"I didn't say it was too much to ask, Reesey. I just asked how long. I'll keep her all week if need be. I'll just keep her. How about that?"

"We don't need you to do all that. Have her back by Tuesday, please."

"What about your other baby?"

"I got him covered, but thanks."

I walked to my car with Portia in my arms, talking to her in baby talk to make her smile. "Your mommy's fiancé doesn't play for the Pistons, he warms the bench," I said as I fastened Portia into her car seat. She laughed at me and slapped me on the side of my face. "It is funny, isn't it?"

"There's my little princess," Mom said as soon as I walked through the door with Portia. Whenever I kept Portia, I took her over Mom's house because she had a lot more space, which provided more comfort and convenience and mainly a woman who knew how to handle an eleven-month-old baby girl.

I passed Portia off to Mom and then removed my leather jacket and heavy scarf. "Where's Winona? I haven't heard you mention her lately."

"We decided to take it easy for a while. T-Things were getting too serious too soon, I guess," I stuttered.

"You never could lie. Never could. You don't have to tell me what happened, just fix it," she said as she walked upstairs with Portia.

"What do you mean fix it?" I asked, walking up the stairs behind her.

"Fix it. I like her and you love her, so whatever it is, do what you know and fix it."

"And if I can't fix it?"

"Then go to who can. I see you reading the Bible. Go to who can."

I woke up at 5:00 A.M., got dressed, and made it to the church by six in time for early-morning prayer. I stood in the prayer room of Faith Church. I realized that all this time I'd been using Belle Isle park as my place of worship instead of where I needed to be, which was among believers and worshipers who could lead me to Christ and help me with intercessory prayer.

"Whom are we praying for?" the young woman asked me as six of us gathered in a circle.

"Winona. She's sick. She has a life-threatening illness."

The woman began to pray. "Father, Heavenly Father, in and of Your mercy we ask that you strengthen our sister Winona and help her with her illness. Place in Winona's heart a spirit not of fear but of love and allow her to know that she is not alone, that she has the love of Christ and that through His love she will be able to triumph into victory. She has the love of family and friends. Place in her heart a desire to accept those who reach out to her. Give her the strength to fight this battle and win in Jesus' name. Amen."

56

Winona

I was sitting in the hospital bed in my private room trying to relax. My parents were watching my kids while I was on what they thought was a business trip to Chicago for a few days. This gave me enough time to get checked out of the hospital the next day and spend a day or two getting myself back together mentally.

The television was turned to *Divorce Court,* and I was caught up in a debate with the tube. "I can't believe you would drag your butts on national television to fight over a stereo. It has to be more to it than a damn stereo. Is a million dollars inside the stereo? Then it would make sense."

I was laughing at the comments Judge Ephriam was making. I remember when her show first started, I thought she was stiff and fake. No Judge Judy, I remember thinking. Maybe that's because she was new. After a few episodes, I started taping every one and couldn't wait to come home to turn it on. Misery loved company and seeing other unhappy couples became my company.

Out of the corner of my eye, I thought I saw Mom's rust-colored coat, but that couldn't be Mom, I thought as I turned to face her. "Mom, what are you doing here?"

"Don't get upset."

"How did you know I was here? Did Gina tell you?"

"She's your best friend. She had to make a decision that she felt was best for you."

"She told you? *What* did she tell you?" I asked.

Mom walked toward my bed with caution in every step. If she would have looked into my eyes, I would have been able to tell what she knew, but she knew better than that.

"She told me what's wrong with you."

I tried to cry but tears wouldn't come, only sounds. "She swore to me that she wouldn't say anything. She promised me! That's it, we're through!"

"Stop, Winona. Don't shut your only friend out, and don't shut your family out."

"I told her not to say anything. You all won't understand. I don't feel like getting judged. I don't want to hear about what I did wrong and how stupid I am, like I don't know all of that already. All I ever wanted from Dad was his love. That's all I ever wanted."

"Well he's outside waiting to see you."

"No, Mom, I can't." I grabbed her hand as she turned away from me. "I can't see him."

"Yes, you can."

I didn't have enough time to think about how angry I was with Gina because when my thoughts tried to turn that way, Dad walked into the room with his hands in his pocket. He strolled in like it was just another day, but even if I wasn't sick, it wouldn't be just another day because Dad and I hadn't been in the same room together alone in only God knows when. I didn't say anything. Just kept watching Judge Ephriam.

"Me and your mama watch that show. What's this one about?"

"I'm not sure. This case is a new one. The last one was about a stereo."

"They sure have a lot of judge shows on the TV now."

I turned away from the television and toward him. "Mmm-hmm. Dad, I know Mom made you come in here, but I won't hate you if you don't stay. You can leave now."

"Your mama didn't make me do anything. You know better than that. She was going to come to the hospital alone, and I said I wanted to go with her and see my daughter. See my baby."

I sat in a state of shock.

"I'm sorry, Daddy. I'm sorry I didn't follow the path that you and Mom had laid out for me. If I had, maybe this wouldn't have happened."

"Your mama never wanted kids. I was the one. That's hard to believe, huh? I was the one. I wanted a ton of 'em. My intentions were to be a good father, even though the only role model I had was a sorry so-and-so. I was going to do better than him, but I never quite got there." He walked closer to the bed. "I'm sorry that you felt you couldn't come to us. I'm sorry that I made you feel so empty. I'm sorry that I was such a bad father that all you could do is get losers for men. I guess you just wanted a man to love you, but I love you and I have always loved you."

He took the check I had written him at the restaurant for seven thousand dollars out of his wallet and placed it on the small table beside me. "You don't have to pay for past mistakes. I don't want your money. I want you to get well."

I found the tears that I had been searching for earlier. I found them and started crying all over myself. This was the first time I'd ever heard my father say he loved any of us, and he was telling me, the one I thought he hated, that he loved me. "I love you, too, Daddy. I love you too."

I don't know how long I'd been sleeping. The last thing I remember were my parents leaving so I could get some rest. When my eyes slowly opened, I saw Porter standing over me. He was holding my hand and staring down at me.

"How long have you been here?" I asked.

"Not long. About five or ten minutes."

"And I don't even have to ask you how you found out I was in the hospital because I'm sure it was Gina."

He sat in the chair beside my bed. "So, you were at the auto show and when they unveiled your design you couldn't take it, you were so excited that you fainted. Is that what happened?"

"Not quite, but that might be something good to tell my boss." I looked over at Porter who was staring deeply into my eyes. His expression was somber. "Say what's on your mind."

"So you still think you can read my mind?" he asked.

"No, I'm not the psychic, you are. Remember?"

"If I were a psychic, I'd know how you were going to respond to what I'm about to say."

"Which is?"

"I really don't care what you say. I want you in my life. I've had you in my life and out of my life and by far my life is much better with you in it."

"Honey, I haven't even been out of your life for a month yet."

"Almost. Next week it will be a month. You dumped me on New Year's Day, and that was lowdown."

"I didn't. It was New Year's Eve. And I didn't do it because I wanted to."

"Then why did you do it?"

"I already explained all of that to you."

"What if I said I had issues? Not the same kind as yours, but it's a deep and dark issue, and it would take a special woman to understand. I think I found her. I know I did. From the first moment I saw you at the health club, it was something there. You were like a magnet. I thought about you several times after that day, and then you appeared again at the restaurant and then I saved your son. You know what, from that alone you have to be with me."

I laughed. "From that alone?"

"Oh yeah, from that alone. I don't even have to talk anymore. I saved your son."

"So you're pulling that card out?"

"I'm pulling it out. It's out right here and right now. I want you. I figure if I can look at you looking as tore up as you look right now and still want your ass, that's love."

"Do I look tore up?"

"Baby, you past tore up. You look threw up."

We both laughed. Mine was much louder. I poured my feeling into it because I hadn't laughed in weeks. But then I remembered. "I'm sick, Porter."

"So am I. So am I."

"Not in the same way."

"It's still eating me up inside. I can't take medication to make me feel any better. I have to live with it."

"With what? What are you living with?"

"I can't just come out and tell you. There's a time and a place for everything."

57

Porter

Y ou gonna have to come down to the restaurant and pick up Portia," Mom said through the phone line. I was just waking up. My mind felt the way my eyes looked—bloodshot. I stayed up all night thinking about Winona, wondering when and if I should tell her. Wondering if it would make a difference. If she didn't want to be with me before, I really doubt she'd want to be with me after she knew the truth.

"Why did you take her to the restaurant, Mom? Nobody told you to do that," I said as I sat up in the bed, yawning.

"Nobody told me to take her; I wanted to take her, but now things are getting a little too hectic down here so come get her."

"Damn!" I said. I was tired after getting up early for prayer service. I felt good while I was there but once it ended and I walked through the church doors, that natural high fell off, and my mind started twisting together the past with the present and making it all seem like one continuous disappointment. That's how I ended up back in the bed. I'd been sleeping almost seven hours, and I didn't want to get up, but now Mom was on the phone stressing me out about another one of her poor decisions. "So now what? I guess you want me to get up and come get her, right?"

"Get up? It's four o'clock in the afternoon. Your ass should already be up. Yeah, that's what I want you to do. Come get your baby." She slammed the phone down.

I walked into the Soul Station and saw Dad holding Portia, pretending to be a grandfather. Not even the coffee I drank on the way down prepared me for this. It was Monday so technically the restaurant was closed, and even when it was open Dad was never around.

"What you doing here?" I asked him.

"Son, maybe you should have a seat," Dad said as he put Portia in her playpen, which was set up in the restaurant near the counter.

Mom walked down the stairs and over to Dad. The two of them embraced.

"What's going on?" I asked, trying to read through their smiles.

"Your father and I have decided to get back together."

"What? You're kidding, right?" I asked, letting my heavy eyelids droop.

"No, and we want your blessing," Dad said.

"That's why I really called you down here, Porter. Not to pick up Portia," Mom said. "I just wanted to surprise you with the news, and I didn't know how."

"What happened to Conrad? Weren't you talking about marrying him?"

"That was almost a year ago. Besides, that was just a little phase I was going through."

"You have a lot of little phases, don't you, Mom? Shit, having kids must have been one of your little phases."

"Porter," Dad said, "you should be happy that your parents are getting back together."

"I should be happy because my parents are getting back together?" I clapped for a moment. "Why is that supposed to make me happy? Where the hell were you when we needed you? Back and forth. Back and forth. Back and fuckin' forth. Make up your damn minds. It didn't work then, and it ain't gonna work now. You know why? 'Cause neither one of y'all is right. Your son died in a house fire. Do you want to know how the fire started? Did you ever ask? Do you even care?"

"Of course, we care, Porter," Dad said. "Our son died in a house fire twenty years ago," Mom turned away from us when her eyes began to water. "And we've lived with it. And as the years have gone by we've dealt with it the best we could. What else do we need to know about the fire, son?"

"That house wasn't right," I said.

"Did it have electrical problems?" Dad asked.

"No, it had Uncle Ray's problems. Uncle Ray did things, perverted things."

"Stop!" Mom yelled as she turned back around to face us. "I don't want to hear no more. I don't want to go back. I don't want to go back there. Twenty years. I'm sorry. I don't!"

"I know, Mom. You don't want to go back. You never want to go back, just like you didn't want to go back to get us. If you'd have picked us up the day you came to tell us you were coming back instead of one week later, my brother, my best friend, would be alive today. That's on you, Mom."

"Don't do that to your mother. Don't hurt your mother like that."

"Don't hurt my mother like that? You never seemed to care about hurting my mother when you had your other women calling the house asking for you even when *my mother* answered. Y'all must be crazy if you think a marriage between the two of you will work."

"Your mother and I got married young. We never intended to hurt our children. I've always loved your mother, but I had to grow into my manhood, and it took a while. I don't know what to say. I don't know what you want to hear. We hate what happened. To lose a child is the worst thing possible. I don't even know how to explain that loss, but like your mother said, we all have to go on."

"Why don't we just think about the better days? Isn't that right? Well, I'm going to have a better day as soon as I leave this restaurant." I walked over to the playpen and picked up Portia, put on her little coat, and wrapped her in a blanket. "I don't need an invitation to the wedding. Starting today, you can start counting how many years go by before the next time you see me."

I picked Winona up from the hospital and we spent most of the day together talking. I told her that I was finally going to open up to her. It was my turn now, but I had to do it at the cemetery.

I stopped at Ben's Florist on Seven Mile. I started not to go by there because I didn't want to run into Damion and his little crew, but something was pulling me that way, telling me not to be afraid, so I went.

"I won't be long," I said to Winona as I got out of my parked car. I was walking toward the entrance and looked to my left at The Perfect Touch. The building was boarded up. The neon sign had been removed and all six of the garage doors were closed.

"Long time no see," Ben Jr. said as I walked in.

"Hey, what's up, man? Where's your pops?"

"On a delivery. You want your usual?"

I nodded. "Two dozen white roses."

"You see your boy's shop closed, don't you?" he asked as he walked to the cooler to remove the flowers.

"Not quite my boy, but yeah, I see. What happened?"

"It was open until last week after the feds raided it. They were doing something scandalous up in there, some kind of big-time fraud ring. You know if the FBI was in it then it had to be serious."

"Yeah, I guess so. So the feds closed it down?"

"That's what I heard. I also heard Damion's probably going to be spending some serious time in the federal pen. I don't know what Pam's going to do."

"I don't either," I said, removing the money from my wallet to pay him for the flowers and taking the long white box from his grip. "Thanks, man."

"Take it easy."

"I will," I said, heading toward the door. "Oh," I turned back to face him. "I'm going to have a big job for you to hook up real soon."

"What kind of big job?"

"A wedding."

"Yours?" I nodded." "Well, Go 'head. Congratulations," he said.

"You'll be invited."

"I'm happy for you, man."

"Thanks. I'm happy for me too."

———

Winona arrived in front of the headstone four steps before I did. "Is Richard your brother?" she asked after reading the engraved words. I nodded. "The brother you never wanted to talk about."

"I always wanted to talk about him, but when my parents didn't even want to listen, I figured who else would."

"I want to listen."

"I don't know where to start."

"How did he die?" she asked, whispering.

"My brother," I said, taking a big gulp right before I closed my eyes in search of a beginning to something that was hidden inside too deep for words. "My brother..." I cleared my throat again. "My brother had a plan when we were little. He wanted to protect me from what he was going through in that house, so he decided to burn it down with Uncle Ray inside, and we were both going to escape. He was going to set the fire in the basement, but first we had to barricade Uncle Ray inside his bedroom so he couldn't get out. After we locked Uncle Ray in, Richard told me he was going to go to the basement and I needed to wait outside so that's what I did, and all I know is a few minutes later the house was on fire and before the firemen arrived there was a big blaze shooting from the roof. The fire trucks came but they were having a problem with some of their equipment and Richard never got out, neither did Uncle Ray." I stared off into space, reliving that day.

"Why did you lock Uncle Ray in his room?" she asked, placing her hand inside of mine.

I couldn't look at her with my answer. "So he'd die. That was the plan. Not for Richard to die, for Uncle Ray to die."

"Why would you want your uncle to die?"

"He wasn't my damn uncle. He was a pervert. Uncle Ray was just some man my grandmother had to have around. Why do some women have to have a man and others could care less, even when they got a good one?" I looked at her for the answer.

"So Uncle Ray abused you?" I nodded. "He sexually abused you?"

"Yes," I whispered, then dropped my head. "He used to watch me use the bathroom. I never knew why. I was a little boy—six, seven years old. I knew it was strange, but it was something he did. One time there was no toilet paper in the bathroom and he went to another bathroom and got some and tore it off, and he got on his knees." I shook my head. "I'm sorry, I can't talk about this."

"I know what you were going to say. I know what he did."

"No, not that time. My brother came in the door and told him to leave me alone, that he'd play with him. At the time, I didn't know what my brother meant. I just know Uncle Ray left and took my brother's hand. I just know that most of the time when my grandmother wasn't home my brother ended up in my grandmother's bedroom with Uncle Ray. My brother told me that Uncle Ray did things to him that he knew shouldn't be done to a boy, and he was going to make sure he didn't do those things to me, but one day Uncle Ray made me go to the market with him. He made Richard stay home, and he took me. Before I left, I looked back at Richard and he mouthed to me, "Don't let him touch you."

"Did he touch you, Porter?"

I nodded. My mind went back there. Back twenty years when I was eight.

"Why we going this way when the market's that way?"

"Don't worry about it," I said in Uncle Ray's voice. "I'm gonna fix your brother. He's always trying to protect you. He don't know what you might like." I took a deep breath. It was hard for me to talk about this.

"It's okay, honey. You don't have to continue if you don't want," Winona said.

"I came home walking funny, and my brother knew. He knew what happened, and he said he was going to kill him dead so we had a plan. We always made plans. They always worked, but this one didn't."

"You never told anybody?" she asked.

"Nope. My brother wouldn't have wanted anybody to know. I guess in a way it was murder. It was. It was murder."

"It wasn't murder. It was self-defense." Winona had tears in her eyes. "I hate that that happened to you and your brother. It just isn't right. It wasn't right."

"I'm not gay, though. I don't want you to think I'm gay."

"I don't think you are."

"I know sometimes boys get abused and when they grow up they turn gay, but I'm not that way. I tried to tell my parents, but they didn't want to discuss it. They just wanted to act like it never happened so that's what I tried to do. That's how I could understand you. Understand how you could keep something inside and not want to tell anybody. Too afraid of what they might think. I understand that."

"How can I help you? What can I do to make it better?"

"Love me. I've been dead ever since 1982. The first time I felt alive again was when I met you. We are meant to be together and I want to marry you."

"But you know my issue."

"I don't care. Did you hear me? *I don't care.* Let me decide on the risks I'm willing to take in order to be happy."

"I'm scared. I'm scared that you're going to change your mind, maybe when we're at the altar or maybe before we make it there, or maybe on the honeymoon. I don't know, and I'm too scared to find out, so I'm going to disappear."

I shook my head. "No you're not. I'm not going to let you. We're going to deal with our issues until they get better. I don't want to look back over another twenty years and my life is still the same. It's not going to happen because I won't let it, and I won't let you leave me."

58

S osha's upstairs cramping," Carlton said, snickering. He was holding the refrigerator door open, looking inside. "I don't want to eat leftovers or pizza today. So what are you cooking?"

I cut him a quick look. "I don't feel like being bothered today." I had just walked through the door. It was my first full day back since I'd been out of the hospital, and my energy was zapped. So much so, I stopped taking the medication because I just didn't feel like swallowing any more of those pills that didn't seem to do anything but make me sicker, and Porter agreed. "And if you were a female you wouldn't be laughing about Sosha, believe me."

"Well, I'm trying to help her. I told her to take one of your Tylenol with some water."

"You told her what? Why did you tell her that? Did she?"

"I don't know. I just told her right before you walked in."

I threw down my things and ran upstairs into Sosha's room. She wasn't there so I ran into my room. She was in my bathroom at the medicine cabinet and she had the large Tylenol bottle in her grip.

"Don't take those!" I shouted as I ran toward her.

"I hurt," she said as she took one out of the bottle.

"No," I said, grabbing her wrist before she had a chance to put it in her mouth. "I said don't take those."

"But I hurt," she said struggling to gain control of the pill.

I slapped her. It wasn't a soft slap either; it was a grown person's slap. I slapped her so hard the Tylenol bottle flew out her hand and all the pills spilled over the ceramic tile and some sank into the bathroom rug.

"Why can't you kids ever listen to me?" I shouted. Sosha stood paralyzed with her face frozen, caught between a cry and a scream. Then she let loose, crying at the top of her lungs like she was dying, but I had to do it because if she had taken one of those pills she might have died, because those weren't Tylenol. Those were the meds Dr. Gant prescribed that I kept hidden inside of my Tylenol bottle.

"You hit me," she cried.

I heard Carlton's size-fourteen shoes hit the steps and start running.

I was on my knees trying to pick up my medication.

"She hit me," Sosha said with her face contorted and one finger pointed in my direction.

My hands were moving quickly to retrieve all the evidence, throwing the pills back inside the bottle.

"Why you hit her, Mom?"

"Didn't I say I didn't feel like being bothered today?"

"You hit her because you didn't want to be bothered?" Carlton asked as he stooped down to assist me. He picked up one pill from the tile floor and examined it closely. "Is this Tylenol?"

"I don't need your help, Carlton. You want to help, get out!" I said, snatching the pill from between his long, thin fingers. "I mean it, get out, and take her with you!"

The phone started ringing, but I wasn't budging until every last pill was up from the floor.

"It's for you!" Carlton shouted. "It's the doctor's office!"

I ran into my room and snatched my phone off the hook. "I have it Carlton, please hang up." He slammed the phone down. "Hello, this is Winona."

"Winona, this is Nurse Smith. The doctor wanted me to call you and see if you can come in tomorrow."

"What's wrong? You got the test results back? Just tell me what they said. I don't feel like coming in."

"We need to see you in person."

———

When the doctor walked through the door he wouldn't look at me. His face stayed focused on my chart. Doctors were used to gloom and doom so if he couldn't even establish eye contact I pretty much figured that after I left I should probably start making my funeral arrangements.

He cleared his throat, still looking down, flipping through those damn pages that I'd heard turn for nearly seven years.

"What?" I shouted. I knew it was rude but I couldn't take it. "Tell me straight. What, I got AIDS now? What, my CD4 count is low, my viral load is high? What, shit? What's wrong, Dr. Gant?"

He cleared his throat again. "I don't know how to tell you this." He looked up at me. "You're not HIV-positive." I heard what he said but I kept telling myself that I hadn't heard correctly but that had to be what he said because he wouldn't have said that I was because I already knew I was, so saying I wasn't would be something I didn't know and wouldn't understand. I sat there staring back at him waiting for him to say it again. "Did you hear what I said, Winona?"

I shook my head because he wasn't getting off that easy. *Hell no I didn't hear you. Say that shit again.* For seven years now, I'd heard it the other way. Heard that I was. Over the phone, in person, through Keith. Say that shit again. Say it as many times as I heard I was. Say it over and over!

"No, I didn't hear you."

"You're not HIV-positive." He said it again, but I didn't believe him. Wasn't this a good thing? So why wasn't I happy?

"I don't understand, I tested positive, so did my ex-boyfriend."

"I retested you because you went more than six years without medication and you were fine, however, the minute we put you on medication you got sick and I changed the meds until we practically ran out of meds to give you. None of my other patients have this much trouble, not over and over. Sometimes people are given a false diagnosis. I can't say it's often, but it does happen."

"I don't believe you."

"I can understand why you wouldn't, but you're not. Under normal circumstances I'd say we'd need to test you regularly for about six months just to make sure, but you haven't had intercourse in more than six years so there really is no reason to retest. I just want you to throw away the meds you've been using. Those drugs are too powerful to use if you're not sick. I need to put you through other tests to make sure there's been no damage to your liver or other internal organs."

"What are you saying?" I looked at him in total disbelief. I spent seven years trying to convince myself that I wasn't sick and now that I've accepted that I am and told practically everyone I know, he's telling me I'm not.

"I'm saying, Winona, you were given a false diagnosis. You don't have HIV."

"Do you think maybe I could've had it and some kind of way something I did or one of these myriad of drugs I've taken cured it? Is it possible you discovered a cure and you don't know it?"

"Anything's possible. We're learning things about this disease every day, but from a medical standpoint it's more probable that you never had it. I believe that the stress you were under probably caused you to develop symptoms that were characteristic of HIV, but you don't have it."

"Okay," I said calmly, "then I'm going to leave. I guess I won't have to keep my monthly appointments." I tried to snap back into my old world. The one I used to live in when everything was okay. No more appointments. Now I could go to the doctor whenever I felt like it. No more blood tests. No more sleepless nights. *This is impossible!*

"No, we won't have to see each other monthly, or ever. I'm an HIV/AIDS specialist. You don't have either."

"I don't have either," I said softly.

"No, Winona. You don't. But like I said I would like to see you next week for some follow-up tests just to see if the medication did any damage."

"Okay." I stood and shook my head while I widened my eyes. I was trying to wake myself from the trance I was in. I walked toward the door then stopped and turned to face the doctor. "Should I call for an appointment?"

"Just come next week, same time, I'll be able to see you then. I'm sorry that you had to live with this for so long, Winona."

"Okay," I said quickly. I walked through the door, taking a moment to catch my breath. I had forgotten how to breathe for a second. I walked like a zombie out into the waiting area, through the swinging doors into the hallway. I was still breathing. Breathing real hard, trying to remember how I was supposed to take in fresh air, the kind that held promises. I stopped in the middle of the hallway and braced the wall. That's when the tears came. I covered my mouth as I wept. These weren't tears of joy. I didn't understand why I wasn't happy. Why I felt guilty. I thought about all the people who would give anything to hear what I just did. I felt like I had just won the biggest lottery in history, one where the prize was my life instead of money. I wondered if the new test results were wrong and whether the doctor was going to tell me next week that I did have it. One thing I did know, seven years couldn't be reversed in one day. Porter and I had a lot of work ahead of us, a lot of healing from the inside out.

Suddenly, my entire body began to shake like I was in the midst of a seizure. I felt it as it was coming on, but didn't know how to prevent it so I let it happen. I let my body tremble, dispelling all the things my mind had been convinced were truth—all my insecurities, all the lies—gone.

People walking by glanced over at me.

"Do you need me to get a nurse?" a woman pushing an elderly man in a wheelchair asked.

I placed my hand on my chest to calm my body. "I'm fine." I inhaled then exhaled, slung my purse across my shoulder and started stepping. This put a new perspective on everything. In one day, someone's life can change forever, for better or for worse. I wanted to call Porter, then Gina, then my parents and tell them all the good news, but I needed to let it sink in first. I didn't want them to get excited for no reason. I'd wait until all my test results came back. Make sure I wasn't sick in another way. My stride became more confident. I tossed my hair back and raised my head as high as I could.

I felt people staring at me as I strolled through the hospital admittance and out the revolving door.

For the first time in my life, I wasn't paranoid. I didn't think people were looking at me because I looked funny or I was too skinny or any of those things I had grown up believing and of which I was having a hard time letting go.

I smiled when the chill of late February smacked me in the face, the wind whipping around my cheeks right before I wrapped myself with a scarf and tucked my bare hands inside the pockets to my long cashmere coat.

"Keep your head up," I remember a man collecting cans on the street telling me while I waited on the Woodward bus to take me home from high school. "Always keep your head up," he repeated. I remember looking at him, his tattered clothing, and dirty skin, wondering how he could afford to give good advice, the kind I needed to hear. I listened to him, despite the fact that others would have dismissed his words as those coming from a bum. I immediately raised my head and kept it raised as high as I could, until I met Derwin. But that was then and this is now. A lot of years have gone by and I'm not the same woman, and I never will be that woman again.

About the Author

Cheryl Robinson is a native Detroiter currently residing in the Dallas/Fort Worth area.

She is a supervisor for Daimler Chrysler Services, Mercedes-Benz Credit Division. She has just completed her second novel, *When I Get Free*, coming the summer of 2003. For a preview of her new book visit the author's Web site at www.cherylrobinson.com